AN EXILE ABOARD SHIP

Shieldmatron #1

An Exile Aboard Ship

M.C.A. Hogarth

STUDIO
MCAH
MCAHOGARTH.ORG

CONTENTS

APPENDICES

A man may fall many times, but he won't be a failure until he says that someone pushed him.

ELMER G. LETTERMAN

CHRONOLOGY NOTE

Though written to stand alone, this series serves as sequel to the Her Instruments series, and this novel in particular as bridge between Reese's adventures and Lisinthir's. Part 1 takes place during the end of the novel *Laisrathera* (and before its epilogue), and also encompasses the Chatcaavan War described in the latter part of the Princes' Game series. I've done my best to neaten up the chronology, but it might not be the most graceful of fits. Fortunately, once we get out of Part 1, we're into a cleaner part of the timeline; Part 2 fits in around the initial Fallowtide period, and takes us up to Sediryl's progression, mentioned at the end of *To the Court of Love*.

If you'd like to read Reese's adventures, start with the novel *Earthrise*; if you want to follow the war, begin with *Even the Wingless*. And for more information on reading order (chronological, series-based, and publication order), please consult the wiki. This page is a good starting point: https://peltedverse.org/wiki/index.php/List_of_Fiction_by_Internal_Chronology

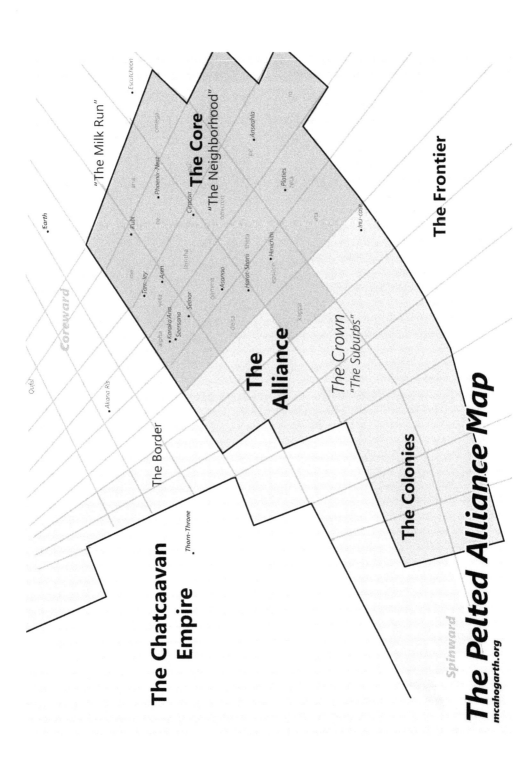

Whereas Incontrovertible Evidence has shown Surela Silin Asaniefa did, of her own Accord, and in full Knowledge of her Actions, commit the Following Crimes:

1. Conspiracy to usurp the Throne, and Importation of unlawful Weaponry in Support of this Effort;
2. Enabling the tearing of the Veil by inviting onto sovereign Eldritch Soil Enemies of the Eldritch People, to wit, Chatcaavan Slavers and Pirates;
3. Complicity in the Deaths of Eldritch Subjects, particularly in the Lands of House Jisiensire, who were slain by a Man acting beneath her Banner;

Therefore, let it be known that Surela Silin Asaniefa has been found guilty of Treason and been sentenced to Death, this Sentence being commuted by the Mercy of the Throne to Exile Permanent from Eldritch Soil.

May God and Goddess have Mercy on her Soul.

Liolesa Galare
Empress Regnant, Eldritch Empire

1

PART ONE
ALL THEIR CHILDREN

CHAPTER 1

"Here are your clothes," said the creature in the hideous mortal tongue, setting a folded stack not even the height of her palm on the seat by the door. "Would you like help dressing?"

The question slammed into Surela with the force of a blow, scattering memories like drops of blood. The smiling face of her handmaiden. The gentle hands that would never rise again to guide her into her elaborate costume. The tender fingertips that would linger on the inside of her wrist. The sweetness of the head resting on her shoulder when the toilette was done, and their excuse for being together evanesced.

And she... she would never see Thaniet again. No one would, because Thaniet was dead, and it was her fault.

The creature had paused, waiting, those animal ears twitched toward her. The thought that her pathos might be obvious to anyone, much less aliens, was so abhorrent it goaded her into speech. "No."

The creature nodded. "I'll get your shoes while you change." A smile. "I bet you'll be glad to be on your feet."

As if she had anywhere to go. And what did it matter anymore? But she had made a promise, so she answered, mechanically, "Yes." This must have satisfied because she was left alone to replace the sack-like gown she'd been wearing since her admission to the alien clinic with her meager new garments. She didn't know how many days had passed... nor could she find it in herself to care. To dwell too deeply on her immediate past and all the deserts she had earned with her arrogance and ignorant pride....

A heart-shaped face intruded into her thoughts, and she pushed it away. So did a different face, the alien one that had said that evidence of her pregnancy had proved inconclusive, and that she had been reprieved, who had asked for none.

The aliens had given her a shirt, pants, and a shapeless pullover: a menial's attire, but she would never again wear the gowns which she had once deserved. Now she deserved this, and only barely, because a human had dared to intercede for her. At least she would never come face to face with one of her kind, who would see her in servants' garb and know her humiliation. Granted that, the garments were at least practical. It galled her to admit they were also more comfortable and easier to don than anything her world had ever produced.

Was it strange that it was her hair that fanned her misery to rage? Her floor-length mane had been dressed daily into coiffures as complex as a piece of filigree. The utilitarian braid worked by some alien hand while she'd been unconscious struck her as incongruous. Who would care for it now that she was a friendless exile? Even the task of washing it would be an immense burden, and a constant reminder of all that had been stripped from her.

The weapon left her by her human benefactor was lying on the table beside the bed. Her motions were jerky with emotion and clumsy with unfamiliarity, but she did the deed quickly for all that... far more quickly than her life had fallen apart, just when she'd thought she'd grabbed the brass ring, the way she was grabbing her braid only to find it connected to nothing. The weightlessness of her head shocked her—but briefly, only briefly. Then, like a girl still in leading strings, she plaited what was left and tied it off. It swung behind her shoulders as she stood to await the creature's return, and her shoes.

It was the least of what she would leave behind, forever.

———

The woman who'd once been known as Surela Silin Asaniefa stepped out of the alien's clinic, expecting to be delivered into the hands of Eldritch guards, men who would not bother to hide their contempt as they shepherded her, formally and definitively, into exile in the nearest non-Eldritch facility in space. Instead, her exit inspired a stranger to stand up and smile at her, flicking his ears forward like an eager dog... which is what he looked like. Someone's cull, because who would have kept a creature of such unhandsome colors and unfortunate conformation? With pelt an awkward mix of gray and red and ginger, and a build too lanky for strength and too thick for speed, the best that could be said for him was that he was well-groomed, his fur trimmed and hair combed neatly. That, and she was forced to admit he had friendly eyes, if in a common shade, the same brown of every loyal hound depicted in the illustrations of countless books.

"Hello, alet," said this newest creature. "I've been waiting for you. My name's Saul Ferry, and I'm here to escort you to the *Earthrise*." When she didn't immediately reply, he indicated the corridor. "This way, please."

Normally she would have led any entourage; certainly, she would not have permitted a servant to walk alongside her. But she no longer led anything, nor did she have servants —indeed, unless she was mistaken she had become one—and she had no idea where she was going. She felt curiously disconnected from the world. Her head was too light, and her shoulders and hips not sufficiently weighed down by her clothes, and nothing made sense. Her body wanted to panic; her mind, to disassociate. Every motion seemed to drag.

"They've been very kind, the Fleet personnel," her escort said, drawing her attention. "You couldn't have had better care anywhere. They assure me you should be fine, once you get your bearings, so I thought you might want to go directly to your new quarters on the *Earthrise*. You've been told about the ship, I'm sure, when Reese made you the offer, but I'm betting she was short on details. The crew's still mustering, so we won't be getting underway immediately, but that's good... it'll give you time to meet everyone sequentially instead of all at once." He smiled again. "Less overwhelming that way."

It was tempting to think of him as an empty-headed chatterer, but that smile disabused her of the notion. It didn't reach his eyes—those common brown eyes that were more sympathetic than enthusiastic. She didn't like their sincerity. It made her feel responsible for not hurting him, and she could no longer guarantee she was capable of living without hurting people. She'd done such a complete job of it already.

Thaniet....

He cleared his throat, pulling her from the memory. "What should I call you, alet? Reese mentioned you might want to use a different name. Eldritch names being so hard to pronounce, I'm guessing." This smile was more natural. "I suppose you might want to take pity on us foreigners."

"I hadn't thought of one," she said aloud, while marveling that the human benefactor she hadn't wanted had seen fit to warn her, obliquely, not to reveal her real name to strangers. And if she wanted to be known as Surela, the Ten Day Traitor? But what would be the point of it? She could never return to that life.

"Reese mentioned you're new to her banner," the creature said. "I'm guessing that makes you part of House Laisrathera."

"Something like," Surela replied, because in all likelihood she was now a peasant without a House name. What else? She had earned all of this.

"Well, you have time to decide."

She glanced at him, but he was staring ahead as he guided them through the unfathomable warren of passages that led to wherever they were going. Before she thought better of it, she said, "You are uncommonly relaxed."

"Am I?" That struck him as humorous, perhaps; his face was close enough to a humanoid template for her to read. The fur and ears made her think 'creature', but his eyes and expressions deprived her of the comfort of dismissing him. "I don't think of myself as easygoing. But I've always liked having a clear directive and a purpose, and I have both now."

"Those being?"

That smile—that was fully sincere, and amused. "An awfully personal question, alet. But I can answer: my clear directive is to work on the *Earthrise* until I'm no longer needed, and my purpose is to be a friend to the friendless."

Such a simple task suited him, with his affable demeanor and kind eyes. They weren't sufficient to steer her intellect away from the obvious. "She sent you. To me."

"Reese? She asked me to help you settle in, yes. I've worked on ships before, I know a little about it."

And if that was all the human had arranged, Surela would wrap herself in a christening gown and declare herself a newborn. Theresa Eddings had saddled her with a literal watchdog. What else, for a criminal whose commuted death sentence had consigned her to hundreds of years offworld? And yet… glancing again at the stolid face of her 'guard', Surela couldn't believe it. Unless she missed her guess—possible, given the magnitude of her mistakes lately

—the creature's report was literal: 'a friend to the friendless.'

"I cannot believe her," Surela breathed.

He pretended not to hear, indicating a door. "This way. We'll be taking the Pads."

She followed, her anger opening her mouth before her better nature quenched the words she would have spoken. She could claim that his services were unnecessary, but they weren't. She knew nothing about the life into which she was poised to plunge—had not even remembered the name of the ship that would be her prison. The simplest questions no longer had obvious answers: how would she eat? Where would she sleep? Would she ever have more than this suit of clothing? So much she had taken for granted in her prior life, because in return for those necessities she had performed a function. Had done it well; even the human had been forced to concede that she was a superlative manager. Now... she didn't know what she was. And her benefactor had supplied her with a guide. It would be stupid not to take advantage of the opportunity.

The creature paused just inside the new room, looking back at her. "Coming?"

Coming where? This room was a dead end. "Yes."

He smiled again, that genuine smile. Nothing hid in it. "Good. If you'll walk across that mat there?"

"This one?" She strode toward it—she would give the peasant attire that, it was far easier to move—and stumbled as her next steps brought her into an entirely separate chamber, larger and darker than the one she'd exited. Whirling, she stared down at the matching mat. She had never used one of the stolen transportation devices supplied to them by the offworld pirates, but she'd seen Athanesin lead his men over them. She had felt an instinctive revulsion toward the incursion of alien technology on their soil. To sully her skin with the experience of using such a device had never occurred to her.

And now she had, and with no experience of having done so. She had taken an entirely normal step, and that step had delivered her to this echoing, ugly space.

Goddess and Lord, was this to be her prison, then?

Her guard appeared, ears perked like the enthusiastic dog he resembled. "Here we are… the *Earthrise*, or at least, one of her cargo bays." A pause. "Is it more comfortable? The gravity on the ship's lighter than Alliance Standard." Perhaps her puzzlement showed, because he continued. "Can you breathe easier? Move with less effort?"

She lifted a hand, let it drop. Inhaled, was surprised to discover less pressure on her breastbone. She'd assumed that weight to be grief. "So it seems."

"Good. You'll still tire quickly, so keep an eye on that, but it should be easier on you than the previous ship. Come on, your cabin's this way. I'll show you."

'Her' cabin implied a private room, which until this moment she hadn't known might have been a privilege denied to her. She walked behind the creature, because to walk beside him would have required them to brush elbows in the narrow corridor, and tried not to cringe from the meanness of the… architecture. Did ships have architecture? It was ugly, whatever it was. Gray walls, darker gray floors of metal grid, gray ceiling with recessed lighting that served solely to call attention to the lack of color. She missed Asaniefa's viridian carpets and creamy marble walls, the bronze busts and the fresh flower arrangements. Her eyes longed for the flicker of a lamp or the purity of the sun, not this… unnatural, steady illumination, pitilessly exposing every flaw.

She hated it. She couldn't believe she'd agreed to live in exile. The human had challenged her by calling suicide the coward's route, but better a dead coward than a living slave, surely?

"Here we are." The creature stood aside as a door slid open, vanishing into a pocket. Alien doors lacked drama or majesty. How did mortals live with such utilitarian surroundings? Surela stepped inside and surveyed the cell they'd assigned her… and cell it was. She would have given a dog a bigger kennel.

"It's a great space," the creature said. "May I come in?"

It was the first thing he'd said that startled her, and it must have shown. The patient regard never wavered, and she hated that it shamed her: that she hadn't anticipated courtesy from aliens, and he'd expected it. "Yes, of course."

"There's no 'of course' about it. This is your cabin, alet. You shouldn't be forced to receive visitors in it."

His compassion drove the blood to her cheeks. "Yes, I understand. Let us not make much of it. Enter, and show me the… features… of this cell." And because she now lived on the sufferance of strangers—and because he'd earned it—she finished, "Please."

"We call it a cabin, or your quarters," the creature replied, stepping inside. "This," patting the door frame, "is a hatch. Just so you know, if people use the terms around you." He walked the perimeter of the room. "This is your desk—the light's here, you can turn it on by tapping, or just ask it to turn on. Drawers here, for storage. And these cabinets above your bunk… it's a fold-out bunk. You can store your linens in this pocket in the wall, or buy extra storage cubage… it can be hooked into the wall with these mounts, so it doesn't move around. Food is served in the mess, and the bathroom is down the hall. You can modify your cabin within reason…."

As he talked, Surela's world shrank. Activities she used separate rooms for at home, like writing her correspondence, or managing accounts, even sleeping and dressing… now she would do them all in this single, featureless room, barely large enough to turn in.

"This is for clothes," the creature was saying. "Reese has

arranged for your things, though if they're not to your taste you'll be able to purchase replacements once we're in the Alliance."

Surela started from her brooding. "I will be able to make purchases?"

He cocked his head. "Yes? You will be a working member of the crew, which means you'll be paid."

"But what will I do?"

"I don't know. Did Reese say anything to you?"

The memory of that conversation was not as sour as she expected, but the strength of her anger and misery made recollecting its particulars uncomfortable. "Something about... management. Social issues."

"Hmm. Well, Ra'aila will want to interview you, I'm sure. We'll figure something out." He smiled. "I'll leave you to familiarize yourself with your quarters. I'm sure you have messages you need to check."

"Messages," she repeated.

He nodded. "On your computer." Pointing now at the desk, which was featureless, innocent of blotter or inkstand. "Just ask. You can also request my location from the computer if you need me later. It's mark one right now, so there will be snacks in the mess. Dinner's at mark five. Ra'aila should be aboard by then, if not sooner."

Before she could object, or ask for clarification, or protest that this was not the life she'd wanted, the creature had gone. Without so much as a bow, either, but she had not observed the aliens to have formal courtesies. They were peasants, the lot of them, and she was now one of them—and with no one to blame for her fall but herself.

This was everything she wanted to prevent her people from being forced to interact with. Become. Was it irony that she should be pushed into that embrace? Or a special and exquisite cruelty?

Investigating the drawers of the crudely-shaped box her

minder had misapprehended as a desk, she found no letters waiting for her. No pens, either, nor ink nor leads. Though she had never handled one, she was aware that aliens used slates to communicate, and no such slate greeted her when she opened the final drawer. What 'computer' was she missing?

He'd said she should 'just ask'. What did that mean? Aloud, as if summoning a servant? Ridiculous! And yet, the thought of searching for the creature solely to ask him to guide her through the use of mortal technology... no, she couldn't. Resigned to sounding a fool, Surela said, "Where are my messages?"

"You have two messages. Play message one at current location?"

CHAPTER 2

Startled, Surela said, "Yes."

An image of the human who'd landed her in this contretemps appeared on her wall in more detail than she liked. It was not in keeping with her dignity to be amazed at mortal technology, at the fact she could count the beads at the ends of the human's hair, or see the reflection of the human's face in their glossy surfaces. She certainly didn't want the recording to render the human's contralto in such high fidelity… as if they were in the same room together.

"I'm sure you're not in the most receptive mood right now, Surela, so I'll go ahead and say I know you're at a loss, so there's no point denying it. Saul's your resource for questions; use him, it's why I hired him. No, I'm not sorry about that… and yes, I know you've probably figured out that he's supposed to help you." The human paused, her full lips twisting. "I'm not good at the high-handed parts of being a liegelady, but I'm working on it. Tell me how I'm doing. Or… don't. Your choice."

It would not be seemly to find this discursion humorous.

There was no liking the female who'd put her in this situation. There couldn't be.

"Anyway, since I know you'll go crazy without something to do, it's for the best that I've discovered I need help. Your help, particularly. I can trust Ra'aila to run cargo, but that would require her to know what kind of cargo to buy.

"And the thing is... we need livestock."

Surela's arms, which had been tightly folded against her chest, eased from it. Livestock?

"I am completely sure Ra'aila has no idea what kinds of chickens or pigs or cows we need. Dogs, we need dogs too. I've promised dogs. And not just for Laisrathera, but for as many Eldritch settlements as we can get those things to. Horses I think I've got covered thanks to the deal with Kerayle, but they don't handle livestock. You used to manage Asaniefa... you've got a much better idea of what people need."

Surela's cheeks burned. *Used* to manage Asaniefa. Did the human have to remind her so pointedly?

"I hope you'll be willing to help Ra'aila with that, because while we'll make do with whatever the *Earthrise* brings back, I really want it to work." The human's body language steadied until it resembled the norms Surela recognized, and that stillness drew her eyes to the human's. They were an uncanny color, blue as gentians. "If you need anything, tell me. Call me anytime. I'll take care of you."

The nerve of the creature, claiming her as if she had a right. As if a human could aspire to the heights of Eldritch nobility. As if Surela could need anything from someone of such mean estate—

She sat, abruptly, on the bed and touched her brow, trembling. No, Surela was the one of mean estate now, and the human elevated to levels of consequence to which Surela was forever barred... by her own acts. Theresa Eddings had not opened her world to slavers and pirates. Had not let them into the palace to rape and kill the people she'd purported to rule, to protect. Theresa Eddings had not loosed a madman on the lands of the Jisiensire, to raze their tenant villages and destroy their ancestral homes.

A voice said, "Play second message?"

Surela's head jerked up. "Yes."

The silence extended, broken only by a strange click. She frowned—how irritating mortal correspondence was! Letters were so much better. And speaking aloud to nothingness, as if to a receptive servant….

Well. That much she could enter into. "Play the second message."

Again the silence, and the click.

As if she'd been sent an envelope with a blank sheet within? She would have considered such a missive a threat. What could she deduce about the mortal version, knowing nothing about how these machines operated? It could be an error. Or a prank?

The chime cut through her puzzlement. Did everything in the mortal world make noise? And what did this sound indicate? It sounded almost like—

Again, the chime. This time, with a voice, a woman's low soprano, brisk. "Ra'aila to see the supercargo."

The door, then. She supposed she could not deny this particular petitioner. "Enter."

What had she expected of the vessel's captain? A human, perhaps, given Theresa Eddings's ownership of the venture. But the individual that stepped through was another of the furred creatures, this one even more animal in seeming than Surela's guard. Rather than a flat, humanoid face, she had a muzzle as long as a fox's, though the tufted ears surmounting the mane were more reminiscent of a hare's. And… she smelled like some exotic desert spice, so intensely that Surela gasped in like the most unschooled of children.

"I'm Ra'aila. It's good to meet you." The creature

17

approached, halting at the edge of the bed. "Reese's contracted me to drive this ship around until one of us gets bored, her or me." A flash of a grin, exposing pointed teeth. "She told me I'd get an Eldritch volunteer, but I admit I wasn't holding my breath. I'm glad I was wrong, though, because my first order is for five hundred chickens and the only thing I know about chickens is what they taste like. Have you got any insight for me about chickens?"

"Do we have room for five hundred chickens?" Surela asked, taken aback.

"Oh, so they need room?"

Goddess and Lord, what had Theresa Eddings involved her in? "Perhaps you should show me the facilities in which you intend to transport the fowl."

"Perhaps I should," Ra'aila said. "Come on, and give me all your advice."

———

The captain of the vessel was not given to idle conversation, thankfully, because Surela wouldn't have had the first notion what to discuss. And she walked quickly, which stole her breath but suited Surela because she did not want to labor long in the company of mortals. That swift gait brought them to a cavernous chamber, as tall surely as Ontine's throne room, but interrupted at intervals with metal beams. "This is the largest of the cargo bays. I don't *think* they pack chickens in bins that we can put on those spindles and hang, so I'm guessing we're going to have to use the deck. Hopefully the cages—they ship in cages, don't they?—can be dogged down the way stalls for horses are. What do you think? Five hundred chickens?"

"How long is the journey?"

The creature scratched her nose. "Depends on where we buy them. We're going to run crew-light up to Starbase Psi, where I'll be picking up the rest of my people. Maybe we'll find something there?"

Surela looked at the creature, appalled at her ignorance. "You don't know?"

"Livestock is a specialty trade in the Alliance," Ra'aila answered. "You're more likely to find it in sectors adjacent to new space, where the fresh colonies are. But there's not much colonization in this corner of the Alliance... most of the push is spinward. It's why we established Kerayle in Sector Psi... not only is this side of the Alliance closer to Earth, but it's also farther from where all the interest is. We were hoping we'd get a better deal on a planet."

This was empire building on a level Surela had never contemplated, though no doubt Liolesa, her former queen, had. Despite the associations, Surela couldn't help her curiosity. "Did you?"

"Oh, definitely. Even granting there's almost no exploration done in this part of space..." The creature trailed off, frowning. "You know, that's really strange. I wonder why there's so little exploration over here? The Alliance is always looking for new worlds. Huh. I wonder if asking about that will get me anything?" She shook her head, ears flapping. "Anyway. The point of this tangent was that we should be able to find a provider at Starbase Psi, or at least, news of one. If we don't, it's because there isn't much colonization in this area, so there aren't the industries to support them. If that's the case, we'll have to go farther afield."

"Is there some... inventory...? Of merchants?"

"On the starbase? Oh, sure. I was going to check once we got underway, now that Reese's sent me her shopping list." Ra'aila eyed her. "Should I copy it to your account? And the vendor data?"

The idea of working was less intolerable than the idea of sitting idle in her kennel. "Yes."

"Great! We should be casting off tomorrow, so if you need

anything brought up from the planet, put in the request now. They can courier it up before we go." Ra'aila grinned at her. "I'm glad to have you aboard. I'm jumping straight into uncharted waters, here, and I'm grateful for someone with somewhat more experience in Eldritch society to help. Which reminds me—I didn't get your name?"

What to say? She couldn't divulge her real name, and even if she could, she was no longer Surela Silin Asaniefa. House Asaniefa was dead, the Silin family scattered, and she... she was now the lowest charity case on Laisrathera's rolls. Her milk name, Sela, she had given to nearly no one since leaving the nursery, and the one person she'd hoped would use it had died... died because of mistakes Surela had made. "You may call me Rel."

"Oh, thank the multiple winds. I was afraid it would be one of the long unpronounceable ones, and then I might accidentally offend you by butchering it." Ra'aila grinned. "Things are going to work out great. I can already tell."

Surela was glad someone could.

CHAPTER 3

The thought of eating should have revolted her; she had as good as killed her beloved companion and nearly destroyed her world, and had been consigned to mortal hell in the company of uplifted animals and aliens. Properly, she should abstain from food until starvation liberated her from breath. Now that execution had been denied her, however, the prospect of expiring like a maid out of a banal romance was revolting. She was no stripling girl to be daunted by... by a complete change in every aspect of her life, including her name. And she was hungry.

Disgraced she might be. But a puling victim—no. That was certainly a bridge too far.

The ship's architecture was not solely unsightly; the sharp, metallic sound the deck made under her shoes made her want to grind her teeth. She ignored it to explore the painfully small world that was all that was allotted to her now, and in this way found the 'mess.' Thankfully, it did not live down to its name, and in it she found Saul-Ferry-her-guard, the assistant arranged for her by her liegelady in an attempt at highhandedness that was laughable in its modesty of scope. True highhandedness would have been far more oppressive. She would have to so advise her mortal keeper.

The canine ears pricked at the sight of her. "Hungry? There's a spread on the counter. Did you meet Ra'aila yet?"

"I did, yes." Surela walked to the counter and stopped, all her limbs locking. The selection there could have graced an Eldritch table, down to the dishes—good porcelain, and with Laisrathera's house sigil. Meats sliced to pink translucency; nuts and cheeses scattered with honey; thin crackers and dense ones; and a bowl of raspberries. A plate of shortbread cookies dusted with sugar; two carafes, one of water and the other—not tea. Coffee, a beverage that had been briefly in vogue when Surela was young, but that had faded in popularity. Tisanes remained the drink of choice for refined palates. This, at least, she could safely scorn. The rest of it....

"Take whatever you want, we're good on stores. And we'll be buying more when we get to the starbase."

Visceral memories now, of her discussion with the Royal Procurer about the origins of the food she'd taken for granted all her life. "How is it done? In the outworld?"

Saul had finished his meal some time ago, from the plate he'd pushed aside. Her entrance had caused him to set down his tablet, and he folded his hands together over it now. "Buying food?"

"Growing it."

"Oh... you like the big topics, don't you." His grin was lopsided. On a dog, it would have been charming. "The answer, like so many answers, is 'it depends.' Because the Alliance is about 660 billion people—"

The number made her stomach drop. She pressed a hand onto the counter. "What?"

"A little more than that. But yes. There are a lot of people, and at least 120 worlds, and there's a starbase in every sector that's as large as a moon, so everything's complicated."

Surela stared at the counter, forced herself to select one of the Laisrathera plates—good porcelain it was, with a pleasing finish beneath her fingers—and began adding some of the crackers and cheeses. Her wrists ached, though it shouldn't have been such an effort. "You are aware…" Could she say this? But the Veil that had protected the Eldritch, the work they'd done to maintain their mystery and their isolation and their safety for so long… it was well and truly destroyed. And she'd had a hand in it. Perhaps the largest hand. She settled herself with a careful breath. "You are aware that we import most of our food."

"Yes. And that's not unusual."

"I beg your pardon?"

"Some worlds grow all the food they need for their populations. Some choose to import some or all of it from other worlds. There are agrarian planets that do nothing but grow food, most of which is intended for export. I'm not sure what your Empress wants for the Eldritch; I get the sense that the Queen wants to see if you can take care of your own needs? But that's going to take some time, I imagine."

So much in this speech to agitate her, and she could allow none of it to master her. "Yes." She stared at the raspberries. "So this food was purchased offworld, and we will be purchasing more such food."

"For the foreseeable future. You can manufacture food with genies, but it's too energy-intensive to be economical for almost any environment. Fleet ships do it, but they have over-built power plants."

"I…" To admit it or not? But what profit in pretense? Pretense had destroyed her life. "Did not understand anything you just said."

"Genies make things from either energy or from spare matter, depending on the type," the creature began, then stopped, shook his head. "That probably doesn't make much more sense, does it."

Surela forced herself to finish filling her plate and then

23

carry it to the table. Sitting across from her minder was too difficult—it would be like watching an animal at a feeding dish, surely? But he was beside the head of the table, and it was natural to sit there. Heading an empty table, or a nearly empty one, was surely not beyond her, even in her fallen state. "I am afraid not. A genie is a mortal device, then."

The creature winced. "I wouldn't use that term. It's a Pelted device, though I assume the Chatcaava have something similar."

"And this device... creates food?"

"Not just food. Anything it has a pattern for. Clothing. Food. Furniture. Tools." He pushed his tablet aside and wrapped his hands around his mug. "Big enough genies can make structures and vehicles."

Her imagination failed her, save in instinctive response: an outraged jealousy, that mortals should have such plenty while her people starved. She latched onto practicalities and climbed them away from her resentment. "Which is the reason for the name. Like a djinn, you wish for a thing, and it is delivered to you. Why then do you suffer from any privation or need?"

"Because it needs power, and power isn't free. That's what I meant when I said earlier that Fleet ships can do a lot of these things because they have the power plant. Power plants create power, and you need access to one to make any modern convenience work. And those plants don't come from nowhere."

"Not even from one of these genies large enough to create structures?"

He paused, then laughed. "Yes, you'd think so, wouldn't you? But it's not that easy, even for us. Who makes the genie? Who maintains it? And then you have a power plant... who understands how to operate it? How to fix it if it fails? How to design it? How to place it so that it can reach all the things that need it, and in the most efficient way? Genies and generators need modern power grids, as well, and designing, installing, and maintaining those is work. So no, we don't live in a cost-free society yet. I doubt we ever will—it's not how God designed the universe."

Aliens with religion… what was his god like? Nothing like hers, she had to believe. "Do we have one of these genies?"

"Not on the *Earthrise*, no. Reese did some upgrades, but running a genic would have required a bigger power plant."

"Back to that," Surela murmured.

"Always back to power," he agreed, and it was as true a statement as she'd ever heard from mortal lips, if less literally than he perhaps intended. "Her other upgrades had higher priority, anyway, like the Pad, and the duster, and better comm facilities…." He chuckled. "It's almost as if she expects trouble, but I can't really blame her. Pirates like small, unarmed freighters that travel alone."

Surela's heart tripped. "Are we likely to be attacked?"

"Not running between here and the nearest starbase. There's too much attention on this part of space." He smiled at her kindly. "Don't worry about it."

As if she could set it aside so easily, when so lately it had been the focus of her every action? But he didn't know. Did he? Surela looked at her meal, watched as her hands mechanically spread the cheese on the cracker. "I have a great deal to learn, I see. Is there a library aboard?"

"A… no. Not a physical one. The computer will tell you anything you need to know. And if you'd like something portable, there are data tablets…."

"But no books?"

"Not unless you want a collector's item?"

She stared at him. "Then how do you write your thoughts? Your notes?"

"People use the computer for that." He looked at her, touched his chin as if in thought. Whatever thoughts the act

25

produced, however, he chose not to share, if his pause was any indication. "I'll make arrangements. In the meantime, your computer will respond to spoken requests for information, if there's anything you want to know."

Surela hardly knew the extent of her ignorance. How would she have stumbled onto the line of questioning that would have led to an explanation of genies? Would a computer be able to understand her queries about the source of alien foodstuffs, or would it be baffled by so complete a naïveté? Goddess, how she hated to be ignorant! And how dangerous ignorance was!

Her minder brought his plate and mug to the counter and did something with both before setting them aside. "I'll take care of that now, in fact, since we'll be pulling out for the starbase shortly. Plates are washed here, under the wand, by the way."

"I see." And again, though it felt like addressing an animal: "Thank you."

He nodded and left her to the meal, and she allowed herself the luxury of relief. It was easier, not to suffer company; she had not loved it among her own kind, and being amidst aliens was worse. Not that her solitude made it any easier to grapple with how delicious the food was, and how fresh the raspberries; that she could still enjoy anything was evidence of a low nature. And yet, she did.

Other than its general shape, the 'wand' did not look like anything she would have classified as one. That it cleaned dishes without water or effort agitated her. She did not want to envy anything available only to aliens. She thought instead how such conveniences made it necessary for people who should be spending their time on more high-minded pursuits to do the work of menials. And what did actual menials do, deprived of tasks that gave them dignity and bread?

There was no graciousness in such a society. There was, however, fresh fruit, in any season. She stared at the remaining berries while finishing her toil—surely she could call it toil, when it was a task she had no desire to do—and struggled. She wanted to deprecate everything, but she was trapped here. What good fighting it, save to make herself miserable? More miserable?

Didn't she deserve to be miserable? She was the One Week Usurper.

Her body was trembling with exhaustion by the time she retired to her cell. Surela tried to lie down but the meanness of her surroundings, and their emptiness, was threatening. If she stared for too long at the walls, they would close in on her... would be painted with the blood that had drenched the palace halls, fill with the noises of battle. Sitting up, she squared her shoulders, breathed until her heart ceased to race.

When the panic receded, the grief threatened to replace it, and she refused that, also. The role of melancholic didn't suit her; even knowing she should be reflecting on her sins, her unworthiness, and her unbearable exile, she couldn't sit idle for longer than a few moments without beginning to fidget. Purposelessness was insupportable. She was alive, and not planning to kill herself—not brave enough, she wanted to think, but the truth was less palatable. She was too stubborn to give up, and too proud, even now, knowing the ugly harvest her pride had already reaped.

Her enemies would be gratified to see her dwindle in exile. That was, she thought, good enough reason to refuse. Rising, she confronted the blank desk. What point a flat surface, if one did not intend to write on it? Perhaps she would learn. She would have to. Surela began to pace. "Computer. What is a starbase?"

CHAPTER 4

That was how she spent her evening. Measuring the length of her cage with her footsteps, and asking one question after another to keep from internalizing how small it was. Rarely understanding the answers; frustrated by the lack of familiar tools to organize her thoughts.

"Computer. What is the Alliance?"

"What are the Pelted?"

"What is the relation between the Pelted and humans?"

"Where do starbases acquire their foodstuffs?"

"Where do the Pelted acquire their foodstuffs?"

She was, she thought, entirely too fixated on food. And yet, it goaded her, the thought that this nearly-700 billion-person nation could feed its populace, and her one minuscule kingdom couldn't. That the kingdom she considered best in all the galaxy was, with each successive question, revealed to be so immaterial to galactic affairs that it could be dismissed... or would be, if its people were not so valued by slavers and pirates... for their beauty, their rarity, and their psychic powers.

"What currency is used in the Alliance?"

"Is barter common anywhere in space?"

"What kind of trade agreements are usual?"

The more she asked, the more agitated she became. The size of the universe was made clear to her in the impartial replies of an automated device that did not respond to signs of affront. At last, she sat on the edge of her bunk and put her head in her hands. She was tired—was it late? There was no way to judge the time. But she felt grimy and worn, and the vastness of the task before her grew with each passing moment. Somehow, she had to learn to navigate an immense and alien world, one that made her prior existence look parochial. Laughable. She had once been one of the most powerful people she'd known, and now… now she was no better than a provincial, smelling of hay and cheap soap.

There was no private bathing chamber. Of course. She would have to wash like the menials she'd been dismissing only a few hours ago while eating berries she still could not have traced the passage of, from soil to plate. Humbled and hating it, Surela picked out something light enough to sleep in and stepped out of her cell.

She almost trod on a package.

Baffled, she glanced up and down the corridor—no one to see her steady herself with a hand to the wall as she went to a knee in her vulgar trousers. It was a box… intended for her, surely, or why was it at her door? She brought it inside, discarding her clothes on the bunk, and set it on the desk. It had been tied with twine, which should have warned her that it had been packed by Eldritch hands. And yet she opened it, expecting another alienation and discovering instead a stack of books, and the kind of ink and pen set gifted to new adults who were graduating from the use of their family's stationery to a set specific to themselves. Ink in every color of the Eldritch language; pens and nibs, multiples of each. And the empty journals, precious and rare; paper was sold loose most of the time, and bound only for rich clients.

29

Saul, she knew immediately. But also Theresa Eddings, because the journals were specialty requests, and only a titled lady would have been able to request them so quickly. Her keeper had heard her need and gone to her lady to ensure that need would be fulfilled before they left.

Surela brought the book to her nose, inhaled the scent of the paper, the smell of home. Her eyes watered, but she refused to cry. Weeping didn't solve problems, and being seen to weep was to reveal weakness. Also, she would ruin the paper.

Hadn't he said the computer would tell her where everyone was? "Computer, where is Saul?"

"Saul is in Bay 4."

"Where is that?"

"Bay 4 is the forward cargo bay on the lower level, and is accessible via lift."

So there was more to this vessel than the tiny area she'd explored? What did it look like from the outside? And did she really want to face the keeper Theresa had assigned to her and thank him? It was demeaning enough to be so completely dependent on others for needs she had once been capable of seeing to herself. To express gratitude would be to acknowledge her powerlessness. And to a creature she considered less than Eldritch: a mortal, to be disdained and repulsed by. Something that looked like an animal out of a tapestry or book.

And yet, it was a mark of good breeding to have courtesy, and to never lose those courtesies in the most extreme of situations. In this fashion, perhaps, she could reassert her self-conception. She was poor and exiled, but she need not comport herself as a rude and unmannered peasant. Yes?

She rubbed her face, hating everything. Only the outworld would create these situations where there were no right answers, only degrees of degradation.

The lift at the end of the corridor opened onto a dim,

cavernous space. Her arrival brightened the area immediately in front of her, which allowed her to spot the mortal near the far wall, and he was… setting a book beside a candle. On what was a small but unmistakable altar.

Had the lift's door not already closed, Surela would have backed into it; to interrupt someone's worship felt wrong to her, so much so that Saul Ferry's species registered as an afterthought. But it was too late, and he glanced up and spotted her. He waved, and so she advanced, torn between an innate respect for the observance of any rite, and her sense that she should not respect alien rites. She had never been particularly devout herself; worship of the Goddess had been a comfortable part of her life, less about belief and more about How Things Were Done. And yet, what she said was, "I did not mean to interrupt."

"It's fine. I was just finishing up." He reached out and tapped the wick, which doused instantly, and perhaps her startlement was too obvious. "It's not a real candle. Fire on a ship, even a ship made mostly of metal, is a bad idea. This is good enough."

"I did not know this vessel had a… chapel."

"Oh, it doesn't. But I don't think anyone will mind me co-opting part of it for God. This bay's in an awkward place for cargo, and used more for longterm ship's stores than anything people need easy access to, so I thought it would be a good place to say a prayer or two. You're welcome to use it if you need a quiet place."

"I doubt we share deities."

"Oh, I'm sure we don't. But an altar's an altar." He smiled at her. "I assume you were looking for me? Is there something I can help you with?"

He was so unrelentingly kind. It nettled her, but she controlled her reaction. How ridiculous it would be to thank him from between gritted teeth. "The books… it was generous. Thank you."

"You're welcome."

He made it so easy; it shouldn't make her angry. The courtesy accepted, no fuss, no uncouth displays of emotion... an Eldritch would have been proud to comport themselves with such dignity and ease. And all she could do was fume. At everything. Particularly since he waited just enough time before adding, "Do you need anything right now?"

"No," she said, grateful for the opening, and angry about that as well. "I won't disturb you any longer. Good night."

The bathroom was an alien contrivance that forced her to request instruction from the computer to operate successfully. Once she had, she hated the shower cubicle for not being a bath and also for being more relaxing than she expected, and more convenient, and having endless hot water at whatever temperature she most preferred. With the water running down her pale head, Surela leaned against the wall and tried to place herself in her life before. Not the nightmare that had ended it, and threatened to blot out the centuries that had preceded them, but the mannered, beautiful life she had inhabited without appreciating. She'd been consumed with ambition for more, so consumed she hadn't realized how good it was: to live in stately mansions and townhouses, to feel rich carpets beneath her toes, and embroidered dressing gowns on her shoulders, to hear the song of harpists and larks and a language that wasn't clipped and lacking in nuance.

Everything she'd been fighting to hold at bay crowded toward her now that the day, full of threatening novelties, was coasting toward its close. Those nightmares were in her eyes when she confronted her reflection, outside the shower cubicle.

She had longed to be singular: to be queen, first among all her people. But even the queen of the Eldritch could not be as singular as one Eldritch among 660 billion residents of an alien federation. Surela tried to see herself as aliens must.

Humans were poor copies of what the Eldritch had become, for even exiled Surela would not deny that they had begun, over a thousand years ago, as part of the human race. However, centuries separated by impossible distance, internal changes, and the mystery cultivated by their culture and the Veil, their habit of never revealing much of themselves, had allowed them to masquerade as a separate species. And they might as well be one, Surela thought; not only did they have the ability to sense emotions through touch—and in some cases, more, as the dreaded mind-mages did—but her kind were taller, more refined of feature and speech, and moved with a dreamlike grace. The latter had been robbed from her by the pressure on her chest, but she remained a faery incarnation, with skin and hair the nacreous white of pearls, elongated limbs, and a delayed aging that would allow her to see nearly two millennia, if pirates, wars, and mortal accident did not befall her.

But what good were the centuries if she spent them divorced from everything that had defined her before? And why, oh why, had she not been content with the riches of her life? Why had she had to gamble for more—and lose—before she understood the magnitude of her blessings?

Her fatigue guaranteed that she would sleep when at last she sought her rude bunk. That she woke several times, her thin garment sticking to her sweaty skin and her heart rushing to fill her ears, surprised her not at all. The memories were sour in her mouth, like the taste of blood.

This would not rule her. She refused.

CHAPTER 5

A mortal spaceship traveled enormous distances at speeds Surela could not fathom, and did it all with only the slightest of vibrations to betray its actions. She often forgot they were underway; knew it only because Ra'aila came by to inform her they would be arriving at the starbase in a few days. Despite the minuscule size of their living quarters, it was easy to avoid two people, and Surela did precisely that, taking her meals at odd moments and spending the majority of her time in her quarters, endlessly quizzing the computer to prevent herself from beating her fists against the walls of her lilliputian cage or surrendering to her nightmare-plagued nights.

"Computer. How many planets are there?"

"How are new planets claimed?"

"Who protects these planets?"

"How many ships does Fleet have?"

She lost a day, investigating Fleet, torn between horror and fascination and avarice. That the mortal navy should have some 700,000 ships…! And yet could not spare more to defend an ally? Or had they decided that Liolesa's problem was so minor it had only needed one ship, barely large enough for a handful of people? How could that be, when pirates loved her people so passionately?

She made notes, and the familiarity of the tools helped—slightly—with the homesickness and the alienation. If she concentrated, she could almost forget she was in a metal box, listening to an inanimate object lecture her, and that the topics her pen described were outlandish, unworthy of a refined intellect.

That they were interesting was a constant, nagging irritation. She had become head of Asaniefa by fighting for it politically, as one must. But having acquired the position, she'd discovered the best part of ruling, which had little to do with people and everything to do with making sure they had what they needed, and building what they didn't yet have... though admittedly, the resources to build anything had been scarce. Food, though, had been plentiful, and ensuring it reached all the necessary people....

But her nearly 8000-person province would have been considered a hamlet by the titans who managed planets and spun off colonies, and the resources and money they moved as casually as she might have ordered a sack of wheat to a village should have daunted her. Or made her angry—so many things made her angry. Just thinking of Liolesa moving on this stage while the rest of them remained trapped on their world....

Except that she had been one of the voices insisting that remaining trapped on their world was preferable to... this.

She gritted her teeth, and continued making notes.

The days passed, filled with solitude and information; the nights remained restless, but now and then her nightmares were chased away by dreams of eating raspberries with someone who agreed that they were delicious. If she could have been assured of their repetition, she would have almost looked forward to putting her head down on the foreign pillow and escaping her cage; the companion awaiting her never spoke but in that way of dreams made her feel comfortable and admired.

When she woke from memories of blood and violence, the thought of those kinder dreams kept her sane.

Sooner than she was ready, the ship arrived. Surela girded herself for the battle.

———

"I'm going to pick up the crew," Ra'aila said, her absurd ears bobbing as she spoke. "I'll probably have them settled in by tomorrow around lunch, so let's meet two hours after that at the north balcony Pad station. We can head to the livestock supply from there."

They'd been summoned to the mess for this meeting, and Surela was very aware of how little she knew, and how unprepared she was for any excursion off the ship. But Saul, who was standing behind one of the chairs at the same table, seemed at ease. "Sounds good. Do you need us to prep anything on the ship for them?"

"No, it's fine. They're used to being itinerants, they don't pack much." Ra'aila flashed a grin that was all animal teeth, and Surela suppressed a shudder. "That's why I'll need all night to round them up. Who knows where they've gotten to." She canted her head. "Anything else? If not, I've got to get moving."

"We'll be all right," Saul said.

The captain of their vessel made a gesture: fingertips to her brow and flung from it, and then she was off.

Her keeper watched, then shook his head. "Either she's going to work out well for this, or it's going to be a disaster, and it's too soon to tell."

It hadn't occurred to Surela that their personnel situation was subject to the same management issues that an Eldritch

House was. And that this ship was a new enterprise for a woman who, for all her mortal origins, was now charged with the prosperity of an Eldritch province in the same way a lady would have been. "Do you suppose there is a second choice for her position, if she is deemed unsuitable?"

"No idea," her minder said, ears flicking back. "But I'm sure Reese will make shift where she can. Anyway... shall we go look at Starbase Psi? It's worth seeing."

"You have been before?"

"I have, yes. It's one of the better staging stops for the colony I used to work on."

To be out of her metal kennel... even to go to a place full of mortals... Goddess, anything to be free of the unrelenting trial of her nightmares. "I am ready," she said, and it was not quite a lie, given her determination to show no weakness to anyone, encroaching alien or memory of Eldritch enemy.

"Then let's go."

They exited the ship through its aft end, and the pressure descended on her, clamping her ribs. She paused on the ramp, causing Saul to stop and look back at her. "Too much?"

"No," she breathed, because she refused to be shut back in her cage. She forced herself to continue moving, down the ramp and into a space so enormous Surela dizzied. She forced her knees to continue rising and falling while around her the horizons expanded past her peripheral vision: other ships, ceilings so high they registered as a sky, metal and glass and people, so many people. She straightened, lifting her chin: of course they lived like ants, crawling on one another in chaos and noise.

"Stay close," Saul said. "The port's a little overwhelming if you're not used to it. You'll like the city better."

This was the *port*? Only?

Saul patted one of the metal legs of their vessel as they passed it, and Surela glanced up the long slope of the hull. Was it traitorous to admit to awe at the sight of it? No

Eldritch had made such a ship in generations, though they must have created one in order to travel to their world and colonize it.

That thought stayed with her, like the cologne of an unwanted guest, all the way through the crowded vastness of the port. That once upon a time, the Eldritch had been adventurers, creating their destiny rather than accepting it. That they had once been masters of ships in space, and the sort of people who concerned themselves with issues as large as this Alliance of aliens did as a matter of course. That they had lost that birthright—no, *squandered* it, and while Surela did not want it herself, that the rest of the galaxy had and could now rightly consider the Eldritch pitiable for their lack nettled her.

"Doing all right?"

She hated that he asked, and that his asking made it necessary for her, out of courtesy, to answer. "Well enough."

He nodded, accepting it at face value. "Here we go, then."

She hurried after him, hating how her lack of skirts made her stride obvious. It had been one of her most difficult flaws to overcome as a young maiden intent on her first appearance in court: that she walked too quickly for elegance. A woman must never be seen to be rushed, for people confident in their power felt no need to be. Impatience was too easy to mistake for fear. And Surela was *not* afraid.

Saul had stopped at a rail, and she came to a halt alongside him at the sight of a sunset as vivid as citrines flashing on a coronet. It smoldered in reflection in a lake so large it looked an ocean, and around it, the empurpled shadows shrouding a city lit with faery strings, yellow and amber and pink, dipped deep into the crevices of its roads that wound down from their perch toward the banks of that water. Beneath her boots, the deck of their balcony shivered with the force of the waterfall cascading beneath them through a channel carved into what looked like grassy hills, for that orange light clung to them as softly as velvet.

Had they somehow come out of the port onto a mountain? The breeze fluttered the end of her rude braid against her back as it gamboled past, filling her nose with the scent of flowers and water, and it hurt because it was the magic and beauty the Eldritch were supposed to have captured in their cities, and hadn't, because they had only ever managed to build a single city and everything else was a crumbling pretension toward the glory that mortals, apparently, had in abundance.

"I thought," she began, and halted when her voice began to crack. When she'd mastered it, she finished, "I thought we had come to a contrivance in space? A station?"

"We have," Saul said.

People were streaming past them on either side of the balcony, heading off it to the paths leading down into the city. None of them seemed to suffer for the weight of the air on their shoulders; it was their movements that had the polished ease of princes, while she labored to remain standing at this rail, fighting for breath. She forced herself to rest her hands on the wood—it was wood, surely? It felt it, to her touch. Polished and still warm from the sun.

"There." Saul pointed toward the horizon. "There are other viewing platforms, if you'd like to sightsee more. It's beautiful at night. You can take paths from here that circle the cup of the city… it's what they call this area, the Cup, because they built it in this valley. Or if you want, we can go looking at the shops. Find something to eat. Everything will be open for hours yet."

Could she eat? Eating would mean sitting. "Food," Surela said. "Then… we will see."

"Lots of choices there. Come on, this way."

Surela followed him mechanically off the balcony, where it split into multiple paths. How did so many people vanish so completely? But she had no eyes for the people once she reached the street, because it seemed like every turning exposed the lake at the base of the city. Standing at the edge, beneath an awning flapping in the evening breeze, she could see the orange glitter of the waves down the incline, smell the freshness of the water.

None of her reading had prepared her for the physical reality confronting her, and to admit to her ignorance, her confusion... it was too difficult. She was grateful that Saul made it unnecessary. "Every starbase is a moon-sized sphere, hollow on the inside, that has spaces in its walls for smaller spheres that civilians use for living spaces, or for farming, or research—whatever that particular group wants. You should think of this place like..." He frowned. "Do you have glass ornaments?"

"Yes."

"Like a glass ornament filled with a small landscape, artificially created. In this case, it's a lot of dirt, a lot of water, and a lot of rocks. Covered with greenery. Like a greenhouse, maybe. You know greenhouses?"

She refused to grind her teeth like a girl new to manners. "Yes."

"This is a greenhouse on the scale of a city, enclosed in a glass sphere set into the wall of the starbase. That's the best I can do to describe it."

"And... this... city."

"Clovellan, they call it. They being mostly Karaka'A, because it was a Karaka'An group that got the grant from the Colony Bureau for this sphere, along with a bunch of Ciracaana and Glaseah, since we're not all too far from their homeworlds. Everything else is..." Saul waved a hand, "the usual mix of people from the Alliance."

Their walk took them downhill, and the sky above them had turned amethystine already, sprinkled with stars that... moved along a ladder-like constellation in the sky. Against it, the stone buildings were silhouettes, where they weren't touched by the last flames of the sunset or the many lanterns.

If it had not been full of mortals and the aggravating sounds of their languages, Surela would have been impossibly charmed by it. But no amount of distant songs or laughter made this place chafe less, and the shrieks of children made the muscles tighten all the way up her spine. It was not fair, that mortals should have children enough to play together, and to dash past them into side streets lit by silver and honey-warm lights.

"Do you like seafood?"

His voice jerked her away from her brooding, and the mounting exhaustion. "I have rarely had it."

He smiled at her. "Is that 'yes' or 'no'?"

Frustrated at what she'd divulged in a moment of inattention, Surela said, "Yes."

"Good. The harbor here has a lot of seafood places."

At the speed of her minder's lanky, loose-limbed stroll, it would take too long to reach the beach, and Surela regretted her reply. But at the next large plaza, Saul turned onto a road that took them to a shelf of buildings perched along the curve of the incline. Their destination was a restaurant that consisted of tiers of balconies overlooking the view, with enormous windows open to the evening wind. Sitting was a relief; the walk had felt short, but moving cost her so much. Would it grow easier? Goddess, she hoped.

She was not so far gone with her body's weakness not to notice her keeper glancing at her throat, where her muscles were leaping with every breath that pulled her collarbones upward. He said nothing, however, and she hated that she was grateful for it.

In that restaurant she was served fish to shame anything she had at Asaniefa, for Silin's manse was well inland and their province's rocky coast had only a single cove suitable for a harbor. She accepted each course with forced equanimity and tried to ignore the mortals crowded around her, and how the murmur of their conversation mingled agreeably

with the wind ruffling the pennants strung from the case-
ments. It was a beautiful establishment, immaculately clean
despite the numbers of people moving through it. The meal
was sublime. She had no idea how much any of it cost. All of
this drove her to distraction. It would be easy—too easy—to
find solace in another glass of the superb wine. Something in
her protested, and she agreed. To dull her senses was the act
of a coward. She refused to be seen as unequal to the punishment her enemies expected to break her.

After dessert, her keeper escorted her outside. "Would
you like to shop? Look around?"

She glanced at him. "You would allow me to go alone?"

His ears flipped sideways, but his voice was unembar-
rassed. "No."

"Do you fear that I might be stolen away by slavers? Or
that I might steal away to conspire with them?"

The acerbic tone should have flustered him, but his face
remained bland: not an Eldritch's courtly mask, but more as
if... he truly wasn't perturbed. "It's an overwhelming place,
even for people born to the Alliance, and you know nothing
about the culture or the technology."

Affronted, she forced her bent spine to straighten. "I can
stand any test."

He sized her up, and it was so obvious she couldn't help
bristling, and hated that her form-fitting peasant clothes put
even her most subtle motion on display. She was so involved
with that frustration that she almost missed his words. "All
right."

"I beg your pardon?"

"You think you can handle it," he said. "I'll let you try. I'll
see you back at the ship. Try to be there before morning."
And then, before she could object, he melded into the river of
people heading up the street, so effectively that he was just...
gone.

Goddess and Lord, what had her anger gotten her into?

An Eldritch alone, among the very aliens who'd made such quick work of her world's paltry defenses, the aliens who harbored those who stole their kind for the harems of dragons? Like Liolesa's benighted heir Bethsaida, who, for all her sickly adoration of her aunt, had not deserved to become their plaything? Oh, that was a pretty piece of work, Liolesa had done, hiding the girl away and giving it out that she'd gone on retreat. Had Surela not had a friend in that convent....

Of course, the threat of abduction was probably minor in comparison to the very real danger that her limbs might cease to work. She didn't know why they were quivering with fatigue from the effort of merely standing, but she couldn't imagine walking any distance.

Standing in the middle of the street would make her look the tourist. Surela forced herself to resume moving, going... she knew not where. Her dismay frustrated her: she was no tyro to be distressed by the unforeseen. She was—had been—Surela Silin Asaniefa, head of one of the Eldritch's ten great Houses, and there was a working mind in her head, unlike so many of her peers. And her body would not fail her, because she would not allow it to.

Toward the lights and the noise... where there were people, there were shops and guides. And up was the direction of the bridge that had led to the port. How different could it be from the capital of the Eldritch world?

———

Many hours later, Surela conceded that a mortal city was like an Eldritch city in the way that a feast resembled bread and water, and she did not love herself for the metaphor. She tried replacing it as she looked at this boutique or that confectionary: as a riot resembled a conversation? A gaudy novel resembled a perfect couplet? A whore resembled a woman of taste and refinement? But no, overwhelmingly her impression was of an abundance, of such affluence and plenitude that she might gorge on it and be satiated long before she exhausted the table.

It mattered little that she had no idea what she would do with the sleek, technological devices on display in the shop she was forced to examine while taking her frequent rests, nor that she found the fashions in the next shop window gauche and unappetizing. It was the multiplicity of the choices that staggered her, the way they asked what she wanted to be and offered her every avenue toward crafting that perfected self. The only thing arresting her awe was the fact that she had no way to interact with any of it, because she had no idea how such things were paid for. That Liolesa had endless rivers of money for her gadgets was obvious to everyone, but like her peers in the isolationist Houses, Surela hadn't cared about offworld wealth. The only wealth that had mattered had been the power and the coin of their world. Until the outworld had obtruded into their sphere through Baniel's machinations, Surela hadn't thought of it at all.

And yet, all this time, Liolesa's offworld wealth had been buying the food they'd been eating, with none of them the wiser.

Surela stopped beside another restaurant, this one small and smelling fragrantly of floral tisanes. The aliens were on its patio and within its walls, sipping from delicate cups and enjoying dainty sandwiches and cookies that could have sprung from one of Asaniefa's pantries. Which begged the question of whether those sandwiches and cookies had literally come from a starbase like this one.

She received all the second glances she'd expected, but had not been prepared for the admiration she saw on alien faces. Such looks on Eldritch ones would have suggested attraction, which was ridiculous, but, she supposed, better than avarice or mockery. When she halted to give her racing heart a respite, the aliens left her alone on the benches, as if they knew and respected the Eldritch distaste for touch, and the two times she stopped to ask for directions, she was accorded great courtesy despite the difficulties created by her clumsiness speaking their tongue.

Surela hated their courtesy. She didn't want to learn that they could behave with recognizable manners. And yet, she appreciated the help, especially as the night wore on and the endless loveliness of this artificial city began to pall. Her choices were to ghost through such cities for the remainder of her life, forever an outsider… or to embrace them, and sink to their level. Contemplating her path exhausted her, and it was easier to retrace her route back to the port, and from there to the ship.

She'd expected to be ambushed by her keeper on her return, but neither Saul nor Ra'aila were in evidence. Surela returned to her kennel and sank onto the bed, where her aching joints set up such a clamor that it was all she could do not to topple. At least the ship did not seem to pull on her limbs quite so avidly.

The computer could perhaps have marked her absence. "How long have I been gone?"

And it knew. "Six hours. It is just past Mark 23."

Six hours! "And… Saul?"

"Saul Ferry has just entered the ship."

Surela frowned. Without consciously choosing to do so, she found herself outside her cabin, walking the ugly metal corridor, and there, near the door to the outside world, was her wolf. She halted, and he looked up, face unreadable and eyes as friendly as his greeting. "Good evening, alet."

"Did you follow me?" she demanded.

He smiled at her. "Not everything's about you." And with a dipped head, slid past her and down the hall.

That… had not been an answer. Had been so exquisitely not an answer that it had felt almost… relaxing. An Eldritch would have replied so to a question they had no intention of answering, but could not in courtesy ignore. It made her want to like him, and she despised it as weakness in herself. As a yearning for home.

She would never go home again, and she would not yield, either, to the alienation of her exile. She would find some way to triumph, somehow. And perhaps, one day, she would not have to lay her head down on a cot in this rude and ugly cage, but would sail the foreign stars in a palatial vessel of her own choosing, and her opponents would remember their plans for her and regret their choices.

———

The morning found her on the other side of the starbase with her minder in tow, staring at the cleanest and most clinical presentation of chickens she had seen in her life. When the human had sent Surela on this errand she'd anticipated arriving at a breeder's yard, there to evaluate—Goddess help her—several hundred animals. Honesty compelled her to admit that she couldn't imagine several hundred animals in one place, and that her mind insisted on painting a picture of a small farmyard with some peasant couple awaiting her.

Instead, she was in what looked like a jeweler's show-room, and the chickens in question were not flesh and blood, but holographic projections, each on a pedestal above another holographic projection, this time of a list of their various virtues and weaknesses. Her 'peasant couple' turned out to be another of the ubiquitous furred creatures, but this one was sleekly groomed, glossy black from head to toe, and had the mien of a court musician. The sole concession to Surela's expectations was the duckling this perfectly coiffed sales-person was holding in one dark hand, and it was incongru-ous. She wanted to rescue the one from the other... put the duck in some pond, and the salescreature in some art gallery.

"Do you know what you're looking for in your stock?" it was saying. Her, perhaps? Surela couldn't tell. A very delicate man, or a very athletic woman.

The question, at least, snapped her priorities back in place. "We seek a hardy breed that can thrive on our board."

"Are you looking for eggs or meat?"

"Can I not have both?"

The creature laughed. "Yes, but not in the same chicken. Unless there's a reason you can't support more than one breed, I'd encourage you not to compromise."

Compromises were for those who couldn't have everything they wanted, and Surela wanted everything. Not just for herself, but for the tenants she'd been forced to abandon. Why should they not have the plenty these aliens took for granted? "We have the funds and the space both, but what we do not, is the knowledge of which breed will do well and which will fail. Would it be possible to take…."

"Samples?" The creature nodded. "Of course. It's just a matter of the number you want to transport, and how. Embryos are easiest, of course, but you'll need the equipment to grow them. Eggs are the next easiest, if you have incubators. The actual birds… we don't keep a lot of grown stock on hand. Your selection would be limited."

Surela glanced at Saul and Ra'aila for guidance; the latter looked bleary-eyed, as if she'd not slept, and there was a slightly rumpled quality to the fur along her cheeks and arms. A third creature had accompanied them, a stranger Ra'aila had introduced as Jorub—such an ugly, curt mouthful, that. He was another like Ra'aila, with the ridiculous ears, not improved by a sullen expression somehow intelligible despite his long muzzle and furry face. Surela ignored him to focus on the captain of their uncertain enterprise. "Do we have any of this equipment?"

"We don't, no. We have a budget, though."

Which Ra'aila had failed to share with her. Surela's mood

was not improved by her shortness of breath and the pressure of the environment on her shoulders, and for once she felt she had cause to vent her frustrations. "Will you excuse us?" Surela asked their host, and then stalked to the other side of the large showroom. There were windows in it, ridiculous windows the size of Ontine's… who put such extravagant panes of glass in something as pedestrian as a farmyard, no matter how radically designed? Once her ragtag band of animals had joined her, Surela leaned closer to Ra'aila than she wished despite the creature's delectable smell and said, "You should tell me what we can spend, or how do you propose that I acquire what we need?"

"You don't know how much money is worth—"

"So, we tell her," Saul interrupted, unperturbed. "She can make value conversions."

On a much grander scale than the purchase of a chicken, at that—

"Fine," Ra'aila said. "Then you've got 150,000 fin to spend on this trip."

Surela glanced at Saul.

"One of those chickens, full grown, is probably 25 fin. The eggs are going to run under five a pop. It's on the labels."

"Goddess and Lord." It slipped out before she could stop it. She had arranged for victuals at home, but nowhere near on this scale, and this was a first outing. She had underestimated the depth of Liolesa's pockets. "And the machinery?"

"Different matter," Saul said. "The incubators should be fine, we can run them off the ship's power grid. The decanters, though… that's as modern a tech as you get in the Alliance, and nothing on your world is going to be able to power them."

"So, eggs," Surela said. "Or birds."

"Right."

"And a method for transporting them."

Saul nodded.

"And, I imagine, some fee for the transfer from here to the vessel at the port."

"She's good," the third creature said to Ra'aila.

Ra'aila scrubbed at her eyes. "I would have thought of it if I hadn't been hung over."

"You could have taken a morning-after."

"Those shots make me queasier."

Ignoring them, Surela headed back to the displays. Husbanding her limited energy, she walked among them, noting the prices and totaling them in her head. When she reached the salescreature, she said, "Tell me about these incubators. Assuming you offer them for sale."

"We do, yes. Over here...."

———

Surela dispatched the captain and her hanger-on back to the ship to prepare for the arrival of the livestock, an errand both were more than willing to use to excuse themselves. Had they been up all night engaged in debauchery? Surela expected no less of aliens. At least the keeper Eddings had selected for her showed no signs of frivolity; Saul remained at her side while she built her purchase list, negotiated for feed, machines, and chicken housing—for the creatures had to live somewhere—and finalized her choices. She was taking a hundred eggs of each kind on offer, and wanted to arrange for the acquisition of live animals in the future. The salescreature had developed a name as irritatingly androgynous as its body, 'Beverly,' and as it summed her purchases, it said, "Yes, of course, we can have them ready for your next run, if you let us know when that would be. A few weeks? A few months?"

It hit her, then, that in a few months, she could expect to once again be here. Buying chickens.

With enough money to deck Asaniefa's entire province in garlands and throw a holiday feast every week for a year.

49

Surela hated the picture of herself stuck in this rut, and craved the high of spending this much as if it was nothing, and the two feelings canceled themselves out admirably. "I'll check our schedule and have a date to you later today."

"Perfect, thank you. We'll have our deliverymen at the docks two hours after lunch."

"Thank you."

Outside in a sunlight that felt real to her skin, Surela paused, allowed herself to admit to the aches in her joints. At least the fake sun also gave warmth. "Did that go well?"

"Excellently," Saul said. "You thought of everything you should have."

She eyed him. "And you know this for certain."

"You wouldn't guess it to look at us, but both Ra'aila and I were part of a group that was dedicated to livestock breeding. We know how it goes."

"Ra'aila? Knows anything about livestock? She divulged to me that she had not the first notion of what to do with a chicken."

"We handled horses, not poultry. The principles might be the same but the particulars don't map to one another."

"Horses," Surela murmured.

"And Ra'aila was a ship driver, not an animal handler." Saul grinned. "I'm also more of a ship driver than an animal handler, but I learned to love it on the trip to Kerayle and after that it felt natural to keep learning."

"And why has Ra'aila not felt it natural to keep learning, if she planned to accept a position transporting livestock?"

"You'd have to ask her. But the Aera... they're nomads, most of them. I think they just like to keep moving."

Goddess, what a horror that sounded. To never have a home? This life that had been forced upon her... who would choose it?

"I like her, though," Saul continued. "She's less flighty than the average Aera. Which sounds terrible, like I'm judging her by my standards of behavior, but I don't mean it that way."

What a convoluted statement. Did all of them have such byzantine thought processes? "What do you mean by it?"

That silenced him as he began walking back toward the Pad that had delivered them to this part of the starbase. Saul maintained a pace surely intended to coddle her, but she was not sorry for it given her condition. The chicken farmer was on the other side of the bay, on a broad and golden, grassy plateau that had a more agrarian sensibility… more like an Eldritch village than a city. Surela had liked it as a place to visit, somewhat, but wouldn't have wanted to live there. She preferred an urban environment, even a crowded one like the alien version on the port side of the water.

"This is something you learn when you head into the broader galaxy," her minder said. "That other people have other ways of living, many of them incompatible with yours. You have to figure out how to work with that, or you have to figure out how to minimize the impact on your life. But you have to choose." He flashed her a grin. "Sometimes you choose both, depending on the situation, at different times. It can get complicated."

It sounded exhausting. But she was more curious, despite herself, about the revelation. "You speak as if you had not always been involved with the Alliance."

"Oh, I was born here, like everyone you see around us. But 'here' can mean a lot of things. For me, that means Covenant, which is the oldest Hinichi colony in the Alliance. It's pretty monocultural. Almost no other species on it as residents, just us. And while we have a bunch of religious sects, on Covenant things sort of collapsed," he made a motion with both hands, bringing them together, "into a single sect that got stronger and more distinct with the passing centuries. So any variation we might have gotten that way vanished, too."

All of which sounded reasonable to Surela. "But you left."

"When I was a kit, we traveled a lot. We had family on Hinichitii—that's our species' homeworld—so we'd visit them regularly, and I got to see what a more populated world was like, and of course, we would stop at all the stations and starbases between here and there. That's what made me think 'When I grow up I should go out there. See what it's like when you're in the thick of it.'"

Only someone without power and influence would ever think it profitable to leave their home out of some nebulous desire to sightsee. Surela supposed she could pity him, save that he seemed content with himself and his choices—how bizarre.

"Anyway," the creature finished. "That's when I learned that you have to make allowances for how other people act, while also not letting them walk all over you."

"I am not minded to allow anyone that liberty."

"No," Saul said with a smile. "And don't let anyone change you, alet. You'll do fine."

She mused on that after they'd reached the ship: how similar 'you'll do fine' was to the ultimate in Eldritch encomiums: 'you'll do.' It should have irritated her to be condescended to by a mortal, but instead it made her wonder if he was right. If her strengths might serve her in this pedestrian world she was forced to navigate.

She thought it again when she found the ship full of aliens. Ra'aila had, indeed, found a crew for them, composed entirely of creatures like her, long-eared, short-tailed, and all of them drunk. Surela had to step over the first in the corridor to reach the mess, and there were two more sleeping on the tables there, jaws agape and tongues spilling from the corners like a dog's. The lingering perfume of alcohol tinted the air, along with the odd sirocco-sharp scent of their species' bodies. If they had vomited or sweated in their cups, Surela couldn't smell it, Goddess be thanked. Thanks to her recent experiences she was all too familiar with the sour scents of vomit and sweat, among less pleasant things.

Ra'aila was in the fore of the ship, dragging an unconscious body by the ankles toward the door. Surela paused to let her by, and when the other woman looked up at her, there was a flash of exhausted irritation in Ra'aila's eyes that boded well. The captain might have joined her crew in their revels, but she did not love being forced to address their excesses the following morning.

"The delivery should arrive later today," Surela said. "As I believe that is all we came for, we should be able to return to my world when it is convenient. Soon, I should hope, as I would like to deliver our cargo to competent hands."

"Still winds, yes. Who on the wayroutes wants to deal with chickens?"

"Those who eat them, I imagine."

Ra'aila wrinkled her nose. "Fair point. I'll get us underway this evening, unless I can't get a departure slot. You and Saul can take leave as long as you're back by dinner."

"I have work to do here," Surela said, because she didn't think she had the energy to fight through the weight of the starbase again. And strangely, she didn't mind, because she wanted to read. About money, and about livestock, and about the creatures they'd bought and the equipment and the power requirements for the machinery Saul had said they could not yet afford. The next time they arrived at Mistress or Master Beverly's establishment, Surela planned to be better prepared.

CHAPTER 6

There was no escaping introduction to the five mortals Ra'aila had acquired for their crew, because they were raucous and restless, flocking hither and yon like nuisance birds. Their hides were brightly colored, reds and golds and blues that had to be dyed, for surely even aliens did not come in ultramarine. They were barely dressed by anyone's standards, in unbuttoned vests and hip wraps, or cut-off leggings tighter than a woman's stockings. Once they recovered from their over-indulgence, they seemed industrious enough, though Surela knew too little about the ship to judge if their efforts were productive of anything other than dramatic display. Her attempts to judge them using Saul's reaction was fruitless—her minder stayed out of the way of the enthusiastic additions, but showed no sign of distress or opprobrium at their behavior, either.

Ra'aila appeared energized by their arrival, which Surela supposed suited, as it kept the alien out of her way. That left her to use their journey back to avoid her nightmares by practicing the ungainly alien tongue in an attempt to minimize her accent and expand her vocabulary, exploring random topics with the computer, and keeping an eye on the chickens. In her weaker moments, she could admit she was proud of the sight of the serried ranks of eggs battened down in the cargo hold. This bounty was traveling home to feed her people, and if it was galling to be forced to turn to aliens for the necessity... then at least, there was a chance, no matter how slim, that a bird in this hold would be the progenitor of an Eldritch breed, saving them from begging for aid in the future.

Surela was not, however, brave enough to leave her kennel when the vessel reached her former home. Her feelings remained a tumult: was she proud that the Eldritch now had a space station capable of docking alien ships? Or disgusted that they'd been forced to bow to the necessity of mortal technology? Was she glad to be home, even if she could no longer walk on the surface of the world? Or angry, because that home was denied her? Or worse, ashamed, because who knew what gossip was bruited about in her absence, about her absence?

Surela, the One Week Usurper. She shuddered.

The cargo vanished in a single afternoon, and then... they idled. From what Surela understood of the conversations she caught in the corridors, the new crew was exploring the station, and Goddess help whatever Eldritch were in their way. Saul remained aboard, and so discreetly that she rarely noticed him. The entire exercise was awkward, and she tried not to dwell on this becoming the routine that defined her life.

She was expecting... what? Another impersonal assignment, delivered by messenger. But she was sitting in the mess hall alone, working on a bowl of raspberries and a cup of tea, when her human benefactor strolled in through the arch which, sadly, seemed not to have a door that could be closed. Surela forgot how short humans were, and how ungainly with their stunted limbs and lack of grace. And yet, how much better this room suited the head of House Laisrathera than it did Surela. The ceilings and walls were sized to hold Theresa Eddings; the casual jacket and pants and boots, in their grays and blacks and oranges, matched the palette.

And none of the finer points of her appearance mattered, because the human looked at ease in her skin in a way that filled Surela with pointless envy. Eddings was *happy*.

"Place looks good," the human said. "Ra'aila's brought her team aboard, I see. Are they giving you trouble?"

Surela would have to participate in this discussion. In person, where her reactions could be seen if she did not control them. She did not love her sudden longing for the distance imposed by mortal messaging. "They are easily avoided."

"Because they're loud, I'm betting." The woman chuckled and checked the carafes available behind the counter. "Aera aren't Harat-Shar, but they're way over on the party animal side of the spectrum. Hopefully it won't bother you too much. If it does, let me know."

"And you will do what about it, precisely?"

The other woman didn't even pause, pouring herself a mug of coffee. "Talk to Ra'aila about it, probably. If you don't decide to handle it yourself… you're pretty good at handling things." Was that a challenge? But no, her savior's face was pleasant, not set in sarcastic lines. "You did well with the chickens… any problems there? Things you need me to fix for you? Lacking for anything? Saul should have told you how to draw down your salary."

Goddess, where to begin with this barrage. "You needn't coddle me. I am a criminal, not worthy of the time."

The human ignored that to consider her. "You look set for clothes, at least. Are you sure I can't get you some entertainment options? I spent most of my shipboard time reading endless reams of romances. It kept me busy."

Being irritated that her unwanted liegelady was ignoring

her attitude was… exhausting. Surela was tired of hating everything, even though doing so was reflexive. How could she retain any vestige of her identity if she didn't cling to the culture that had rejected her? "I am spending my time studying. There is a great deal of context I lack. If I am to buy foodstuffs and materials, I cannot be ignorant."

"That's a good start, but all work and no play is going to drive you crazy. Unless you enjoy manipulating numbers?"

Did she? "I never thought of it as something to enjoy. But it is satisfying, to be proficient in one's chosen arena."

"That's a long way of saying you want to be useful. But I get it." The woman tapped her brown finger on the wall of her mug. "Do you want to take up watercolors? Or playing the harp or… uh… the pianoforte?"

"I… beg your pardon?" Surela asked, confounded.

"I don't think 'learn foreign languages' is something you get taught as an accomplishment—"

Surela stared at her. "Dare I ask where these wild notions are rising from?"

"In my fevered brain? I should have remembered it's the men who have to have the accomplishments and the women who get to pick their spouses in your society." The woman looked wistful. "Honestly, though, I always thought it sounded… great. If the most your society wanted out of you was to mess around with art and be good at talking."

"Leisure does not interest me," Surela said. Which she thought was true. Her life had been filled with duty, and if most of it involved political maneuvering… still, that was work.

"I guess learning about the Alliance is going to keep you occupied for a while. When it stops occupying you, let me know."

"You need not be so unceasingly *helpful*."

"That's where you're wrong." Eddings sipped from her cup, set it deliberately down. "I rescued you and that makes you my responsibility. I took you into my House and that makes you twice my responsibility. I might be new to this Eldritch liege stuff, but I'm not stupid. And I'm not going to let you fail because you didn't have help." Her blue eyes were uncomfortably direct. "Too many people are hoping you will, you know."

Surela didn't grit her teeth because the return of this uncouth habit she'd been forced to break as a maiden would have mortified her. But it was a near thing. "I am aware, yes. And you... you would be shamed before them all if your investment failed to produce, wouldn't you."

"I'd hate to be wrong. Doesn't everyone? But that's not the real point, not for me. I'm the one who talked you into taking this chance. If I don't support you while you make it, then your failure is as much my fault as yours. I owe it to you."

"You owe me nothing," Surela hissed from between her teeth. Was this anger? Humiliation? Something of both.

"You're wrong, but I'm not going to argue about it. When you're calmer, you'll know better. I'm not Eldritch, but I do get obligation, and I get taking care of your people." Eddings rested a hand on the back of one of the mess hall chairs. "We're going to need a lot of work from you and the crew. These eggs were a good start. Can you go back for more? Everyone tells me that chickens die with ridiculous speed on your world."

It was not the change in subject that disarmed her, but how completely the human refused the offense. The woman she'd met in their prison cell had been waspish, swifter to both attack and defensiveness. This one... had her mind on other things. More urgent ones, and as they involved the vulnerability of her people—hers, not the human's—Surela could not fail to appreciate Eddings's priorities. "I have arranged for adults, though it will take the breeders several weeks to produce them."

"Good. While we're waiting on that I need to send you

out again for staples… flour, sugar, salt, that sort of thing. We need a lot of it. I'll tag you with the list. Do you know how to get those lists now?"

"I can command the computer."

"Good enough. If not, Saul can help, or Ra'aila."

The human's concern was smothering. "You are doing enough."

"I worry that all our efforts won't be enough, some days." Eddings sighed, shook her head. "No use fretting about it, though. We're on our way, hopefully." She rose. "Think I'll take a look around… it's hard not to be nostalgic. You'll call me if you run into any problems?"

Surela had hoped that would have been offered as a rhetorical question, but annoyingly the human paused alongside the door, waiting.

"Yes," she said at last. "Yes, I will, if your hired guardian does not solve my problem for you."

Eddings grinned. "Good enough. Keep fighting, Surela."

Was she insulted at the intimation that she was? That she should continue? That the grin suggested pride in Surela's obstinacy? That a human should believe herself entitled to pride over the accomplishments of a woman three times (or more!) her age!

Had Theresa Eddings come aboard merely to be assured of her comfort?

Goddess, the preposterousness of it. That a human would believe herself owed vassal duties, and to owe liege duties in return! It was presumptuous, and it chafed her, that the woman might be good at it. But it was impossible not to honor her for the effort to ape her betters, surely.

Surela scowled at her raspberries and almost didn't finish them… but they were good, and something in her insisted that she should have them. By the time she'd scooped the last from the bowl, she could admit that her pique was unjust. Eddings had saved her from execution, after trying to save her from rape. The least Surela could do was tolerate her attempts to undertake her duties.

———

Within a week they had embarked on their journey back to Starbase Psi. Surela learned to take her meals early, did she want to avoid the boisterous Aera Ra'aila only somewhat kept in line... this put her in the mess at the same time as Saul, but his company was restful in compare. She needed only one supper with the new crewmembers to know she wanted nothing to do with them. Sloth disgusted her, so she could not argue with their energy... but their vulgar conduct nettled her. They asked too many questions, talked over one another, grabbed for things they wanted, made too many abrupt motions. They left messes they only sometimes remembered to tidy, and laughed off attempts to be shamed into better behavior. Saul had shrugged and said, "Think of them as members of a family," and that... helped, oddly. At least, as a context for the way they interacted with one another. Surela hadn't loved her cousins, but she'd had a great many of them, too many, and reunions had churned with their restless ambitions and scheming. The crew's lack of spite could be construed as relaxing, in that regard.

Surela's absence troubled them not at all if their behavior was any indication, and that lack of interest freed her to prepare for their next expedition. This time Eddings had advanced her a budget directly, along with the list of necessities, and there was something satisfying about the contemplation of its fulfillment. Eggs that might or might not become useful breeders were one matter... flour in fifty pound bags, however, was a more direct solution to their problems. When her nightmares woke her, she dragged herself to her desk and looked up commodity prices until her eyes began to close.

On their arrival to Psi, Surela dressed in her peasant wear

and set off with Saul in tow, and while the Aera went on furlough—having done what to earn it, she had no idea—she procured the staples on the human's list, and, with the spare money, purchased the extras dear to Eldritch palates: dried fruits to ornament their feast breads; cheeses in multiple varieties, spreadable as well as hard; the verjuices and vinegars that gave an appealing contrast to the sweetness of their sauces; and of course, the almonds that went into their cuisine and their liqueurs both. Though it dragged at her breathing and joints, Surela tarried in the open air markets, for there were multiple such in the city, with everything from seafood to fresh vegetables, and while she longed to send back tender, new fruits and salad greens delicate enough to gratify a debutante, Saul shook his head. "We couldn't bring back enough of it, not with the facilities we have."

"There are facilities that make it possible? To transport this as cargo without preserving it?"

"Oh yes. We're not there yet."

That drove Surela back to her research, where she learned about stasis fields and their applications in everything from medicine to cooking. The endlessness of what she didn't know agitated her, made her feel she would never be equal to mastering the mortal world's inexhaustible capacity to surprise her.

For several days, she acted as Laisrathera's procurer, and with Ra'aila and Saul's aid, organized the deliveries. Once those deliveries arrived at their cargo doors, the new crewmembers loaded it, and it could at least be said in their favor that they did so without complaint, and with much sport and laughter. But soon enough, they had sealed the ship and headed back to Eldritch space, there to offload the cargo and leave again, this time for more chickens.

Surela had so much to accustom herself to: the language, the bizarre routine, the unexpected tasks and the steps needed to undertake them. It kept her busy enough not to notice the passage of time. If she drowned herself in the minutiae, she no longer had the energy to notice how small her cage was. And if she was often hungry, and often tired, and often irritable, then surely all these things were understandable.

But hers were not the only troubles, which she discovered when her early morning raid on the mess ambushed their captain in a state of dejection. Surela stopped at the arch. Had Ra'aila been another Eldritch, Surela would have backed away instantly to preserve the fiction of privacy... had that Eldritch been someone she respected, anyroad. An enemy, she might have advanced on in hopes of using their weaknesses against them. What would an alien want? To be left alone? Or to be comforted? Goddess, as if she could comfort a mortal!

Alas, Ra'aila's long ears were more than equal to the task of hearing even the slightest of motions. She looked up from the plate she was ignoring and exhaled. "You're not here to complain about our itinerary, are you, alet? Because I can't take more complaints about our itinerary."

Comfort, Surela could not offer. Solutions to problems, however, were within her métier. She advanced on the counter in search of tea to soothe her agitated stomach. "What possible problem could there be with our itinerary? We are fulfilling our duties by making these passages to and from the starbase. That is what we are hired to do, is it not?"

"It's what you were hired to do, and what I was hired to do, and what Saul was hired to do... but we were picked by Reese."

Surela looked over the counter at the creature, who hadn't raised the head she had resumed cradling in her furred hands. "And?"

"And Reese told me to find a crew and hire them to fill out the roster."

"Which you did, yes?"

"Which I did, yes, and they're great crew. They know how

to run a ship. But they're unhappy." Ra'aila sighed, turned her cup on the table. The scraping noise made Surela's eyelid twitch. "They didn't sign up to run the same route over and over. They want to know when we're heading off to explore the galaxy."

It was too early for the tisane to have been prepared for the carafe. For once Surela was glad of being reduced to the manual labor of making it, since it gave her an excuse not to sit alongside the creature and weather the brunt of her glum demeanor. She need not be a mind-mage to find such obvious emotion distasteful. "I was not under the impression that trading vessels did much exploratory work. By their nature, they would seem to travel between predictable destinations."

"They do, yes. But it's not unreasonable to expect an Alliance trading vessel to do its shopping in more than one location."

Was it? When the starbase seemed to have everything a world might need? Yet another thing to research when bad dreams drove her from her bed. "Can their dissatisfaction be addressed with higher wages?"

"I doubt it."

"Well, then," Surela said, filling the carafe, "you shall have to dismiss them."

Ra'aila looked up sharply, enormous ears sagging on either side of her shoulders. "I'm... sorry?"

"Dismiss them. They are not the proper people for the work. Free them to do something else, and hire new employees who value routine and a steady wage."

"Just like that!"

"What alternative do you have?" When the Aera began to speak, Surela waved a hand. "Make no excuses for them. Are they your relations? That is not enough. You have tasks to fulfill, and you need people to do them. You can either waste your time bullying your existing crew into doing their work —an act you tired of the first day you brought them aboard—

or you can sever their contracts and put yourself in possession of people who will be assets to your enterprise." There, the tea was made, and to her taste. She filled her cup. "Laisrathera engaged you to do important work on her behalf. You accepted that charge. Do you not owe her your best effort? And how can you remand it to her if you are worn down with the petty irritations and frustrations of an untrustworthy company?"

"They're not untrustworthy! Just... unhappy."

"Then make them happy by setting them loose to seek employment better suited to their natures."

Ra'aila rubbed her brow with a crooked finger, grimaced. "All right. They are bad for what I need. But... I don't *know* anyone else."

Goddess, these mortals. With all the riches of their ridiculous society, and as helpless as babes when pushed past their meager limits. "You cannot convince me there is no guild for hiring employees for trade ships such as this one."

"Well... no. I mean yes, there is one."

"Then consult it, interview candidates, and hire them. Provisionally, to see if they suit."

"It's just... it'll be a pain."

"More of a pain than living with this situation?" Surela said. "You are miserable, and the wolf and I do not leave our kennels, the better to avoid your confederates. Do we all not deserve a better environment?" She couldn't help wrinkling her nose. "It is a poor enough one without burdening it further."

"Put that way..." Ra'aila shook her head. "But I've never been a ship's captain before. Not for strangers. That's not how it works in the clans. We always rely on one another for crew. It's one of the reasons I volunteered for this job, because I thought some part of it would be familiar."

Goddess help her. "Then we shall help you."

"All right, you've talked me into it." The creature glanced

64

at her, rueful. "I don't suppose I could convince you to be the bearer of the bad news?"

"To your crew?" Surela sniffed. "No. That is your duty, certes. Help hire their replacements, yes. But it is for you to tend your own errors, or are you not the head of this vessel?"

"I guess I am. And I thought it would be easy!"

"Did you put yourself forth in the expectations and hopes that it would be?"

Ra'aila's puzzlement was oddly evident, despite her animal face. "Well... yes? Why would you volunteer for a job you weren't sure you could do?"

"To discover within yourself the wherewithal to do it, naturally."

The creature chuckled, and seemed surprised by her own change in mood. "That's an interesting way of thinking of it. I think I'll try it on for a while. See if it helps."

Surela wanted breakfast less than she wanted to escape the vexation of this conversation. "Indeed. And I shall look into the hiring now. If you will excuse me."

Ra'aila twitched a hand. "Go on, it's not like we're Fleet here. You don't have to ask me permission for anything."

Did she not? No wonder this first crew had been such a disaster. How could one run anything with no hierarchy? No doubt her wolf keeper would say that family could manage without a properly defined authority, but Surela knew better. Running her family's enterprises required more such rules to keep her many cousins from deciding they should topple her from her position.

Surela had not expected or volunteered to become more involved in the Eddings human's goals, but sitting back while Ra'aila turned what little shelter they could claim into a divisive and noisome prison... no, that she could not do. And she knew something of managing people. She could only hope her knowledge would apply equally to aliens.

CHAPTER 7

"All right," Saul said, tapping his stylus against the edge of his tablet. "Crew roster. Did Ra'aila say how much money she had to spend on wages?"

"No," Surela said. "But she hired five people."

"Ah, but if they're all basic crew, they'll be paid lower rates than a specialist."

They were meeting in the ship's fore, a compartment Surela had seen very little of... but Saul was on duty in the early mornings while the Aera slept off their madcap nights, and it was one of the few places they were certain to be uninterrupted. It was an oddly compelling space, with its enigmatic consoles and bizarrely slanted windows, and the stars seen through them as if in a permanent midnight sky. Surela preferred the windows. Her kennel's lack of them made her feel as if she'd been shut in a stall. A mean one, for even horses had windows on her world. "Forgetting for now the expense, how would you go about the hiring?"

"She's a small ship, and we're trading, not fighting." Saul stopped tapping. "You have a captain, of course. Captain's usually the financial person, and the big picture person, but

Ra'aila's the one Reese tapped for that job, so she's going to end up the manager. We'll need other people for the roles she's not filling." He began counting. "Pilot, because we might eventually want someone who can fly this thing on manual, or land on a planet. I'm the mechanic, but it's a secondary job, so a mechanic or engineer. A purser, to handle the money. You're proving good at what you're doing, alet, but you're too new to the Alliance still, and a ship this small should have cross-training anyway." He paused, fingers still up. "Healer," he said after that pause.

Surela frowned. "You sound uncertain."

"I am. Healers aren't essential crew, usually, and they get expensive. But…" Saul grinned. "It's something of a tradition for this ship to carry one. And it's a good idea if you can afford it. So… healer. Then we need to fill out the roster so that people can work in shifts. One more, maybe two at most. Someone who can haul cargo around, or drive an antigrav dolly."

"So, still at five. But perhaps five requiring more money."

Saul nodded, canted his head like the dog he resembled. "You're serious about helping with this."

"It needs to be done."

"And you don't think Ra'aila can do it?"

"I hardly know the cre—woman." Surela finished writing the list. By hand, as she preferred. "I was given to understand you knew her from prior to this assignment. You would have a better notion of her fitness."

"She can do it, and I think Reese was right to give her the chance," Saul said. "But she's new to it, and she's got to figure out she's got it in her first."

Goddess, was there no end to the human's need to give people chances? And did she have to saddle Surela with quite so many of them at once? It would have been less irksome to have come into a situation managed by competent people, so she would have had the luxury of being the sole confused and alienated one. No... she'd been thrown into exile in a foreign civilization, only to have to take charge while sweating through nightmares and struggling with her deficient physical fitness. "So then. Five people, six at most. And the chickens."

"We might not find all of them at once—"

"We made the first trip without help."

Saul was nodding. "We did, and we can run the ship on a skeleton crew. But it's not a good idea. Redundancy is key in space, alet. It's the most hostile of hostile environments. Just because we've found ways to tame it doesn't make it safe."

"We will make haste, then. If you might show me the process by which we might access the list of potential employees."

That occupied them for the next hour, and Surela left for her room resigned to the necessity of using the computer interface to dig into the mountain of information Saul had guided her to. Indeed, the aliens had guilds for the employment of their subjects... but unlike the Eldritch, whose guilds covered solely the minuscule middle class created and supported only in the capital, the aliens had literal millions of available people for hire. Where did they *find* so many people, much less feed them and keep them gainfully occupied? It bothered her that she, who had found numbers so simple to manipulate, could not imagine a population this size.

Was this what made people like Liolesa so dismissive of their own? Or was that fair? Was it unavoidable that any Eldritch who went into space must develop a perspective that could look upon a single squalid kingdom and perceive solely its inconsequentiality?

And yet, dragons had coveted them, and pirates and slavers. And their kingdom was not squalid, but beautiful, ornate, mannered.

Surela pressed the heel of her hand against her brow, fighting the headache and the despair that never ceased stalking her in her weakest moments. Again, she refused the latter, and again, resigned herself to the former, and set her list of needful personnel on the desk alongside the floating projection of the guild listings. Saul had taught her how to search it, and all the terms that described the process: she had them written down the side of her page, 'database' and 'query' and 'keywords' and so many more. She was not looking forward to the exercise.

Except that, once she'd embarked on it, it engaged her. Like her procurement sorties on Laisrathera's behalf, but instead of shopping for foodstuffs, she was shopping for people. The Eldritch were uniform in demeanor: pale-skinned and –haired, with almost universally light eyes, and all tall, with little difference in build. She'd thought it harmonious, and still did… but there was an allure in these aliens with their constant and exotic differences. Tall, short, stout and dainty, in every color… and texture as well, for while some were furred, others were feathered, or scaled, and some had solely skin. The humans from whose stock the Eldritch had sprung came in far more hues than she assumed. Nor did all of the aliens have humanoid faces, for there were beaks and muzzles to go with the flatter style she found more readable in Saul. And there was no homogeneity in how they dressed, or how they coiffed their hair, and their personal styles ranged from absurd to austere, and she had no context to evaluate what any of it meant. She could tell in an instant the generation, social class, and family of any Eldritch she met. But these creatures? Was that oddly patched vest an heirloom, or a sign of rebellion? Was that grotesquely shaved hairstyle a tribal affiliation? A personal choice? Or did the alien's mane grow that way naturally?

And yet, there were some portraits she looked at and liked immediately, and couldn't tell why, or if she was right to trust those instincts. But she marked those anyway.

Supper came and went, and she was spurred to the mess

to collect something to bring back to her room, for she had no wish to tarry with the Aera having their late meal. She would have skipped it, sooth, but something in her insisted that she fuel herself. No fainting maidens, it seemed to remind her. She was no longer Surela, the friendless exile. No, now she was Surela, the manager of wayward aliens a fraction her age. Mere children, asked to do the work of adults grown. From that perspective, it astonished her that they accomplished all that they must have, to have created the enormous mortal Alliance.

It was good to keep busy. And fortunate that there was so much to be busy with.... And if the chores she was using to keep her confrontation with her past at bay involved mortals and the labor of menials, it was still preferable to that confrontation. The past felt unreal after weeks in her claustro-phobia-inducing cell, and the longer she went without wrestling it, the more she could tell herself it was solely the province of nightmares. Right now, that was what she could live with, particularly given the signs that were growing more difficult to ignore... that the healer on the first ship had been wrong, about 'inconclusive evidence.'

She would face her days one task at a time, and cram them so full of tasks she could use them like beads on an abacus, counting out the sum of her new life in increments she could handle.

CHAPTER 8

The dock at Starbase Psi was beginning to have the familiarity of her former apartments at court. Surela wasn't sure she was happy about it, but she supposed she should be grateful that the sharp edges of her confinement were being worn away by conversancy. Certainly the sight of the departing Aera did a great deal to soothe her irritated nerves. They were well quit of the creatures, and not even Ra'aila's gusty sigh moved her from that conviction.

"Firing them went better than I expected," the captain said. "They were glad to go. Now, we look for people, I guess."

Surela handed over the tablet she'd borrowed from Saul.

"What's this?"

"A preliminary list of possible hires."

"Already?" Ra'aila flicked through it with a swiftness Surela envied, slightly. It had taken her much longer to become comfortable with the device. "Winds of the Wanderer, have you seriously already set up interviews with some of them?"

"Neither Saul nor I could guess at our budget," Surela replied, ignoring the incredulity. "You will have to inform us if we overreach."

"This is… a lot of people."

"There are a great number of them in your Alliance."

That startled the creature into a laugh. "Yes, you could say that." She lifted her face, and for the first time Surela saw something in it: a hint of steel, of discernment. "I hope you're prepared, alet, because you'll be sitting in on all of these interviews."

"I… beg your pardon?"

"You and Saul picked them out of the pack, fine. But it's one thing to read a résumé and another one to look someone in the eyes and listen to what they've got to say." A grin, full of appalling teeth. "Consider it a learning experience."

What about her life since her exile hadn't been… one long and exhausting lesson in humility and resentment. "Very well. The chickens shan't be ready for another week. Will we be able to stay that long?"

"Oh, sure." Ra'aila shook her head, long ears pressed toward her neck. "I'd rather not leave without hiring at least one person, if we can. Nothing on your world is so urgently about to break that we can't layover long enough to pick up a crew."

Was that true? Surela wondered.

"I'll see if I can't add some people to your queue here," Ra'aila continued. "I don't see anyone here who can do training, and I want one. You need it, and so do I, if we want to keep this outfit running." Her! Be trained? In what, Goddess help her? "I'll let you and Saul know when we're due for the first interview. He's a good judge of character, his opinion will be helpful."

And that was unmistakably a dismissal, an impertinence Surela would have found appalling in a mortal had she not wanted Ra'aila to show some signs of leadership. In no universe did Surela wish to be captain of this ugly alien vessel. To prevent being forced into that role by the incompetence of her fellows, she would gladly act as a subordinate to an animal.

Well, perhaps not *gladly*. But with relief, certainly. She went as bidden.

———

Interviewing aliens was a curious and unpredictable process. The first candidate, a male who had looked likely for the position of first mate, struck her immediately as a poor choice and she had not the first notion why, only that Saul and Ra'aila concurred because after he'd left they glanced at one another and made similar noises. "Too full of himself," Saul said. "He'll want your job."

"I don't know if I want my job yet, but I want to decide, not have it decided for me," Ra'aila agreed, and that was the most promising statement Surela had heard out of her yet.

So it went. As each prospect arrived, they were shown to the mess, where their attitudes about the vessel's size and age informed their initial responses so obviously Surela wondered whether any of these aliens troubled to school their faces. She was no mind-mage to read their emotions from a distance, but she didn't need to be either. They communicated their curiosity, their contempt, their desperation, or their interest quite admirably without the need for greater effort. Most of her initial choices proved unsuitable immediately.

And then, the first appeared that she liked on sight. A short, ivory-furred creature with the ears of a fox and who sported seal points that made the silver tattoos on the insides of her dark ears all the more striking. Stocky, with hair in long ropes bound behind her with a braided cord, she somehow looked more the animal than Ra'aila despite her humanoid face with its bright blue eyes. But it was her demeanor that attracted Surela: an easy cheer that hinted at self-assurance. She was a pilot, and her name was Merina 'Meri' York, and both Saul and Ra'aila said after she'd gone: "Yes."

"Good pick," Saul added to Surela.

"Grant me no credit for it, as I have shown little by way of talent in this endeavor yet."

"That's one down, at least, if she'll take the offer," Ra'aila said. "Let's keep going."

They had another piece of luck a day later, when an engineer fell into their laps. Saul had not quite salivated over her record, but Surela had observed him long enough to see his interest in the way his ears were too perfectly still, his eyes too perfectly fixed. The woman in question was not what Surela had expected in a maintainer of mortal technology, though what she'd imagined, she didn't know. Erynne Seyvald was a curly-haired bon vivant, an easy conversationalist who revealed in that conversation occasional glimpses of intellect and practicality that shimmered like gems beneath a jeweler's spotlight. She had all the previous crew's endless enthusiasm for parties without their unsteadiness of purpose. "I'm looking for something small," she said when Saul asked her why she was willing to ship out on a freighter the *Earthrise*'s size. "I've done big engineering departments before. I know how to manage people. I miss being more personally involved in the nuts and bolts, though. I'm going to end up the chief engineer of some big liner eventually, but I don't want to hang up my troubleshooter's hat yet." She'd looked at the mess's ceiling, floors, the hatch. "This is a Martian clipper, probably a Vesta... they've been building these for almost a hundred years without changing the plan much. I'd love to have a look, if you'd give me a tour?" A grin, nearly impossible not to return. "Even if you don't hire me, I'll at least have put my hands on one of these beauties. You don't get a lot of clippers with Pelted crew, they're usually a human thing."

There was nothing for *that*, but to hire her, particularly since the tour put to rest any questions they might have as to her competence.

"Two down," Ra'aila said after that. "I'm feeling pretty good about this."

The chickens were ready for transport before they'd agreed on anyone else, however, and the breeder was politely obstinate on the delivery date. They had no facilities for the number of animals Surela had requested: they would be sent on the specified date, and there would be no delays.

"Can't they hold off even for one week?" Ra'aila asked in despair.

"Not even one day," Surela said. "Make the offer to York and Seyvald, so we might have at least some aid on the way back."

"I'm less worried about that than that we've got two more interviews coming in along with the chickens!"

"We'll make do."

But they more than made do, because amid the mayhem of the delivery—for loading live chickens was a different proposition from accepting crates of eggs—they found their next two hires knee-deep in the fray. One, a short woman with strikingly bicolored fur, had begun directing the delivery people, having grown frustrated with their inefficiency and confusion… and the other, a svelte male with golden mane, was cheerfully taking her direction and laughing about having become an animal handler. Surela was not the only one who stood back and watched that interaction… but unlike her, Ra'aila strode forth and introduced herself, and they secured thus their final crew: Danica Blakesley, who had done work as a first mate and could also train nearly every job on a cargo vessel; and the irrepressible Leonid, who was as safe for this crew full of women as one of the more flamboyant traveling Eldritch jongleurs. Surela did not know mortal mores, but she didn't need to in order to recognize his type, and feel, perhaps, a little empathy for him.

Within a day, all four were aboard, and Surela liked the tenor of the company then. The clannishness that had caused the Aera to act like a tribe apart from those who didn't share their species was absent in these disparate personalities, so they conducted themselves with more care to one another's comfort. They had specialties and duties that apparently pleased them, and none of them eschewed hard work. They cleaned up after themselves... Erynne, who preferred night shifts, even started the tisane and coffee before repairing to her bed, which saved Surela the inconvenience of doing it herself.

It was all quite proper and she was feeling satisfied with herself when Saul requested entrance to her room, on an evening prior to their arrival to Eldritch space.

He made no small talk—she appreciated that, since she had no desire to spend a great deal of time in mortal company—but she was not sure she liked his expression, or that she could read it so easily. "Ra'aila thinks the hiring is done, so we need to convince her otherwise."

"Do we? What have we missed?"

"The healer."

A very long pause. Surela was certain she didn't want to know where the conversation was going... and was resigned to their traveling there anyway. "You will tell me why, I suppose. To win my aid."

"Because you might be pregnant."

There. That was the sentence she'd been awaiting, more merciless than any exile. More inevitable, also. "I assume you have reason to say so, when no such verdict was spoken over my head when I was released from the mortal clinic into your care."

His smile was slight, and did not shape the skin around his eyes. "You smell different."

Goddess. That she might have a scent discernible to these creatures with their animal noses! Should she be more appalled that they could detect it? Or that she was emitting it?

"It's not evidence, one way or the other," Saul said. "But I was informed it was a possibility. And if I'm right, I don't want you to lack the expertise."

"And here I thought you had it, having been involved with breeding animals."

He shook his head. "Don't, alet." Don't what, she wondered? Make light of it? Turn that cruelty on herself? What was it, specifically, that he disliked? But he hadn't finished. "Even if you aren't pregnant, Eldritch are feather-worlders, and eventually you're going to need that addressed if you stay in the Alliance. Reese runs this ship at closer to Martian hab gravity, which is easier on people like you without being too detrimental to the health of those of us who grew up at Alliance Standard Grav. But if we end up spending more time off the ship I don't want you crippled by the environment. You're already working too hard at it when we're out."

So her problems were a phenomenon with a name and a cause. Yet another topic for her notebook. "I am forced to take your word for it—"

"Don't," he said. "Do the research. Or ask Reese, we'll be home tomorrow. But I want that healer, and Ra'aila's going to be hard-headed about it. She'll think adding more people is asking for trouble... she's feeling too new to her role to be comfortable with the thought of growing the crew past her ability to convince them she's in charge. She'll get the hang of it, but she's going to want to coast in her comfort zone a while."

"You are resolved on this course," she guessed.

"If you don't help, I'll go over Ra'aila's head to Reese. But it'll be better for Ra'aila if the request comes from below so she can deal with it herself. She needs her authority shored up, not undercut."

An analysis Surela agreed with, for the maid was as green as a debutante—surely she could say so of a mortal, no matter how adult that mortal thought herself. Ra'aila's flailing was patent to eyes that had seen dozens of youths and maidens launch themselves into the cutthroat Eldritch court.

"A healer," she said at last, "would be useful to all aboard."

"They would, yes."

"I will back you," Surela said stiffly.

He nodded. "Thank you. Good night, alet."

He left her to the quiet of her kennel, and her resignation. She did not need an alien with a hound's nose to tell her the obvious. The voice inside her that delighted in raspberries when Surela herself didn't think of hunger, who encouraged her to rest rather than spend her evenings staring at the ceiling in restless frustration, the voice that barred some of her nightmares, and suffered through the ones that couldn't be prevented… that voice was not some inner wisdom surfacing, but belonged, very obviously, to a passenger in her body. She couldn't say what she felt about the prospect, either. None of the obvious responses fit. To acquire an heir without the trouble of marrying a man—a relief, and a coup. To be unmarried when bringing forth that heir—scandalous. To bring to term the issue of a rapist and an alien—unthinkable.

What Surela felt most was… nothing. Save that it was restful to eat raspberries for that wistful presence. Perhaps when her body began to change more visibly, she would grow anxious or angry. Too, it was pointless to grapple with her ambivalence before it became obvious the child would stay, and not die before term like so many Eldritch infants.

The storm of emotion that wanted so urgently to blow her away pressed at her edges, and she forced it back, again. She would not remember Thaniet's passage. She would not think of Jisiensire burning. She would not linger on the past, recent or deep. This was what she had now, and she would not break.

CHAPTER 9

The captain made noises Surela could tell were intended to bruit her authority when she and Saul submitted their request, but as the wolf had predicted, Ra'aila surrendered to their argument... if with ill grace. She sighed her way through the listings for healers, growled at the necessity of scheduling interviews, and grumbled about the wages and the crowding aboard ship. Surela left her to stew, having decided that encouraging Ra'aila to fulfill Saul's request constituted the limit of her responsibility —or interest—in the matter. She did not expect to like or even interact with the physician, beyond the necessary.

Prudence MakeShift, though, enchanted them all. Even Surela, who still thought of the various aliens of the Alliance as creatures, could not look into Prudence's face and think of her as an animal. Was it that her demeanor shared something in common with Lord Hirianthial's? The quiet self-control that suggested depths inaccessible to the casual and commonplace? She was beautiful, also, with a face flat enough to be read like an Eldritch's, and fur as short and soft as velveteen. Her eyes could have come straight from an Asaniefa noble's, the rare "first blush" green, delicate with pinkish flecks. And she put herself to work the moment she unpacked, by scheduling physicals for each of the crewmembers. "To establish a baseline for my records," she said. "And we'll get to know one another."

"She takes her assignment here seriously," Ra'aila told them in the mess later, bemused. "As if we're not a two-bit freighter with all of eight crew."

"We hired her to take us seriously," Saul said. "So that's working out well."

One by one, they reported to the cramped compartment that served as the ship's clinic. Surela's appointment fell halfway through their return journey, and she presented herself at the clinic and tried not to react to what could charitably be called its modesty; the healer, at least, seemed unfazed by its size or the meanness of its appointment. "Please, have a seat."

Surela sank onto the edge of the padded plank that passed for an examination table. She had never seen anything similar outside the slab used by the house's kitchen for butchering meat, and the sight discomfited her.

"So," said Prudence. "I know nothing about your species, alet, and our security hire tells me I'm not likely to have access to any information I could use to remedy my ignorance. You'll have to forgive me if this is a perfunctory check."

"Of course." Surela watched the woman drop her eyes to a tablet as she passed a narrow wand over the Eldritch's body. She waited for the shock, but the healer remained composed. A faint pursing of pink lips, perhaps, examining the results, but that was all.

"Not too far off humanoid. Enough that I think I can be helpful." The woman raised her head. "Is the child wanted?"

It was so similar to the question the Eddings woman had asked that Surela felt herself transported back to that clinic, to the challenge she'd been issued: to live, or to give up and leave her mistakes to others to fix. How could she begin to respond to this question? Was the creature developing inside her another mistake, and if so, how should she fix it? Except that she might not be able to do anything at all, given Eldritch issues with pregnancy. "It is... rare... that we are able to bring them to term."

"Her."

A hiccup in her thoughts. "I'm sorry?"

"The evidence is slight but clear enough. You're carrying a girl."

A daughter. An Asaniefa daughter—no. She was no longer Asaniefa, but the lowest tenant in an outworlder's House.

And yet... a daughter.

"I have a specialty in obstetrics." Prudence turned away to put her instruments back in their slots, and Surela was aware of it as kindness, a gesture intended to give her time to compose herself. "An accidental one, but it goes that way for Tam-ileyan medical educations. We accrue time in maternal wards. I'll do all I can if that's your wish."

"Is it what you would recommend?" Surela asked, remembering her mortal liegelady's reticence to discuss alternatives to her state.

Prudence shook her head, wisps of chestnut-colored hair swaying around her face. "I'm not here to tell you what to do, alet. Just to keep you in one piece while you do it. But if one of the things you want to do is have a baby, I can help."

Hearing it aloud didn't make it real to her. To have a child? And do what with it? Foster it with Eddings, as the woman had suggested? No... foster *her*. A daughter. An Eldritch daughter.

Or... was it? Eldritch? There had been more than one rapist. The humans would have seeded her with an Eldritch child, but the Chatcaavan... could the shapeshifters appropriate wombs for their get?

No... she would not dwell on it. The likelihood of her pregnancy persisting was slight. To invest too much in it, be it distress or hope, was impractical.

"I will keep that in mind," Surela said. "If I may ask after a different topic?" At the healer's nod, she continued. "I have been reading about a process that acclimates those of my biology to moving through the different environs of the Alliance. Is that a process you can administer?" Because researching the gravity differentials had appalled her. Surela didn't want to be trapped anywhere in the mortal worlds, unable to breathe easily or move, subject to physical stresses that could shorten her lifespan. That she didn't know what she'd do with the remainder of her centuries fell away before her horror that those centuries might be truncated without intention.

"I can, yes," Prudence said. "But the regimen can cause miscarriage. Would you like me to begin it now, or do you want to wait?"

They returned, inevitably, to the topic she had wanted to avoid. How patient the healer was, and how careful not to influence her decision. And now she would have to make one. Putting it off was a coward's choice, but Surela could barely convince herself of the reality of a possible infant. Planning for one was beyond her. "I shall wait, then."

"All right, alet. Unless you have questions, we're done." Prudence's smile was slight but genuine. "Maybe when we reach your world someone will be able to release data to me that will make it easier on us both."

Surela wondered. Would Liolesa release such information from beneath the Veil to succor the woman who'd deposed her? But there was no Veil anymore. What would Eddings say, if asked? "Perhaps."

Outside the clinic, Surela allowed herself to accept that

she found the healer restful. That her composure approached Eldritch levels of self-control; that the care with which she chose her words made her predictable and therefore trustable; and that, Goddess on high, she was lovely to look at, and if Surela was to be trapped amongst aliens for the balance of her life, it was some small mercy that they might not all repulse her.

She could say this about her exile: even the most basic of routines in it required so much amendment of her ignorance that she was not forced to count its hours. She was busy. That was enough.

———————

"How are you finding the work?" Saul asked her a week later. They were once again underway to Psi, and the morning mess was thankfully absent the slack bodies of sleeping voluptuary aliens. Arriving early to the mess had become a matter of preference, because Surela was grateful to leave her bunk, rather than an attempt to avoid tripping over someone's arm or picking her way through their discarded plates and cups.

She looked through the offerings this morning: waffles, she had little fondness for, but there was a promising loaf of bread in the warmer, and even better, poached eggs that somehow stayed perfect while floating in their stasis container. Working with poultry had granted Surela a new appreciation for eggs in all their manifestations. "The work has been, until this moment, encompassable. I cannot pretend to understand the cargo Laisrathera sends us for now."

Saul nodded as he considered the breakfast line-up. Like her, he skipped the waffles. "Machine parts. They're building out the power grid on your world, looks like."

"And a generator," Surela said, remembering the word.

"Will we be making many such runs? How many such items will we require?"

"To furnish your world? I don't know." The wolf chuckled. "You could look into it, if you're curious… figure it out on your own."

"I thought that would have been a realm barred to anything but a specialist?"

"Sure, but you could learn. You're not like us, after all. You could become an engineer, a healer, a naval officer, a ship driver, a farmer, an artist… and master all of it. We only get the one lifetime, so we have to be a little more picky."

The notion startled her. She already had a position, or… rather, she'd had one. The work of an Eldritch noble had kept her occupied. Mostly. Would it be disloyal to admit that the work she'd considered consuming while on her world now seemed lacking in variety and depth compared to everything she was learning now? Surela frowned at her plate, forcing herself not to toy with the fork. "And how long would all this education need?"

"You could probably get the basics of any one field with a few years of concentrated study. That would fit you to start out in an entry-level position, anyway."

Ra'aila, entering with a yawn, said, "What's this? Does Rel want my job?"

"Goddess, no," Surela said. "Keep it, please."

That provoked a laugh from the creature, an easy one that matched her relaxation. The new crew did not require as much supervision as the old, and as the days passed, Ra'aila's stress had visibly subsided. "All right, all right. No fears, alet. But seriously—" stopping to fill a mug from the coffee carafe, "—why wouldn't you want a ship of your own? You people live so long, you could have dynastic shipping enterprises. Make money hand over palm. Your long-term investments would make ours look like kits' play."

Proclaiming that overmuch attachment to money was

vulgar… it was what she would have done in the past, to put such people in their place. But the knowledge of what Liolesa was doing with money, and how much money the Empress appeared to have, and had had for centuries… much was said of the Galare fortune, but Surela Silin Asaniefa had depressed such discussions as beneath notice. She no longer thought of this topic as beneath notice.

"If you're interested," Saul said, "you can look into investing your salary."

"My salary," she murmured.

"Or you could spend it," Ra'aila said.

From the door, their purser chirped, "What are we spending?"

"Our supercargo's salary," Saul said, amused.

Leonid seemed to overflow with enthusiasm, until his entire body vibrated with it. Would he burst into dance? She half-expected it. "Oh, sweet desert peach! You must do something about that wardrobe, it is *not* at all flattering. And your hair! You deserve so much better! I support you fully in your decision to embrace a new style."

Ra'aila choked into her coffee. "I don't think we've decided she needs a makeover."

"Then I'm in time to talk her into it!" He clasped his hands in zeal.

Impossible to look into that face without toleration. Perhaps even more than toleration. To mingle with players and actors had been beneath her as Asaniefa's head, but Surela had always ensured that musicians could spend the dark winters under her roof, and had been pleased by her role as patroness. "Do you sing?" she asked, suddenly.

"Me! No." He shook his head sadly, pressing a hand to his chest. "The angels didn't give me that gift." A wicked grin. "The inverses made sure I could dance though." A shimmy that was positively scandalous, and answered admirably Surela's conjecture on whether he would break into some performance if given the impetus. On the other side of the table, Saul shook his head with a smile.

"Never a dull moment, anymore," Ra'aila declared. "In a good way."

Ignoring her, the purser—he preferred 'Leo' to Leonid, she remembered—dropped into the chair across from hers. "Say you'll let me dress you. You're mouthwateringly gorgeous, but it's like you're trying to go unnoticed! You've got to let that amazing light shine!"

"I will consider it," Surela said, because he was in such earnest that she couldn't respond any other way. It would have been like cuffing a child.

Leo squealed. "I can't wait! How far are we from Psi? I need to make a list of boutiques. You're rich, aren't you? Everyone knows all Eldritch are fabulously wealthy! We're going to have such fun. You won't recognize yourself when we're done!"

"Zleayron help you," Ra'aila said after he'd darted from the mess, without so much as pausing to refresh himself from the counter. "I think you're going to have to take him up on it." A grin. "Good luck with that."

"Thank you. I believe I shall need it." That left her with Saul, who had finished his meal and was bringing his plate to the counter. She watched him clean it. "I am waiting for you to tell me it would not be prudent to allow my 'light to shine', being Eldritch and the target of slavers."

"I won't let you be taken."

That was all. Neither dramatics, nor fervor. A statement of fact. He did not stay to explain it, or to meet her eyes significantly. Did nothing that a liegeman might have done while speaking a vow.

And yet vow it was, and it stunned her silent. That vows should exist in the mortal realm, and be cherished as Eldritch might cherish them. Did that mean the world of duty and high romance extended even here, into her benighted exile?

Or was she grasping for anything that might remind her of what she'd lost?

She thought again of Saul's matter-of-fact reply, and the calm with which he'd issued it, feeling no need to explain or qualify, and set down her fork to compose herself... and failing, put her face in her hands.

CHAPTER 10

Leo was not the only one eager to accompany her to Psi's markets: he convinced Erynne to go as well, and the pilot, Meri. The latter seemed content to orbit the first two, or drift on her own errands, but engineer and purser were a friendship ordained: two sybarites, Surela thought, eager for entertainment and unmoved by the opinions of passersby as they laughed and joked. Erynne could sing well, and did, snatches of outlandish foreign songs that inspired Leo to sway or break into occasional dance, inspiring appreciative calls from nearby strangers. Had Surela feared she would be noticed as the sole, valuable Eldritch on the starbase? She shouldn't have. Leo and Erynne were a two-person traveling act, and weren't afraid who knew it.

Saul had come, because he had to: after his promise in the mess, Surela no longer expected less of him. Even Eldritch hounds had been capable of loyalty, and they had not had sapient eyes, nor words to express their devotion. It embarrassed her that she should merit a guard of any kind after what she'd done, and that she should need a guard because of what she was to these mortals who knew nothing more than her species. It stressed the differences between the Surela who had been Asaniefa, and traitor, and the Surela who was now an Eddings employee, and a visitor of romantic stripe to a civilization enchanted by the myths of such guests.

Their destination was a part of Psi's coastal city Surela had not yet seen—not difficult, given how little of it she had—but like everything else it was unfairly lovely: a permanent market carved into the cliffs along their edges, overlooking the city or the bay, with high stone arches and glass walls and stores, restaurants, and what appeared to be dwellings lining the inner walls. It was known as the Arcade, and it was busier than the town byways while also being airier, with ceilings high enough to serve a palace.

Ostensibly they'd made this outing so Leo could dress Surela, but when she had not entered into his efforts wholeheartedly, he had let it go... and so naturally it was obviously kindness and not sulking. Surela was grateful: she was not ready to embrace wholeheartedly the Surela who could outfit herself on the advice of mortal companions on one of their starbases. It was hard enough to be the Surela willing to go on such an expedition, and to face how relieved she was to escape the confines of her cell, the ship, the reminders of the terms of her exile.

After returning to the ship, Surela returned to her kennel and called up her finances. Numbers, at least, remained the same from society to society, and several weeks of spending Alliance fin had given her some sense for its value. She had accrued nearly two months of pay thus far—had it truly already been so long?—and she was paid on par with the ship's healer, a ridiculous sum for someone who did so little and had such a paucity of expertise. Saul would no doubt remind her she was the only one who understood Eldritch needs; she didn't have to apply to him to hear his voice in her head, firm and unruffled. 'There's no replacing you,' he would say. 'You're the only one with an Eldritch perspective, alet.'

She'd researched that, also: the endless words inserted into their tongue that did not translate cleanly. 'Alet' was what one called someone formally; 'arii', what one called a friend. The latter had as many modifiers as an Eldritch word had moods, for levels of friendship, and familial relations. Was there, she wondered, a word for whatever Saul was to her? Her tongue had many, but in this, Universal was clumsy. She could take some small pleasure in that.

Surela collected her dinner late, when she was sure the mess would be empty. It had been her custom for most of her life to eat alone, if she could; long association of meals with the jousting of politics had soured her on eating in company. Family dinners had been the worst, simmering with aggression and cutting remarks. Not that her parents had been cruel, but her cousins were so frequently with them that it was hard to escape the constant jockeying for primacy. Once her mother had died, her father's increasing intimacy with his brother's family had ensured she'd been forced to grow, cheek by jowl, with some of the most ambitious of her set.

No, the silence was welcome. The only thing that could have made it better entered when she was lingering over tea and dessert. The healer paused, smiled at her. "How'd the outing go?"

"I beg your pardon?"

"The outing Leo took you on. If you're wondering how anyone knew, well... it's a small ship. There was no avoiding the gossip." Prudence showed her a smile that would have seemed slight had her eyes not been so merry, and so sympathetic. "Everyone was very excited about playing dress-up doll with their very own supermodel Eldritch."

Some of these words made no sense to her, but she had

the gestalt well enough. "They soon found other diversions, thankfully."

"They weren't too pushy? That's good. What's Clovellan like? I haven't explored it much."

This puzzled Surela, as they'd hired Prudence from the starbase. "Did you not live there?"

"Not in the city-sphere." The healer filled a bowl and brought it to the table: something that looked like porridge but smelled savory. "I'm from Tam-ley. That's my species's homeworld. I was adjunct at a family practice there after medical school, and I enjoyed it, but I was getting to a point where I had to ask myself whether it was everything I wanted."

How strange it must be to have so many choices that the knowledge of one's desires might be difficult to grasp. "Was there some other path that seemed good to you? More so?"

Prudence's smiles continued to trend toward the small, almost private. Had her gaze not been so candid, it would have made her seem haughty. "I wasn't sure. I was wavering between working in a big hospital, or seeing more of the Alliance. So I did both, and took a contract job here, in the aquasphere."

This time, Surela's reading afforded her some hint of what that meant. Sadly, it was only a hint. "The aquasphere. That is... another part of Psi."

"Right. The city is in a sphere of its own. The aquasphere's on the other side, and it's basically a big globe full of ocean water. They have aquatics there... not just the Naysha, but the Platies, the big ones that need a lot of space. The people there do research, and farm, and fish, and there are some big islands and platforms. I was the on-call physician for one of the communities there." Her eyes brightened. "So fascinating. And I did a lot of swimming, which was novel. I didn't know how to swim until I arrived! I never got good at it, either, but I had plenty of opportunities to try."

"You enjoyed it," Surela observed.

"I did! And you're about to say: 'but you left'." Prudence's chuckle was quiet. "I don't think I'm done exploring. I'd like to go home eventually, but maybe not yet. Your captain showed up at the exact right time with her contract, and it's not a long-term one, so... I'll do this for a while. See what I think of being a ship's healer."

"And if you love it? Will you still go home?"

"Oh yes. Absolutely. My family's all there, you see."

Surela did. As much as she hated her family, they would always be part of her history, her context. Her memories. Her understanding of her place in the universe. How bizarre it was to have been cut free of them. What had happened to them after her sentencing?

"Would it be impolite to ask what brought an Eldritch here?" Prudence went on to ask as she ate. Delicately, despite the potential for untidiness of her chosen dish. "We're bringing a lot of colony materials back and forth, it looks like. It's not what I would have expected of a settled world... but of course, no one knows anything about your homeworld, alet."

"We are expanding," Surela said. "And we seek greater congress with aliens." That, at least, was truth, and if she had no desire to have that congress, or to court that expansion, she need not share her feelings, nor her history.

"How exciting it must be to be part of that," Prudence said. "And you have such long lives, you'll be able to oversee so much of the expansion yourself."

"I am anticipating the results," Surela said, which was still true: she was anticipating the results would damage everything she thought of as important about their culture and people. But language, even this curt and inelegant alien tongue, could be used to obfuscate as well as illuminate, thank the Goddess. Disappointing this beautiful woman, no matter how furry, would have been dreadful. "Would you tell me a little about your world? I have not seen much of your Alliance yet."

Prudence brightened. "You should take a tour one day. I've only ever seen Karaka'Ana, once, when my school organized a study abroad program. But it's really something, to step foot on another planet."

"I can only imagine."

"But you asked about Tam-ley." This smile was so sunny it lit the woman's eyes, and the dart that smote Surela was unavoidable because of how it reminded her of Thaniet. Of Thaniet's unsophisticated joy, and her willingness to be vulnerable when she felt safe. Surela had prided herself on furnishing that safety to her lady-in-waiting. And how wrong Thaniet had been to trust her with it, in the end. The memory tightened the muscles along her ribcage and she forced it back into a box before it could rise to her eyes.

The healer spoke of her world, of its universities and its learning, of its prominence amongst the other alien home-worlds, of its history and beauty, of the meadows where she'd grown and the cities where she'd studied. Surela listened, and tried not to think about how much it had once mattered to her, that she could give shelter to musicians and impoverished noblewomen fallen on hard times, and tenants who needed food and shelter. That she had wanted to be, and prided herself on being, the head of Asaniefa because she wanted to help her people prosper. That in fact, she'd wanted Liolesa's throne because she thought she could do a better job of taking care of the world... because she'd believed with all her heart that Liolesa's aims would pollute them, make them less able, less safe. That sitting on that throne would have slaked her private ambitions had been a large part of her motivation... but if ambition alone had mattered to her, she would already be planning to build up some new empire, one to compete with Liolesa's... not mourning all she'd destroyed in her hubris.

94

Their machine parts were purchased, ferried to Eldritch space, and unloaded at the orbital station. Mewed in her cabin, Surela accepted the newest shopping list... more parts having to do with power generation, but also a flurry of requests for smaller electronics, like the tablets that were so ubiquitous. She'd been neglecting her notetaking in favor of reading the computer's floating displays, so she brought out her paper notebook and smoothed it to a fresh page. The date first, of course, and what little she'd learned about Tam-ley and other planets from her discussion with the healer, and then she paused to look up the data herself: eighteen home-worlds, these aliens claimed. Nineteen if one counted the Alliance capital, which was not solely a city but an entire planet. And an additional ninety—ninety!—colonies. Her fingers paused, the pen sagging against the join between thumb and forefinger. One hundred and nine worlds.... Goddess. How many people? Saul had told her, hadn't he? Some ridiculous number, but surely he'd been inexact, or misremembering. She asked the computer.

"Last census," the computer reported, "the Alliance population numbered 663 billion."

So, he hadn't been wrong. Surela's mind choked, attempting to visualize the size of the populace. Asaniefa had been one of the largest Eldritch Houses, and she'd been proud to claim nearly 7,800 people to her banner. Only Galare had boasted more tenants.

She forced herself to write the number down. And then to parse it out. How many different ways could she multiply numbers to reach 663 billion? She had filled half the page when the door chimed. Looking up, Surela said, "Yes?"

The door opened on the bicolored female, Danica, who served now as Ra'aila's second in command. Could she call the creature older, when most Eldritch were still considered children at her age? Surela couldn't gauge maturity in these mortals, but while both Ra'aila and Danica were practical, Danica was calmer than the captain. It was hard not to be reassured by her demeanor.

Her guest was holding a package. "This came for you from the surface."

"Thank you. You may set it on the bed."

Danica did so, and as she turned... halted, eyes arrested. "Are you... writing? With an actual pen?"

Surela felt anew the familiarity of the barrel in her fingers. Black ink was made with carbon, usually from soot or burned bones, and had a grounding smell. It remained the most common ink used by her people, which in her youth had made her wonder if all correspondence was bad news. Even knowing that only those who diluted their blacks would use colored inks for mood shadings, she couldn't help the association. Using it now felt appropriate. "I am, yes."

She expected a challenge, or a dismissal. To see the creature's eyes light with wonder and curiosity... should not have been so gratifying. "Like an artist!"

As with all the gently bred, Surela had been taught to draw, and had shown no talent for anything other than reproductions of facades. Straight lines and geometries, she could do. The mercurial textures and curves of flesh had been beyond her. "I am no artist. But I am used to writing in this fashion."

"Is it hard?"

Depressing the pretensions of outsiders would have been easier had this outsider not been so obviously eager to understand. "I... am not certain it is much different than how you employ your stylus."

"It's not the same, though."

That was inarguable. "No," Surela said, and had no idea why she continued, "Would you like to see?"

"Oh, could I?"

96

Surela also had no idea why her initial demonstration turned into another, and how that evolved into nearly an hour spent talking to the creature about the relative viscosities of ink colors, of the shapes of nibs, of papers and drying time and penmanship. By the end of that hour, she'd coached Danica through the process of writing her name, painstakingly, five times. The woman was elated at her success, and crestfallen at her lack of skill. "It's so wobbly! I'm used to the tablet correcting for the spaces between my letters... I don't know how to make the proportions right on my own."

"It comes with practice."

Danica glanced at Surela's examples, her ears sinking. "A lot of practice, I see." With a sigh, she rose, smiled. "Thanks for showing me, though. It's so beautiful. And it was a nice break from..." She waved a hand idly. "The madhouse out there."

"Is the unloading done?"

"Probably not for a couple of days. There's a lot going on downstairs. But we'll be underway again by the end of the week."

After Danica had gone, Surela looked at the spare page, with its spidery scrawl, full of ink spatters. Like teaching a child... but how determined the woman had been, and how delighted at the difficulties. Because 'it felt real,' whatever that meant. Surela didn't perceive the interfaces and glowing displays as any less real: if anything, they forced her, constantly, to confront the reality of her exile, and worse, the puissance of these mortals with their technology. But she remembered better when she wrote by her own hand, and there was so much she needed to retain, and quickly, that there was no other way.

Had she really spent an hour teaching one of these aliens the fine points of handwriting?

Had Danica's eyes become a person's eyes in that time?

Yellow eyes were not unusual among the Eldritch; Danica's dark amber irises would have been unremarkable.

Surela made herself rise and go to the bed, there to unwrap her package. As she half-expected, it was more paper. On top, however, was a copy of the broadsheet, and her hands seized in place. Did she want to know what was happening on her world? She couldn't even think of what time of year it must be. Was it still late winter? Had the spring come yet? It brought its blessings late to Asaniefa in the north, and visiting Ontine for the winter courts had granted her welcome respite from the harsher weather.

No, knowing would be too hard. Except that the front of the broadsheet was a sketch so large she couldn't avoid seeing it: her new and unwanted mistress, her hand bound in a wedding cloth with Hirianthial's. 'Laisrathera's Lady Takes a Consort!' read the headline, followed in only slightly smaller letters: 'The World's Lord of War Is the Newest Male to Leave the Marriage Mart. We Felicitate the Newlyweds, and Express Condolences to the Hopefuls.'

To have news of the mortals on her homeworld had to be less painful than to see what her old rivals were doing, and her peers, so this article was surely safe to read. That was her excuse for lifting the broadsheet from where she'd dropped it atop her stack of blank journals and ink refills. The sketch... so well done, she wondered if it had been made at the event. It wasn't always so: more often than not, the broadsheet artists worked off reports. Had Eddings allowed her cere-mony to be witnessed by vulgarians eager to make her into the next gossip item? Surela couldn't guess.

But that the artist had known Hirianthial, that she could see. She recognized the breadth of his shoulders, and the proportions. The hair was... poignant, shorn so. Like a child's. It bothered her more, seeing it against the backdrop of a normal occasion, than it had amid battle and strife. Her fingers traced the line of his spine. She had not wanted to marry, not really. She'd accepted it as part of the necessary consolidation of power, but it had always felt like a chore to be brushed past as quickly as possible. And it could have been done without fuss, if she'd selected a biddable man, easily appeased with the many divertissements Asaniefa could offer, with its hunting lodges and fine horses and the promise of ships at the coast. She'd held onto that vague plan until she'd seen Hirianthial at court.

Such a man. So earnest in his passions. The romance in his eyes. The way he danced, laughed. She'd never imagined she would meet any noble with so little interest in the games of the court. Hirianthial had wanted to be a knight, not a lord. He'd longed for the honor won in fights against monsters, not political opponents. That such Eldritch existed had staggered her... and she'd craved him, suddenly and shockingly. To be yoked to someone who found meaning in the impractical poetry of their intended lives....

He'd been the only man she'd ever thought of that way, and he had thought nothing of her. Had married that dab of a girl, Laiselin. And now, Goddess help her, he'd married again... and to a mortal.

A mortal who loved him, and whom he loved, and that love had been obvious even to her. Perhaps especially so, for having seen Eddings in extremis, in a prison cell.

It was too much, that article. The waste disposal in the crude bathroom shared by all the parties aboard accepted the broadsheet as easily as it did anything else. Surela consigned it to recycling and returned to her kennel, there to tuck her new stores into her crude desk. She had thought so little of the manufactured drama of Eldritch lives, preferring the pragmatic... and her devotion to 'realism' had delivered her to those who believed in ultimate practicality, something they'd proven on her body. Her exile had granted her no reprieve, either. There was no romance in her ugly cell, no elegance in her pedestrian wardrobe, no glamour in her trips to and from the starbase, as regular and as mundane as a tenant's to the market. It was the least of what she'd deserved, perhaps. But she was not minded to flagellate herself with what she'd lost. As boring and predictable as her routine was, it kept her moving, and as long as she kept moving, her enemies were cheated of their vengeance.

CHAPTER 11

Once again, underway. The healer, catching Surela at breakfast, asked about Danica and the pen. That telling the healer about Danica's game attempts at writing her name didn't strike Surela as a nuisance was... painful. Vexing. She didn't want to find any part of her durance bearable. First because she deserved punishment for her crimes, and this exile had been conceived as the worst possible punishment, outside of the execution originally pronounced on her name. And second because... how could she find pleasure in the alien worlds? It was gauche.

But at night she sat on her rude bunk with her arms slung around her knees, and she concentrated on the warmth in the center of her body, the one that trusted her without question, and she... she was afraid. Afraid of the future, of what she would discover inside her head when she stopped moving. Stopped focusing on the next task.

Repressing the sigh that was barring all the other emotions she couldn't afford to face, Surela groped for her notebook, and gave herself back to learning.

———

Erynne and Saul did most of the negotiation for the mechanical cargo, with Leo along as their keeper of the purse, but Surela went with them, hoping to divine through their behavior some notion of how she should value mortal technology, was she ever called upon to do this part of the work herself. That expedition proved mostly that delegation was a key leadership skill for a reason, because to approach their facility with hardware would require a lifetime of learning. A mortal lifetime, anyroad. That she had that time to spend didn't help her people now, and if Liolesa thought their homeworld needed power grids... it was hard not to agree, when confronted with the luxury that aliens lived with as a matter of course, luxury that was denied the greatest of the Eldritch as well as the least.

They were halfway through their purchases, and their stay, when Surela received a flat message from her human benefactor... and how different this one was from the first, because Eddings's warring emotions were more than enough to overcome her otherwise adequate control over her face. The woman was glowing... was that exaggeration? Or was Surela reading too much into the power of a wedding on a woman in love? But no, a tension had fled the human's arms, her jaw, and she smiled more easily.

But she was also worried. "Just touching base," said the projection as Surela watched with folded arms. "I've already talked to Saul and Ra'aila, who gets to decide how much she wants to share with the crew. You, though, need to hear it separately, so... don't find reasons to go farther into the Alliance than Psi. In fact, if you can load up on some more staples before you come back, that would be great. We might want you close. The war's... either broken out or about to, and we don't know how it'll go." A pause. "I don't know how much background you have on that, but for all I know, you know more than I do. Baniel might have been filling your ears with it, or the pirates. But the Chatcaava are about to hit us, and no one knows what that's going to look like. We doubt they're going to make it all the way over here, but I'd rather not assume."

That sudden dryness of throat, and the quiver in her back... that was surely excusable. She had been raped by a dragon, by pirates.

After that warning, she expected the starbase to be different... to be shadowed with impending danger the way a poem could be shrouded in the ominous black mode of speech. But the creatures of the alien Alliance went about their business as carefree as they had the day before, and try as she might, Surela could sense no indication that things had changed. Saul, behind and to one side of her, murmured, "They probably don't know."

Surela glanced at him, but the wolf was scanning the crowd with the same vigilance that characterized Liolesa's Swords. "How can they not?" she said, "Is it not their nation?"

"It is, yes. But you forget that you're directly involved with the highest levels of your government. Reese has your Empress's ear, and her fiancé—sorry, husband—is the war minister. Even if you weren't hooked into that, you'd be one of the only Eldritch in the Alliance, and I'm betting someone would have sent you a memo. 'Come home,' probably, or at least 'beware.' Especially with Chatcaava. The Chatcaava want you people."

"I know," Surela murmured. "Should we even be abroad?"

"The border is way spinward of us... and doing our errands at Psi takes us farther from it. Omega's technically closer to your homeworld, but it's also closer to the Crown of the Alliance, and I'm betting Reese didn't want you heading that way or she wouldn't have suggested Psi in the first place." His ears flipped outward, tracking some sound. That ripple of laughter? Some scuffing of shoe or luffing of tunic? Something else her ears were not keen enough to discern? "I don't think we have to worry. But there's no harm in being careful."

Surela allowed that. Then: "Your people will stop them, won't they?"

"I hope to God they do."

Which was not the confident reply she'd been expecting, and she glanced at him again. But he said nothing more, and she had no desire to press.

———

There was a certain injustice to her bargaining sessions, Surela began to understand, because of her species. The aliens found her glamorous and distracting, and many of them obviously wished to please her in the hopes that she would tarry where they could stare their fill… and she in her poorly tailored mortal clothes, with not even a servant to braid her shorn mane with a rope of pearls! What would they have fallen over their feet to offer her had she arrived in the garb of an Eldritch noblewoman, with flowing gown and gems at throat and ears and brow? Or would they have assumed her to be richer, and raised their prices? That she was reduced to haggling like a milkmaid should have galled, but it fascinated her to watch the inevitable bewitchment in the faces of her opponents as it warred with their desire to secure the best terms possible.

It was most noticeable in the open air markets, where she earned more than her share of double-takes, even with her every gesture weighed down by the gravity. But pressing the miller for better flour prices, or the farmer for extra eggs, she saw it, now and then... that softening that stiffened abruptly when the owner realized the advantages he was surrendering. Even among the blacksmiths who were responsible for their machine parts, there was, perhaps too often, a glimpse in the direction of the woman who was contributing nothing to the discussion, save her attention.

After the last such session, Erynne made it halfway down the street before she fell prey to such a paroxysm of giggles that she had to halt and lean on a wall. Wiping her eyes, she said, "Sun... and... *stars*. I feel like I'm wielding a Fleet-grade graser."

"It is hilarious," Leo agreed with false solemnity, his eyes dancing with merriment. "Can you imagine what it would be like if we could convince her to dress up?" He considered Surela. "Black catsuit, maybe, with spike heels?"

Erynne had another fit, golden curls shaking over the arm propped against the wall.

"Or, you know, a crown and a ball gown... that'll probably work better with the baby bump. Either way it would be deadly." Leo grinned at Surela. "Don't mean to talk about you, gorgeous, but..." He waved a hand extravagantly. "Erynne's right. You are *deadly*."

But all thought had stopped. And all sound too, because Erynne had frozen, and Saul had come to an abrupt halt.

"I—I'm sorry, was it supposed to be a secret? But it's noticeable, you know, you're so slim—" Leo clapped his mouth shut. "Let's... just... move on. Yes?" A weak but desperate smile. "That way. Back to the ship."

"Yes," Surela said, because if he continued talking he would make things worse.

On reaching the privacy of the *Earthrise*'s halls, Erynne paused before following Leo down the corridor—Leo, who had fled as if the monsters of the forest were on his heels—

and the engineer's gaze was somber. "We don't mean to talk about you that way. As if you're some exotic foreigner."

"And if I am? Which I patently am?"

"It can still make you feel objectified. We don't mean to do that."

How to tell the alien that she and all her furred compatriots were as exotic to her as she was to them? And how would Erynne react if Surela confessed to preferring to be treated so? That she thought it rightful that mortals should conceive of the Eldritch as a breed apart, beautiful and unattainable? That it flattered her pride to believe they might be entranced by her mere existence? What did she owe these creatures, anyroad?

Why did she answer honestly, as honestly as any Eldritch could? "It does not distress me, to be considered attractive."

She'd expected this sop to the creature's disquiet to be cheering. But Erynne searched her face as if seeking evidence of palliating lies, and when she spoke it wasn't to be glad. "As long as you're all right with it. But if you aren't, we won't tease you." The woman smiled, and it was such a... such a real smile, so complex with regret and whimsy, that she snapped into focus: no longer an alien, but a person. "Teasing is how most of us show we're part of a group, and I forget... you might not think of yourself that way. As someone on the inside. But you're our Eldritch, no matter how rare and fantastic. We want you to know you belong with us."

"Is it truly 'us'?" Surela asked, surprised. "When you all have known each other so short a time?"

Erynne's smile was more natural then. "Sometimes things come together, like falling in love. You just know from the beginning it's going to be good. This already feels like that to me. But you can rush things, knowing where they're going, and then ruin them by going too far too soon. You know?"

That the mortals should have the concept of a thing's end being written in its beginning, and acting accordingly, should not have struck her so powerfully. Surela did not want to continue to think of Erynne as a person rather than an alien, while also feeling, suddenly and desperately, that if she did not begin to accept mortals as such she would be consigning herself to centuries of desolation. The only way to make her exile bearable was to treat those around her as capable of entering into her confidences and enriching her life. And as much as she felt she deserved no such reprieve given her crimes, she was too selfish to want to live her life in misery, and too desperate for distraction from those crimes to turn away.

"I do know," Surela said after a long pause. "And I am not offended." And it was true. She was too tired to be offended: tired of suffering, tired of hating everything, tired in her joints with the constant shift between the *Earthrise*'s gentler gravity and the starbase's standard one.

"All right. But if we ever do offend you… let us know." With one last searching gaze, the woman headed up the hall.

Saul had been still through the exchange, as still as any courtier caught in an uncomfortable moment between two nobles. Now he straightened in a manner suggesting an infinitesimal pause that in an Eldritch would have been an offering: 'you may begin a conversation if you wish, or not.' Was she misreading him? She had not thought the aliens capable of subtlety. How many other ways would she be wrong, if she was wrong about this? And her fatigue continued to mount, which made her waspish. "Oh, don't fret. I am not about to hold mortal manners against them. They would have to be mind-mages to know my ways, given how little anyone knows of our ways. How then shall I judge them?"

"By your standards, I imagine," Saul said, voice quiet, as if calming a fractious child. "We don't expect you to know ours any more than we do yours."

Which was so reasonable and so sudden an inversion that

she felt dizzied. "How do you go on in such a manner? Never understanding by whose standards you are being judged, or knowing on whose you should be operating?"

He considered, then said, with a twitch of his mouth that was almost a smile: "Practice."

It was so pragmatic, and so unexpected, that she couldn't help smiling back, and that grew his expression until it almost reached his eyes. Did, she thought, if only faintly, like a tea just beginning to steep. She said, "Some things apply across every culture, perhaps."

"Probably."

———

Prudence stared at her tablet, holding the wand over Surela's belly before slowly drawing it upward. Lying down for this procedure should have been comfortable, but it made Surela too aware of the pressure on her chest. She knew she was breathing, but the sensation reminded her of suffocation... something she was not glad to have personal and direct memories of. One of the pirates that had raped her had done so with his hands around her throat.

"I don't like how fast your resting heart rate is," Prudence murmured, and she sounded almost distracted. "But we have to accept that's going to be normal for you until we've done the gravity acclimatization. The baby..."

Another long pause. Surela waited, wondering how her daughter fared. Hearing about the infant had become her favorite part of these sessions—that and watching the quiet, self-contained healer move around her domain, mistress of all she surveyed. It was pleasing, that sight of competence and ease in another woman, especially an alien one.

"Would you mind if I ran a longer scan? I want to double-check what I'm seeing."

"Something amiss?"

Prudence shook her head, but it was less a response to the question and more as if she was clearing her thoughts. "Rest there." A slightly harried afterthought, again, to herself. "There's no projection above the bed. There should be."

This made no sense to Surela, so she ignored it and waited, watching as Prudence hovered over the larger display on the desk. The woman's brow had tightened, tracing thin wrinkles through the velveteen pelt, and her lips were compressed as if she feared to allow them license. Would she be frowning, if she loosened them?

When the chime heralded the end of that scan, the healer's face didn't change. If anything, it grew more masklike, an act that made Surela brace herself. The aliens did not retreat behind such careful facades often.

Prudence drew her stool to the bedside and settled on it with all the neat grace of a gently bred woman. She composed herself with a slow breath. "What I'm seeing is, I thought, a medical impossibility, but that's the second scan that's confirmed it. Your daughter has… extra limbs."

"Oh," Surela said without thinking. "It was the dragon, then."

The alien froze on her stool, which brought Surela back from disassociated memories, made her realize what the statement must have sounded like. What it must be implying. Had the aliens assumed that her pregnancy had been the accident of some secret liaison? They had cast her in the role of dramatic heroine perhaps: the blushing virgin, seduced into the bed of her lover and left with an unplanned souvenir. Surela had heard similar enough tales in her youth, passed down by elders who used them as exhortations against choosing poorly in one's lovers… because though it was rare and rare again for any woman to conceive so easily, a noblewoman gave her virtue in tandem with her fortune, and a fortune was a far more important prize than any virgin body.

But these aliens… did they believe in marriage? What had

they assumed? She couldn't decide, because Prudence, usually so composed, was failing to hide her horror. The mouth, the cheeks, the brow, remained blamelessly smooth, but the eyes, too wide, betrayed her. "Alet—"

"I know what you fear, seeing it," Surela said, to save the woman from further anxiety. "You are not incorrect. But the deed is past, and my attackers were repaid in worse kind. I was avenged." And she had been. Strange to realize it, suddenly. That, in fact, knowing for certain that her child had been a product of the dragon and not the human pirates meant that *she* had avenged herself: had killed him with the weapon given her by the human who had gone on to claim Surela for her House.

Surela had not saved herself from imprisonment or her people from the fate she'd drawn down on them in her hubris, but she had killed her rapist, who'd led the invading force. Was it wrong to be proud of herself? At the time, it had been nothing she would have prided herself on, but a hideously painful and sordid event. The monotony and mundanity of her exile since had put enough distance between herself and the event that she could consider it in a new light, though, and perhaps be pleased that she'd taken at least one step toward addressing her sins, when it would have been so easy to give up.

A hand shocked her back from her thoughts, because someone was touching her. When had she last been touched? And it was such a gentle one, resting on her wrist, and with it came a swirl of feelings: compassion, sweet as fruit in winter; purpose, steadying as a lamp in evening; concern, bright as exposed steel. The mélange nearly drowned the tactile impression, of the warmth of that hand, and the unexpected smoothness of the fingers and palm. Surela had been expecting fur.

"You're certain about keeping her."

"I did say," Surela said. "You did not know how she was conceived, healer, but I did."

Prudence's shoulders rose and fell with her careful sigh. "All right, if that remains your choice. Then I can go on to the technical part, which is where I confess I have no idea how you can have conceived from an alien—a true alien—much less how your body hasn't rejected it yet."

"They are shapechangers, are they not?" She could think of the creature dispassionately, strangely enough. That rape had been part of Surela Silin Asaniefa's life, a life that had been free of aliens and violence. She was this new person now, without even a family name: Rel of Eddings, she supposed. The box she'd pushed her feelings in had closed, perhaps finally. "Could it be that the shapechanging fools the body of other aliens?"

"She did look Eldritch earlier," Prudence admitted. "Nothing in my earlier scans made me think otherwise, but maybe that was my complacency preventing me from seeing any clues." She shook her head. "We know too little about your biology. I assumed anything I didn't understand had to do with you being Eldritch, not with this pregnancy being... unusual... in other ways."

"Is she safe?"

"She seems fine. Developing normally, or at least, what would be normal for one of us. We gestate within nine Alliance-standard months, like the human template we were based on. I have no idea what the gestational milestones are for... well. For Chatcaava." A wry smile. "We have biological data on the Chatcaava, but it's almost exclusively for the male of the species. I don't think we've run into a pregnant female yet, at least, not on record."

That struck Surela as strange until she tried to imagine allowing a pregnant woman to stand among those receiving an alien delegation. "I imagine not."

"Alet…" Prudence was struggling for words. She had not yet let go of Surela's hand, though, and through it communicated the urgency of her desires: to be helpful, to offer comfort, to make good out of the tragedy not just of the conception, but potentially the birth, because in that moment Surela understood that to the aliens it was unacceptable that women should have frequent miscarriages. That it might not even be normal. How bizarre, and how staggering. "Alet, if you ever need… anything…."

Was it perverse that Surela wanted that hand to linger on her skin? Surely to hold the hand of an alien was less hideous an impropriety than to hold an Eldritch hand. An Eldritch would have been able to divine Surela's feelings from the contact in a way a mortal couldn't… but Surela had the uncomfortable sense that the healer was guessing too accurately at her state of mind, solely from her numb responses. "I appreciate—" What? "Your discretion," she said at last. "And your aid. You have been all that is helpful."

"Even when discretion hasn't prevented your situation from leaking to the rest of the crew?" Prudence asked ruefully.

"I should have found looser clothes. I will not blame you for my own lack of foresight." Surela thought of Saul. "My minder has already divined my state, and that apparently from my scent alone. Is that typical? Should I worry about all your noses?"

"What?" Prudence started with a self-conscious laugh. "Iley, no. We're not usually that sensitized to scent or… gods, pheromones, probably. Though some people pay attention more than others." She smiled, a little more naturally. "Should I ask about the 'minder' business? Is that Ra'aila? No, let me guess. Saul seems more the type, and he follows you around."

"I am new to your society," Surela said. "He was assigned to me to… introduce me. To the many differences."

"Oh, I believe it. Even other Pelted get culture shock with

one another, so being another species must make it even harder."

"Do you?" Surela asked, surprised to hear Saul's cautions about dealing with other societies repeated. She'd assumed that had been particular to his personality, not a general rule. "Have such troubles? Also, may I rise? I don't love lying down."

"Go ahead, you're fine. Well. No, your body is working much too hard and I don't like it. But beyond that, you can get up." Prudence let go of Surela's hand. "As for the culture shock... yes, of course. Our societies can be very different from one another's. If you're from a cosmopolitan destination like Selnor or one of the starbases or major world capitals, you'll be more used to it. But if you're not...." Another self-conscious laugh. "Iley, the Harat-Shar are enough to make all of us a little crazy."

"Which race is that?"

"Like Leo. The great cats. Their people are exempt from some of the rules that the rest of us live under. It makes them more alien than some of the aliens, to be honest. The Aera are... strange, too, probably because so many of them spend generations roaming the stars in family ships, never settling anywhere. They end up with these microcultures...." She trailed off, shook her head. "The Phoenix are inscrutable. The Hinichi... let's just say putting them in a room with people less dedicated to duty can be a problem. It's..." A laugh, quiet. "It's good, actually. We'd get too comfortable with ourselves if we were all alike. A family needs different kinds of people in it."

An extraordinary statement, this ardent defense of diversity. Surela didn't want to agree with it, but she remembered, with sudden and painful clarity, what the first sight of Hirianthial had done to her after years of dealing solely with Asaniefa's infighting. A hint of a different way, not because she wanted to give up her own, but because as in a song, a harmony line had to diverge from the melody to serve. Too many lines led to cacophony, but who would live without harmony?

"Tell me about the crew's species," Surela said. "I don't know them. I think. I have read about the creatures of this Alliance, but I have failed to associate them with the people on this vessel. Some of them look so similar. Saul is... a wolf person of some kind?"

That earned her an odd look. Someone else might have been offended; the healer, though, was thoughtful. Perhaps this depth of ignorance could only be pitied. Pitied, and corrected, and this Prudence did in full as Surela listened: lying on her side, now, which made breathing easier. Many of the aliens were, in fact, based on animals, but they had been modified by the application of a human template. So Saul was, in fact, a wolf person... or at least, a person whose long ago ancestors had been contaminated with wolf bits, based on some science Surela did not properly understand. How long ago had that been, she wondered? Had Liolesa already been alive before humans made the first animal person? Had she? Sobering thought.

Thus, Saul the dutiful, the religious, and the wolfine—not lupine, because such adjective was reserved for actual animals—was Hinichi. Leo was one of these libertine Harat-Shar, whose culture did in fact seem to Surela to be composed of players and musicians, at least morally. He was perhaps part lion? Surela didn't understand that explanation well. There was more than one kind of lion, and what did she know about lions?

Danica, the first mate, was some kind of cat as well, but somehow completely different from Leo, from a more retiring race called the Karaka'A; also, inexplicably, the pilot Meri was of a race known as the Seersa that borrowed fox-like characteristics but was somehow more alike, culturally, to Danica's than Danica's was to Leo's. Surela had assumed the two catlike creatures would share societies, but no, that was not how that worked, and it had something to do with their flight from Terra.

They had fled Terra—she hadn't internalized that, and perhaps should have from her reading. That the furred creatures, like the Eldritch, had engaged in an exodus from Earth. Were humans so awful then, that everyone wanted to distance themselves from them? Or had it been the rebellion of an immature spirit, longing to establish itself apart from its parents?

Erynne was another kind of partial cat, but again, from a radically different culture and world from either Danica or Leo: she was Asanii, to Danica's Karaka'An and Leo's Harat-Shar. And Prudence herself, another creature touched gently with foxish antecedents, shared nothing with Meri except that very distant history.

"How do you remember all these names and cultures?" Surela asked finally.

"It's easier if you grow up with it," Prudence replied. "People born in more isolated places are just as baffled by it when they head out into the wider worlds as I'm guessing you feel right now. It won't take you long to figure it out, though, not with such different people aboard. You'll see."

———

That perhaps would have been enough for a day. Certainly she retired glad of the chance to barricade herself against the onslaught of new ideas and taxing interactions. Her intent had been to study until dinner, but instead she slept through the intervening hours and well into the evening shift, and without nightmares; she dreamed instead of lullabies, and raspberries, and woke hungry and wondering. The mess was empty and she was not sad to have it to herself; she tarried there for some time before heading to her ablutions, and then to bed. If she was not glad to be tired despite the nap, she had heard stories from her extended family. Pregnancy was exhausting, so what else could she expect?

But when she returned to her room, she found a package awaiting her. Puzzled, she bent to fetch it up from the ground, wondering as she did so if she should install a mailbox given the number of such packages left on her non-existent doorstep.

Inside, she undid the cloth wrapping on a small jewelry box and a note. She opened the former first to reveal a silver barrette, a startling one: three parallel lines, sleek and sharp edged, evoking... what? Feathers, perhaps. They were inlaid in places with pale green lacquer and something that looked like mother-of-pearl. It was not at all Eldritch, and yet beautiful, and better suited to her unornamented garb than any more baroque piece. And the back... how did it even work? There was no catch, only a slight raised area. She tried brushing it, and was startled when the air seemed to stiffen over her finger. Like an invisible pin? She tried sliding it into the hair at her temple and her mouth gaped when it stuck there, better than any piece of metal.

Still amazed, she looked at the note. No hand-penned thing, this, from how smooth it was. Another ridiculous mortal contrivance, no doubt. But the words were no template.

Alet—

If I made you feel less beautiful, or less welcome, I'm sorry! I saw this and thought of you. It's not an invitation, so don't feel uncomfortable about accepting it. I just wanted to give you something.

I'm really not good at this, when I have no idea how to make it clear what I mean! If any of this makes you uncomfortable, I'm sorry about that too!

—Leo

And the absurdity of it struck her, suddenly and power-fully, and she began laughing. Her alien crewmates had even less idea how to handle their interactions than she did. It shouldn't have made her like them better, but it did.

CHAPTER 12

Theresa Eddings's message was sufficiently terse to give one cause to wonder why she'd recorded it at all; surely sending another of the itemized shopping lists would have been sufficient. But the human had bestirred herself to create a recording, in which she confessed to frustration with the chickens' failure to thrive, and could Surela find other strains and bring them by? What was behind the woman's curtness? Not the marriage, surely, because the looseness of shoulders and gestures remained. Something else was putting the lines on Eddings's face, and Surela doubted it had anything to do with the vicissitudes of the planet's poultry. The war, perhaps, if war there was yet. Surely not, no matter how avaricious the dragons. Surela had lately seen the aftermath of battle in Ontine's halls: what was worth that carnage? Who would countenance the waste?

She dreamed still, but the nightmares were fewer, and she woke feeling stronger despite the energy consumed by her condition. Perhaps that was why she faced Saul in the mess, after they'd docked at Psi, and said, "I would like to reprise my outing alone."

He continued filling his plate. "All right."

Surprised, she watched, waiting for his body language to illuminate... something. Some clue that might inform her why he had capitulated. Was his swift response a trick? Why bother? But if he had been detailed as her guard....

He looked up, for she had surely left it too long. "It's fine, alet. You have enough experience with the gravity to pace yourself, and I doubt you'll get lost after this many trips out. But I need to get you a telegem before you go and teach you how to use it. Promise me you'll wait on that."

"I—of course."

She'd not known what her keeper was talking about, but half an hour after breakfast Saul chimed for admittance to her kennel and brought with him what appeared to be a single earring of modest style: a flattened ball in silver. "There are fancier ones," he said. "But you can buy yourself a more decorative one if you want. Here, it goes on the inside of your ear."

"The *inside*?" she repeated, taking it gingerly.

He began to tap his own as if to demonstrate before grimacing. "I keep forgetting that's not going to map well, since you have human ears. Will you let me apply it, or do you want me to demonstrate how in a mirror?"

She did not love the idea of letting a mortal touch her, but she'd permitted Prudence to do so, and Saul was, whatever his other sins, hers—assigned to her by what she was forced to concede was her liegelady, to guard her safety. To interfere with his duties was distasteful. She had a responsibility to him, to not make his work more difficult. "You may affix it."

"All right. Do you have a dominant hand? One you prefer to do fine work with?"

"Yes?" she said, bemused. "The right?"

He moved to her left side and halted for so long she wondered what he was about. His breath was warm near her neck, as if he was staring there. "All right. Slight pressure, now. I'll keep it minimal, it doesn't need much to stick." With that, his fingertips brushed her ear. How it stole her breath, that touch, in so intimate a place... near her face, and that was before it was compounded with her impressions of him, emotionally. Of his calm purpose, and devotion to something —what, she wondered? What had made him so adamant on the inside, and without agitation? And how could she linger in those impressions, when the use of the mind talents was anathema to people of good breeding?

Saul drew back. "All right. Shake your head, make sure it stays?"

She tried a twitch, and felt nothing other than the slight pressure near her ear canal.

"All right, looks good. The telegem works like the computer. You talk to it to activate it. You can use it to contact the computer, or you can tell it to connect you to the ship. Let me walk you through that."

How precipitous all these mortal communications were. No pages to take messages to and fro, only this instantaneous and impersonal connection. She could trouble anyone without warning, no matter their station, solely by asking... and with the link to the computer she could request any information and have it whispered in her ear. Was it different, really, from the imposition of a mind-mage's legendary telepathy, the one that could be extended over long distances? In a way it was worse, she decided... at least a mind-mage was forced to reveal something of his mind, and take into his own something of his target's. The computer breached privacy with indifferent power, and paid nothing for the imposition.

"All the crew have one of these," Saul finished. "Don't be afraid to ask for us if you need us, it's why we have one."

"Is this... device... typical? Of crew of cargo vessels?"

"It's pretty common. Not just for crew, for most people. I wouldn't say everyone's got one, but more people do than don't. It's too convenient, especially since they're easy to apply... not like an eyefilm that you'd have to have done at a healer's." At her blank stare, he said, "An eyefilm projects a computer display for you wherever you are. It's generated by another device, this one a thin layer, that they put over your cornea."

Surela shuddered. "Goddess. What a horror."

"It's comfortable and easy to use," Saul said. "I honestly think it's a cultural thing, that it's not more common. Some distance from tech is considered good, probably because of our bad experiences with nanotech. That would be when you inject the machines into your body."

The thought was so outlandish she couldn't be horrified by it, because she couldn't make it feel real.

Saul finished, "Since we didn't do well with that, there's some pressure not to get too deeply invested with integrated tech. And really, what's the point if it gets too intrusive? The ideal, by most Alliance standards, is that the technology allows you to live the life you want, and most people want what people have wanted since time immemorial: love, plenty, time to spend with your family, less stress. Obviously a spacefaring society can't eschew technology completely, but we can choose not to let it run our lives. Now... you've got a telegem, it's linked to the ship, and you know how to use it... and if I've forgotten anything, you can tell the telegem to walk you through it yourself if you ask it for help. You're good to go on your own now. Don't do anything unwise."

"No," she said. "Of course not."

He nodded and left, and that puzzled her: that he should abandon her so readily. Or was it that this device yoked her now to some invisible leash? If it could reach the other crewmembers, that suggested it could also tell her where they were....

Perhaps not a bad thing, at that, if it meant kidnappers could not hide her from her rescuers. Not that she feared kidnappers, not anymore. Weeks spent running Liolesa's errands on Starbase Psi had acclimated her to the reactions of aliens, and overwhelmingly they ignored her. When they didn't, they treated her with a refreshing deference, and if it sometimes bordered on yearning, that could be construed as a compliment. Or at least, it was easier to do so than to consider it encroaching.

It was for the best, she thought, that her room had no mirror. She could dress in her ugly, untailored garb, braid her cropped mane in a way that now exposed her alien technology, and never see how far she'd fallen. But she did, after a hesitation, use the barrette. The strands near her right temple insisted on sagging out of the braid after a few hours, and it would be useful to keep them out of her face.

———

To be out on the base now, after familiarity had made the weight on her body expected and the vista less staggering, was... refreshing. She hadn't anticipated that. That she would one day find the mortal world perilously close to exhilarating. Or perhaps that was solely that she was out on her own? One of the things she'd liked about ascending to the final tier of power in Asaniefa had been the ability to send her subordinates away. A great lady had little free time if she took care with her duties, but she could steal some of that time back from the endless management of expectations, needs, and complaints if she was willing. And when Surela had become Asaniefa's head, people no longer felt entitled to her time, and often apologized for bothering her, which had been... relaxing.

She had enjoyed her independence as a great lady, and to be walking here, among dangerous aliens in a foreign environment, with neither fear nor confusion... that was an independence she would have been hard pressed to explain, save that the scope for freedom was greater in a society this much larger than her own. Was it traitorous to think so?

Had Liolesa walked alien halls in this way, and was that what had made her so apt to jerk the reins from anyone who held them? What did Surela really know about the woman she'd attempted to depose, other than that she'd apparently been arranging, all this time, for the material aid that would prevent the starvation of the Eldritch, and secreting it to larders all over the world?

To reach the opposite shore required Pad transit, and Surela lined up to use one with all the confidence of a native. She gave the destination, stepped over, and immediately headed toward the farm. The outrageous diversity of the people passing her on the thoroughfare no longer disarmed her; she could even recognize some of them by name, though the fact that three separate races looked like cats, and three separate ones were dog-like, led her to uncertainty now and then. She had grown accustomed to the deliberation with which she was forced to move while under the influence of the heavier gravity, and no longer mistook it for fatigue. The cadence of Universal took less time to parse, and while it remained an outlandish tongue, lacking in nuance and clarity and possessing far too many hard consonants, still, she managed. And when she entered the showroom, she was recognized: knew not only Beverly, whom she now knew to be female, but the two employees that worked for her in the showroom, and several of the individuals who managed the animals in the back.

Today, Stuart was in the front, another Hinichi wolfish man like Saul, but unlike her uncomely guardian, a sleek and striking creature, silver-furred with yellow eyes. He could not have looked more dissimilar to his employer, but like her, he wore starkly formal garb and had an animal companion... a gray and white goose, in his case, who waddled in his wake with imperious dignity. "Alet," Stuart said on seeing her. "How can we be of service today?"

Surela sat, feeling the need. That, too, had become habit: knowing when she needed rest, and for how long. "You can tell me if you have shown me all the breeds you have for sale. We are having little luck with the ones I've purchased thus far."

His frown was slight; she appreciated his ponderous movements, and how he never indulged in extreme gestures or histrionics. "We've sold you everything we commonly carry, so this is where I inform you that anything else would constitute a special order. It'll be more expensive than if you went direct to those salespeople."

"But I would have to reach these people," Surela guessed. "They are not here, on Starbase Psi."

"No."

How much more would they have to spend to travel to distant ports? Surely it cost something in fuel to move the ship. Not that it mattered, for Eddings had said they shouldn't stray far from home. "I would prefer, perhaps, to work with people I already know."

His eyes brightened. "We won't let you down. Tell us the problems you've been seeing, and we'll see what we can do for you."

That was a productive interview, and during it she watched Stuart take notes on a tablet. He had a telegem as well, she saw, discreetly nestled on the inside of his ear... why, then, did he not dictate to it? Or—Goddess, she hadn't thought to ask—make a recording, such as the ones sent to her by Eddings? Was it personal preference, or etiquette?

"This may take a while," was the last thing Stuart told her. "We'll have to contact other breeders and requisition the birds, and shipping live cargo isn't as quick as static cargo. But we'll contact you as soon as we have some candidates for evaluation."

That left her on her own, and without an errand, and how strange that was: to be subject only to her own schedule. Surela could go… anywhere. She even knew how to use money, now; reassuringly, the Alliance exchange worked much like the one she was familiar with from her stays in the Eldritch capital. There, she would browse the merchant shops and make her orders, giving them her name so they could draw on the account held by the Asaniefa House purser. It was the House pursers who exchanged coin with the capital's small middle class for their goods; everything else was handled through vassal-liege ties: tithes owed for duties exacted.

The aliens also needed only a name to debit her funds. The familiarity of the exchange soothed her… and she admitted to preferring to have knowledge of her balance without having to engage the purser. Asaniefa's had been effective, but peevish.

Without having to answer to anyone, Surela could linger where she liked. Look at the boutiques and wonder if Leo was right, and she should choose something different to wear —and what? Wander slowly, cautious of her energy level, through small markets full of wares that were superficially commonplace, candles and jewelry and foodstuffs and art items, while also being the product of this bizarrely advanced society. Did that woman handmake those candles as an Eldritch would have? Or did she oversee some complex technological process? Who bought those kites and where did they fly them? Were those grooming tools for fur or hair? And what did the feathered aliens use instead?

Surela had a light lunch near the edge of town, overlooking the plains from a sunlit balcony. What did it mean, to be an Eldritch alone, here? There had been other wanderers: the (formerly royal and now imperial) House Galare was famous for producing them, though Surela hadn't concerned herself with anything other than the rumors of their disappearances abroad. Other, of course, than Hirianthial's, because the departure of a former head of Household had been noteworthy, especially after such a scandal. His parents dead... come to think of it, they'd died at their own hands, hadn't they? She rested her hand on her wine glass, frowning. Yes... something about the weight of the years, accumulating on shoulders that knew not how to bear them. The Eldritch had been breeding for longevity, and precipitously, since Jerisa had come to the homeworld to establish their people, and the stories said each subsequent generation added another four or five centuries to their potential lifespan.

Would they all go mad, absent something to fill those increasing years with? Did they even know how long they would keep adding centuries to their lives? What would they do with functional immortality?

Except, of course, that they could be slain. And they could die of disease and injury. Her hand stole to the slight swell beneath her ribs.

After lunch, Surela stopped outside and tried, hesitantly, a low command. "Computer?" A chime in her ear, so soft to be so clear. "Is there a bookseller in this place?"

"The nearest bookseller may be found by walking down Tassel to Freiyet. Make a left and continue to Dormanne. Pardeen's Books will be on the right, at the intersection."

Goddess. She had no idea whether to be appalled or elated. Was it empowering to rely on no one for aid, or distressing because she had no idea how that aid was provided? Surely what she did not understand could be taken from her, leaving her with no idea how to replicate its effects. She set off, ignoring the shiver in her joints and the persistent and annoying fatigue.

Pardeen's was, indeed, a bookseller, and sold items she recognized as books; not a given, with mortal technology. The store also offered texts that were read using mortal display, which it advertised in the same way the farmer advertised their nonexistent chickens, via representations… in this case, of lurid cover art. Since the oldest books in Surela's libraries had been encrusted with gemstones she felt she had no basis for contempt. That those gemstones might have made her books more valuable did not, in most cases, make them less gaudy. She preferred a more understated treatment for covers than many of her peers.

Surela knew enough about the alien society to guess that this single store, which represented treasure beyond counting on her world, was probably the least of what aliens took for granted. That in all probability books were commodities rather than heirlooms to be cherished and maintained for centuries. That she could probably buy any of these books—more than one!—and pay less than she would for the meal she'd just eaten. She paused along one of the shelves, resting her fingers on the spine, sobered by the realization. How did the aliens know what was worth saving, when they could afford to save everything?

There was a single proprietor in the back, sitting on a stool and reading from a paper book: a handsome woman with ragged spots on her tawny pelt and a lush tail that curled around the stool's three legs. She lifted her face long enough to smile and nod, then returned to her reading. Surela was glad of it, for it left her to her perusal without the burden of conversation.

What to buy? So much fiction… Goddess, she couldn't imagine a single improving novel among the thousands available, if only because she couldn't fathom that there were that many authors willing to produce them. They were unpalatable fare even at home. And nonfiction as well—she took down one about climate zones and found color illustrations as vivid as any she might have seen in her own library, though not painted onto the page. The aliens obviously had some technique that allowed them to print… like the broadsheet, but in color. Perhaps that was why she was startled by the second book she selected at random, because it was about starship types, but the illustrations were so obviously hand-drawn that she kept turning pages, looking and enjoying the juxtaposition.

She brought that one to the creature on the stool. "How much is this, may I ask?"

"New Edition of Wiley's? Good choice. It's twenty fin, alet."

So little! "I will take it. And... do you have perhaps a history book?"

"Whose history?" The woman set her book aside and clasped her hands on her lap, giving Surela her full atten-tion... and from someone with those round, blue-gray eyes, flecked with silver, it was astonishing. "Human? Pelted? If Pelted, early history, late?"

Too many choices. "An overview, perhaps, of the Alliance's?"

"Lot of good overviews. My favorite is Tandeyra's, though. Here, I'll get it for you."

The creature returned with another book, smaller than the starship book, and denser. It also had illustrations, or... perhaps not. Perhaps these were reproductions more specific than any drawing.

"It's thirty-five," the creature said. "But worth it."

Surela bought them both, and thought herself rich, or poor, and didn't know which. To walk into a store and purchase a book for so little! And not have to commission a copy? It was impersonal, certes, but faster. Was faster better, or simply different? Imponderables.

Leaving the bookseller made her uncomfortably aware of how tired she was. Tired enough that she stopped to lean against the wall of the store and wait for the dizziness to pass. When she straightened, she wished she hadn't. How ridicu-lous it would be to faint on her first foray alone since her first trip to Psi!

Determined, she set off. The Pad could deliver her to the dock, which would make for a shorter walk to the *Earthrise*. She had only to reach it, and reach it she did without remembering clearly how she made it there, only that it took far too much effort. She rested a hand on her belly, but beneath her hand she sensed no distress. Good enough—to lose the child would have been too dramatic by half. As head of Asaniefa, Surela had never gotten further than acknowledging she would need an heir, save briefly when Athanesin had pronounced his undying devotion... but some part of her had believed that she would be the exception to the Eldritch rule, that women should find baby-making impossible when it was not perilous.

No, she was keeping this child. They had gone through enough, the two of them, without also being parted untimely.

Stepping over the Pad at last, she moved out of the way and waited for gravity to stop dragging so hard at her limbs. It was a walk to the *Earthrise*'s berth, but surely she could make it?

Was she relieved or irritated that Ra'aila and Meri melted out of the crowd near her?

"You're back," Ra'aila said cheerfully, fooling Surela not at all. "Meri and I were just on her way to the ship, too."

"How fortuitous." And as long as they were there: "Could you take this for me, please?"

Meri accepted the bag. "Ooh, Pardeen's! I haven't been there in a while. I should go."

"You know it?"

"Sure, it's a chain—I mean, there's one owner of the business, and there are multiple shops in it, all selling the wares. There are Pardeen's all over the place."

How fascinating, and appalling, revealing as it did the scope of the mortal federation. She would have to add 'store chains' to her research topics. "It was worth the stop. I have also arranged for our next livestock shipment."

"Excellent," Ra'aila said. "We're about due to bring back more food. When we offload this cargo at home port, we'll come back for more staples."

Thus the conversation, all the way back to the ship, and they proceeded at a pace Surela would have found infuriatingly slow had she not needed it. The two delivered her to her room, even, with Meri handing off the bag at Surela's door before following the captain toward the mess. Surela looked after them for several minutes, then entered and waited for the door to shut before saying, as she'd been taught: "Saul Ferry, please."

A moment, then, in her ear: "Saul here."

"Did you set your minions on me?"

A pause, and with astonishing fidelity she could hear the reply, so that the smile that shaped it was obvious: "My minions?"

Would her exasperation be likewise obvious? "The captain and pilot."

"Would it upset you if I said 'yes'?"

She started to reply, then sagged onto her bunk and sighed. Eddings had hired him to ward her. To blame him for doing that work was ill-mannered. "No. In retrospect, I perhaps overextended myself."

"You'll get used to gauging what you can handle; stopping to eat was a good instinct. I'm glad you had a nice time."

"Thank you." She paused, remembering both her purported name and the bizarre grammatical construction that ended these conversations. "Rel out."

She brought her purchases from their bag and set them on her desk, opening the history to the first page and thumbing through the next few. Her fingers paused. He'd known she'd stopped to eat... how? Had he been following her?

What else?

Surela laughed. She would have been charmed and proud of an Eldritch guard who did such work, with such zeal and discretion. How could she hate Saul for it, no matter his ungainly appearance and outlandish origins? Did he continue in this vein she would owe him a guerdon, and what a ridiculous notion that was: an Eldritch with mortal vassals. When did aliens give gifts, and on what occasions? She would have to find out. "Computer, note more research topics. Gift-giving, and store chains."

"Added to your list."

CHAPTER 13

To and fro—to and fro. With the metronomic predictability of a music lesson delivered under the glower of a withered taskmistress. Surela could almost hear the songs as the ship ran its path, as if she could sing the ship into harbor, and off again on the waves in space. Did space have them? She asked the computer, and frowned through explanations of solar waves and the theorized creation of the universe. She brought back eggs in her incubators, and parts that began to have recognizable names: a gem grid was for power and was set in the floor, and could heat or cool it as well as feed the devices favored by mortals; a Pad allowed transit between two spaces instantly; a genie created new things using a pattern and either mass or energy; a generator created that energy, from various sources. And of course, all the smaller devices, that kept plates warm, and food from decaying; the tablets that supplanted pen and paper; the endless conveniences that replaced the things she'd always known, or would eventually. Cloth she bought back in reams in Galare blue and Mathanith yellow and Laisrathera peach, to be transformed by tailors into livery… how soon before those tailors no longer sewed by hand, but instead used the holographic visualization tools that showed her what sort of chicken would hatch from her latest eggs?

The fabric gave her pause, when she lifted one of the ells between her hands. No Asaniefa green would ever have passed through a hold like this. How many bolts had been brought to Ontine in secret, all these years, to clothe Liolesa's servants?

It was enough to drive a woman to melancholy, and Surela refused. She chose instead to consider it as past due, that the Eldritch should be as rich as their mortal neighbors. She was having some small part in creating that parity. It would have to do.

———

Ra'aila held up her hands in the mess, which was the most comfortable place to gather the entire crew. It was the first time she'd summoned them to it for a meeting like this. Surela didn't need to puzzle at the animal face when the body language was sufficient... because a similar emotion had once animated Surela the head of Household in her bounty years. Their captain was about to spread some largesse she was excited about sharing.

"I'm happy to report that our employer is pleased with our hard work," said the Aera. "And that means—"

"Bonuses?" the first mate asked, bicolor ears twitching forward.

"Bonuses!" Ra'aila agreed. "And I'm using mine to buy us lunch at Idyllic, in the aquasphere's Beach Town." She laughed. "I see the healer knows what's in store."

Prudence had, in fact, straightened in her seat. "Do we get the hats?"

"We get the hats. Tomorrow, when we get into port... we feast!"

———

The hats were explained in due course, when Surela was seated at a table too sunny for a bare head. The waitstaff had handed them out amid the laughter and delight of Ra'aila's crew, and even Surela was hard pressed not to smile at the sight of them threading their ears through the holes in the straw. She could settle hers without the effort, and while the cord that held it fast lacked something in elegance, there was no doing without it, given the breeze. The restaurant lived up to its name, for in typical mortal fashion it made profligate use of technology to offer an unbelievable dining experience: each party was assigned to a table mounted on a clear disc, which floated at whatever height its participants preferred above the waves in a secluded cove. Some diners left it hovering so close over the water that stronger waves slopped over their feet; others chose to float at the maximum allowed distance alongside the cove's cliff ceiling, some two floors up, Surela judged. The waitstaff reached them on their own translucent discs, sailing as if flying to their sides.

It was ridiculous, and she had to fight not to find it astonishing. And charming, that also, because Ra'aila let their table drift near the surface of the water, and the nearness of the surf, the smell, the breeze, the sun, the *novelty* of it, and the outrageously near-magicalness, worked on her relentlessly. These aliens, she thought, were determined to be admired, and very much wanted to be loved. She looked down, saw a school of fish darting between her feet, and struggled to maintain her emotional remove.

The menu was all seafood, and delicious. The company... she ate, listening to the banter. Did she like these creatures?

"...and what are you going to do with your bonus?" Danica was asking Leo. "Should we assume something outrageous?"

"Want to finish dressing the Eldritch?" Erynne asked, eyes merry.

That drew Surela's attention, but rather than tease, the man lifted his chin and sniffed. "I already have, and none of you noticed." He pressed a hand to his heart and bowed to Surela. "The lady honors me."

He'd noticed the barrette, then. "It keeps my hair from falling in my face," she said, because she guessed they would expect this sort of demurral from an Eldritch. And added, because she was not solely a caricature, "And it is lovely."

"I have excellent taste," Leo agreed, nearly purring in pleasure.

"That? That's too understated for you to have picked it," Meri said, peering at the hairpiece.

"I can do understated! I just wish I didn't have to. I mean... swimsuit and sarong on her would be amazing."

"Are you sure you're an accountant?" Danica asked, amused. "Because you talk like a fashion designer."

"A man's got to have hobbies, sweet peach. What about you? What are you spending your funds on?"

"Oh..." The woman pursed her lips. "I like food."

An easy ripple of laughter, because the evidence of how much all of them liked food was still cluttering the table. Dessert plates now, and there had been one for each of them, and some of the others had stuck spoons in their neighbors' choices.

"No, really," Danica said after the laughter had died down. "Good food, when you're a spacer... it's a big deal. And it makes you feel rich, to eat well."

Murmurs of agreement that surprised Surela, for she hadn't thought that these aliens, who were so prosperous, might feel the same way about food that an Eldritch tenant might.

"What about you?" Danica asked Meri. "What's your pleasure? Vacations?"

Their pilot grinned. "I see plenty of places flying ships. I like ConEd."

Beside her, Saul murmured, "Continuing Education."

"We going to lose you to some more impressive job soon?" Ra'aila asked, ears twitching forward—a sign of interest, rather than dismay.

"Oh, no. I just like learning." Meri said with a blush. "I already have certification in two other disciplines—"

"What!" Ra'aila exclaimed, laughing. "I read your bio before we interviewed you! How did I miss these specialties?"

"Because they weren't on my bio! It wasn't relevant!" Meri's amusement was patent. "One of them is in industrial psychology, and the other one's in metallurgy."

"Oh, no, this is a story we have to hear," Erynne said, and they did, and Surela couldn't follow more than half of it but apparently their pilot could design stores that enticed people to make more purchases, or restaurants to make people linger, and also that she knew a sufficiency of smithing to have made swords for Eldritch lords. Perhaps. Goddess knew what a Pelted-created sword would look like.

Prudence, when asked, confessed to spending her spare money on music, and interestingly, in a way Surela under-stood: these aliens also had patronage systems, choosing specific artists and investing in their future endeavors. Erynne, the engineer, was a '3deo buff', which involved plays, but recorded as holographs, and this was a common enough pastime for the table to devolve into debate over their favorites and give recommendations. Saul disap-pointed everyone by being the type to save money rather than spend it, and endured the good-natured teasing about his stereotypical lack of irresponsibility. Ra'aila liked jewelry, but not cheap pieces, and was hoarding her money until she could afford a full set that she showed them on one of the ubiquitous floating displays: a torc with large, rectangular cabochons in teal and orange, with matching armbands.

"And you?" Danica asked Surela at last. "What will you be spending your bonus on?"

"Books, I'm betting," Ra'aila said. "I've never seen anyone hitting the u-banks on so many topics."

"The searches on a small ship aren't private by default," Danica hurried to say. "You should have warned her about that, Ra'aila, she probably didn't know."

But Surela had never believed her questions to be private. Perhaps she should have, but one assumed the servants were listening, and perhaps discussing, one's actions. "I have few needs," she chose to say, because it was true enough. "I suppose I'll let the money accumulate until something strikes me as worthy of the use."

"See, that's practical," Meri said. "'Wait and see.'"

"Unless you decide you need a degree in architecture? Or flower arranging?"

"You'll be fine for a while if you want to keep her," Erynne opined to Ra'aila. "No one's going to know how to hire someone who can arrange flowers, erect a building, make you spend more money in a boutique, assess the flaws in your latest alloy, and then fly you to the border."

"I can't talk," Ra'aila said. "I'm a ship's captain who can breed horses!"

That inspired a fresh round of laughter and questions, and Surela marveled at the ease with which they interrogated one another on matters an Eldritch would have considered private. They revealed their interests and desires so casually, and with such enthusiasm, and even Saul and Prudence, who tended toward a reserve Surela recognized, were more forthcoming than an Eldritch tenant, much less an Eldritch noble.

Their meal came with a cabana on the beach, reserved until sunset, and there the crew repaired to do what could only be called frolicking in the waves. Glad to be relieved of their nearness, Surela drifted away and bent to touch the water. Small wonder the others threw off their clothes to reveal swimwear, for it was warm as a bath.

That they played like children shouldn't have surprised her, given their lack of inhibitions in other arenas. What did was that her own reticence exhausted her. What good was all that she'd learned as Surela Silin Asaniefa when she would never use it again? What Eldritch would ever see her to judge her behavior? And granted that, why should she not dive into life with all the enthusiasm of the mortals she now worked alongside?

And yet, it was all she had left of who she was. And the nightmares, though receding in frequency, remained.

Surela set off to walk the beach, because it was beautiful. When Saul followed, she said, "You needn't. I can hardly fall into trouble here."

"I know. You just looked like you needed company."

Had she? When she glanced at him, she caught a glimpse of Prudence, who was also strolling her way. "And now I have earned the attentions of both of you. Do I look so doleful, then?"

"It's less that and more that you're not participating in the group activity." Saul's smile was whimsical. "I'm glad, because I don't want to participate in the group activity."

"You do not swim?"

"I know how, but I don't enjoy it."

When she drew abreast of them, Prudence was all smiles and damp fur, a towel wrapped around her hips. "What are we not enjoying? I'm guessing swimming. No, don't be surprised... I have to be in the mood for it, myself. I don't swim well."

"Really?" Saul asked.

"Not even a little, and despite being taught over and over by very zealous instructors. And let me tell you, there are a lot of instructors in the aquasphere...! I can wade around, but swimming for real?" She shook her head. "I asked for a tow whenever I had to go out somewhere." At Surela's canted head, the woman finished, "From a Naysha."

A Naysha… had she read something about them in the table of alien species? There were not many water creatures. "The ones like merfolk."

"Yes, them."

"You worked here?" Saul asked, and the two of them were off again, sharing their backgrounds with an appalling lack of concern. Though in these two, who were the least forthcoming of the group, it proceeded at a pace Surela found slightly more comfortable.

"The environment was definitely the best part of this sphere," Prudence finished. She waved toward the false horizon, where a sun appeared to be dipping toward the waters, tinting them orange. "They paid so much attention to the modeling of the light and gravitational forces. The moon'll be coming up soon, and it'll pull on the water just the way it should so that all the flora and fauna that evolved in an ocean with currents will thrive."

"They generate a magnetic force," Saul guessed. "I never thought about how that must work."

"Neither did I until I worked here."

"What wonders you take for granted," Surela said, without planning.

"We do, yes," Prudence said after a hesitation.

"That's what prayer's for," Saul said. "Say thank you daily. Eventually you stop taking things for granted."

"Is that how it works?" the healer asked him, smiling.

"Don't you pray?"

Another of those pauses. "Why would I?" she said at last. "Your religion is organic, arii. You got it from humans, who got it from some source they claim to be true. Mine… mine was constructed. I appreciate it as a cultural touchstone, a shared reference. But Iley isn't real, is he?"

Saul smiled. "I'm definitely the wrong person to ask about that."

"Then I'll ask Rel." The woman turned her lovely eyes to Surela, arched her brows. "Do you pray?"

"I didn't," Surela said. "But I should have, more."

————

She thought of that later, undressing to shower after the long afternoon out, in the quiet of an empty ship. She'd been the first to return, wearied by the expedition and grateful for the time alone.

Did she believe in Goddess and God, Lord and Lady? She had sworn by them all her life, attended the rites, defended the church. That had been her duty as a head of household, and an Eldritch noble: to set a good example, to hew to the principles set forth by their religious institution. There had been pageantry in it, and solemnity, and that had struck her as appropriate. But would she ever have attempted to create an altar in a foreign land, the way Saul had in the cargo hold?

And if she dared believe, would she have to ask why she lived, still? And why the Goddess had permitted their world to be opened to slavers and pirates through her hubris? Could Surela believe in a divine plan, having suffered evil? Worse, having wrought it?

Something in her grieved at her melancholy, and she rested her hand over the swell in her abdomen. "None of it is attached to you," she promised, quiet. "I am a survivor, and you, a victim." No, that sounded wrong. "A bystander."

The distress quieted, and Surela sighed, rested her head against the cool, metal wall. So hard to live here, and so easy.

CHAPTER 14

They hauled their cargo to the Eldritch homeworld and out again, and this time Surela read the broadsheet. She learned in this fashion that her world now had a name, and apparently had had one since the winter holidays: Escutcheon. Who had chosen it, and why? The columns and articles in the broadsheet assumed that the name was broadly known, but as long as Surela had been alive, no one had ever called their planet anything other than 'the world.' As one ought, if one planned it to be the only world that mattered.

Escutcheon. She rolled the word around on her tongue under her breath, alone in her room. *Eihiun.* So difficult not to take it personally, when she'd chosen a shield as her particular mark when she'd ascended to the head of House Asaniefa. She knew what shields meant to her... the question was what this shield had been intended to convey. Why the silvered mode? The word, unmarked, *hiun,* would have been enough. Coloring it transformed it from simple shield to something more. Not gold, to make it the strongest and best of shields, nor white, to make it the holiest and purest. But silver, as if speaking of something out of tales of knights intent on acts of glory and sacrifice.

Of course, Liolesa had done it. The question was why.

Summer was approaching, and with it, preparations for the summer court. Who was going to seek a groom, or a bride? Who was hoping to establish stronger ties with another ally or divest themselves of a troublesome one? Who would be seen, and wearing what? How many years had Surela spent seizing on these details, every year, twice a year... and how had they seemed so important? She had eaten at Ontine's banquets without understanding the real power that moved beneath the surface, the one that had made that food possible.

And here she was. What to do now? And could she have power again, by Eldritch—new Eldritch—standards, when she could never go home? Surela fought back a wave of desire and anguish over the loss of Surela Silin, the shield of the Asaniefa family. She had lost that right forever. She had to move on.

Eihiun. What threat was Liolesa holding their world up against? And what would serve as her sword? And would Surela bring her the component parts of that defense in the hold of this ship, all unknowing?

———

After arranging for half the list of necessaries on this trip, Surela took herself to lunch on the far side of Clovellan, thinking perhaps inevitably of Danica and her assertion that food was luxury. Food was not sufficient, she thought. True luxury included solitude. To be waited on by strangers who expected nothing of her, unlike the servants who had been hers to care for... to choose whatever she pleased, without concerning herself over whether there was a sufficiency of that dish for everyone. To be able to please herself in silence, to read, or watch the aliens go by, without being forced to make conversation… all of this was luxury. She could admit to enjoying it.

The book she'd brought was forgotten on the table alongside her plate. It was enough to savor the breeze, and if the bay in the city-sphere was less engaging than the mock ocean that filled the aquacultural sphere, there was a poetry to the swoop of the shore birds, diving past the cliffs.

Her telegem chirped once. Then it emitted a terrible sound she hoped never to hear again, and all around her people were straightening.

"Attention," it whispered in her ear. "Attention. Please proceed to the nearest source for news."

Then… nothing. Surela frowned and paid for her meal, waving the account chip over the table. Rising, she said to the telegem, "Connect me to Saul."

A rising arpeggio, another chime. Then her minder's voice, brusque. She didn't know why she thought he was jogging somewhere. "Alet. I'm nearly at your location. We'll be heading back to the ship."

"Saul? What has happened?"

"The war's caught up with us."

Her body clenched. What did that mean? Was she presently in danger? She glanced at the people dining around her… some of them were still eating, laughing. Others were staring at tablets, and the silences around them were growing the way pools of blood had around the dying bodies in Ontine. She started walking, and as she left the patio, she espied Saul. Until that moment she hadn't realized how much of a comfort he was, in his constancy, and in his homely competence.

Except she did not like at all the tension on his face. He fell into step alongside her. "The nearest Pad is this way, and we've got to get there immediately."

"Immed—is it so bad?"

"It's going to be."

She glanced at him. "You know what's happened."

"Yes." He shocked her by wrapping a hand around her upper arm, stabbing her with the adrenaline swiftness of his heart. How was he not shaking with the force of it? "Can you move faster?"

"Y-yes?"

"Let's go."

They were entering the Pad station when the world around them erupted. Yells, first, then a scream of such anguish the hair leapt upright all along Surela's nape. "Don't look," Saul snapped, and had her over the Pad before she could disobey. The device delivered her to a space alongside the *Earthrise,* and then he was pushing her up the ramp and his urgency infected her through two layers of clothing. He wasn't talking to her, though, but to his telegem. "Get them all aboard now, Ra'aila, I mean it. They should have been moving before I finished talking to you the first time. I know you didn't know but what the hell did Reese hire me for if you're not going to listen to me about security issues? Yes, I know you didn't know I was actually good at it, now will you get everyone back *now*!"

Had she ever heard him use such extreme language?

"What do I do?" she asked him.

"Sit in the mess. We're going to need a conference when everyone's aboard. And if someone raps on the external door, don't answer. No deliveries, no messages, nothing. If they don't already have access to the ship, they don't get in."

Would they be mobbed with strangers? What could possibly be happening? Saul had gone, swift as flowing shadow, and it hurt that it should make her think of song. He was an alien, and no beauty besides, but the steel in him stole her breath and left her staggered. She sank onto a chair in the mess, thinking that she could look up the news—that she could ask the computer in the silent well of the room and it would fill that silence with information, and then her ignorance would end. But she kept remembering the stench of violated bodies, strewn on the palace's carpets. The smell of her own body after the violence visited on it. The clamor that had filled Ontine's halls, loud enough to vibrate through closed doors.

The next people in were Danica, Erynne and Leo, and then Meri. Prudence entered last, puzzled, with Ra'aila: "I hadn't left yet," said the healer as she sat in the chair alongside Surela's. "What's this about?"

"You were right," Ra'aila told Saul, her face grim. "It's getting crazy out there. Should we cast off?"

"No. I think we might be safer where we are."

"Safe from what?" Danica asked.

Leo was too still. "I saw," he whispered.

"The Chatcaava have attacked the Bright Belt." Saul glanced at Prudence. "There's no good way to say this. Tamley was the worst hit, along with the colonies Luminous, Pelara, and Trade Winds. They also went through Karaka'Ana and Seersana's system, but the planets look intact."

"The pla—" Meri's teeth clicked together. She licked her lips before continuing, "You're saying the other planets… aren't?"

"Luminous and Tam-ley are gone. Pelara and Trade Winds probably aren't coming back either."

Prudence listed, toppled into Leo's arms. The leonine lunged to catch her and held her against his breast, eyes wide. "She's breathing," he reported in response to all their stares. "I've got her."

Meri turned back to Saul. "What does it mean? Are the Chatcaava coming here?"

"No one knows. My guess is no—the damage follows a broad but consistent trail—but we're on one of the borders. If they decide they like broaching borders…." Saul shook his head. "I think we're safer here than back at the Eldritch world, which is in the isolated fringes. This is a sturdy harbor and we've got the naval base right over our heads. Nothing's going to attack an alerted Fleet base unless they like a fair fight, and what happened out there wasn't a fair fight. Having said that—" Looking now at Ra'aila, "People are going to be crazy for a while."

"Riots?" Ra'aila asked.

"Unintentional, maybe. But definitely people not in control of themselves. I'd suggest staying put until things calm down."

"What do I do with her?" Leo said, his breathing too rapid. "She's fainted."

"Was she from Tam-ley?" Erynne came to his side and took Prudence's hand briskly, checking her pulse at the wrist. "I never asked."

"She was." That was her voice. Surela cleared her throat. "She had said."

"Sun and stars," Erynne muttered. "We shouldn't leave her alone."

"I can carry her," Leo said. "And one of us should wait in her quarters until she's awake. Do you need to do anything special for fainted people?"

"Since she's the healer, I guess 'wait until she wakes up and ask her,'" Danica said. Her white ear was an unhealthy color on its inside surface, bloodless, and her voice was shaky. "Bast. I can't believe what you just told us. It's real? The Chatcaava... they've started a war? People have died? Tam-ley is... gone?"

"How gone is gone?" Meri wanted to know.

"They hit it with an asteroid," Saul said. "From what little we know right now, it's looking like what they missed with it, the weather will take care of."

"That's... that's a core world!" Meri sounded offended. Angry. "They can't... you can't kill off a core world!"

Danica touched the other woman's arm, and Meri looked

at her as if seeking agreement. What she saw in Danica's gaze made her ears collapse.

"This isn't real, is it?" Meri whispered.

"It is, yes," Saul said.

"Right." Ra'aila, who'd been silent and pale throughout Saul's briefing, squared her shoulders. "No one leaves. At least for a day, until we get more news. Leo, would you get Prudence to her cabin? Erynne, do you want to do first watch on her? Or you, Leo? Treat her like someone in shock, keep her warm and… put her feet up, I guess. Unless the computer has better advice." She turned to Saul. "You'll keep us apprised of the news?"

"Of course."

"Right. I'll contact our employer, make sure nothing's happened over there. The rest of you, try…" Ra'aila paused. "Try to keep busy. There are some routine maintenance tasks we've been putting off, this seems like the right time to handle them."

Murmurs in return; Leo was already rising with Prudence in his arms.

"I'll help with her later," Surela said, and no longer cared that the offer surprised her. "Later tonight, if you wish someone to sit by her bedside when someone tires."

Leo nodded. "I'll get you after dinner, then. If we're doing maintenance, you're going to be busy, Erynne."

"Right."

That left five of them, and the ensuing silence filled with their mingled ignorance and fear. Ra'aila scratched at her head, drawing some of the bright red hair from its braid. "Is it going to keep happening? More attacks? We fight them back now, isn't that how it works?"

"It would, if they'd stuck around to get hit," Saul said. "But they took us completely by surprise. Raided us… vanished, as far as we know."

"So they could be anywhere?" Danica asked, shaken.

"We're going to win," Ra'aila said firmly. Glancing at Saul: "We're going to win, right?"

Surela was surprised to discover that she knew Saul well enough to see he was unhappy with the question. "I don't know how big their military is—"

"But we know how big they are as an empire, right?" Danica again. "They're not as big as we are...."

"We know that's what they told us," Saul began.

"In the treaty," Meri said. "That was a requirement for the treaty, we learned it in school. I still remember."

Saul's reply made perfect sense to Surela. "They might have lied."

"You can't lie at a treaty table!"

Surela met her keeper's eyes, and in them she saw a world-weariness to match her own, and without the years to have earned it.

"They might have lied," Saul repeated. "So they might have a lot more people than we thought."

"Or less?" Meri asked, hesitant.

"Or less," Saul said, and no one needed to guess his opinion of that possibility. "And even if I did have numbers, to make assumptions about whether we'll win, I'd need to know what they want."

Danica looked from one to the other. "How is that a question? You start wars to make people leave you alone, don't you?"

Goddess, their naiveté hurt. "That presumes," Surela said, "that what they want is to be left alone. They may want to conquer you, to hold your lands. They may desire plunder. Or they may wish to destroy you utterly."

"No one starts a war because they just don't like you!" Danica protested. "There's so much space in space! You might not understand that, you're Eldritch. But if they didn't like us, they could just... expand in some other direction—"

"Rel's right," Saul said. "And we don't know what they

want out of this fight, or how much they're bringing to it. We don't know almost anything, aletsen. Which is why I wanted us to sit tight until we learn more. Docked but inside the ship, we're as close to mobile as we can be without being exposed outside the starbase."

"If something happens, we might end up trapped in here," Ra'aila said, quiet.

"I know. But it's the best of a lot of bad options. And if we're trapped here because the starbase is being attacked by the Chatcaava, we're not going to want to be on the outside of the hull."

"We're really at war," Danica breathed. "Bast preserve us. The Chatcaava attacked us."

Ra'aila gripped her shoulder as the first mate shivered. "I'll go check with Reese, make sure there's no local bulletin."

"Good plan," Saul said.

"And me?" Meri asked, ears flattened.

"Go help Erynne," Ra'aila said. "You too, Danica. At least until dinner. You're still our best cook." She managed a smile, one which Danica was too stunned to return. "Seriously, get moving."

The two left, with Ra'aila chivvying them before her. Surela admired the work the Aera had done with the two of them—with the entire meeting, certes. She hadn't been sure Ra'aila would rise to the challenges of being their ship's captain, and had someone pressed her for an opinion she would have guessed that Ra'aila would crumple beneath an emergency of this magnitude. That it had galvanized her instead impressed Surela... impressed, and relieved her, because she wasn't sure how much help the remainder of the crew would be.

Saul was watching her. "All right?"

Was she? Could she imagine the death of a world? Surela remembered her terror when she thought she'd delivered her own to pirates. But more, she remembered what death looked like, and violence. If she saw images from this Tam-ley, would they look like what Athanesin had left of the lands of Jisien-sire when he razed them in her name? "It feels impertinent, to feel anything. They are your worlds to grieve over, not mine."

His eyes lost focus, and perhaps he was listening to some memory of his own, because his ears were flicking—this way, that. Then, abruptly, "Fair. Maybe you can help me with them."

"Does it not affect you?" she asked, unable to help the question.

His smile was crooked. "Someone has to keep it together until the crisis is over."

"You don't think it's over."

"I don't like the situation," he said. "I can't make it make sense. Why do this much damage and then vanish? If it was a feint, where are they now? If it was a raid, then what does it say about the size of their forces that they can commit to a raid that size?"

"Dragons," Surela murmured. "Where then, the pirates? Do they not always come together?"

His glance was sharp, but the response calm. "No matter how many pirates there are, they're not going to be as numerous as the Chatcaava. But you raise a good point— we're more likely to see pirates out here than dragons. And the chaos is likely to create an excellent environment for them to operate."

Surela said, "I have said a useful thing."

"You have, yes. Thank you, alet. I think I might see if I can catch the tail end of that call and ask some questions of my own." He dipped his head to her and departed, animated by the same grim focus that had characterized his rescue of her from the other side of the starbase. She wondered what he would learn from the call. If her experiences at Ontine might in some way equip anyone else to resist the depredations that had brought her low… that was worth it. No matter how she felt about mortals, pirates she hated. And dragons—

Something in her protested, not verbally or mindfully, but viscerally: a cry of grief, that dragons might be unworthy of love. Surela soothed the sleeper, passing her hand over the slight slope beneath her ribs. "Not you," she murmured. "You did not ask for your estate."

No question whether the words mattered, for they didn't. But the emotion did. Surela made herself—made both of them—tea and wondered if she was the only one aboard who could bring herself to drink. And eat, that too, and she tasked herself to that as well before returning to her cell. As Saul said, someone must have the strength to see them through this. What good all she had suffered, if it could not armor her against similar troubles?

A war on the level of planets, though… she swallowed. Had she been able to ask, would Liolesa have told her that preparing for such a thing had been her plan all along? Come to that, there had to have been a treaty between Eldritch and Alliance, just as there had apparently been between the almost-certainly duplicitous Chatcaava and the Alliance. Maraesa's doing, that treaty… did the Alliance have records of it? They must. She woke the computer to ask, first after the Chatcaavan treaty, called the Treaty of Za'ara… signed eighty-nine years after the Eldritch treaty, called the Vetch Agreement. A backhanded insult, no doubt, to name it after an undesirable but indestructible weed. One could only compromise with vetches, for there was no wishing them away. Surela brought up both agreements and began to read, ignoring the pounding in her head that was the emotions and memories she'd locked away, pushing closer.

CHAPTER 15

She had barely been an hour into her studies when Leo fetched her, his distress palpable. "She's awake, but she's just... staring at the wall. I don't know if I should hug her or talk to her, but I'm worried."

As if Surela would know what to do! But she allowed the purser to pull her back to the healer's cabin. As Leo had described, Prudence was curled up on her pallet, facing the bulkhead with her blankets drawn around her shoulders. Leo turned that expression of mute appeal on Surela again, and Surela ignored him to perch on the edge of the bed. To touch a stranger... not done. It was uncouth among some Eldritch to touch beasts, much less thinking persons, for even an animal's thoughts could whelm an Eldritch of acute sensitivity. Surela's empathy had always been better-behaved, and she had prided herself on not being laid low by its blandishments as easily as her peers. If talents every Eldritch must have, she could congratulate herself on one easily ignored.

But to touch this level of suffering....

Twisted this way on her bed, Prudence looked a little as

Thaniet had, near the end, and Surela slammed the wall between herself and that memory. She drew in a shaky breath, holding up a hand when she heard Leo shifting as if to approach.

If paucity of talent she had, then surely she could weather this, and do so for a woman who had been... kind. Prudence had been: endlessly kind, and patient with Surela's ignorance. To leave her in this state was unconscionable. Surela allowed her hands to hover over the healer's shoulders, then, decisively, drew her away from the wall.

Nothing answered her palms but the catch of fabric over fur. Surela guided Prudence's head to her breast and felt the fine tremors in the long torso, the arms. The healer's mind... her mind was a blank. Surela recognized the numbness. She'd fled there when she could, during the torments she'd suffered. Had, she thought, fled there shortly after exile, and it was an open question whether she'd left that comforting numbness yet.

But this moment was not about her. She tightened her arms around Prudence and met Leo's gaze over the healer's tumbled hair and limp ears. Whatever he saw in her eyes caused him to draw over a chair, the one he'd been using, perhaps, for his vigil, and sit. Should this evidence of camaraderie surprise her after her time among them? But mortals had shown themselves more willing to care this way. To be seen to care, anyroad. It should not astonish her that she valued this about them. That she had things she valued in them.

How facile, to bond with them over their mutual victimhood. What a pretty story that would be, to say that it was the Chatcaava who taught her that the aliens were no different from Eldritch, not at the heart. She could even imagine reciting the lines: 'It was then, seeing them laid low by the same enemy, that I realized we could both hurt. That we were all children before God and Goddess, and tragedy comes to us down the same roads and through the same doors.'

But that would have been a lie, and Surela was done with comfortable lies. Comfortable lies had led her to depose Liolesa, and learn how fragile their society was, and how much of it relied on mortal aid. Comfortable lies had allowed her to believe Baniel, who'd told her exactly what flattered her pride, the better to control her. Comfortable lies had seen pirates introduced to the halls where she'd once walked in winter and in summer, among peers who upheld those same lies so they could spend their lives as they wished, without caring at the cost.

The truth, sadly, was that her exile had forced her to choose between living her life forever alienated… and living her life among people that interested and moved her. She had chosen not to suicide. That had closed the door on mortals as animals beneath her notice.

Surela closed her eyes and rested her chin on the healer's hair, and held her.

———

She woke, abruptly, unaware that she'd fallen asleep with her spine against the bulkhead in the healer's room, and all her limbs cramped from keeping Prudence against her. But the door had opened, and the silhouette had Saul's proportions, the rectangular lankiness of his torso, the set of his ears.

His voice was brisk. "Rel, we need you in the fore."

Leo, voice husky with sleep, rubbed his eyes. "I'll take over," he murmured, and slid onto the bed. Would that distress the healer? Surela thought she knew something of aliens now but couldn't guess at the mores dictating behavior between male and female. The woman's distress surely over-rode any other concern. More importantly, she trusted her sense of Leo, who acted the scapegrace but was so swift to apologize that he betrayed his tender heart. Gently, Surela arranged Prudence against Leo's side, then pushed herself from the bed and followed Saul into the corridor.

"It's Reese," Saul said without preamble. "She said to expect a call in ten minutes. You should be there."

Her? But why? Who was she anymore, but Eddings's latest employee? Not even that anymore, at the rate Lais-rathera was no doubt expanding. But Surela wanted to know what was passing more than she wanted to argue, so she paced Saul to the fore of the ship where Ra'aila was hovering over the comm panel. The Aera glanced up and no extraordinary knowledge of alien physiognomy was neces-sary to read her expression. Surela rested a hand on her shoulder, too, and could measure Ra'aila's terror by how long it took the Aera to travel from the shock of what had been done to the Alliance, to the shock of an Eldritch touching her. The woman looked at Surela's hand, then at her face, mouth dropping open.

"Nothing threatens us at this moment," Surela reminded her, and wished the mortal tongue wasn't so damnably imprecise. "Nothing threatens us, the people on this ship. Right now. Right now nothing is happening to us. Be aware of this, if you can bear it."

"But I can't," Ra'aila said, hoarse. "Because so many people have died." She waved a feeble hand toward a display and on it was a number, an enormous number that was incre-menting as Surela watched. "They... they keep updating the totals...."

And Goddess help her, but the woman was subjecting herself to the sight. Would Surela have had the strength to turn from that knowledge if it had been available during the fight in the palace? Would the grief and guilt of her actions have crushed the life from her, had she been able to learn of each individual death as it was discovered by those moving through Ontine's corridors?

Saul leaned past them both and snapped the display off. "We need to be focused for Reese's call."

"What if they're still attacking?" Ra'aila asked. "What if the Chatcaava are hitting someplace else, while we're sitting here? And we don't know, because they've killed everyone—"

Surela shook the Aera. Just one twitch of her hand, enough to send a wave rippling through the woman's long spine. "Master Saul is right. If danger there remains, then we must be equal to responding to it. You can permit no course of action that robs you of that power."

Ra'aila dropped her head into her hands, her long ears falling on either side of her neck.

The incoming message alert sounded, and Saul woke the display for all of them. There, before them, was their employer, and—in this moment—Surela's liegelady. Because to be without one during this crisis felt insupportable. To be isolated without hope of the material aid of a House when at war... no. Even a human would do. Perhaps especially a human, if it was this one, whom Surela was forced to concede had been a true companion, no matter how briefly. They had conspired together, Theresa Eddings and she, against their mutual enemies, who had been pirates and Chatcaava both. Perhaps another Eldritch would have been slower to that alliance, and slower to the need for violence against foes who respected no dueling code.

Looking at Eddings through that lens, Surela could appreciate the stern expression, and the gravity that firmed the full mouth. In Eldritch legend, dragonfire was said to burn a blue brighter than a summer empyrean, and it was of fire that Surela was reminded, looking at Eddings's gaze. "Stay put," was the woman's first words, her contralto abrupt.

"Reese," Ra'aila began, but the human held up a hand.

"I mean that. I've been told that we're assembling a bulletin for all our shipping, telling them what to do... but it's all dependent on where they are, and the *Earthrise* is exactly where it should be. Until you hear from us again, I want you to sit tight. We'll handle the docking fee if it becomes a problem."

"All right," Ra'aila said. "But... what's going on? Do you know?"

"Not as much as we want to. But more than some people, probably." A breath that lifted the woman's chest until the light caught on her House pendant, running its edge. "There are Eldritch in this war, if you'll believe it, and they're embedded in some of the biggest parts. Liolesa won't tell me everything, and Hirianthial can't, but there's some evidence that the Chatcaavan Empire is... fracturing. Part of that fracture's on our side, but we don't know if our side is bigger than the bad guys' side yet."

"They're having a civil war?" Saul asked, intent. "Is that what this is about? We're just collateral damage?"

Eddings met his eyes. "I haven't heard it put that way, but now that you have... it does look a little that way, doesn't it?"

"And there are Eldritch involved?" Ra'aila asked for all of them, her incredulity patent. "Fighting a war between the Alliance and the Chatcaava? How does that work?"

"Apparently that works when the Alliance borrows an Eldritch to be their ambassador to the dragons. Like I said... I don't know a lot about it yet, but the pot's boiling over now. Either it's going to be over quick, or it's going to be over quicker, because there's no long drawn-out conflict in our futures. We either have enough manpower to fight them off, or... we don't."

This was not an analysis guaranteed to gentle Ra'aila's fears, so Surela was grateful when Saul stole the conversational baton. "So you want us to stay docked in Starbase Psi until we get the signal from you. Do you have any hints as to

157

how long we're looking at? We took on live cargo this run, and some of it's already in the holds."

"Try to keep it alive," Eddings said. "But if you have to, dump it. There will be more money for animals. Your safety's more important."

Surela, unable to help herself, said, "Eldritch. In this war."

Eddings's gaze met hers, and its directness reminded her of their time in the catacombs. "You know we can fight them. And you know why we had to be a part of it."

How strange to accept that 'we', as if Eddings was one of them. But the human had suffered at Chatcaavan hands. "Did we send many?"

"Enough to make a difference, is what Liolesa said." That accompanied by a slight snort, as if remembering a... frustrat- ing? Or amusing? Conversation? Perhaps both, knowing Liolesa. But Eddings was continuing. "I don't know if you'd know them, they're all much younger than you. I think. Liolesa said one of them was the Nase Galare heir. The other three were also Galare, but I don't remember their names. Two were brothers, and one's a girl who got exiled years ago. She's been in the Alliance all this time."

Surela doubted Theresa Eddings could truly imagine what it was like to be Eldritch, to live centuries among the same people, who produced few children and many scandals. She'd gone to court twice a year, every year, for over four hundred years... and while she would have had to concen- trate to recollect every new noble introduced to society, it was not hard to recall the Nase Galare heir, who'd come to court on the coats of his parents' crass quarreling, nor one of the few sets of brothers to have come out of that generation... and the disinheritance and subsequent departure of Nuera's sole heir had been fodder for salacious gossip for decades. And these were the unlikely soldiers Liolesa had sent to this fight?

"There might be others, but no one's telling me all the

details. You people hold things so close to the chest, even when all the horses have already fled the barn—if I'm using the metaphor right." Eddings turned her attention back to Ra'aila and Saul. "I'll get back to you when I know more. But it won't be long. I have that on good authority."

"What authority is that?" Ra'aila stammered.

"The Eldritch Queen's pretty good at figuring these things out. If she says we'll be wrapping this up sooner than we think, we can probably bank on it. I'm going to, anyway. Send me the bills. Try to keep the crew calm. If anyone wants to break contract for family reasons, let them go." The human chewed her lower lip. "That's all I can think of, but shoot me your questions if you have any urgent ones. Saul, you've got the situational awareness. Keep them out of trouble."

"Will do."

"Ra'aila?"

"We'll… we'll handle things," Ra'aila said. Her smile was wintry but at least she'd essayed it. "Thanks for the realtime call. It's probably some weird hour over there, isn't it."

"Trust me, no one's sleeping right now." Eddings glanced at Surela. "Alet?"

"I have no questions," Surela said.

"Good enough. More later, aletsen." And then the projection emptied, left them in the hollow quiet of the fore of the ship.

"This is really happening to us," Ra'aila whispered.

Surela reined in her impulse to snap at the woman, knowing it to be the product of her own disquiet. She was glad when Saul said, "I'll see if I can set up some deliveries. It'll help with the monotony of being aboard if we can get some random food or entertainment at intervals."

That roused Ra'aila from her stupor. "How long do you think she means us to stay here? 'Wrapping up soon'… how soon is soon?"

Saul shrugged. "A week? A month? Hard to say. She's

159

human, so we can hope she's using human metrics, not Eldritch ones." He glanced at Surela, lifted his furry brows. "Do you know the people who went into the war?"

"Not well." What could she in good conscience reveal to strangers? Once, the Veil would have prevented her from speaking at all. What did the Veil matter now, if there were Galare hip-deep in the matter? Of course, they were all Galare, and would come home heroes! She could appreciate as humorous her irritation that none of the isolationist houses had thought to arrange for future adulation by booting their more vexing family members into exile... because of course, it would have been absurd for them to foresee the need. And yet, Surela wanted to blame all of them for it, herself included. "The younger ones, very poorly, though from what I understand the Nuera heir was a strong-willed girl, and not likely to be brooked." Rumor had claimed the Nuera heir a lightskirt and a jade as well, but Surela had dismissed those stories on hearing them; accusing a noble of poor taste in the bedchamber was the first refuge of gossipmongers. "The Nase Galare heir, however...." She remembered the spate of duels, though she'd attended none of them. It was enough to know the man didn't fear the circle, had been, in fact, accused of loving violence so much he'd created situations that would allow him to call his detractors out. Had he been the bestial aggressor whispered of in hallways, or was that also embroidery? But what better man to send to a war? "I can see him being...." What? "Useful. Inasmuch as any one person can be useful to a war of this... scale. I am correct, am I not? What good one warrior?"

"I don't know," Saul said. "Sometimes, though, one person in the right place, at the right time...." He shook himself, like a creature troubled by midges. "You want to handle the crew, Ra'aila, or do you want me to take care of it?"

Ra'aila rubbed her arms, but her voice was resolute

despite her morose expression, and Surela liked her better for it. "No, I'll handle it. It's my job, and they need to see more than one person aboard not falling apart."

"Then we've got our marching orders. Rel?"

Surela looked up.

"You don't have to help with Prudence."

"But it was her world," Surela said. "This… Tam-ley. Will she see it again? I admit I can't… quite… imagine how it would work. To… lose… a planet."

Saul glanced at Ra'aila, but the Aera shook her head. "I know you're about to give me some excuse to leave so I don't have to hear what you're going to say. 'You can go on, and we'll watch the bridge.' But I have to… I have to grapple with this. Don't spare me, all right?"

His study lasted several calm breaths Surela counted by watching the rise and fall of his chest near the arm, where the vest he was wearing flexed at the seam. Then he nodded. Turning back to Surela, he said, "It depends on the world. The colony worlds the Chatcaava hit… most of those were small. Think one city, at most three. If you've got one city on a world and a pirate comes by and bombs it, then that colony world is gone. You can build again, but the civilization that started on it the first time won't come back."

Surela imagined someone destroying the capital of their world… like a storm wiping it from the cliff. Her skin rashed with gooseflesh, but she nodded. "And a world like Prudence's?"

"You've probably never seen a capital world. That's a good way to describe it, actually. Think of a capital city, but as large as a world. People spread all over it, on every continent. Several billion people. To kill a Core world, you have to make it totally uninhabitable." Saul flicked his eyes toward Ra'aila, but continued talking, his voice as steady as a foreman's holding forth on some unexceptional topic. Crop yields, or the birthrate of kine. "If you throw enough ordnance at a world, you can destroy entire continents. You can set the atmosphere on fire, and it'll flash-fry everything under it. There are a lot of ways to do it."

"But the Chatcaava used an asteroid." Ra'aila was trying for Saul's calm, and Surela commended her for the effort, no matter how poor the imitation.

"Right. And what preliminaries we have say the asteroid did for half the world. But the explosion will clutter the atmosphere. What it didn't kill immediately, the change in the gas mix and the weather will, unless we can get in there and reverse the process before it gets going. The terraforming protocols might make a dent. We'll have to see what happens next. The people closest to the ground will make that call."

"How does one stop such attacks?" Surela asked. "You create metal worlds." She tilted her chin toward their portals, which were showing the dock, or would have had they been lit. "You have ships. You have, one presumes, some sort of military. Is protecting a world against such an attack an insoluble problem? Is there no defense?"

"We can prevent most worldkillers," Saul said. "But even we need to spin up defenses against something that overwhelming. They took us by surprise." His eyes grew harder. "They won't a second time."

That did for their impromptu conference, and Surela left Ra'aila with Saul to begin arranging for a schedule of deliveries, and to discuss what was to be done with the livestock. She stopped on the way to her cabin to check on the healer: Prudence was asleep on her bunk with Leo slumbering alongside, his head near her feet and one arm lying off the bunk's edge. Both looked haggard, worn by their worries and horrors: no escape, even in dreams. She sympathized; she also wrestled with pity as she retired to her cell, and there contemplated her computer. Had it been a living creature she would have been concerned that any queries she made on planetary disaster scenarios would have distressed. But a computer was not a living servant, and could not be dismayed by her questions. And questions she had, because what she nursed as a result of the day's events was nothing so harmless as curiosity. Curiosity could be sated, or ignored. Her need to understand was a whip... because what had been done to these incredibly technological worlds could be visited on her own. Her own, which was alone and off the beaten track, exposed now to outsiders and filled to the brim with the most valuable kinds of slaves, by dragon standards.

How could their world be protected, when the Alliance with all its might had lost one of its capitals to their enemies? What was Liolesa doing to shield them? Because the woman had named their world for that shield—surely, or why 'escutcheon'? Why truck with the outworld, if not to prevent just such disasters? No queen would have reached out to mortal ally to avert the death of her people from starvation, only to be so witless as to miss the potential that they might die anyway, from external provocation.

Surela had hated Liolesa for most of her life. But the woman wasn't stupid. And now... now with dawning horror and anger, she understood the stakes for which the woman had been playing all this time, planning. How infuriating it was, and how humiliating, to learn just how wrongheaded her own schemes had been. To take the throne from Liolesa, thinking that would solve their problems! And all along, the dragons had been creeping nigh, their empire growing, and the pirates accreting around their advance like the clouds before a stormfront?

Surela pressed the heels of her hands to her brow and forced herself to slow her breathing. So, she had been unaware of the true scope of the play, just as she'd been ignorant of the size of the galactic theater. Her coup had died, as it inevitably had been destined to, because of that shortsightedness, and now she knew better. Now she could... do what? As a woman forever barred from returning home?

Learn, she guessed. Knowledge could not be wasted. Not if lack of it had destroyed her previous life so completely. How urgent such learning could feel, and yet, how frustrating. She brought up her prior reading on the treaties, and resumed, as much as possible, her study.

CHAPTER 16

But there was no sleeping that night, for all Surela tried, lying on her bunk and staring at the ugly gray ceiling. Not so much as a coffer or molding to distract the eye, and the dark was pierced by ugly glows in blue or green that gave the room a ghoulish cast. It was not in her nature to respond to crisis with idleness; her limbs craved activity, and her mind, a plan, any plan. She returned to the bridge and found it unmanned, and was not sad at the silence. Ra'aila had left several displays running, showing the news reports from various places, and even muted they arrested the attention. Surela checked the tenebrous corridor for anything more distinct than its shadows, then, assured of her solitude, she retreated to the pilot's chair, there to sit and watch… and after a moment, to listen at reduced volume.

The Chatcaava had not attacked again, but damage reports continued to be refined by those assessing the sites. Pirates harried the borders yet—Surela checked a map and discovered the border in question was on the other side of the Alliance from Starbase Psi—but those attacks were not, it was posited by most, affiliated with the Chatcaavan raid. There was a great deal of noise and speculation about what might come next; some said the Chatcaavan Empire was massing to continue the attack, others that the Chatcaavan Empire was dissolving into internal squabbles. All of it had the weight of one of the gossip columns in the broadsheet. Surela couldn't take the reports seriously; they were too obviously making gowns from faerie cloth.

But the pictures of the devastation… those, she believed.

Leo stumbled in… when, she didn't know. Perhaps some hours later. He halted at the sight of the news. "Angels. Tell me there hasn't been anything new."

"No new attack, at least. Much about the aftermath."

"Worse." He dropped into the chair beside hers and put his face in his hands. "Worse."

"Prudence?"

"Asleep." Leo rubbed an eye with the side of his hand. "Normally it wouldn't matter that everyone's asleep, but I feel… I feel vulnerable."

"Surely the ship is protection?"

"It's something. Whether it's enough is another matter. Especially when I couldn't say what I'm afraid of. Someone throwing an asteroid at the starbase…."

"Would that work?" Surela asked.

"Oh, it would work."

"Perhaps you also need sleep," she guessed, because he hadn't seemed comfortable on the edge of Prudence's bed.

"What I want is a lot of cuddle and sex. But there's no way in the battlehells I'm leaving this ship to find it." His smile was wan. "Do you think Ra'aila would mind if I ordered in?"

"Ordered… in…" She paused. "As in, send for prostitutes?"

That made him laugh, weakly, but it was something. "The way you say that is hilarious, Rel. I hope you don't mind me saying so because right now there's no wall between my brain and my mouth and I'm too scared to try to put one in.

Because then I might… actually… look at the inside of my head too much. You know?"

"Yes." She watched more agonized aliens gesticulate over scenes of death and waste. "Is it a thing that can be purchased here? Prostitutes?"

"You really want to know? Because it would be… it would be good, to talk about something normal." At her expression, his eyes lit, just a little. "Oh, you do." And then he began to talk, and Surela… did not listen, not as she should have. She couldn't concentrate on alien copulatory customs, and how they differed across species and cultures within the mortal Alliance. Not when she was distracted, over and over, at how mortal that Alliance was.

Sometime later, she left Leo on the bridge to walk the silent corridors, and even the rattle of the floor beneath her boots was subdued. The chickens were sleeping in the main cargo hold; the other bays were empty, save the one Saul used for his devotions, and in that one she found the single candle shedding a dim orange glow over the makeshift altar. Left there for the dead? Or did he always have it thus? Would she ask? But this ship, she thought as she went up the ladder instead of using the lift, had become familiar to her. Her apartments at Ontine had been larger, but the modest size of the *Earthrise*'s living area had allowed her to make the entirety of it known that much more swiftly, and that felt, urgently and abruptly, like a blessing.

Prudence was still sleeping when Surela checked on her, and rather than leave the woman to wake alone, Surela took up the vigil Leo had left… if not on the bed. It had been… many… years since she'd slept in the same room as another woman. Thaniet had been too aware of their differences in estate to be comfortable with any more obvious a sign of devotion than the occasional touch. And Surela had believed —Goddess forgive her—that she would have centuries to show Thaniet otherwise.

Could she think about this now? But thoughts of Thaniet felt very distant when her head looped the images of the destruction on Tam-ley and the orbitals of the Alpha system. Her life before this fresh war's imagery was dreamlike, and that allowed her to analyze it from a remove... enough to see that her behavior would never have permitted the gap between liegelady and lady-in-waiting to be bridged. She had been too cognizant of her own position, and no matter how she'd attempted, her affections had inevitably been shaped by that knowledge. Her very desire not to create situations where Thaniet would have felt compelled to accept her advances, because of Surela's power... that had been a form of condescension, if conceived from the best of intentions.

A muffled sob scattered her thoughts, and the decision to touch Prudence made itself, and to perdition with the consequences of allowing that storm of emotion ingress through her skin. Surela slid onto the bed and drew the woman into her arms, tensing at the shock of the anguish. She firmed her mouth and bore it, resting her head against the disheveled hair. How good it was that Prudence at last resorted to tears! Not that tears had ever seemed to cleanse any of Surela's woes, but these sobs were accompanied by such agony that they had to represent a first step toward facing the magnitude of the loss. Prudence's world, and presumably her family, and all the context that had shaped her... yes, that could be worth the discomfort Surela felt, standing the embrace. Indeed, long before the sobs should have stopped, a wash of shock and humiliation interrupted their flow. Too well could Surela guess the woman's thoughts: that she imposed on the sole empath on the ship, that this near stranger was witnessing her breakdown.

So Surela said, "You wondered, perhaps, at my pregnancy."

Prudence gulped in her exhale, stopped her struggle to

free herself before it had fully developed. Surela sensed the woman's receptiveness and continued.

"There was a… civil war, perhaps you might call it. A much smaller one than anything on this scale. But it was abetted by pirates, and the Chatcaava. They wanted to turn our world into a private harem, to be plundered for merchandise when they fancied. We would have become…" Surela made herself face it. "We would have become another pirate outpost, and all our people their slaves, and that would have been the last anyone heard of the Eldritch… save as exotic pets scattered throughout the zenanas of the worlds." She stroked Prudence's hair back from the quivering ears. "I was in the palace when the fight to take back the world began, and the pirates slew many in response. I had already been their captive, and they and their Chatcaavan master had had their way with me. Thus, my condition."

Surela could hear Prudence swallow. When the woman spoke, her voice was a bare whisper. "You… you've been through this already."

Such an unjust statement could not be allowed to stand. Surela shifted, settling the woman more comfortably against her side, for there was no doing it across the front of her body anymore. "No. My grief cannot compare… for my world remains, if somewhat reduced in circumstance. I do not fully understand how your technology works, but from what has been explained, your home may never be habitable again."

That caused a shivering in Prudence's ribs, but the tears didn't resume. Surela could feel the healer clinging to their conversation as a shield against her suffering. "You kept the baby. Because she was a victim, like you?"

What a horrendous story that would be, if Surela chose to tell it so. She didn't. "I kept the child because I am the actor in my life. To allow my emotions about the event that saw me pregnant to dictate my actions would be to surrender volition."

Prudence was still. The whirl of her emotions slowed. "That's what matters to you. That you're the one making the choices in your life. Not other people."

"Does that not matter to all who breathe?"

A long silence, churning with the healer's feelings. One solidified, rose above the turmoil. "And after everything that happened to you, you came here. To be somewhere the dragons couldn't hurt you again. And look what we let happen...!" And again, the tears, this time commingling grief with guilt.

Goddess, how revelatory a statement that was... to take Surela's description of personal agency and apply it somehow to their nation entire. As if it was natural, that choices should apply, not only to individuals deciding how they should conduct their lives, but also to events obviously beyond their control. Such breathless arrogance: to have been attacked successfully, it had to have been because they allowed it... because it could not be because their foes were too great for their powers. Was it true? What would it be like, to be so powerful that one could believe such a thing, without reality contradicting?

Reality had contradicted at last, and how it had. Surela bit back her sigh and petted the woman's back, waiting for this second bout of weeping to peter out before speaking. "Will you have a touch of something? Broth, perhaps. Tea."

Prudence whispered, "I just want to sleep."

"Only if you are willing to eat when you wake. It need not be much."

"I'll try."

With that Surela had to be content, because she knew she would induce no better promise. Would she have been willing to sup the day after Escutcheon's fall? Certainly not. The day after, though... to begin planning her vengeance, or her escape, most probably. Eddings's words rang in her memory, the response to Surela's claim that she was no sword to be her own defense: *"You stabbed a man in the eye, Surela. IN THE EYE."* Healers were not known for their vengeful spirits but Lord Hirianthial had certainly made good on his vows against the pirates attacking their world. Perhaps he was a healer second, and a warrior first, as Eldritch men should be. Though why the stabbing should be reserved to the men, Surela was no longer certain. It had been terrifying to kill the attacker laboring over her body. But looking back on it, she could be glad that she had been the one to dispatch him. To wait for rescue would have galled, and worse, given the ruffians more time to savage her and everyone else, including Araelis, who had been pregnant at the time.

Tired of holding her memories at bay, Surela went to eat.

———

She had had all of an hour's sleep when an alert woke her. The lights in her cell were strobing, each flash pricking her mean surroundings into sight and then dousing them in shadows. "Lockdown commenced," the computer said. "External access unavailable. Please wait for further instructions."

Had they been attacked? To perdition with awaiting further instruction. Surela flung her blanket off and dressed in haste, then hurried from her cell to the fore of the ship. There Saul and Ra'aila were huddled around the displays, and Erynne was joining them, shrugging on a robe that trapped her golden curls against her back. Most of the pictures continued to display the news from distant worlds. The largest, however, hovering over all the others….

"Is that the city?" Surela asked, appalled. "Here? On the starbase?"

"It is, yes." Saul was grim. "They should never have let that crowd get that big. Now it's a riot."

"So we are not attacked?" Surela edged closer, trying to

make sense of the seething mass on the screen. So many people, their faces distorted by anguish and rage.

"Not from without," the Hinichi answered.

"What happened?" Erynne asked, sounding far more awake than she looked.

"As far as we can tell, it started as a prayer service," Ra'aila said. "Or something like that. 'Gather together to mourn the dead.' But it kept growing, and people started getting angry, and now…."

Now they were streaming through the streets Surela had trodden, destroying whatever responded to the violence of their grief, no doubt trampling some of those who fell beneath their feet. It had become a mob, like a crazed and wounded animal, and the uniformed people trying to diffuse it were not succeeding. Indeed, the throng seemed to be growing. Surela said, uneasy, "There are… a great number of people on this starbase, are there not?"

"And you're wondering if they're all going to end up in that stew?" Saul nodded, jaw tight. "You're right to worry."

"If that gets into the port… it's heading up, isn't it?" Ra'aila sounded nervous.

Erynne belted her robe closed. "I'm going to check things over."

The engineer's departure increased Ra'aila's anxiety noticeably. "If that mob ransacks the port, they can't hurt us, can they?"

"Not unless a bunch of them start driving antigrav lifts into ships," Saul said. "Which is possible, but not probable. The lifts big enough to hurt even something the *Earthrise*'s size aren't going to be left unguarded. In fact… I'd be surprised if the port wasn't already battening down."

"How could they do it?" Ra'aila whispered. "People are going to die. It just makes everything worse."

"They're angry and suffering, arii," Saul said to her. "And

they can't face their adversaries directly. Where else was all that grief going to go, except inward?"

Surela slid slowly into one of the vacant chairs... just as Leo burst in, followed by Danica. The Eldritch did not listen to the explanations, only watched the news. How often was this scene replaying all over the Alliance? Her eyes caught on their faces, the stretched mouths, the streaming eyes. She would have liked to turn from them. To dismiss their ugliness, their agonies, so gauchely displayed. But her own face had been twisted into such shapes. She had cried into Theresa Eddings's shoulder. It had not been beautiful. There had been nothing in it of the elegant scenes depicted in tapestry or referred to in dirge.

She had called them animals, and thought of them as creatures, and referred to them as mortals. And they were animals, and they were creatures, and they were mortals.

But so was she.

"We should start keeping station watches," Saul said to Ra'aila. "More than one person."

Meri hurried into the bridge, her beaded hair bouncing around her shoulders. "What's going on? Are we under attack?"

As Ra'aila began to explain anew, Surela turned to her minder. "How do I stand one of these watches? I assume it is something I can do."

"You can, yes. And we should probably teach you to shoot a palmer. Anything more strenuous will have to wait until after you're done with the baby. But anyone can aim a gun."

CHAPTER 17

That ushered in a new routine, equal parts tedium and tension, for the crew could neither leave the ship for the starbase, nor leave the starbase for some other, less fraught sanctuary. Watchstanding was not the release Surela had hoped for, as it involved sitting on the bridge and doing several hours of nothing. Most of the time she had the fore to herself, with her counterpart in engineering, but now and then she'd have company. Briefly, as most people's attempts at diversion exhausted her. Meri was the only one who made the hours bearable.

"As long as we're stuck here," she'd said, "we could do some cross training? If you feel like it... I could teach you basic piloting."

"Does the ship not need to move for this?"

"Oh, we'll use simulators. That'll get you pretty far along, if you're starting from the beginning."

Surela felt she'd done nothing but study since her exile. She'd thought paper would be her problem, having filled one of her notebooks already. But it was ink that frustrated her, for the black ran low so swiftly she was forced to make do with the other colors which, she was forced to admit, served better as ornament than they did when filling an entire page. Acclimating to the tablet and stylus was less of a pain than dealing with that eyesore, and the irritation of discovering that there were many advantages to them that paper failed to provide faded quickly beneath the pressures of recording everything she needed to remember. Piloting, at least, required interesting exercises in addition to memorization of information, so she was not tied to the note-taking part of the endeavor as completely.

The riots lasted several days, and like some noxious vapor spilled into different parts of the city-sphere, and then into different spheres. They never penetrated the port past its door, though for several terrifying hours they tried. The death toll was absurd and unnecessary, and Surela surprised herself by feeling compassion for the freshly hurt aliens. But Ra'aila resolved that the watchstanding should continue, "just in case," and no one gainsaid her. The routine might have been stultifying, but it was better than sitting in their cabins, waiting for a reprieve.

One week into their self-imposed imprisonment, their cargo began to show signs of failure. Nothing so obvious as disease... but the lack of sunlight, and the confined spaces, were taking an obvious toll on the poultry. No one on the crew was willing or able to nurse them back to health, and despite the happy presence cushioned beneath her skin, Surela had not a maternal bone in her body, to do any better. Lacking that, and figuring the crew needed distraction, Ra'aila ordered the chickens to the pot as they lost condition. Danica cooked, and brought food and coffee at intervals, and Surela ate what she could and allowed herself to find the sweetened coffee soothing, and if her stomach cramped more than she wished, it was hard to fault it. The news never stopped playing on the bridge, and while she kept it muted, she didn't need the sound to watch the totals of the dead increase, and see the increasing agitation on the faces of reporters wondering whether the Chatcaava would attack again.

Prudence did not join the crew on the watch; she remained in her cabin, much to Leo's dismay. Danica's advice was to 'let her mourn,' which Surela supposed was sensible advice. She could not help wondering if Leo had the better understanding, however. To be alone with grief of that magnitude was surely ill-advised. Especially when Leo divulged, exhausted, "The worst part of it is that there's no direct news from Tam-ley. There's no way for anyone to find out if their family's all right. The infrastructure's gone, the satellites, the stations, all of it. The only people in the know are on rescue vehicles, and they're all busy. They report casualties as they find them, and you just have to... you have to wait. Can you imagine?"

Surela could, but the scope of what had happened on Escutcheon was so minor in compare she didn't feel comfortable raising the issue.

The monotony of their routine combined poorly with the war's pressures. Her nightmares returned, and she made herself lie down solely because the little voice in her begged for rest. To keep herself occupied, she began transcribing her earliest journals from paper onto her tablet, separating them into fields of study... and added, on a whim—or inspiration? —the study of the dragon language. Learning Universal centuries ago had been a way to protect her interests, for even if the nobles who trucked with Maraesa and later Liolesa didn't use it to hide their aims, their servants spoke it, and some information could be gleaned thereby. Learning this new alien tongue would surely pay similar dividends, and it allowed her to feel as if she was making some effort toward fighting them directly. Too, her daughter would be a dragon.

The language was her birthright, and surely there were dragons who spoke it who did not love war and slavery. This, Surela reminded herself frequently while stumbling through the first lessons, because the Chatcaavan tongue was singularly hideous. Even Universal shone in compare like a diamond of better waters.

Some two weeks into their durance, Eddings made another call. "Everything all right there?"

"We're managing," Ra'aila said. "We'd like to leave though. Do you think it's safe to cast off?"

"Not yet." The human looked worn, but subtly so, in a way Surela could appreciate: slight tightness around the eyes, and a faint darkness under them that suggested hollows without definite evidence. For a mortal Surela knew to be emotionally volatile, Eddings was comporting herself with unexpected poise in her new role and under considerable strain. "The Alliance put out a war warning a while back, and there's some talk that's going to tick up another notch—"

"Wait, we haven't done anything in response to their attack?" Ra'aila interrupted, ears sealing along her skull. "I thought 'we need to fight people who are already attacking us' was the obvious response here. We are going to fight back, aren't we?"

Eddings waved a hand in a curt motion. "Of course we are, but there's 'use your existing fleet of warships to defend yourself' and 'start raising taxes so you can retaliate', and I think we're going to end up going there."

"You don't sound happy about that...?"

"I'm not, because the people I trust who know more about it than I do aren't," Eddings said. "We've got one of our people at Selnor now who's convinced that things are more complicated than we think, and a lot more dangerous, and 'more dangerous than what's already happened to us' is going to result in a lot of dead people. Even if we win."

Surela was sitting behind Ra'aila, and so was in an excellent position to watch those long hare's ears crumple. After a significant pause, Ra'aila said, "*If* we win?"

The swift and palliative reply... didn't come. Instead, their liegelady said, "I'm not going to say I know everything, because for all I'm married to the war minister and the Empress comes to dinner once in a while, I'm still not privy to everything that's going on. But the one thing I am sure of, alet, is that it's... optimistic... to talk about 'winning' a war on this scale. For either side."

"Is de-escalation possible?" That was Saul, at Surela's shoulder.

"I have no idea. But if you're the praying kind...."

Surela heard the slight smile in her minder's voice. "Right."

"That's all I've got, unless you need something?"

"What we need is to stop hunkering down here like a frightened animal in a burrow," Ra'aila said. "There were riots here, did you know?"

"What?!"

That occasioned some explanation, and any exaggeration Ra'aila embarked on was reined in by Saul. Between the two they conveyed the mood of the starbase, though, and Eddings's eyes had darkened and grown less focused as she listened. "I didn't guess anything like that would happen. You think it might again?"

"Not without something spurring it on," Saul said. "But if there's some new bad news...."

"If there's some new bad news bad enough to inspire riots, you might still be safer in the port." The human's mouth firmed, as if she disliked the words she was saying. "At that point you're going to have to use your best judgment."

After the call ended, no one left. Ra'aila rubbed her brow bone. "I hate to say this as a card-carrying member of the

Aera, but I've never wished more for a home. Someplace I could run to and hide for a while."

"That does seem out of character." Saul leaned past them and tapped the com. "Mess, this is the bridge. Anyone up?"

Danica's voice: "I'm here, planning our next chicken dinner. What do you need?"

"Send up some coffee." He glanced at Surela, who made a slight motion of assent. "Three cups."

"I'll bring the pitcher."

Straightening, Saul said, "I think the Aeran take would be 'the only safety is movement.'"

"And I want to move badly, but where would I move to? They could be anywhere."

"Space is big," Saul said.

"And space will kill you if you stray too far off the trade routes." Ra'aila shook her head. "We like to wander, but that doesn't make us explorers. The point is never to commit to any one place, because every place is exciting and you want to experience them all. Not to wander off into sensordark so you can die in the cold when one of your engines trips an error."

What a bizarre philosophy, Surela thought but didn't say.

"But every home, now, and every exciting place, is a potential target," Ra'aila finished. "So movement isn't safety either."

"What is safety, then?" Surela asked.

They both looked at her, and neither answered before Danica's arrival with the tray. Then they were distracted, accepting their cups and setting the pitcher aside. "What did the boss say?" Danica asked, and Ra'aila explained that they were to remain. "So, more of the same. Could be worse. I'll go finish off dinner prep. I'm thinking of stuffing this one with something." A flash of a grin. "I was a decent but not very creative cook before this, but boredom is inspiring."

"Ducks," Surela said, surprising herself. When Danica

glanced her way, she roused herself to finish, "Next time, I shall arrange for ducks. Or geese. At very least, we'd have variety."

"Sounds good to me."

After the first mate's departure, Saul said, "'What is safety' isn't a minor question."

"So what's the answer?" Ra'aila asked. "Because I want to know."

He shrugged. "Safety for me is God. I don't think that answer would work for you."

"I don't even believe in the gods I swear by!" Ra'aila shook her head. "Maybe there is no safety. It's all an illusion, one we're clinging to because if we don't, we'll collapse into useless puddles." Her smile was wry. "I guess by that standard, your solution is the best one, because an imaginary god can't ever fail or betray you or change, right?"

Surela expected this to offend the Hinichi, but Saul said only, "Yes." And then, more gently than she expected, "It's all right to be afraid, arii. If you're going to be thrown into existential crisis at all, 'galactic war' is certainly a good reason."

"Except I could fix a minor problem like 'I don't know what to do with my life,' or 'I don't like my family' or 'I'm lonely' or 'I just realized how much I hate my job.' I can't fix..." Ra'aila waved a hand at the displays. "This."

Saul said, "Drink your coffee. Tonight we're having stuffed chicken experiment, and tomorrow, probably baked chicken experiment. For now, we take it day by day."

Ra'aila let her head sink, sighed. Chuffed a laugh. "Maybe you should be in charge."

He chuckled. "No, thanks. I'll let you wrangle the personalities and the schedules and the red tape and the bills."

She snorted, but her shoulders had opened again, and Surela thought that her keeper was better at the personality 'wrangling' than might be assumed. But then, one might be good at a thing one did not enjoy doing.

Dinner was not bad. Surela had hers alone, late at night, because it took several hours for her stomach to relax enough to permit it. She was glad of the quiet, and frustrated with the monotony, and wasn't sure how she wanted that détente broken but she was ready.

CHAPTER 18

When things changed, however, Surela was not glad. She was on the bridge when the news displays switched from constant speculation and updates on the rescue efforts, to frenzied reporting of a fresh attack force, this time in the capital system of the Alliance. Surela froze. With numb fingers, she reached to the displays and swept several new ones open, and more and more clustered at the corners. She foregrounded one and dialed up the volume, and the hysteria was palpable. "...Chatcaavan forces, estimated at thirty thousand ships, at least, these numbers are preliminary, scouts are on the move—"

Surela couldn't breathe out the Goddess's name. The numbers were simply impossible. Here was surely the culminating event Eddings had warned them was coming... but thirty thousand ships? At *initial* counts? What had Saul said? That the Alliance had half that number?

She made herself touch the com. It was the middle of the night, and both Saul and Ra'aila would be sleeping. Neither of them would want to sleep through this. "Rel to Saul."

A pause, and then his voice, slightly sleep-roughened but alert. "Alet?"

Surela wetted her lips. "The war has recommenced." Which didn't make it clear enough that they were not in danger. "The fighting is in the Alliance capital system. Shall I wake Ra'aila?"

"I'll do it after I see what we're dealing with. On my way."

Saul had one look at the multiple displays, eyes darting from one to the next, and then he hit the comm. "All hands, to the bridge." When Surela glanced up at him, he said, terse, "They deserve to know."

She thought about that choice of phrasing while waiting for the others to arrive. 'Deserve to know.' As if to bear witness to such atrocities was a thing to be deserved? Or did he mean that they deserved to be treated as adults, and participants in their destinies? In history? 'Deserve to know.' Had the Eldritch deserved to know what she'd done when she'd arranged Liolesa's short-lived expulsion from the planet? So brief, that exile. Liolesa had come home. Surela would never. She watched the displays, the confusion of images, of ships and diagrams and maps and wretched aliens, terror distorting their mouths and wracking their limbs. Perhaps there would be no home for any of them after this.

Leo had one look at the news, then squeaked, "Warm things." And dove back into the corridor.

All of them stayed on the bridge, and most of them accepted the blankets Leo brought back. Ra'aila chose a single news channel to bring to the fore, though the others remained silently playing in the background, and the crew kept what Surela realized was a vigil. They were watching... what? Their deaths? If the dragons destroyed this capital world, would that end the war in the dragons' favor? Possibly, if all the Alliance's warships were gathered there to do battle, and were routed. And then what?

No, this was far more than a vigil for her companions. What happened here would either reprieve them... or condemn them to a life of flight from conquerors. And the Eldritch would not be exempt. Without the Alliance's warships to bar them, nothing would stop the Chatcaava from raiding Escutcheon.

How calm she was, given that.

The wait stretched on, interminable hour after hour, as those reporting on the news grew more and more desperate. From what she could understand, the Alliance military was attempting to shroud some of the battle in secrecy, so they might have the benefit of surprising their enemies—if such was possible, when the surprise was so patently on the dragons' side. But unlike the Eldritch world, which had the one station, the capital system of the Alliance was cluttered with such stations and habitations, each full of some inestimable number of ships belonging to traders and private individuals and every sort of business. Hiding what was happening was impossible. And unlike Tam-ley, the Chatcaava had not stooped from the darkness, hurled a rock, and retreated... at this Selnor, they had arrived with all the arrogance of their superior numbers, bearing down on the world with intent to subjugate. The people of the system had ample time to see their ends coming, and were reacting as predicted.

Finally, Danica said it, quiet. "We're going to lose."

No one replied until Erynne at last broke the silence, and the words were brisk but without animation. Like an engineer facing a problem that would doom the ship, Surela thought. "It was over the moment they showed up. The numbers are on their side."

"But... numbers aren't always everything?" Leo asked. He was propping up Prudence, who was staring fixedly at the display with tears seeping down her cheeks. "It's only two to one—"

"Closer to three to one at this point," Erynne said. "Almost four if you're comparing tonnage rather than hulls. The Chatcaava like carriers. They build them big." At the glances this earned her, she said, "I researched them after Tam-ley. Thought I might as well know."

"What do we do?" Meri asked. "When they wipe out..." She paused, visibly composed herself. "When they wipe out Selnor, and most of Fleet?"

Saul said, "We regroup, and start over."

"With no military left?" Meri asked him.

"Space is big," Saul said. "And the Chatcaava will be busy digesting the Alliance. If we go far enough, we can start over. Maybe bunker down somewhere before they decide they're done picking off our richer planets."

"All those people, though," Danica said. "The ones we leave behind... on all those worlds...."

"There can't be enough dragons to enslave us all," Leo said, his tremor in his voice. "Can there?"

"Oh, Four Sisters," Meri whispered. "I can't even get my arms around this. It's too big. It's too big to be happening. How did they make something this big happen?"

Ra'aila roused herself for the first time in hours. "Same way the Alliance happened. We started with Joy. Remember? And Holly. Holly set our entire interplanetary civilization in motion, and she was one person. So maybe one person will save us all, someday."

"One day," Erynne said. "Because it won't be today."

————

...but amazingly, Erynne was wrong.

They lived on the bridge through the endless anticipation of their ending, and that feeling had prisoned them so completely that when something shifted on the side displays, none of them noticed. But that change rippled inward until it reached the one they'd been watching, and the shearing shock of it was so extreme none of them understood the words.

"...reinforcements, reporting there are reinforcements entering *behind* the attacking force—"

Ra'aila sat up, shaking so visibly her ears were bouncing on her shoulders. And then all of them were moving, shedding blankets and paralysis, sucked into a circle around the display which was reporting—Goddess above them—that there were reinforcements. *Chatcaavan* reinforcements. Some of the ancillary channels were reporting further doom, that the new force had come to bolster the attackers, but no, now there was confusion. Sensor readings that were impossible to believe, but the evidence kept mounting.

The new force was cutting into the rear of their invaders'.

Had they come to squabble over the spoils? Surely that was more believable than that there were Chatcaava on their side? But no, Fleet was coordinating with these new dragons... was that true?

"I can't stand it!" Danica gripped herself in a hug that looked painful. "Which is it? Are they on our side or not?"

"Choose to have hope," Saul said, clipped.

If the vigil had felt interminable prior to this development, now it was nerve-shattering. Were they reprieved? Or had this accelerated their end? Ra'aila widened more of the ancillary newsfeeds in an attempt to make sense of the conflicting reports, splitting their attention between four more views, and slowly Surela's settled on one of them because the energy level in it drew her eyes. The people discussing the news were neither panicking nor numb, but as focused as hounds on a hunt. And that energy was becoming more excited, not less, as time went, until she could no longer take her eyes from them.

She found herself repeating their words. "They're fighting on our side."

Everyone on the bridge swung toward her, and from her to the screen she was watching. Ra'aila raised the volume on it, shoved the others into the background, and the words washed over them like the wind clearing a storm from the air. "…we have definite confirmation now that the new arrivals are coordinating with Fleet's highest echelons. The fleet that attacked Selnor is not—repeat—not authorized by their government. They are traitors, attacking on their own recognizance. The Chatcaavan Empire denounces their actions, and has come to do so in person."

"…that's right, we have preliminary reports that the reinforcements are being led by their emperor."

"This is a big fight, though. We shouldn't expect resolution for hours. We'll be on top of it as it happens, minute by minute, until it's over."

"They're right," Saul said, walking in front of the display. "Hovering isn't going to help. If those really are reinforcements, we're going to pull out of this. We'll be hurt, but not down for the count. I recommend we eat, clean up, get some sleep."

"Sleep!" Meri yelped. "How can we sleep?"

"He's right." Danica rose. "I don't believe in dragons helping us out of the goodness of their hearts, but dragons who are angry at rebels starting trouble they didn't want? Yeah, I bet this emperor brought everything he's got to swat them down. They've ruined his chances."

"Doesn't that mean when it's all over, he's going to move in and take Selnor for himself?" Meri asked.

"Choose to have hope," Saul said, and turned off the last of the news. Without the illumination from the displays, the bridge vanished into the gloom of the few lights on the consoles. "It's late. Get some rest. Pray if you can't. There's nothing we can do about Selnor, it's half the Alliance away from our position. We'll know more in the morning."

Ra'aila stood. "Let's go. I want something from the mess. Anything. A piece of toast."

"You can eat?" Leo muttered.

"Not only can I eat, you should too. We'll make things worse on ourselves if we don't keep ourselves running. If we need to respond to any changes in our situation, we want to be sharp, not exhausted and dragging."

"She's right," Danica said. "It's too late for coffee, but I'll make…" She glanced at Ra'aila, who spoke.

"Kerinne, herbal tea, and hot cocoa."

"Right. We can do that."

"I'll put Prudence to bed," Leo said.

Ra'aila eyed the Tam-illee, mouth open… then she closed it and shook her head. "Right."

Had she been about to take their healer to task for ignoring her health? Perhaps. Surela wished she had, for she guessed that without that whip the woman would succumb to her depression. How not, with so much more weighing on her than the others?

"You too," Saul said to Surela after the others had filed out of the compartment. "If there's nothing the Pelted can do about a galactic war with the Chatcaava, that goes double for the Eldritch. Don't stay up worrying about them."

How could she not? And yet he was right. "I will do my best. But it is not the sort of day that commends one to the tender embrace of sleep."

Saul snorted. "No, it isn't." And something in his voice….

"Do you know someone? That you worry for?"

"Other than everyone in the Alliance?" he sighed. "I won't be the only one with a personal investment in this, alet. But I do have family in Fleet, and I'm hoping they're on the capital ships that survived."

Surela hesitated, then said, "As do I."

When she retired to her room, she did not ask the computer to show her the news. But she did bring up the crew's records. Prudence, of course, had lost her world... but Erynne, the golden-locked engineer, had done some of her training on an orbital facility in the Tam-illee's home system. Danica and Meri both hailed from planets in one of the systems that had lost significant infrastructure to the first attack. Leo had been bred on the homeworld of his race, the Harat-Shar, and she could find no evidence of any ties to the conflict... but Saul's file would not have warned her of his family ties to Fleet, so it was hard to know for certain. Ra'aila, who'd been born on Aren, had spent most of her life on ships before settling briefly on the colony world that had begun supplying the Eldritch with its purebred horses, but Surela could imagine someone who'd spent her life in space being distressed at the possibility that space would no longer be safe.

No one, Surela guessed, would be sleeping tonight. As she shut down her display, she wondered whether the dragons who'd arrived had come as salvation, or the final log on their pyre.

CHAPTER 19

"We're good." Eddings sounded as exhausted as she looked, and the triumph that should have accompanied the words was markedly absent. None of them had had time to check the news before the real-time comm alarm had jerked them from sleep. So far only she, Ra'aila, and Saul had made it to the bridge, but Surela wouldn't bet on the others remaining abed long. "It's over."

"Over, over?" Ra'aila asked cautiously. "Or 'we're waiting for yet another shoe to drop' over?"

"Over as much as any war is ever over," Eddings said. "The Chatcaavan Emperor is on our side. They're going to sign a formal treaty in the Selnor system while he's there."

"He really was on our side," Ra'aila repeated.

"He was, yes." Eddings looked past her at Surela. "Your ambassador's doing."

"My... what?"

"The Eldritch Liolesa sent the Alliance when they asked for a candidate as their ambassador to the Chatcaava. No idea how that worked, but somehow he turned the emperor."

"God Almighty," Saul murmured.

"Unfortunately, there are big chunks of his empire that disagree with him," Eddings continued. "That's the 'as much as a war is ever over' part. But Fleet's backed down on the shipping warnings, so you can leave as soon as you pack us up something to eat." Her smile was wan. "We could use some cheering up, so if you can bring us some ice cream, we wouldn't be sad about it."

"We'll leave as soon as we can," Ra'aila said. "All of us are sick of being stuck here."

"We'll be glad to see you back. Reese out."

They exchanged glances, then brought up the news, and it was full of trauma and the shock of their reprieve. The battle had been heinous—Surela glanced at the casualty figures, added on top of the existing ones from the first attacks, and closed her eyes. Did it matter anymore that they weren't Eldritch? The size of their disaster staggered the heart. She would have grieved for millions of birds, or horses. How much more so for these people who wore their animal seem-ings like dominoes for a masque?

"What's going on?" Danica asked, popping her head into the bridge, and her eyes were grimy with fatigue, or with weeping. "Is it over?"

"The good dragons saved us," Ra'aila said. "Our employer would like us to box up some chickens and ice cream and come home."

Danica's mouth worked in shock and nothing came out initially. Then: "You're... not jesting."

"Trade winds, no." Ra'aila pressed her fingertips against her brow and let a laugh out. "Let's go find some supplies. I can't think through all this stillness."

"I... I could buy supplies," Danica managed, as if the prospect of doing so was novel and distant. "We could leave the ship."

"We are leaving the ship. All of us." Ra'aila rose. "Get everyone up, we're rhacking leaving this ship."

———

An hour later, Ra'aila had chivvied all of them off the vessel except Prudence and Meri, who'd offered to sit with her. "Something's going to have to be done about her," Danica murmured to Ra'aila, when Surela was certain the shorter woman thought no one was paying them mind.

"She'll come out of it when she's ready," Ra'aila said. "Maybe faster now that there's been some resolution." Louder, meant to be heard by everyone, "Stay close, aletsen. Just in case."

Surela was too glad to be free of the ship to care that it might not be safe—that current events might inspire another riot in what was apparently a volatile populace. Saul orbited near enough to raise the hair on the nape of her neck, and that comforted. The others also clustered close, but she couldn't blame them for their anxiety. Their restlessness ran through her veins as well. There was something in Ra'aila's philosophy: movement was preferable to paralysis, and their huddling in the ship had begun to loom too large in their minds, until it bade fair to define them as victims rather than survivors.

The mood in the port was... shocky. The people around them had the glazed stares of those uncertain that their shattered world had been restored to normalcy. Some looked fiercely glad, but they were rare compared to those who looked numb or exhausted. How not, given the battle's cost? But like the *Earthrise* crew, they were at least in motion again. And oh, to be in motion again. How good to see the city of Clovellan, smell the freshwater in the air climbing the byways from the shore. And while the shopkeepers lingering near their doors looked lost, or like convalescents fresh from a long illness, it pleased Surela to see them upright and refusing despair.

Their captain took the state of the city's merchants personally, for she strode purposefully to a shop with all her crew in tow and there asked for 'bulk rates on your ice cream.'

"I'm sorry?" stammered the youth behind the counter.

"I'd like to buy everything you have," Ra'aila said.

"E-e-everything?"

"Within reason," said their captain. "If you need to keep some stock back—"

"No! I'll… let me talk to my uncle—"

As the boy scampered through a door, Ra'aila said, "Anyone want ice cream?"

Erynne said, "Hell, yes. Why not. I'll get a sundae. Where to after this?"

"I dunno. What do the Eldritch like for special occasions, Rel?"

Startled to be singled out, Surela said, "Champagne, if you please."

"Angels, yes," Leo said.

"Right, next stop, alcohol. Hell with the chickens."

"Turkeys," Danica murmured.

"Think bigger," Ra'aila said.

"Uh, buffalo?"

"What's a buffalo?" Leo asked.

"Like a cow, but even more cowy," Danica said.

"Not refined enough," Erynne said. "They drink champagne. They need quails or something."

All of them looked at Surela, who said, "Quail are good."

"But?"

She thought of the coast. "Fish are rarer."

"Oh, yes," Leo said. "*Fish.*"

"Fish next," Ra'aila said. "After the alcohol."

But everywhere they stopped, they had samples. Surela tried chocolate mousse ice cream, thought it rich and sublime. The champagne delighted. A few bites of fish, both flaky, delicate white fishes and red fishes that melted on her tongue, fatty and rich. She tried mussels, which she had never had,

193

and was startled by them. By then, most of the crew was tipsy, either with drink or relief or both, and their shopping spree took on the character of an adventure, one that reassured them that all they valued had not vanished with the convulsions of the past month and a half. As Surela accepted wedges of oranges, bred for their sweetness and tang, her mind returned to Eddings's words. *Your ambassador's doing. He turned the emperor.*

Goddess, she thought. That the Eldritch should have been a part of this, and so pivotal a part. Had he done it alone? Did it matter? It proved something to her—that Eldritch could be significant, even in the wider galaxy. Perhaps especially so.

What did that mean?

At station's nightfall, they gave up their shopping because Clovellan's population came out to celebrate as ferociously as they'd mourned, and the rising elation filled the streets with song instead of shrieks. The amber lights smoldered in the city and the lanes filled with people hugging, laughing, kissing, and then dancing, long lines of celebrants stopping up the thoroughfares and no one cared. Surela allowed their emotions to sweep her away, until the constant touches of shoulders and arms no longer troubled her. Saul was the only member of their party who had not become inebriated; he was also the sole member of their party who remained fast to her side, loyal as the hound he resembled. She was glad of him, and glad of the catharsis, that it was joy this time and not despair. It should have overwhelmed her, but it buoyed her up instead. Perhaps not as intimately as it would have, had they been her people... but that was for the best, for she might otherwise have drowned in their emotions.

She was glad to return to the port, fatigued not only by the gravity and the length of their excursion, but also by the number of meals they'd had, for her stomach was assuredly not well with it. At the hatch, Saul watched her with narrowed eyes, and to that gaze she said, "I am fine."

"All right."

That was not agreement but acquiescence to her whim, she thought, having known enough servants to have learned the difference. But she was fine, insomuch as her physical state permitted. And she was glad to have gone out. "Have the others returned?"

"I'm going to check, but I'm sure they'll be all right. Good night, alet."

"Good night, Saul."

———

But she jerked awake in the middle of the night, panic spurring her heart rate. Not hers, either. She was coiled around her own middle as the cramps rippled through her body, and it was her daughter's fear that moved her, not her own… though her discomfort was intensifying, and rapidly. Tasking herself to calm, she said, "Computer. Saul, please."

A chime. Then, as she'd expected, her minder, voice lower in pitch but clear, as she'd hoped despite the hour. "Rel?"

"I believe I am in physical crisis. I don't know if the healer will respond without physical incentive."

A sound like a snap: had he jerked his jaws closed? "I'll get her. Hold on, alet." The connection ended, leaving Surela to lie in her bunk and confront how little she wished to lose the child she'd told herself was of no moment to her. She had accepted her daughter as a passenger, and strove not to devote too much thought to what that meant… but now….

Another chime, that was the door, and then a confusion of voices and blurring movement. She was in Saul's arms and he was carrying her in Prudence's wake. The healer looked like a woman woken from her lover's bed, hair trailing from her fallen chignon and robe fluttering around her body, but her urgency felt too pointed, and Surela was not glad at how it punctured the pleasant fantasy she'd been building, the one that dispelled her growing fear.

"Here, here," Prudence said. "Onto the bed. Rel, give me permission to treat you, I'm assuming you want to save your baby—"

"Yes," Surela said.

"Then close your eyes, deep breaths now... you'll feel like you're falling asleep...."

And she was, and took with her the pretty dream, the one where Prudence was cast as a lover in an assignation, rushing to her bower to greet her beloved, and her beloved had pearled skin and open lips—

CHAPTER 20

She woke. Barely. The weight of her thoughts drew them out of her grasp, and it was hard to hold them together. She had been in crisis... was she out of it? Had the aliens saved her with their medicine again? Again—that was important. They had done this before. Surela forced her eyes open and saw only the ugly ceiling common to all the compartments in the ship that had become... expected. She wouldn't call it home, but familiar, certainly. No longer threatening.

"She's awake!" That was Leo's tenor. Was he forever to be consigned to someone's bedside? Or was it only because he cared that much when people hurt?

Prudence's face swam into focus above her, and the words wobbled, like the surface of water struck by rain. "—with us? Are you with us? We need to talk about next steps."

"I am." Was that her breathy voice? How ridiculous. She strove for clarity and volume. "Of course. Continue."

"The gravity we run at is lighter than normal, and you and the baby seemed to be responding so well to it that I didn't think—" Prudence stopped, and when her words resumed they were terse. "The changes, going between Psi's Alliance norm and the ship's were probably responsible for the microtearing. But the short of it is that you might lose the child unless we take measures. You have three choices. The one I recommend least is bedrest, because the second choice is better: we can set up one of the cargo holds at reduced gravity and put you in it for the duration."

Surela had no idea what that meant, but bedrest for the remaining months of her confinement would turn it into true captivity, and she was not eager to stare at the inside of her cell for that long without reprieve. "And the third option?"

"We transfer the baby to a float chamber. That would require us to transfer you to the starbase hospital."

"What... what is a float chamber?"

"It's like what we do for those chicken eggs." Leo's voice, from behind Prudence. "When we incubate them."

Astonished, Surela said, "That can be done with people?"

"It can, yes. But the float chamber's not going to move," Prudence said. "Once we put your daughter there, she's not going anywhere. You can leave her at the hospital—"

"No," Surela said instantly.

"Then you'd have to stay there."

They presented this as a viable solution, but all Surela could grasp was its isolating promise: her child, rent from her and put in some machine, and Surela herself... where? Hovering nearby in some medical facility? Where would she sleep? What would the crew do? Not stay, she imagined, not with Escutcheon in such need.

"No," she said. "I would rather remain on the ship."

A pause. "I've been talking with Ra'aila about hiring a different healer for the *Earthrise*. I missed your condition, alet. I should have been keeping up with your checkups, even with the war...."

"Don't," Leo muttered.

"But Ra'aila says she's not willing to replace me. If you

stay, I need you to know that I'll still be in charge of your care, even though...." Prudence stopped, struggling.

How amazing, that an alien should have such different mores, and still react in a way Surela understood. She reached for the woman's wrist, wrapped her fingers around it and the thundering pulse of Prudence's remorse. "You feel you have failed me. But I do not perceive it so."

"I got so caught up in myself—"

"You had cause." Surela squeezed once, let her fingers slip away. "What do we do next?"

Prudence wiped her eyes. "I tell Ra'aila to get the hold ready and then we move you there and keep you monitored. I'm not going to let anything new happen to you. But... I also won't lie. It's going to be a monotonous few months. We won't be able to let you onto the parts of the ship with normal gravity. You definitely won't be able to visit the starbase. You're not going to enjoy it. And... after all that, we might still have to rush you to Psi and get your baby into a float chamber."

"It is the best of poor choices, perhaps," Surela said. "But there is no use repining. We must pick a path and move forward. Yes?"

Prudence nodded quickly. "Yes. I'll get that moving right now."

It was Leo who brought her something to drink. "She would have," he said. "But... she's not herself."

"Goddess, I should hope not," Surela said. "If she could weather the death of her world, the enigma of her missing family, and then a war on her nation without a hiccup, how could one trust her to enter into one's concerns without contempt?"

Leo hesitated. "That's... an interesting perspective." He accepted the cup from her and tucked the blanket back around her shoulders. "You're an interesting person, you know that, Rel? Nothing like I was expecting, the way you people get talked about."

Though she wasn't sure she would like the answer, she couldn't help wanting to know. "And what were you expecting?"

"Well... mystery. Glamour. Romance." He chewed his lower lip, then finished, "Snobbishness."

Surela hadn't had any argument with the first three, but the last surprised her, because in her thoughts, hadn't she disdained every member of this crew, and all the aliens she interacted with, and the worlds full of them? She hadn't thought herself that good at hiding it, mostly because it hadn't occurred to her to try. Or at least, it wouldn't have occurred to the Surela of House Asaniefa. The Surela claimed as lowest tenant by House Laisrathera had undergone significant adversity with a human, been rescued by one, and then been saved from her wounds by aliens, and accepted as she was, by aliens.

"If that was too hurtful—"

"No," Surela said. "No, not in the least. For you say I am the opposite of these expectations, yes?"

"And that would be great, in the snobbishness department, but I also implied you weren't glamorous and romantic and mysterious, and who'd want to hear that?"

She stared up into his earnest and worried gaze and saw the absolute conviction in them, and couldn't help a peal of laughter. "You are perfect just as you are, Leo. Let no one tell you differently."

His ears flushed and he patted the blanket near her shoulder. "I'm not sure what I did to deserve that but I'll take it? Also, you *are* glamorous. Seriously!"

"I believe you," she said, and was amused at the revelation that she did... or at least, that she trusted the picture Leo had constructed in his head, after he'd remade her in the image of his fondest fashionable dreams, was indeed, as glamorous as could be imagined.

———

Began her confinement, then, and the novelty of being installed in a space the size of Ontine's Blue Room, where the Empress received petitions, soon palled... for it was not a space intended for habitation, but for cargo, and not all the hasty changes made for her comfort could transform it into anything else. She had a hammock in one corner, and a cubicle for showering and necessities. They'd installed a trunk for her worldly possessions, and for once she was grateful at how few she had, for the 'reduced gravity' caused her to float in a way that made normal movement impossible.

"With enough time, you'll come to rest on the ground," Saul said, clinging to a handle on the bulkhead. "But don't count on it to save you."

Various implements helped either push her in space, in the case of the small jets she could affix to her wrists and ankles and waist, or cling to the walls, in the case of the sets of pads. Sleeping required clipping the hammock around her body to keep herself in position; the shower cubicle was the one place gravity approximated the norm in the rest of the ship, but she didn't stay long in it. Perhaps it was her imagination, but she thought the baby grew distressed when she tarried. Was it because she was bearing a child born to fly that the girl disliked the weight so? Pretty to think so.

The entertainments that had suited her previously were no longer practicable: reading paper books while floating was an exercise in frustration, and writing in one with a dip pen, impossible. The one consolation was that Erynne had set up the computer for 'maximum fun.' Surela could bring up as many displays as she wanted, and wave them to any size; could float through them, and configure them to surround her. She could even project complex and complete simulations of other locales, though the pretense frustrated her... especially when she couldn't mimic the behaviors natural to those settings, like sitting in the chairs of restaurants, or on the backs of horses.

She tried once floating in simulated outer space, complete with gaseous nebulae, and couldn't decide if she liked the sensation or found it unnerving. When she removed the nebulae, though, the simulation looked like the night sky and that interested her... as did a daylight simulation, which made her think of flying as her daughter might one day. The displays could be reconfigured into glowing rings, so she entertained herself by aiming herself through them, and this was apparently a common type of game, and so engaging that she played it daily.

Prudence approved: "You don't want to overdo it, but you should keep active. If you like micrograv aerobatics enough to keep doing it... by all means."

"There are those who don't?"

"Most people get bored of it eventually."

Surela didn't, though perhaps that was because the game kept giving her more complex puzzles to solve: moving through the rings in the right order, or at specific times, or when the rings themselves were in motion. That, she thought, was her favorite permutation. Who could tire of flying?

The *Earthrise* resumed its schedule of transports, except that now Surela could only recommend what they should buy, not leave the ship to procure it herself. Nor could she wander the venues, eat at restaurants, follow this crewmember or that while they embarked on shopping expeditions or pleasure walks. And while the crew visited, possibly more frequently than Surela liked, it was not the same. She'd grown accustomed to living with them, which was a different matter from entertaining them as callers.

If her body was shackled to this chamber, at very least her

mind need not remain so—must not, for she now knew that the greater universe impinged on her own smaller one in a way she'd never been willing to admit. She continued her investigations, formalizing her interests into a course of study she tackled as rigorously as if she'd been enrolled in a formal program. And always, she maintained one display for news to stay apprised of the war's aftermath, which is how she discovered that Liolesa was in the Alliance.

Arrested, she enlarged that display as the cameras followed the Empress in all her magisterial calm, walking the halls of some mortal facility—Surela turned up the volume in time to hear that a formal treaty was being signed in the Selnor system between Alliance, Eldritch, and the Chatcaava. A switch then, to the sight of the Emperor of dragons greeting the Empress of Eldritch in what looked like a palatial conference hall: a modern one, set against the backdrop of the stars.

The juxtaposition should have irritated her. To have the purity of the Eldritch aesthetic ways sullied by the imposition of a mortal setting, and alien concerns. Her emotions now were far more complex. Anger, because of, she suspected, her own helplessness, trapped in exile and now more completely, into this box. Relief, because Liolesa's presence in the Alliance implied the Empress's willingness to take the threats of the galaxy seriously, and do something to avert them. Pride, because the Empress put on such a good showing... how easy it would have been to be overshadowed by the implied power of the aliens with their technology and riches! But Liolesa was effortlessly regal, and made of the alien corridors and compartments a setting that existed only to set off her magnificence. Longing, certainly, because how she missed the world she'd been forced to leave... and satisfaction, that the Eldritch would not be excluded from galactic politics. A threeway treaty between Alliance, Chatcaava, and Eldritch put them all on equal footing. It left her only to wonder what Liolesa was promising to these greater powers to make them take her seriously.

And at the last, there was regret... that she had to stand outside history, barred from involvement with it. Had she not meddled, perhaps... "But no," she told her baby, resigned, floating alongside the display. "Even had I not, I would not now be among Liolesa's intimates, preparing to celebrate her successes. I would be on the other side of the court's aisle, insisting that she not waste her time on mortal concerns when her place was here, among her own people. More fool, I."

The girl did not like cruelty, no matter where it was directed, so Surela left off self-flagellation. It had never suited her, anyroad. "Shall we practice flying, then?" And this met with approval, and perhaps it was some small thing to be redounded to the credit of her prison, that she could take her exercise like a bird on the wing, twirling and rising in the vast, echoing space of it.

CHAPTER 21

Her confinement dragged on, week after week, until it stretched into months that felt interminable. And yet despite that, the cramps started too soon. This time the healer answered the call without external intervention, was floating alongside her with her instruments tethered to her when the cramps came again, and did not relent. "Computer, bridge!"

"This is Danica. What's up, Pru?"

"We have to go back. Immediately."

Through the nauseating pressure clamping her spine and torso, Surela could appreciate how swiftly the reply came, and the trust it implied: "Changing course. I'll ping the captain, you do what you have to, to keep things on track."

How calm that statement: 'keeping things on track.' Nearly Eldritch in its refusal to engage with ugly possibilities while referring to them.

"Thanks, will do." Prudence swam Surela to the hammock, her soft hair drifting around her face like a halo. "Everything's going to be fine."

"I may be forgiven for believing such statements optimistic? It is too early, is it not?"

"She'll be premature, but not by much," Prudence said. "I think. There's no literature on Chatcaavan births." She tucked the hammock around Surela's belly and clipped it. "I'm more worried about you, alet. Our employer released some medical data about Eldritch to me and you're a finicky bunch to treat." Her smile was bright, despite the worried eyes. "I'd like to avoid surgery if at all possible."

"So would I, come to that."

"It won't be long. We just left Psi yesterday," Prudence said. "We should be back tonight. I'll stay with you, just in case."

———

Everything Surela had heard about labor from the few Eldritch women with experience, and from managers discussing livestock, suggested that it was the work of hours, sometimes days, of exhausting effort and pain. Her labor, on the other hand, was abrupt and bloody. Painful, that, certainly. Confusing, also, and she remembered... very little. Prudence's voice, lifted in a commanding tone; the exhaustion that rendered her limbs sodden and unresponsive; bubbles of blood floating alongside her like a spray of cabochon garnets, and then great lacy blankets of it. She spoke, she thought: "This would be the outcome you were concerned with, I believe." Or maybe she dreamed the words? Surely she did, and the part where the blood wrapped around her like a wet shawl.

Her next clear moment involved waking pressed down into the softness of a bed with all the longed-for inevitability of gravity. The window beside her framed a garden and the finches conferring at its sun-lapped birdbath, and their musical chirping eased through the crack with the scent of soil and growing things. Nothing interrupted her view when she looked toward her toes, and this had become novel… something she observed with a lassitude that made the blankets and the birdsong a great comfort.

In the corner of the room was a chair and in it, Saul was napping, his chin propped on his chest and arms folded on his lap. He looked the gangly patchwork he had always been, with one leg outstretched and the other cocked, and tail limp along the cushion…but his homeliness was no longer the first thing she noticed, but rather the rightness of the sight of him. That he should be here felt proper; that he was asleep, soothing. If Saul was sleeping, it was safe for her to do so. So she did.

The second time she woke it was to the sound, not of birds, but of voices, one of which she recognized. She roused herself. "Prudence?"

"Alet, you're awake!" Her Tam-illee sank onto a stool beside her bed. "Doctor Hurst and I were just discussing you."

"You look good," said the stranger, a human woman who could have been Eldritch from her milky complexion and blue eyes. The hair, though, was an orange threaded through with silver, impossible and startling. "We don't usually have trouble with placental abruptions but yours required blood transfusions, and your physician told us you might reject those."

"Did I?"

"No, thank Iley," Prudence said fervently. "You're fine, and the baby is too."

That made her struggle to sit up. "Where…."

"Meri's got her next door. Shall I have her come in?"

"Please."

Prudence left her with the human… who was not, Surela noted, fascinated by the novelty of an Eldritch patient. The healer's businesslike demeanor was reassuring. "I don't see any reason to keep you in the hospital, alet. There's nothing wrong with you at this point that you can't heal on your own, in the comfort of your own home. Do you have any questions?"

What did it mean, to heal on her own? She didn't know what had been done to her. "Need I... be cautious of anything?"

"I wouldn't do strenuous exercise for a couple of weeks, but I doubt you'll want to." A smile, professional but sympathetic. "You won't be sleeping much with a newborn."

Surela pressed a hand to her heart that now beat for itself alone, without the echo that had become familiar and necessary. "My care in this facility... what do I owe for it?"

"Your employer's already squared that with the hospital."

What else? "Then... I can think of nothing. Thank you."

The human smiled. "What we're here for."

Through the door that opened for Meri, Surela espied the edge of Saul's body, standing alongside like a guard. The nurse escorting Meri glanced at the baby in the Seersa's arms with an ambivalence out-of-place among the staff's cheerful or impassive faces. But of course, she thought as Meri brought her that bundle: her daughter was a dragon, and Chatcaava had attacked the Alliance.

What had she expected of an infant dragon? Something too brutish to be loved, perhaps. Had Surela still seen aliens as animals, dismissing her daughter as one would have been easy, for a baby dragon looked nothing like an Eldritch infant, other than a shared, squashed plumpness of limb. But the spirit that had been riding in her for months was so obviously tucked into this tiny shell of flesh that she noted that shell as an afterthought to the overwhelming gratitude, that they should be reunited.

Hurst, who had watched this interaction patiently, smiled when Surela looked up. "She's a cutie."

Startled by this break in the human's reserve, Surela said, "Is she?"

"They all are. But the little wings and the big eyes..." Hurst shook her head, still smiling. "If you like, I'll start the paperwork to get you released."

"Yes, if you would."

"The healer's right, she's the cutest," Meri said, sitting beside the bed. "And so easy to take care of. I have some younger siblings and they were much fussier."

How easily the pilot accepted that Surela had produced a child of a different species. Had the situation been explained to the crew? "Is it true that I might simply walk out of this place?"

"If you feel up to it, sure. But you've only been here three days, alet. Don't feel like you have to leap up and get back to work! None of us mind idling while you're recuperating. Ra'aila even said if you wanted you could stay on the starbase while we make the run back to Escutcheon. There's no rush."

And no doubt Eddings would pay for that as well.

"I will... consider it."

"Do that." Meri rose. "I'll let you have some alone time with your daughter. We've been monopolizing her while you were sleeping! All of us have had a turn, even Ra'aila, and she's not much of a kit type." She grinned. "I'll go tell her they're processing your release."

"Thank you, alet."

Which left her to the quiet, and the baby in her arms... the baby who sighed in her sleep, her eyes tightly closed and little fists clenched.

And what now?

Now, she thought, the inevitable. If the others could have the courage to go on in the face of what had befallen the Alliance, it was the least of what she should ask of herself.

CHAPTER 22

Her decision to leave the hospital despite her uncertain limbs netted her the inevitable interview with Saul. It went... just as she expected it would have gone with an Eldritch liegeman: he merely entered her presence and, by that, made it clear that her plans were hers to make, but that he was not comfortable with them. Had they been that pair, Eldritch liegelady and Eldritch guard, she would not have deigned to make explanation. To Saul, however... "There is a thing I must do, and I believe it must be done alone. But if you feel I will come to harm outside your protection, then I will concede to it."

He had surprised her by studying her face, then saying, "No. I think you're right. And you'll be fine."

Thus she began this... interstitial period. A woman truly alone among aliens, for she knew that Saul was not tracking her now, that the *Earthrise* had pulled away from the dock and set off for Escutcheon without her... and the baby.

The crew had arranged for the room—Danica, perhaps, if not Ra'aila. No one had consulted her, nor drawn money from her account. It was adjacent the Arcade, and looked out on the bay through windows framed in the rock. She had a receiving room and a bedroom, hewn from the stone as if she was living in a castle, but with the amenities of the mortals at her disposal. Sitting on the bed and watching her slight weight crease the sheets, she wondered if one day her homeworld would be thus: the luxuries of technology subtly integrated with the existing styles and mores. What would that be like?

And she would never see it.

The baby was drowsy, and she tucked the girl into the crib the hostel had provided before returning to the receiving room. "Computer," she said. "Can this room be made impervious to noise, so that I might not disturb the infant?"

"Soundproofing can be enabled at any time. Be advised that the owners of the Selle at the Arcade will not be held liable for emergencies that occur while noise is canceled."

Surela touched the windowpane, looking out at the serene aquamarine edge of the bay. "Understood. Please enable."

She sent for lunch first, and with it, a bottle of wine: some vintage specific to the hotel, deep gold in color. The lunch she left aside. The wine she sampled, sitting on the sofa and watching the artificial sun set. Her shoulders loosened; the muscles between her ribs ached from the strain of breathing in the heavier gravity. She would ask Prudence for the regimen when she returned. It would be time.

The first tears streaked from her eyes.

The feel of Prudence's body in her arms, so similar to another body she'd held, so much more briefly. The sight of Prudence's body curled into a rictus of grief and pain, so like the body she'd held as it failed, and took the gentle spirit in it from her, forever.

All the grief she'd been holding at bay, all the loss she'd forced into a box, chased into nightmare, hammered behind a wall until she could focus on surviving, on moving, on whatever it took to keep going when her enemies wanted her shamed, humbled, defeated, *dead*....

Dead, like Thaniet, whom she'd loved and never made her lover. Dead like the dozens of people in the palace, who'd been slain defending it from the pirates she'd allowed— without understanding what she was doing—ingress to their world. Dead like the hundreds of House Jisiensire and its province, razed because Athanesin had used her as an excuse to attempt his own coup when she'd refused to marry him and give him power that way.

All the things she'd done. All the things she would take back if she could. All the love she'd lost, without ever recognizing it or valuing it as she ought to have.

The first sob led to the next, hideous and painful, worse in this heavier gravity; her jerking ribs felt like they were shredding something in her sides. As nightfall spilled the dark into the sky, she wept, and when the first scream shocked her on its way out, she let it go. She howled—beat her fists on the wall until they felt broken and the skin pulped... wept until months of denial and horror and anguish crashed out of her.

And then... she was done. She gulped, nose stopped up and head pounding and hands aching.

Into the quiet, the baby burbled as she woke.

"C-coming," Surela said. Realizing the child probably couldn't hear, she said, "Computer, soundproofing off, please."

"Soundproofing disabled."

Surela wobbled through the arch into the bedroom, where her infant daughter was making noises so small and so tender that they bypassed every rational thought and engaged something more primitive. Gathering the bundle against her, Surela hunted for the bottles the hospital had sent home with her. "Don't worry," she murmured to the child. "Don't worry. We'll survive. No matter what, we will survive."

As she fed the sleepy child, she thought of Thaniet, and could, at last.

———

Infants were so rare among the Eldritch that there was no reason a noblewoman would know how to care for one. Surela certainly had not the first notion of what it entailed, and that was part of why she'd sent the crew away. So she could have the experience of fumbling through it alone, consulting the alien's resources when she came to the end of her knowledge. And slowly, as the hours became days, she grew more deft; her daughter, fortunately, was forgiving. And how she loved to be nestled against Surela's chest, wrapped in a sling and taken into the city with its song and sound and bustle. With the child tucked close and hidden by the fabric, Surela was free of concern for their safety. She could also admit to that concern, for the war's conclusion had been as abrupt and traumatic as her pregnancy's. That both she and the Alliance had been reprieved mattered less to them than it did to her, and talk in the cafes and streets inevitably revolved around the Chatcaava and whether the alliance was real this time, or another lie as the first treaty had been.

Strange to think that her daughter, an innocent, might not be safe in this radically multicultural haven, and yet… she couldn't escape the conclusion that to raise her daughter personally might put them both in danger. Too, it would estrange her child from the culture Surela had grown in, and she wanted her daughter to be raised Eldritch, as much as her seeming allowed. There were compensations to the life to which Surela had been exiled—she could admit it now—but none of them compared to her daughter growing up beneath a sky, knowing the scent of spring flowers, and the sound of autumn storms… and being surrounded by people who would protect her.

The calm that had followed her private catharsis had yet to dissipate, and tarrying at Psi with the crew absent had been necessary for that release. But sitting by the shore with her baby close against her chest, Surela knew this had been the other reason for her request... because she needed these days to resign herself to the necessity of surrendering her daughter. She kissed the little head and watched the shore birds wing past overhead.

———

The return of the *Earthrise* was heralded by a chime at her door, and Surela opened it not on Saul's affable countenance, but on her liegelady's. For several moments she could find nothing to say, until finally she regained her tongue. "My lady."

Eddings studied her face, said, "Interested in lunch?"

What did one say to one's liege? Except: "Let me prepare."

The human said nothing to the sight of Surela with child wrapped to her body; Surela said nothing about the sight of Theresa Eddings here, so far from Escutcheon, her husband, and her duties. It was far, was it not? And yet, Liolesa herself had been offworld recently, and Eldritch abroad had been involved in the war. If her people belonged amid the fray, why not Eddings?

The café was on the roof of the cliff, overlooking the waters, and despite the outdoor seating involved linen table-cloths and fine china. After the water was poured by the waiter, Surela said, "If I may put forth a proposal?"

If Eddings was unsettled by this dispensation with pleasantries, she showed no sign. Was, in fact, looking hale again, if more serious than she had as a newlywed. "Go ahead."

"When we first spoke, in the clinic... you said you might raise the child for me. Is this offer still open?"

"It is, yes. If you're sure. Are you?" The woman's eyes

flicked to the baby sleeping contentedly at Surela's chest. "You seem comfortable with her."

"I am, yes. But I would like her to know my world. My tongue. My culture."

Did the woman know how much Surela was carefully avoiding with those words? The sense of loss? The potential pathos? The regret she felt at not being in a position to raise a daughter, and not knowing whether she would have been fit for motherhood had she tried? But all Eddings said was, "I'll make sure of it. We'll keep her safe and give her everything a girl should have."

That put it to bed. No questions, no unseemly prying. Just this easy exchange, as it should be, tacit and accepted. Liege-lady and—not vassal. Tenant.

In her heart she felt it: that she was not as divorced from her home as she'd believed. Through Theresa Eddings, who had taken a chance on a traitor and a harpy, Surela had a relationship that re-integrated her into the society she'd thought she'd lost. She was no longer one of Escutcheon's great peers... but a villein in the Alliance could become a power in her own right, and knew freedoms that Surela Silin Asaniefa had failed to understand were not only possible, but necessary to her fulfillment.

"Tell me the news," Surela said. "Of the war, and how it finds us."

That filled the remainder of their lunch, and it surprised Surela by being bearable. Enjoyable, even: she could admit that now, on the other side of her grief. She liked the human... liked her even more in this setting. Liked the Alliance, more than she'd planned or wanted to. Was it knowing that Eldritch had participated in the war that made it possible for her to conceive of remaining Eldritch despite her sojourns abroad? Or had it been the sight of Liolesa on foreign newscasts, so supremely herself despite her surroundings when she'd journeyed to Selnor to make peace with dragon and alien?

Or was it the long weeks in company with such congenial individuals, realizing that they were interesting, and she could see a life among similar people?

"I'll send someone over for all her things," Eddings said as they left the café. "I'll leave her with you until then."

Startled, Surela said, "You didn't arrive aboard the *Earthrise*?"

"No, I took one of Liolesa's couriers." Eddings smiled a little. "I wanted to check on you after the hospital visit. Sometimes Eldritch don't do well in hospitals. I wanted to make sure you were one of the 'you survive transfusions' types, rather than the 'you go into shock' types."

"I... see."

The human continued, as if knowing there was no graceful response to this show of concern. "What do you want to name her?"

"I hadn't... I hadn't thought of one. I thought she should have a Chatcaavan name. Surely?"

"She's part Eldritch too, you know."

"She is, yes, but... I would not make trouble for her. Names can be." Saying that naming her would also make her feel too attached would be too pathetic. She touched the little face nestled against her collarbone.

"So you've been calling her 'child' or 'daughter'?"

Surela hesitated. "Little gift, usually. It was what a... friend's... mother called her." Calling Thaniet a friend did her too little justice, but preserved her privacy. Now that she could face those memories, she didn't want to share them with others for different reasons.

"I'll see what we can do then." Theresa glanced at the baby and smiled. "I had no idea the Chatcaava were born so cute. I bet everyone will love her."

"I hope they do."

———

"We missed you!" Erynne exclaimed when Surela boarded the *Earthrise.*

"Did you?" Surela asked, and could mean it as teasing now.

"Oh yes," Danica said. "Everyone except Ra'aila, because she likes berries and you eat through them like no one's business."

"The solution to this seems obvious," Surela said. "And yet no one has thought to enact it?"

"Good point. We'll lay in double orders from now on."

"Baby!" Meri squealed, holding out her arms, and Surela delivered the girl over as Leo burst into the corridor.

"You're back!"

"I am," Surela said. "And indeed, I think you and I are long overdue for a shopping trip, alet."

The leonine gasped, clasping his hands together. "Don't say you're ready for a makeover!"

Surela lifted a finger. "Nothing too outré."

"Never! You will be the soul of dangerous elegance when I'm done!"

"Oh, this I'm going to have to see," Erynne said. "Count me in."

"Me too!" Danica said. "Hells, I think we'll all want to see."

"I leave you to arrange the expedition," Surela said, and watched the child make the rounds through everyone's arms. It hurt, allowing her to see the future she might have had, had she been able to keep the child. But it also gave her the leisure to look on the familiar faces of the *Earthrise* crew without their realizing it, and to know those faces had become welcome.

After they'd done all the doting they could, Surela reclaimed her daughter and returned to her cell. Setting her bag on her bunk, she reflected that it was nowhere near so pleasant as her hotel had been, but it was also... hers. And for the next few hours, the baby was, too. She sat, cradling her, and there she was when Saul chimed for entrance. How good it was to see him. She no longer thought of his features as bestial, and his conformation unfortunate. He was... he was simply Saul. Her keeper, and a reminder that not everything in this alien Alliance would be strange to her... because how could anyone have described their relationship more properly than the Eldritch?

His voice was quiet. "All well?"

Could she admit to uncertainty? "I think so."

He nodded. "The baby?"

"Theresa is coming for her shortly."

"I think it's the right decision. Things out there are... chancy."

She tucked the blanket closer around her small gift's body. "Do you think there will be a healing?"

"There's always a healing until we're done with this life," Saul said. "The toughness of the scar... that you can't predict."

Startled, she glanced up at him, but he was looking at the child. And she was suffused, abruptly, with the strength of her fondness for him, could understand it as fondness without thinking of it as betrayal of her origins, her past, and her values. "Thank you, Saul. You have been staunch."

That flushed his ears pink. "You're welcome. I'll leave you with her." He paused at the door and added, "Welcome aboard, alet."

"Thank you," she said. "I'm grateful to be here." And she was.

Came her liegelady, and took the baby from her, and Surela kissed the girl goodbye while weathering the hot flush of tears pushing at her eyes. Thankfully, not ten minutes after Eddings's departure, the crew descended on her, and she didn't have to guess to know they'd been waiting for that moment to do so, to distract her from her regret.

"Ready for adventure?" Leo asked, eyes bright with compassion.

She chose to answer the cheer of his tone, and to look forward, rather than back... again. Strangely, she no longer felt it to be a lie. "I believe I am."

PART TWO
TRAITOR'S CHOICE

CHAPTER 23

"Fetch!"

Two black blurs darted across the field, their bodies smudges against the dramatic backdrop of the cliffs outside Clovellan's city limits. Surela shaded her eyes, watching them recede in pursuit of the ball. "Remarkable. And they were bred to hunt?"

"They were, yes: foxes, badgers, wolves, deer. And in the mountains... you said you were interested in something that might do better in light gravity, and the immigrants took these from Earth to Mars in part because their increased lung capacity gave them something to work with. Pavonis Taigans aren't as famous as marshounds, but I think they're closer to what you might be looking for."

"They are handsome creatures," Surela allowed while wondering if two dogs alone could take down the monsters that had been rediscovered in the northern wilderness—in what used to be her province, at that. Who would have thought that the ancient menace that had nearly destroyed the Eldritch settlers could have escaped extinction, when so many men had devoted their lives to ensuring the end of that threat? According to her liegelady, the beasts were as dangerous as legend had painted them: the chimera, who hunted in packs and could paralyze with auras of terror, and the larger basilisks, that mesmerized their prey with their minds. The monsters had announced their survival by attacking a village and killing several before they'd been stopped by Eldritch mind-mages.

One of whom had been the princess.

As the hounds loped back, curled tails flagged, Surela conceded that they need not be effective hunters, particularly to companion a woman who was so apparently dangerous on her own. Theresa's request had been specific: "I want a dog for Sediryl. I promised her one and she hasn't had time to pick, and I get the feeling she'll never have time... so I'm doing it for her. Or rather, you are. Get her something that'll keep her alive. But pretty. You know."

Since Surela had spent the past year looking for dogs that might keep the tenants of Escutcheon alive in the face of the renewed threat of chimera and basilisk attacks, she had some sense of what she should be seeking. And whether she liked the princess or not, the imperial heir was due something more rarified than the impressive specimens Surela had already procured. Thus, her research, which had led her to these two creatures, sitting now before their master. They were attractive: elegant with intelligent faces, speaking brown eyes, and coats that grew thicker around their legs and chests. Andromeda, the female, was entirely black; her mate Perseus was black with splotches of white at the belly and haunches.

That, in the end, had driven Surela's choice. The Eldritch mania for matching creatures inevitably drove them to prefer pale beasts. Giving the princess two black dogs would set her apart. And if these creatures could chase off the mountain wolves of Earth, surely they could account for one or two chimera before a basilisk tore them apart.

"They look suitable," Surela said.

"Then while Amie handles the paperwork, let me take you through their commands."

Over an hour later, Surela departed with the two dogs jogging at her side. While the succession of livestock she'd been forced to handle in the year since the Chatcaavan War had acclimated her to animals, nothing had convinced her of the merits of pets. The *Earthrise* crew inevitably cooed over the dogs, the lambs, even the baby chickens… Surela mostly wanted the goats to stay in one place, the sheep to stop excreting, and the dogs to shed somewhere else. Ra'aila was the lone crewmember who agreed with her, but even she could be caught sneaking a serving of meat to a well-behaved dog, and all the dogs Surela had procured were mannerly creatures.

The year had been… perhaps kind was an overstatement. But Surela had put it to good use, both academically, studying everything from languages and history to the economics of the galactic stage; and physically, by undergoing the acclimatization regimen that allowed her to tolerate the Alliance's standard gravity. To be free to roam without fearing her body's failure had been such a relief that she'd become something of a tourist. The prospect of exile lost some of its sting when a year's worth of exploration had not acquainted her with all the nooks and crannies of a single city-sphere on one Alliance starbase. The thought of the worlds open before her… well. She would never grow bored, certainly.

The telegem woke: Ra'aila's mezzosoprano. "Hey, Rel, you done?"

"I am, yes, and on the way to the port with both animals."

"Oh, so they worked out? Great! For everyone else."

Surela hid a smile. "At very least the crew doesn't complain when you set them about cleaning the filters."

"The way they pet the things, scattering hair everywhere…." Surela could almost hear the Aera's resignation.

"Anyway, Prudence's ship is docking, so get back here. It won't be a party without you."

————

The mess glittered with streamers and swags of fabric and floating stars: literal ones, because they hung in the air with no obvious strings. Leo was fluttering from one side of the compartment to the other, checking on the refreshments, the table dressing, and the decor. The dogs were well-bred, indeed: they responded to the commotion by sitting at the hatch like matching andirons, their ears alert.

"Rel!" Leo squeaked. "Should I change the colors? Is pink too much? As an accent color, I thought it might set off the gold, but maybe I should have gone with teal...." Before Surela could assure him that pink was fine, the purser touched some control and all the pink streamers and stars shifted to an oceanic aquamarine. Leo hugged himself, staring dubiously at the results. "That's more elegant, maybe, but is it more fun? I could add fish, maybe... a beach theme? If I hurry, I could sketch some extras out—"

"It's fine," Erynne said from the hatch. "Keep it just the way it is, she'll love it." She crouched to lavish attention on the dogs. "Look at these cuties. They're so cute. Look at their long, long noses. What long noses you have! Such cute long noses! What precious babies!"

"When are we going to be able to keep some of these dogs?" Leo asked.

"When you are willing to answer to the captain for the inconvenience," Surela said.

"Such a pity." Erynne straightened, dusting off her trousers; Surela foresaw much housekeeping in the princess's future, if the fur flying from the engineer's hands was any indication. "Danica and Ra'aila went to get Pru. Meri's—"

"Right here! Ooh, punch? Is it alcoholic?"

"No," Leo said, "but extremely sugary? You can add alcohol to it if you want, though, I put a bottle under the counter."

"You are a gem among lions," Meri declared, and vanished behind the counter. "So did you hear the news from home port?"

Something in Surela's chest tightened. Her habit of avoiding the broadsheet had become entrenched; it was easier to move on if she put her homeworld's concerns behind her, beyond their need for supplies.

But Meri continued, "The Eldritch have a navy, and Pelted can join! As servants!"

"Servants?" Leo asked, confused. "Do navies have servants?"

"Yes, how does that work?" Erynne asked, one ear sagging.

"I don't know, but I got it from their village news net." Meri dipped a cup into the punch bowl. "Oooh, I should have used the ladle, shouldn't I. Anyway, I assumed those ships we saw wandering the system were being crewed by all Eldritch, and it turns out I was wrong. Pelted can join, but they can't be officers. Which means the Eldritch are always in charge."

"That... sounds reasonable?" Leo pulled a stool out from under the counter and perched on it. "The Harat-Shariin homeguard is all Harat-Shar. Why wouldn't it be? It's our solar system. If Pelted want to help the Eldritch out in theirs, it's just that, isn't it? Help."

"Thinking of abandoning us for the elf military?" Erynne asked the pilot, who chortled.

"Don't look at me! I don't even know any Eldritch, except Rel here. I just thought it was interesting. You can't get any scuttlebutt about those warships, everyone on the station's very hush-hush about them." The Karaka'An glanced toward Surela. "Have you heard anything?"

How good it was not to have to lie… and also, how irritating that she hadn't thought to wonder what plans Liolesa was laying in for their defense. "Not a whisper."

"See? Top secret."

"So top secret you found out from the gossip network…."

"We're here!" Ra'aila called from the hatch.

"Party time!" Leo crowed, and launched himself from the stool, across the room, and into a startled Prudence's arms. The healer laughed and hugged him back, and then it was embraces and greetings for everyone. Surela hesitated, hanging back, but Prudence dispensed with her reticence by setting a hand carefully on the Eldritch's arm and smiling up at her.

"We're so glad to see you!" Meri said.

"And I'm glad to be back—oh, cake!"

They ate as they hadn't since Prudence left them half a year ago for a family reunion: her family had been one of the fortunate ones, for their residence had been on the opposite side of the planet from the attack. Two cousins who'd been abroad had died, along with an uncle, but the rest of the Tam-illee's family had been spared. "They don't know what to do next," Prudence said, nursing her second cup of punch. "The weather's bad, and not all the work they're doing to prevent it from crashing the climate is going to keep things from being unpleasant for a few years. We have some distant relations on Rem-ley… that's where they're thinking of going. But no decision's been made yet. What have things been like here? And do I get to ask about the dogs?"

Surela leaned back, content to listen to the banter. Prudence had been missed, and not solely because Danica had been forced to doctor her own toe when she'd dropped a shipping crate on it. Their company had a wholeness, one that had been lesser for the absence of the healer's gentle energy. But to mend the nervous anxiety that had plagued Prudence prior to her leave request, Surela would have granted her far more than half a year. It was a merry convocation, this one, and its modest size compared to the parties Surela had overseen as Asaniefa's head was more than compensated by the company, and the casual richness of the repast.

Several hours later, Erynne and Danica reported to their evening watches, and Meri to her bed. Leo begged the privilege of toting Prudence's luggage to her quarters. The dogs had fallen asleep near the door, and that left Surela with the healer, the captain, and Saul.

"Do I get to say the obvious?" Ra'aila said.

Prudence had her cheek in her palm and was smiling. "That being...."

"You came back. We're grateful, because we really did miss you. But if you'd wanted to break contract I would have understood."

The healer traced a line through the crumbs on her plate. "I considered it. When I thought I'd lost my family... I understood how important they were to me, in a way you don't have to when you assume they'll always be there." A slight sigh, revealed only by the rising of her shoulders. "And it was really, really good to see them. But they went through the attack together, and you could tell. There was a bond there. Shared experiences. Things they were moving through together. Things they remembered." Prudence shook her head. "It made me realize that going through the attack here, with all of you... that created the same kind of bond." Her eyes rose, just enough to meet Surela's. "We traveled through our own, specific hell, one we could try to explain to outsiders, but it would never make them part of it. You know?"

"Don't we," Ra'aila said, glancing at Saul, whose smile was crooked.

"There's something reassuringly normal about what we're

doing here. Trading cargo like this. I like it. So... for the fore-seeable future, I'll be here."

That conversation returned to mind later, after Surela had retired to her quarters: how shared experience had yoked her to Theresa Eddings, and that bond had been stronger than anticipated. Had, in fact, kept her alive, more than once. She paused the tutorial she'd been studying as she remembered the harrowing hours spent in their shared cell under the palace. How astonishing a thing shared experience was, that could create amity out of antagonism, and seal unfriends more closely than friends who'd been parted by separate lives, events.

As if summoned by her thoughts, her computer chirped, heralding a message... one marked with a routing address she didn't recognize. All of the *Earthrise*'s assignments came to them from Eddings: no one should be contacting her directly from the homeworld, much less... she glanced at the name, and froze. Thuliven Mel Deriline, the Royal Procurer, had sent her a letter? Surela remembered him: there was no forgetting the man whose advice had led her to the horrifying epiphany about the Eldritch economy, in her very short tenure on Liolesa's throne.

For your timely execution of the last set of requests, I must thank you... and particularly for the delicacies you thought to append, which were not on the list. The supplies are destined for twin feasts designed by the imperial heir to open the summer court, and your choices will add to the consequence and elegance of both affairs.

—TMD

The stylus sagged from nerveless fingers. A thank-you note? From someone who'd been forced to serve her while she labored as the One Week Usurper? The heat that stung her eyes made her shake her head, angry. She would not cry; she had put to bed her regrets and made peace with her new life. There was no returning.

"Mess Hall to Rel."

Dashing the tears from her eyes, Rel said, "Erynne? What is it?"

"Did anyone tell the dogs they were free to go? Because they're still here, and they look awfully uncomfortable about it."

Goddess, what time was it? Well into the night shift. Surela rose. "On my way."

CHAPTER 24

As usual for early mornings, the fore of the vessel was empty of everyone save the watchstander, and now, the watchstander's student. A mug had been set out for Surela on a warmer, filled with coffee the way she took it. How casually these aliens performed services for one another, like menials, and yet with such affection. They took care of one another in a way Surela continued to find inexplicable. Now, though, she also found it touching. "You have left the weapons console active. Am I the tactical officer for this round, then?"

Meri clipped back her mass of braids, made a gesture with her hand that suggested ambivalence. "I'm not sure. I'm looking at Quadrant 18 on the take from Selnor Welcome Station. Have a look."

The display woke in front of her with such a mass of detritus spiraling from multiple explosions she was hard-pressed to choose something to focus on, even after months of similar exercises. She had run through Meri's pilot training and both of them had grown bored with simulations. When sensor data from the Battle of Selnor became more widely available, Meri had begun analyzing it as a way to teach herself tactics—"because why not, I like learning"—and Surela had joined her, for more practical reasons. Or at least, more personal ones. If dragon enemies there remained, she wanted to understand how they killed.

"Selnor Welcome," Surela said slowly. "That would be the station farthest from the star."

"Right." The pilot put up a map of the solar system, cluttered with habitats, and pulled the focus in toward an installation swinging through a wide orbit around it. "It looks like this squadron—" Meri circled a group of six ships. "—separated out to handle the station."

"Only six vessels?"

"Six was enough, since they didn't want to capture it. I think this is one of the few times we see mostly energy attacks from capital ships, or... I don't know. I don't think these are big enough to qualify as capital ships. But they're not using carrier tactics to deal with the station, they're just lobbing weapons' fire at it from a distance."

"But why?" Surela asked. "When they love prisoners? That is why they prefer to swarm their targets with small fighters, yes? To deliver the dragons to their enemies' ships to hijack them, and procure slaves?"

"That's what I've heard... and it's how they attacked once they got close enough to the mass of ships heading for them."

Surela frowned. "Was it about needing to surprise their victims...? Except they had overwhelming numbers, what need had they for surprise? Indeed, one would think they would prefer the reverse: to strike fear into their enemy's hearts by giving them a sufficiency of time to count their numbers."

"I'm not sure," Meri admitted. "Maybe it has something to do with the reports that the attacking group wasn't commanded by a single person, but by a bunch of competing interests? Someone might have disagreed with the strategy.

Come to think of it, the raid that started all this wasn't carrier-fought. It was also 'stand back and lob rocks at things.' Or at least, initially. Reports say the dragons came back and picked through the mess for prisoners."

"Were any of them stopped?"

"Some, yes. Maybe there's some sensor take of that. I'll look it up later. For now... you want to do defense or offense first?"

Surela pursed her lips. "Offense. My aim is... to whelm your defenses by striking repeatedly, until there is not enough power to respond?"

"And without getting hit."

The Chatcaava had done it, so it must have been possible. "Let us see if I can reproduce the results."

For the next hour, they played out the scenario. The Alliance had not released tactical data about the capabilities of their stations, but much could be inferred from the sensor data, and there was no hiding the sensor data. It was appallingly easy to reconstruct nearly every facet of the Battle of Selnor, so much so that Surela wondered how the Eldritch Veil had ever held. Surely obscurity was not sufficient to prevent the Alliance's citizens from assembling the pieces necessary to reveal everything about the Eldritch.

When they exhausted the possibilities offered by that scenario, they resumed another of their pastimes: worst case piloting sims, or as Meri called them, 'hell no's. Their last such scenario had involved being tumbled off course by the failure of one engine into a dense asteroid field, which had killed them both despite multiple resets. For their edification today, the computer conjured multiple attacking Chatcaavan fighters, darting by on wildly erratic vectors.

They both died every time they attempted this scenario, but Surela lasted a few minutes longer. Meri, laughing, congratulated her. "You never know when a few minutes will make the difference between dying horribly and dying slightly less horribly."

Surela eyed her. "That would have been more encouraging had the second option been measurably more optimal. Or perhaps even desirable, such as being rescued."

"I try not to bank on miracles." Meri grinned. "So do you want to formally certify to fly? You could, you know. You'd pass."

"So that Ra'aila might fret over my ambitions?" Surela shook her head and rose from her station. "I think not."

"Fair enough. If you change your mind...."

"...I will inform you the next time you ask, which will be in approximately two weeks, given your habits."

"That's telling me!" Meri laughed. "You off to shop?"

"I am, yes. The hounds are with Erynne... I believe she means to remand them to Danica when the latter wakes. If something goes amiss, would you have me contacted, please?"

"Will do."

Which left her at liberty, and glad of it. She told no one that she purchased gifts for her daughter for milestones and holidays; the thought of the crew's pity tired her, nor did she want them to participate. It hurt to receive news of the child so Surela had asked Eddings to refrain from passing any on... but she couldn't dissuade herself from the shopping trips, and those gifts her liegelady accepted without comment, save to say she would ensure they were received. It was the only way Surela could remain part of the girl's life. Anything more involved would inevitably entail heartbreak, but she didn't know how to turn her back completely on her daughter.

How pleasurable it was to shop for a child in the bounty of the Alliance! Books for Eldritch children were jealously guarded heirlooms, read aloud by adults who held them out of reach of grasping hands; toys, all handmade, were meticulously repaired as they were passed down. But Surela could browse any number of stuffed animals and choose one fresh, as if her daughter was the first scion of a line, rather than the fourth generation who could hope for nothing but her mother's playthings. And if the books were not as glorious and singular as those in the Asaniefa library, they were indestructible and brightly colored.

What had happened to the riches of the Asaniefa manors? Had they escheated to the crown? Or had they been looted?

Surela did not allow herself to wonder. Was a plush dragon too strange for a dragon child? Or would it be like an Eldritch girl receiving an Eldritch doll to dress? A duck struck her fancy, and had the added advantage of not being too closely related to the heraldic animal of any particular Eldritch House. Perhaps with matching yellow ribbons for the girl's hair? Did dragon children have hair enough to braid? The Chatcaava depicted on newscasts had manes.

A long amble through Clovellan eventually saw her over the Pad to the opposite side of the bay, there to stop at the bookstore and then make her way to what had become one of her favorite places for lunch. Umbrellas had only outdoor seating under its titular umbrellas, arranged in a wide apron around what she presumed to be a kitchen, but could only presume because there was no seeing inside the squat, fortress-like facility. She liked the long view over the fields, and the distant glitter of the water, and the sun. The airiness of it appealed to her after weeks in the ship.

Surela was addressing herself to her salad when a man slid into the seat across from her as if he was expected. She lifted her gaze from her plate and subjected him to its brunt for his temerity, and he was not at all discommoded. A human, middle-aged, perhaps. But unprepossessing, in the same sort of ship boots, trews, and shirt that served many in the Alliance as casualwear, and with a loose-limbed ease that would do nothing to suggest to onlookers that he was a complete stranger.

His face was unremarkable, until he met her eyes. She'd seen eyes like that before. Her skin flushed cold, and then she remembered how she'd last served a creature with similarly ruthless eyes. She was no longer a helpless prisoner.

"It took you long enough," said the stranger. "Our mutual benefactor said you'd be along but you're cutting it a little close, aren't you?"

Between one breath and the next she understood that this criminal thought she was his confederate. Why? Who had told him so? And why now, almost two years after her exile? Surela patted her mouth with her napkin. "I'm here now."

"Much good it'll do us if the window closes. I assume you're willing to do business?"

"That would depend entirely on the terms," Surela replied. "What are you prepared to offer, and what precisely would you want in return?"

He smiled as the waiter arrived with a glass of water. "Thank you. Could I get the special? Perfect." Returning his attention to her, he said, "We want the princess, as promised."

"Good," Surela's mouth said. "I'd like to see her taken care of."

"We can grab her during the procession. We just need a ship count, make sure we've got the numbers on our side. That's your job: get us details on the escort, and which ship she'll be on."

Surela reached for her water. "You want significant work from me. Dangerous work. What precisely do I get from this arrangement?"

"Vengeance against the people who exiled you." At her cocked brow, he smirked. "Our mutual benefactor told me about you, Asaniefa."

Goddess, who precisely was this benefactor? Who was betraying their people to pirates, and how could they possibly, after what pirates had done in the halls of Ontine? Surela sniffed disdainfully. "One cannot live on vengeance."

"Oh, so you want money, is that it?"

"If you succeed," Surela said, hoping she was guessing correctly, "you will have any number of slaves to sell to lucrative markets. Quite lucrative ones. And I do not love being forced to subsist on an ancient and battered excuse for a freighter."

He laughed. "The lady wants a yacht, is that it? Understandable. We can arrange for money. Two percent of sales?"

"You disrespect me. Fifty."

"I've got crews to pay. Five percent."

"Twenty-five, and half prior to delivery."

"Highest I'll go is ten."

Would it be enough to convince him she could be bought? She didn't like the look in his eye: too skeptical by half, and perhaps not particularly of her. One could not be a criminal without a habit of suspicion. What would break through that crust? Ah. "Ten percent... if."

"If?"

"There is a particular man I want delivered to me. Personally. For my amusement."

His brows rose. "Only one?"

"The minister of war," Surela said.

The criminal laughed. "Let me guess... he rejected you?"

She made a point of looking away, as if to disguise her reaction, and this had the desired effect.

"Isn't it always the way. Well, it's no skin off our backs. We had his little wife targeted for payback anyway. The organization has a score to settle with her. You can have her spouse, and—as you would say—we'd like to see him taken care of. We assume you will."

"Oh, I have plans."

His smile did not reach his empty blue eyes. "I bet you do." As the waiter arrived with two sets of plates, that smile tinted them until he looked normal. "Thank you, that looks delicious."

Surela waited, all her skin alive to the dangers, to his nearness, as the waiter arranged the table, refilled their glasses, and withdrew. "You mean to dine with me."

"Of course. Why wouldn't two old friends do so? And we are friends, aren't we?" Another of his smirks as he dug into the fish.

"At best we are comrades in arms," Surela replied icily. "I would hope for nothing better."

"Unless we profit from our mutual arrangement? Our benefactor suggested we might have long term aims in common. I could certainly see the value of someone on the inside. There's no way into the damned system anymore, it's crawling with sensor platforms."

"An inevitability, given how badly the affair was handled previously. How your people could fail when I wrapped the entirety of the planet for you and gifted it...."

"Don't look at me," he said. "If I'd been in charge, we'd be kings several times over by now and you...." Another of those ugly smiles. "Would be queen."

Surela forced herself to eat, though she couldn't taste the morsel her fork delivered to her mouth. "You need throw me no sops. I know your aim would be to be rid of me the moment it was feasible... just as you know it would be my aim, as well."

"Should I be worried about you building an empire of your own, then?"

"Only if you mean to stand in my way. On the other hand, we might have some profit from one another. Yes?"

"Possibly." He chuckled. "You know, I didn't know what to expect from our benefactor's description of you. I should have known someone who wanted a throne would be thinking long term."

"Indeed. And long term for one of my kind is very long indeed." She eyed him. "Dare I state that I doubt your ability to overcome the escort?"

"Obviously you do. Don't worry about it. You tell us what we're facing, we'll handle it. It's just a matter of… shall we say… diverting resources. My, what a delicious meal this is. You have impeccable taste."

"Naturally, not being a savage."

He laughed. "Like the rest of us? Rhack, you Eldritch are such elitists. You have no idea how much fun it is to chain you up."

She let her lip curl into a sneer. "So long it is my enemies you chain, I care not how you find your entertainment."

"I thought it would bother you to hear about our plans for Eldritch."

"Don't be stupid," Surela said. "I have no more loyalty to my race than any other person of wit and ambition. I have allies and enemies, that is all… and to the extent that the latter include other Eldritch, I am only too happy to see them suffer."

"Like your minister of war, is that it?"

"Just like."

He tossed his napkin aside with another of his reptilian smiles. "Looks like I'm getting called away on urgent business! So sad to have to leave early." He tapped his wrist in a gesture that made no sense. "Remember, the clock's ticking. The procession's leaving in a month. Get us the info."

And then he was gone, leaving her to stare at the meal she'd picked at.

Goddess help her. What now?

What had Saul taught her? She assumed surveillance, and forced herself to resume eating as if untroubled. Her innocent purchases struck her as perilous—had the pirates watched her buying toys, and guessed at a way to control her? She hoped not. After paying for both meals, Goddess damn the man, she rose and embarked on a leisurely constitutional, strolling past the shops and wondering whether her enemies were watching her from behind some of the storefront windows, or in the crowds passing, or if they were using some technological device beyond her ken to track her. If they were....

Her thoughts spun. She meandered until she felt she had made her nonchalance evident, and then her footsteps carried her toward the port at a decorous pace, when what she wanted to do was flee for the shelter of the ship... even knowing that her time as an anonymous exile had run out.

CHAPTER 25

T he war had altered a great deal about the routine of
the *Earthrise* crew. One of those changes had mani-
fested in the conversion of one of the cargo bays into
an exercise room… one with targets for armed and unarmed
combat. Danica had learned to shoot in a desultory fashion to
repel pirates ("I thought boarders were a myth; guess I was
wrong"). Leo, surprisingly, knew some hand-to-hand work.
Nearly everyone spent a few hours a week practicing some
form of self-defense, and Saul had a standing class for those
who wanted personal tutelage; he was committed to daily
practice so, as he said, he might as well teach.

In the beginning, Surela had attended these sessions
because Prudence had encouraged her to do some form of
exercise to help the acclimatization take. Those first few
lessons, learning to shoot a palmer, had provoked a fresh
spate of nightmares, but she'd wrestled them down. To be
impotent again… no. She refused. So she learned to shoot,
and when she'd realized that dragons preferred to transport
themselves to enemy vessels so they could fight in the corridors, she'd put herself forward for tutoring on uglier, more

direct fighting methods. At first, Saul had taught her solely how to 'get out of the way.' When she proved her dedication, he and Leo began in earnest.

"You have incredible reach," Saul had said. "But you're a lightweight, and no matter what living in higher grav does to your bone density, you're still going to crumple if someone tackles you. We'll get you a collapsible shock-lance, and teach you to keep from being hit. If you do…" He'd glanced at the dagger she now traveled with in her boot. "Surprise will be your best option."

Surela hated fighting. But she'd been the helpless victim of violence, and she would never again allow it.

Saul offered his practice session in the afternoon, which gave her enough time to drop her bag in her cell and repair to the shower. A long session under the water soothed her shattered nerves. Then she dressed and took herself to the cargo bay, where she hoped to be the sole student; thankfully, when she entered, the room was empty of everyone except the Hinichi. Saul had been at the punching bag for some time, from the sheen on his body: she didn't understand the relationship between sweat and the furred members of the Alliance, but some of them could lather like horses and Saul was definitely dripping.

At the sight of her he paused and smiled… and then instantly, the expression folded away. "Something happened."

How could she begin? "We must talk."

He grabbed a towel. "My cabin."

Almost she objected: to intrude on the personal space of a retainer was ill-bred. But for no reason she could articulate, his space seemed safer than hers… and, Goddess forgive her, but she was curious… curious, and satisfied, because when she entered, it was exactly as she imagined: uncluttered, with bedding in dark, neutral grays and browns barely picked out by the low lighting. On his desk was a thick book with a scuffed cover, and a small holographic family portrait with so many people they barely fit in the space. Had he liked his extended family more than she had hers? They were all smiling.

Her keeper pulled out the chair for her before perching on the edge of the bed. "Tell me."

"I was approached today by a pirate seeking my aid," Surela began. "My aid to betray my people." His expression didn't change, so she forced herself to continue. "He had reason to believe I would be amenable to this offer, because... I have betrayed them before." She looked at her hands, folded on her lap. Until this moment she had not realized that she valued his estimation of her so. "Liolesa—that is to say, Empress Liolesa—and I were on opposite sides of an internal debate on our homeworld as to whether we should deepen our relationship with aliens. It was her opinion that we would be enriched thereby, and mine that it would demean us. I thought I could do her job better than she could. Thought, in fact, that it was my duty to wrest the throne from her and prevent our people from becoming more entangled with offworlders. This flaw in my thinking left me prey to an Eldritch priest, Baniel Sarel Jisiensire, whose goals were far more extreme. He told me everything that I longed to hear: that he could help me onto the throne, and that this would give those who hated Liolesa's politics the voice they'd been denied by her autocratic acts."

Saul had not yet said anything. She dared not raise her head to evaluate his reaction. "I believed him, and gave him license to equip my partisans with offworld weapons, thinking... oh, that no one would dare fight if they knew themselves so vastly outmatched. I wanted a bloodless revolution. I wanted to rule, not to... not to destroy. But I was alone in this, for the man with whom I had allied myself had established a relationship with pirates and Chatcaava, because he wanted to destroy our world, and sell us all to slavers. I should have wondered how he came by his alien arsenal, but at the time I... I didn't want to ask questions. I feared I would mislike the answers."

She was now gripping her hands so tightly they hurt. "My coup succeeded, inasmuch as it put me on the throne. But I was a puppet for Baniel and his dragon partner, no more. When I discovered that Liolesa had been strengthening our ties to the Alliance because we could not survive without their aid, I realized..." She freed a hand from their clutching and massaged her forehead. "Everything I'd believed about her, and her reasons... they were all wrong. And in my naïveté I assumed I was the power on Escutcheon, and discovered otherwise when I was thrown in a cell, when I was not tied in someone's bed. Too, my ascension gave license to the worst malcontents among my people, including a man who razed an entire province purportedly to please me, but in reality, for... for some other purpose I never divined. Even now, I don't know why he did it. But my acts brought pirates and dragons to our world, and fire and ruin to multiple villages, and I should have died for it, save that Theresa Eddings interceded. We were trapped in the same cell in the latter part of the coup, and she equipped me to fight my rapists. When Liolesa returned with our rescue, and the fighting swept through the palace, I was able to kill the Chatcaavan with the weapon Eddings lent me. Through her kindness I was able to relay a command to what few loyalists answered to me, to stand down and accept judgment. I wanted no more fighting. Liolesa's was the only path. I didn't understand until I tried it my way."

No response. She forced herself to look up... and there he sat, his shoulders relaxed, his face unchanged. So casual, with his elbows propped on his thighs and his hands hanging loose between them. No revulsion. No anger. Which meant: "You knew." One corner of his mouth drew upward. Not quite a smile, except that somehow it expressed his sympathy better than any declaration. "Theresa. Theresa told you—and you... you told me when you arrived to escort me to the *Earthrise*... 'to be a friend to the friendless.'" She touched her fingers to her brow. "I am correct, aren't I. She arranged the entire affair. And you..." She looked up. "You said yes. But why? I am past redemption."

"It's because no one is past redemption that I said yes." He paused, shrugged a little, and the slight smile grew into a private, gentle thing that transfigured his unprepossessing countenance. "My religion believes in deathbed conversions. Do you know what that means?" At her slight head shake, he said, "If you live a life of sin and evil, if you murder, blaspheme, steal and destroy, but with your dying breath you ask for God's forgiveness, and feel sincere contrition for your acts... then you get to go to Heaven with all the saints and angels, same as the person who's lived a life of perfect virtue."

Arrested by the power of the image, and its unlikeliness, Surela said, "That... hardly seems fair."

"Salvation isn't. That's what makes it so hard for us to accept." He studied her with his patient eyes. "And you aren't without remorse, are you, Rel."

"No," she said, softly. "I regret all that I did. From beginning to end." She sighed. "But that brings me to today."

"Yes," Saul said, and his demeanor changed so completely the hair on her nape rose: no more the gentle confidant, but the wolf... and an angry one. "Tell me about today. You're not bugged because I rigged the hatches to check for them on every person who exits and enters. That means they've been watching you once you leave the ship. Tell me exactly how it went. Start with what he looked like."

Surela related the entirety of the conversation, and had the encounter not disturbed her enough, Saul's expression would have dripped the wax on that seal. "I... I am in trouble, I know."

"Yes, and thank God they think you're a criminal yourself. If they'd believed they had to suborn a virtuous person, you'd be in far worse danger. As it is…" He leaned back, exhaled. "What do you want to do?"

"I… I beg your pardon?"

"I can make suggestions, but I can't make your choices, alet. Do you want to play their game? Report them to the Fleet presence on Psi? Go back to Escutcheon and tell your local authorities?"

"I don't know enough to make such decisions!" Surela brought her voice back under rein before it further betrayed her fear. "Who is this mutual benefactor? Why did they give these criminals my name? Who was the other possible contact? What are the details of this personal grudge they appear to have against Eddings? I don't even know what procession it is they would have me gathering information on!"

"That one's easy," Saul said. "It's in your local news. The princess is going to visit the new Eldritch colony world. Something about a summer court."

"Could the criminals succeed?"

"In capturing her? I don't know. If they have enough ships that they think they could fight off the Eldritch Navy, then… maybe. I guess that's the question." His eyes were steady. "Whatever you want to do, I'll help you do."

"And if I told the Alliance authorities? Would it concern them? This is an attack against Eldritch interests, not theirs."

"Pirates always interest them, but you're right to say they might not prioritize it, especially now. The war junked a lot of the Alliance's capital fleet, and diverted the rest of it to active patrolling on the coreward border."

"Then," Surela said, stomach knotting, "I must lay it in my liegelady's lap. There is no other answer. If navy we have now, this threat is their charge." She met his eyes. "Is the *Earthrise* in any danger?"

He tilted his head, smiled.

"You mean that I should note I have changed," Surela said. "But I assure you that all my worst impulses remain in me."

"That's fine. They remain in all of us. Otherwise, virtue would be meaningless. As to the crew…" He closed his eyes. "I don't know. I'd guess the pirates aren't going to make any waves until they're sure of you, but it's for the best that we're due to cast off tomorrow morning. If you're planning to tell Reese…?"

"When we dock."

He nodded. "Then I would wait on her response. She might want fewer people to know what's going on."

"Then… we do nothing."

Saul stood. "Then what we actually do is go back to the bay and practice." His eyes were somber. "You're going to need it."

"Surely… surely someone else will handle the particulars?" But she stood, and her knees only felt a little weak at his intimation.

He shook his head. "Rel, they're already following you. You're in this up to your neck. It's not a matter of if you'll have to defend yourself, but when. So let's keep working on your skills, shall we?"

CHAPTER 26

How grateful she was that the ship's schedule made her decision to stay in that night natural. To pretend to normalcy in the face of confirmed surveillance... she had done, in the court, when it had been necessary to drive off opportunistic predators. But Surela was now far too aware that showing weakness to a passel of over-bred Eldritch courtiers was a very different proposition from doing so to pirates and slavers. Best not to test herself again, at least, not so soon.

The following morning, Prudence happened on her in the mess. "Oh, Rel! You can't imagine how happy I am to be back. Is it silly that I love my little clinic?"

How beautiful the foxine was, and how terrible she would look in chains. Those dainty wrists, the soft hair, the long limbs. Surela forced a smile. "Not in the slightest."

"You're just saying that to be nice." Prudence beamed at her and picked through the mugs behind the counter until she found the one she preferred. "Did you eat already? Oh, I see your empty plate. You always cross your utensils so neatly. Danica's waffles! Oh no, I love her waffles."

Surela couldn't help laughing then. "Truly you are delighted by everything today."

"I am! And..." The healer brought her plate over, set it down... and frowned, ears flipping back. "You look tired. Is there something on your mind?"

How could she lie to this woman? But to tell the truth before she understood her liegelady's mind... had she been in Eddings's place, she would have expected discretion from her servants. "I never sleep well when I am escorting hounds. To shut them into a single cabin is heartless, but a ship of this type is not an ideal environment for them to run loose."

"I was wondering about that. What's with your world's mania for dogs? Why never... I don't know. Cats? Parrots? Gerbils?" At Surela's quizzical look, Prudence laughed. "Other things humans keep as pets."

"A parrot is a bird, yes? But what is a gerbil?"

"It's about this big... and related to a rat. I think."

Goddess, who would keep such a thing for pleasure? "I see. But no, the dogs are not intended as pets, but as working animals. They guard livestock."

Prudence nodded, applying herself to the waffle. "And... you'll tell me when you're ready to talk about the thing that's really bothering you, right?"

Surela began to object, thought better of it. "When I am at liberty to do so."

The other woman speared a small square and ate it, swallowed. "As long as you know... we're on your side, arii."

Just that easily, they arrayed themselves in her vanguard, without knowing her history, her sins, or her enemies. Saul knew but the wolfine was... an unusual case. She'd spent some time before bed researching the common beliefs of the Hinichi until she located his homeworld's. Reading its basic tenets had frightened her because of the resonances she'd felt between his religion and the Eldritch's. Only her people were not quite so radical. Saul's people might forgive her sins...

she was not certain about her own. No Christ-like figure had sacrificed himself for her salvation, and the saints and martyrs the Eldritch portrayed in stained glass and tapestry were commonly held to be stories, not reality. Beautiful stories, certainly, but fictions all the same.

"I am honored," she said at last. "Thank you for your trust." Goddess, the poignancy of it. Would they still trust her when they found out? Because they would, inevitably. Surela curved her lips into a smile. "So, did you find a new musician to patronize during your stay with your family?"

————

Try as she might, Surela could not decide what figured foremost in her heart when they docked at the station in orbit above Escutcheon. Relief, that she was nearly quit of this burden? Or dread, that she would have to relate the encounter to Eddings? Theresa would believe her when she insisted she had done nothing to encourage pirates to believe her their ally. Surela did not like to guess what anyone else would believe, once Eddings passed that information on.

As per usual after delivering the cargo, the crew dispersed to take liberty on the station, leaving the *Earthrise* empty of everyone but Surela and the hounds... well, and probably Saul, knowing the Hinichi. The last of Surela's decisions passed from her when a message from Eddings arrived, informing them she was coming in person to accept the princess's dogs. Surela brought the pair to the mess and sat to wait, and it wasn't long before her liegelady appeared, and with her a stranger.

"Alet," Eddings said, and whistled at the sight of the dogs. "Now that's a striking set. They look well-behaved, too."

"They are," Surela said. "I have written down everything I was told about their care...."

"I'll make sure it gets into the right hands. Austin, if you'll take them? Thanks." As the hounds trotted off behind the man, Eddings grinned. "I'm grateful for the Eldritch instinct for drama. Those two will be shockers, showing up at her heel."

"It was my hope," Surela said. She pushed a small bag across the table

Taking it up, Eddings shook her head. "You know I can bring her up to see you. Anytime."

To see her daughter would be to miss her. "It is best that we maintain the distance."

"If you say so." Eddings pulled out a chair. "You said you had something you wanted to talk about?"

"There is no one in the corridor?"

Eddings paused before sitting, one hand on the back of the chair. Without asking for more information, she stepped to the hatch and looked out it, then returned, seating herself. "All clear. You've got my attention."

This was the moment. Best to get it done. "I have been contacted by pirates," Surela said. "They want my help capturing the empress's heir during her visit to the new colony."

The human's eyes widened, and the pupils dilated so quickly it reminded Surela of the sea darkening beneath cloud-shadows. Then Eddings's mouth pulled into a taut line, and her expression became determined. "This should be good."

Startled, Surela said, "It should?"

"If they want another round in the ring... this time with Hirianthial aware of what he can do, at least three other mind-mages on planet, and an entire navy on our side, plus the Chatcaava? Oh yes." Her liegelady's eyes were hard. "You want revenge, Surela? Because blood and gods forgive me, but I do."

Surela allowed herself the license to envisage her situation thus: not as a woman surrounded on all sides by the enemies that had engineered her planet's victimization, but as the defender chasing down monsters to protect her people. A modern Risaliel, Star-Crowned Huntress… except unlike the woman of the tragic fable, Surela would survive the encounter. "I… believe I rather like the notion. Save that they seem to think they are equal to anything we might bring to bear. They know of our navy."

"They think they do," Eddings said. "I doubt they understand it, though." She rose, checked the corridor again, paused. "Saul's at the end of the hall."

Guarding it, no doubt, while she spoke with her liegelady. "He knows."

"Good choice. Did you tell anyone else?"

"I did not, no. He recommended I wait on your decision before informing anyone else." Surela hesitated. "I fear for the crew."

"So do I. We'll take it step by step. But this isn't the best place to discuss this. Let's—oh, freedom curse it all, I can't take you on station, that's technically Eldritch soil. The bridge, then. And if Saul's going to play guard, I'll get him to do it formally."

On the bridge, with the compartment sealed and Saul standing outside the hatch, Surela related all the pirate had told her. Unlike Saul, Eddings did not press her for details, only listened, leaning forward with her hands on her knees, until Surela reached the end of her recitation. "I can't say I like it," Eddings said. "But it was only a matter of time before they started sniffing around here again. I'm going to take this up the chain, see what we want to do about it."

"And what shall I do?"

"Just sit tight. It won't take long to get a response on something this big, and then you'll have your marching orders."

Whatever that meant. Surela escorted her liegelady to the

hatch and watched her vanish around the bend in the corridor, then said to Saul, "She was angry."

"What did you expect?"

What had she? "Fear."

After a long moment of looking down the hall, Saul said, "Same thing."

———

Surela had expected Eddings's return the following day, or perhaps not even that: it was as likely that she would receive a message with instructions in a day or two, and Goddess help her for did she not have a deadline? But she should have known better, granting a threat to their empire. She had been in her quarters less than two hours when Saul's voice summoned her via telegem. "They want you in the mess, alet."

'They'? Her chest tightened until it throttled the breath in her throat.

Nor did the sight awaiting her in the mess hall resolve her trepidation, for while Saul was there, standing tense and alert against the wall, and Eddings, arms folded and face set... there were three more people, and one of them, Goddess and Lord, was the man she had sentenced to death for being a mind-mage in her short tenure as queen, the man who was now Theresa Eddings's husband and the world's Lord of War. Not only that, but Hirianthial Sarel Eddings Laisrathera had once been Hirianthial Sarel Jisiensire, the head of the House that had been razed by her out-of-control liegeman in an attempt to impress her into marrying him. If wedding Theresa Eddings had improved his temper, she couldn't see it in the cold sentinel brooding behind her other two visitors, and his eyes conveyed all the distrust that his impassive face was too well trained to reveal.

The Eldritch before and to one side of him was in an unfamiliar uniform, very smart, a white double-breasted tunic with silver braid and buttons and a looped sash from shoulder to opposite hip. It took her a moment to recognize him as Haladir Delen Galare, because she'd seen Haladir infrequently at court after his marriage to Thesali Nuera. Haladir was also—Goddess save her—the father of Sediryl Nuera, the empress's new heir and the woman the pirates wanted for themselves. In short, another man predisposed to dislike her.

That left the third attendee, and the third should have been the most alarming: a Chatcaavan male, his brown hide glossy like a dark bay stallion's. An impressive crest of horns framed his blunt face, one softened by the tumble of dark mane over a shoulder. His tunic implied some sort of shipboard activity; by now, Surela recognized the types of closures and boots favored by spacegoing crew. If she was not mistaken, his bright magenta eyes were more curious than predatory. Certainly he was less threatening than Hirianthial. A dragon could only kill her. A mind-mage with a grudge… who knew. She wouldn't, because he could ensure she would never remember.

"They wanted to hear it firsthand," Eddings said, and if Surela wasn't mistaken that was an apology. Before she could respond, however, Hirianthial spoke to someone past her shoulder.

"If you'll leave us?"

She'd forgotten what Hirianthial's voice sounded like. That clear, cultured baritone, like something out of a ballad. Saul's response, in his unremarkable tenor, sounded thin and scratchy in compare. But there was nothing in it that backed down, either. "Sorry, no."

Before a cordial fight could erupt, Eddings said, "He knows all of it already."

"He doesn't know what we'll discuss once we've heard it," Hirianthial said.

255

"Then we can discuss it elsewhere, if we feel it necessary." That was Haladir Delen. He, at least, appeared to be focused on the reason they were there and not past wrongs. "But let us put ourselves in possession of the facts first, Minister."

A very long pause, during which her wolfine keeper and the man she'd wronged stared at one another, had one another's measure. Then Hirianthial said, "Very well."

"Why don't we sit?" Eddings gestured toward the table. "I'll get a pitcher of water."

"Excellent notion," said the dragon. He drew out a chair and sat on it backwards, allowing his wings to swing free of the arms. "Let us hear about this glorious opportunity. For opportunity it is, isn't it, Eldritch lords? Bait for a trap!"

"That bait," said Haladir Delen, low, "is my daughter."

"One of the dangerous powers of your people, yes? Ha, even better. Sit. Let us learn something." The dragon turned his great glowing eyes on Surela. "Speak, Eldritch woman. I am curious. Tell us what our enemies desire."

Eddings, determinedly pouring glasses of water for everyone, said, "Yes. Tell them what you told me."

It was an admirable attempt on Eddings's part to make her claim on Surela, and therefore her protection, plain to those listening, so Surela honored it. "Yes, my lady." And forced herself to sit, and to begin speaking. Since addressing the dragon felt perilous, and the two Eldritch men impossible, she kept her chin up but her eyes lowered to the hands she folded on the table. For the third time, she related her encounter with the pirate, sparing herself nothing, not even the request she'd made for her particular Eldritch slave... for who knew if Hirianthial could not hear her thoughts, and know her to be adjusting the narrative to flatter herself?

"And that concluded the meeting," she said.

The silence was ugly, and ended when a chair scraped against the deck. Hirianthial had risen, and in his wake, the other Eldritch. They were nearly to the hatch when the Chatcaavan, his sinuous neck twisting to follow their progress, exclaimed, "You are not leaving? We haven't asked any questions!"

"She has told us what she knows," Haladir said, though he sounded uncertain. "Now we make plans. Is that not so, my lord?"

"It is," Hirianthial replied.

"How can you make plans without questioning the asset?" The Chatcaavan's wings were sagging, as if disbelief had robbed him of the power to maintain their posture. "This is a priceless intelligence windfall, and you are walking away from it? They want details from her, details we could feed them, to fool them!"

"Anything she knows and shares," Hirianthial said, "is compromised."

The dragon looked toward the other Eldritch, and Haladir flushed. "It is that she is a traitor, alet. She cannot be trusted."

Now that head swung back to her, and Surela found herself the object of the alien's regard. Given her single experience of a Chatcaavan prior to this, she expected that stare to disturb her... but nothing about this new dragon reminded her of the first, save in gross physiognomy. Her attacker, consumed with lust and frenzied with greed, had seemed an animal. She could not look into the magenta gaze now considering her and see a beast. "You," said the dragon. "Challenged your empress for her throne? Is this what they mean?"

"I... yes. I did."

"You fought her for her position and lost? And for this you were punished, presumably?"

Surela could sense the stares but dared not look away. "Exiled, yes."

"A mild punishment, but you have no horns, so who could strip them from you?" He studied her with interest before saying to Haladir, "She dared much, and you did not think her dangerous enough to kill outright. Why did you keep her, if not to put her to use?"

Haladir was as flummoxed by this as Surela felt, if his stammer was any indication. "I... beg your pardon?"

"She was sentenced to death," Hirianthial said, and his voice was cold. "But the sentence was commuted."

"So, you *were* deemed threatening." The dragon sounded approving. "Your ambitions were worthy ones, given the limited scope for power among your people. You failed, but supposedly this empress is a magician like Third, so it would have been shocking for you to succeed. And now, we could use you to prise information from these pirates—"

"She cannot be trusted," Hirianthial repeated. And at a quiet noise from Eddings, said, "On this I will not be gainsaid. The Empress gave me the duty of protecting the empire from its enemies. This woman gave them license, Theresa. She tore the Veil, brought pirates to our soil, oversaw the razing of Jisiensire."

"Impressive," the dragon murmured, eyes widening.

"You do not help your people's case," Haladir said to the dragon. "When you speak so of her crimes."

"You do not measure her as my people would," said the Chatcaavan. "Very well. Shall I use your values against you? Where did my Queen learn forgiveness if not from the lips of your ambassador?" He tapped his chest. "Here sits a traitor, in fact... who gave the Breath of the Living Air to pirates as a plaything. Do you understand this? My Queen, the consort of the Chatcaavan Emperor, was the avatar of change that my religion has been awaiting for thousands of years. And I... I handed her to freaks and thugs. From this hell she returned, and rather than condemn me, she gave me the opportunity to prove myself. I am here because of that chance." He tilted his head back toward Surela. "I too was an ambitious male. I sought the throne of the Chatcaavan Empire, which I assure you was a greater prize than your petty planetary fief. That is the way of things: males of power seek more power. This, my Queen knew of me. But she told me that if I wished power now, I would have to seek it her way. Here you find me." He peeled his lips back from his teeth and directed that expression at the two Eldritch men. "Will you send me away now that you know this history?"

The unease in the room had nothing to do with her now, and it was Eddings who forded into it. "I think he's right about the opportunity to learn more. If these pirates were connected with any of the pirates that have been problems for us before, we need to know."

"She can't be trusted," Hirianthial said.

"She could be," Haladir said, unexpectedly. "If she were to be tested. By a mind-mage."

The word exploded from her before she could cage it, and the only surprise was that it was spoken in unison with Hirianthial. "No."

"Not by you, my lord," Haladir said. "But you are not the sole mind-mage on Escutcheon." He eyed Surela. "Would you consent to the test from a different man? The high priest, perhaps."

Who was the high priest, now that Baniel was dead? And did the man who'd replaced him have a similar lack of scruples? Surely not, or Liolesa would not have instated him.

"Val's good people," Eddings said, and she sounded certain. "I'd trust him with you, Surela."

"Then we do this test," the dragon said. "Because lives will be lost if not. I will stress this, as it is important to you: if you do not make best use of this female, Eldritch will die who need not have died."

"We have enough ships—" Haladir began.

"You think you have enough ships," the dragon replied. "And you guess you'll be able to overwhelm whatever force attacks you. But why guess when you can know, to the last detail, how many ships will be sent against you? Their armament? Where they'll set their ambush? When? Why by the Living Air would you forgo the chance to learn these things? Send her back with false information to lure them into complacency! Arrange things so that we will be the hunters, and they the prey! To do elsewise, because an ambitious female did what the ambitious must?" The Chatcaavan shocked her completely by flipping to the Eldritch tongue and shading the words in the black mode for direst effect: "It is folly!"

In the stunned silence that followed, Eddings raised her gaze to Hirianthial. They were not a liegelady and a minister of war for a fleeting moment, but a wife and a husband. It was the latter who sighed, and with that sigh revealed the extent of his feelings for the human he'd married. "I will talk to the high priest."

"Excellent." The dragon thrust himself from the seat and mantled his wings before sliding them neatly behind his back. "I look forward to the blooding." He grinned at Surela with every evidence of camaraderie. "We shall hunt together, yes?"

She jerked her head in a nod, because to speak with Hirianthial looming was beyond her. Her relief when the three departed flooded her so powerfully that she started trembling.

"Sorry about that," Eddings said, refilling her glass. "Especially the dragon. I didn't know they were going to bring him, but he's the head of the visiting Chatcaavan forces and they've been teaching us everything they know." She looked toward the corridor. "He's not bad, for a Chatcaavan. Though I didn't know that about him betraying the Queen Ransomed."

"So now what?" Saul said from behind her. "What's the test they're talking about?"

"They will enter my mind, I imagine," Surela said, subdued. "And assess my loyalties thus."

"They'd do that to you?" Saul sounded so offended that

both she and Eddings looked toward him. "It's wrong," the Hinichi said. "Shoving your way into someone's heart. God hears our innermost thoughts because He can put them in context, and love us when we're at our worst and most vulnerable. No one born has that wisdom, except the one who died to save us."

Eddings's braids bunched over her shoulders as she leaned over the table and cupped her glass. "There was a time I would have agreed with you. Now... now I still don't know how I feel about it. But it's not my decision. It's yours, Surela. I don't know how they'll involve you, but it won't be safe. You don't have to get any deeper into it than you already are."

"And if I do not? They make plans, assuming the pirates will attack the procession, and presumably prevail, but at greater cost?"

"Probably, yes. Or maybe the dragons go with them, and the convoy will look too dangerous to take on."

"Then the pirates will withdraw," Surela said. "And we may never know their numbers, or when they next might strike."

"That... would be the size of it, yes."

"How could I do anything other than volunteer?" Surela said. "I will weather the high priest's evaluation. To prevent our people from falling into the hands of pirates. To perhaps end their threat completely. How could I not?"

Eddings looked over at her, tired. "It kills me how wrong they are about you."

"They are acting as they ought," Surela said. "I cannot blame them."

"I can," Saul said, and said no more.

CHAPTER 27

After such a shattering meeting, Surela was glad of the ship's empty halls and the prospect of a long evening alone. She spent it working through exercises assigned by Erynne on advanced shipboard maintenance; as with seemingly every topic she undertook, the basics could be covered quickly, and exploded outward into a vast constellation of more complex permutations that gave her to wonder how people with shorter lifespans became expert in anything.

She carried those studies to the fore of the ship the following morning, for while there was no need for watchstanding while docked, she appreciated the change in scenery. With everyone still at liberty, and Saul about his business, she had no expectation of visitors, which is how she came to nearly drop her mug at the curious and confident tenor that spoke from the hatch in Universal.

"So this is the famous *Earthrise* that carried Reese Eddings to the Eldritch homeworld."

There, without fanfare or announcement, was another Eldritch, underfed, too short, and with hair shorn like a child's around a pointed face. His clothing claimed him a peasant; his slovenly posture, a marked indifference to proprieties... and his eyes... were alive with mischief, like the youth he resembled but almost certainly wasn't. She had no idea who he should be, nor why he'd escorted himself aboard... nor indeed, why Saul hadn't stopped him or warned her.

That was when her heart skipped. "Goddess," she said, starting to rise. "Tell me you did not do aught to Saul Ferry's mind, or it will be the worst turn we could serve him."

The man paused, both brows jerking upward. "That matters?"

"He deserves just treatment, and believes mind-magery an offense against his god!"

"Interesting. But no, I didn't do anything to him." Surela began to relax, halted when the stranger grinned. "Hirianthial, now... is having a talk with him. I'm sure he's enjoying that."

"No!"

"Don't fear, it's nothing too strenuous. We'll just say your guard dog's rush to defend you has made him wonder if you suborned him with *your* mind powers."

"My... my... Goddess, no! I have no such ability, thank you kindly!"

"I see that you don't." He dropped into the pilot's seat and spun it to face her before propping a boot on the console. "A very comfortable ship. Do you like her? They call ships 'her', you know. Humans do, anyway, and Reese is human."

Slowly, Surela sank back onto her chair. "So this is my test. High Priest, you need not delay. I am certain you have many demands on your time."

He waved a hand idly. "Nothing more pressing at the moment. Not even slightly. You will object to the characterization, but how can you? I'm the high priest, and you are a wayward soul." Was he serious? She couldn't tell. As she strove not to stare, he finished, "Drink your coffee. It is coffee, isn't it? Shocking! Not a very Eldritch drink."

"No," she stammered. "But it was a thing shared during the war. There are associations."

"Ah? Interesting." He let his boot drop from the console and leaned forward. "I was there, you know, while you were sitting—briefly—on Liolesa's pillow. In fact, Baniel nearly killed me. His lackeys tossed me out with all the other bodies, in a big pile on the back lawn." He grinned, showing teeth. "If it hadn't been for Reese's tiger girl, I might have finished expiring there, buried under the rotting corpses."

Surela flushed. "It was never my intention."

"I know," he said, disarming her. "You aren't a killer, Surela once-Silin Asaniefa."

"But I did. I killed the Chatcaavan—"

"A cornered animal gives no quarter," the high priest said. He tossed her something, and startled, she caught it with her free hand. "Nicely done. Recognize it?"

She opened her fingers, but knew before her eyes lit on the medallion what she would see. She'd worn it for so many years its contours were familiar to her palm, from its smooth surface to the little imperfection in the curve of the top right corner, the one that caught on whatever fabric it rested against. Surela swallowed, facing the House token that had once proclaimed her the head of the second largest political faction on Escutcheon: on its vert lozenge, a centi-core salient in electrum. "This is the medallion I gave Theresa, so that she might command those who looked to me."

"What's on the back?"

She didn't have to look to know. "A shield."

"Your personal emblem, isn't it. Why'd you pick it?"

Her cheeks heated. Was it necessary to drag the past out for examination? Was this worse or better than submitting to a direct reading of her mind? "Because the head of the House stands between her people and what would trouble their peace."

The high priest nodded. "Liolesa's personal emblem's a sword. Why do you think so?"

"You ask me to guess at the mind of the empress?"

"You very lately thought you could be queen, so why not?"

Surela looked away before she could snap a response, and her eyes snagged, inevitably, on the display, where she'd been studying engine schematics and shutdown routines. "It would seem to be obvious. Liolesa has known for longer than we have been denying the importance of the outworld that our enemies would attack us, and that we were vulnerable. She has been planning for it: to become useful and necessary to the Alliance, so they might aid us until we can defend ourselves."

He nodded. "That bother you?"

"That we should be defended by aliens? I much prefer it than to become their slaves."

For a long moment, he studied her face, and if he was using his powers to probe her thoughts she sensed no evidence. And then… he smirked. "Did you really tell pirates you wanted Hirianthial for a personal toy?"

"I thought it would convince them I had a weakness they could exploit to control me."

He laughed, shaking his head so that the edges of his hair swung around his sharp chin. "You really are something, you know that? Too smart for your own good. Obviously, because your smarts landed you here, and it didn't serve your good. Maybe. The Lord and Lady working, as they do, in mysterious ways. Here's the real question, Surela, child of the Goddess and God… would it be worth your life to save the Eldritch?" He held up a hand. "Before you give me a glib answer from the catechism, let me paint you a picture." His eyes no longer seemed merry or mischievous. They saw into her too well. "You, in a barren cell that looks like your cabin, but with nothing in it, and a quarter the size. With your clothes ripped from you, and your body covered in bruises and scratches and some man's spend dripping down your leg. One of your eyes is swollen shut from a punch, and the sharp bright pain when you breathe too deeply is probably a broken rib. And you know, intimately, that in the next hours, they're going to put a palmer to your temple and trigger it, and you'll die... impossibly far from home, disgraced, in pain, and alone. Would you die like that, to save Sediryl Galare, a maiden you barely remember, who will one day succeed to the role you wanted for yourself?" He lifted his brows. "You remember what it was like. To be a prisoner. I see it behind your eyes. Would you risk it again for the people who exiled you and the empress who preferred you dead?"

Her body tried to choke, not on her revulsion, but on her desperate need to reply. "Yes. Goddess, yes. To save *anyone* from that, yes."

"Even your worst enemy?" His eyes grew sly. "Would it bother you, truly, if someone were to lay Liolesa low? She could use the humbling, couldn't she?"

"No one deserves that humbling, and I will not distract the woman while she is busy being the shield I could not be in my useless and laughably short tenure as queen. What do you think I am? A villain of Baniel's cut? Goddess! I wanted us only to be left alone! And what a naïve wish that was, for without the power to enforce our desires, we are prey to everyone who disagrees over whether we should have that privilege or not!" She shook her head, set the medallion on the console between them. "You want to know if I am comfortable being Liolesa's pawn? I only regret that I am not a more powerful piece in the game she is playing to ensure our survival. I miss my home, and I miss my family, and I miss my daughter—" Her voice cracked. "I try not to think, daily, that I can never smell the breeze off the coast, or hear the night loons, or wake to a summer morning in Silin Manor. I have lost everything that mattered to me. But to steal that from every other Eldritch out of pique… I could never. If I knew I had had a hand in the destruction of Escutcheon and our people, for true, then truly I would have no reason to wake again." She stopped short, her breath coming too hard.

He plucked up the medallion, studied it, and tucked it back into his robes as he rose. "That was all I needed to know."

Mastering herself, Surela said, "And will you tell them that I am an adequate tool for the task?"

"No," he said. "Because I'm a priest first, and everything else after. You don't want to distract Liolesa while she's working? Laudable. I don't want to distract the God and Goddess while they're about their business either." Another mercurial mood shift, accompanied by a smirk. "But don't worry. The right people will like my report, and the ones who won't will do the expedient thing despite their feelings." He nodded toward her mug. "Drink, it'll make you feel better."

And then he was gone, leaving her stunned and trembling. Following his advice did steady her nerves, but not enough to decide what she thought of the man Liolesa had set in the position of the highest of the male clergy on the planet. She was still struggling when Saul stepped into the fore of the ship, and then she did stand. "Are you well? It did not go hard with you?"

Her minder looked tired, but not discouraged. "No." A slight smile. "Hirianthial and I have some history. It needed to be put to bed."

"You… knew him?"

"We met on Kerayle." Saul eased into the seat vacated by the high priest. "He ran into trouble there, and I admit, he deserves to dislike his memories of the colony. I was the administrator's assistant at the time. I think… he thinks I have a habit of choosing bad people to help."

Surela suppressed the urge to sigh. "He warned you off me, I presume."

"He did, yes. Which is ridiculous, because I told him I knew your history. He wanted to know if I really understood it so I had to prove to his satisfaction that I did." He looked up, and there was the simmering anger again. "They lured me off the ship, didn't they. So you'd be alone when they sprang the mind-reader on you."

"It appears that way. But... the high priest did not use his powers on me. I don't think. He merely..." What? "Interviewed me. Rigorously."

That drew a hesitant smile from him. "Rigorously."

"His methods were... unexpected." She considered. "Effective, however. But not predictable. He is on no one's leash but his own."

"So will they do it? Involve us?"

She paused.

"You know it will have to be 'us.' There's no not telling Ra'aila, at very least."

And her keeper would no longer be content to allow her to roam unattended, she suspected, and couldn't blame him. She would welcome the guarding. "I do know, yes. And... I think so." A pause. "It is not what I wished for us. But the dragon was... not wrong. It is... satisfying. When one contemplates the matter as an actor, rather than as the one acted upon."

"Then we'll do everything we have to do to make sure they give us the tools to turn it into a hunt, not a trap where you're the expendable bait. I trust Reese, and I think she'll look out for you. I'm not sure about everyone else."

Surela thought of the whimsy in the high priest's eyes, and the unexpected adamant of his faith. "I am sure of at least one of them, and I think he counts for more than we might expect."

———

"There was a debate about what to do next," Eddings began.

"We won." A second human, male, slid onto a chair in much the same way the dragon had the previous day, with every evidence of relaxation. Behind him was a woman Surela no longer needed to consult a guide to recognize as one of the Karaka'A, the short felinesque race. A charming-looking individual, that one, calico-patterned with earnest hazel eyes. "Is that a coffee carafe?"

"I'll get mugs," Ra'aila said from the door, "if someone will tell me what in the blistering stillness is going on. We're here, as usual, delivering cargo, as usual, and suddenly my ship is crawling with strangers, most of them scowling, dangerous types. Reese? What's going on?"

"I'm afraid you've been recruited for an operation in much the same way I got recruited for an operation back when I was running this ship." At the Aera's arch expression, Eddings said, "You told me once that risk was interesting?"

"You didn't say you were hiring me for operations of the type I think you're suggesting. You especially didn't say you were hiring me for operations on ships that have all of one working laser on them for clearing debris."

"You have a duster?" Eddings offered.

"So I can run *away* from danger. Am I running into it?"

"No," said the Karaka'An female firmly. "All you'll be doing is driving to Starbase Psi, same as you always do. This time you'll be ferrying two contractors who needed to swing by civilization to pick up some supplies for their work on Escutcheon. Since you were the first ship heading out that way, we booked a cabin. Paying passengers, you know. Nothing could be more innocuous."

Surela was not the only one skeptical of either of these two being taken for normal passengers. Ra'aila's ears were still flattened. "What will you actually be doing, since you're obviously not innocent civilians?"

"I wonder that too," Saul said.

Eddings cleared her throat. "Aletsen, these two are Montie Dawson and Mina Brown. They really are contractors—"

"This should be good," Raila'a said.

"—on loan to the Eldritch Navy. Intelligence types."

The Aera raised her eyes and appeared to take several long breaths before continuing. "Why am I carrying spies to Starbase Psi?"

"Because," Surela said, "a pirate has attempted to recruit me for an attempt to ambush the heir's procession to the colony, and I am—I believe?" She glanced at Eddings, who nodded. "Going to involve myself with them in some fashion that will allow the Eldritch Navy to turn their ambush against them."

"More specifically," said the Karaka'An, Brown, "you'll make contact with the pirate and divulge the information we want them to know, and then leave the rest of it to us. All you need to do, Captain, is deliver your passengers to the star-base, and once we're there we'll do our thing."

"You're making it sound simple and I bet it won't be," Ra'aila said.

"You won't be involved with those parts."

"Probably," Dawson murmured.

"How did I not know that pirates were sniffing around our heels?" Ra'aila asked Saul. "Did you know?"

"I did, yes."

Ra'aila paused while she evaluated that piece of information. "You're good with what they're planning?"

"As far as I know."

The Aera looked from Eddings to Saul, then stood up. "I suppose it's no worse than getting shot at with arrows every few weeks, which is where I was at when you hired me. Let me know what you need me to do when you're done here. I'm guessing the less I know, the better."

"That would be best," Dawson agreed.

Ra'aila eyed them, then left. After, Surela noted, distributing the coffee mugs and taking one for herself. Eddings watched her go, then turned back to Surela. "Last chance to say no. I mean that."

"Alet—" No, that was too mortal for either of them. This was not a request from a foreigner to an Eldritch, and she could not answer as an Eldritch to an alien. "Lady Eddings. I must do this."

Eddings searched her eyes, relented. "Fine. But don't call me Lady Eddings. It's Reese. Or Theresa, if you want to do the Eldritch mania for multiple names. We're... doing the Eldritch mania for multiple names, aren't we."

"What's this about a mania for multiple names?" Brown asked, calico ears perking.

"I'll explain later. Surela?"

"Tell me what I am to tell the pirates."

Brown nodded. "All right. We'll lay it out, and rehearse until you can sell it in your sleep. But we want to be clear about this: you hand over the intel and then you're done. Your captain's right about that much: this isn't going to be simple, and we need your involvement to be minimal. This is what Montie and I do, and what your empress hired us for. Let us do our jobs."

"I would not dream otherwise," Surela said.

CHAPTER 28

Two days out from Escutcheon, Leo plopped himself across from Surela in the mess. "I want in."

She heard Saul setting his tablet down at the head of the table, but didn't consult her keeper for his opinion. "I beg to understand your mind... is this some new adventure you are about to advance to me?"

For once, the purser sounded serious—almost angry. "No. I want in on whatever's making Ra'aila unhappy, and you quiet, and those two military types involved. Don't try to sell them to me as 'agronomists,' alet, those people are farmers like I'm a virgin."

Had Surela not known Dawson and Brown's true profession, she would have been convinced by their guises. "How...?"

The leonine's ears slicked back. "The way they look at one another."

This drew Saul from his silence. "They look at one another like people who know one another."

"No they don't," Leo said. "They look like people who've been in tough places together. And when you get a fit-looking human paired with one of us Pelted, looking at one another like that, it's military."

"Well, damn," Saul said. "That's a good guess."

"And I'm right, and I know I'm right, and I want in, so what's going on? Or should I keep guessing? Slavers, isn't it? It's always slavers with Eldritch."

"I fear I may have underestimated you," Surela said slowly.

Leo blew out a breath. "Of course you did. Everyone does the same thing with us. Harat-Shar, sex-crazed party animals. No self-control. It's fine, we really are that way. That doesn't mean it's the only thing we are."

This, for some reason, provoked a bark of laughter from Saul. When they glanced at him, he said, "I went to Kerayle to escape my own species stereotype."

"Oh, right." Leo nodded. "Steadfast, religious sticks-in-the-mud. But good to have at your back in a crisis. Right?"

"Right."

"And you actually are steadfast, religious, and good to have in a crisis. And I'm actually a sex-crazed party animal. But not stupid."

"Whereas I probably am a stick-in-the-mud," Saul said, amused.

Surela interrupted. "And I am high-handed, mysterious, and supercilious. But Leo, we are hoping there is little to participate in. I have a part to play for but a single scene, and then I am quit of the stage."

"So, take me with you."

"Now that would be dangerous," Saul said.

"I bet you're going."

Saul's ears dipped.

"You are not!" Surela exclaimed, urgently. "They would surely know you for what you are."

"Your bodyguard," Leo agreed, and held up his hands.

"Don't look at me that way. If you'd wanted to hide it, you should have done better. It's obvious to anyone with eyes."

"You must not," Surela said to Saul.

Saul toyed with the handle of his mug. Ceasing, he said, "Don't ask me not to."

"There, see," Leo said. "You won't be able to stop him, so you might as well bring me along. So where are we going and what are we doing?"

———

"No," Brown said when Surela brought the request to the twain in their cabin. "Absolutely not. You show up to that rendezvous with backup and they'll—"

"Be completely unsurprised," Dawson said. "In fact, it might make them more suspicious if you show up alone. A woman who's trying to carry off 'I want to rule a planet' should be arrogant."

"It puts them in danger," Brown said to Dawson.

Dawson studied Surela. "They volunteered?"

"I fear greatly that if I forbid them, they will follow me without permission."

To the Karaka'An, Dawson said, "You have to work with reality, not with what you wish reality would be."

"We're supposed to be imposing our will on reality, remember?"

Dawson held Surela's eyes as he replied to his partner. "That only goes so far, though. And when it stops, you have to adapt."

Surela answered what she saw in his face. "Shall I send them to you for instruction?"

"Do that," he said. "And you come too. If you're going to have muscle, you're going to need to act like someone who hired them."

———

After that, it was Danica. The first mate bearded Surela in her cabin. "Don't try to tell me there's nothing going on," she said. "Between you, Leo, and Saul spending all this time with the passengers and Ra'aila putting on a stoic face like something out of a 3deo movie, it doesn't take a genius."

"Alet—"

"Rel. Just tell me. Ignorance kills."

That spurred Surela's heart, because it was inarguable.

Hearing this fresh news, Brown threw up her hands. "Operational security's blown all to hell. We might as well tell the whole ship at this point!"

"Not a bad idea," Dawson said. At the woman's fulminating stare, he continued, unruffled, "Half of them know about it, and it's too small a crew for the secret to keep. We fold them all in, we have a chance of getting them to behave."

"Goddess," Surela said. "I wish you luck of that."

———

The silence after Brown explained their errand was... illuminating. Surela had expected the news to daunt the remainder of the crew, but around her she saw only signs of resolution, even in Prudence, the gentlest of their number, and Meri, the most timid. It was the latter who said, "So, how are we helping?"

"We're not helping," Raila'a said. "At least, not any further than delivering the people who are involved in this to Starbase Psi."

"That's definitely a lie," Meri said. "Because if I'm hearing this story correctly, these people are surveilling us. And possibly have a grudge against the ship."

"They have a grudge against Reese," Ra'aila said dryly. "We're just collateral damage."

"You're not going to be damaged," Brown hastened to add. "Your captain is materially correct: you're bystanders. No one is going to start shooting you because you were employing an Eldritch turncoat."

Surela did not flinch solely because hundreds of years of practice overrode a bare two years of life among more demonstrative offworlders.

"You're going to need a healer," Prudence said confidently. "These things always go sideways, and then someone ends up in a clinic. I'll have to pick up some extra supplies, but I was going to resupply this time anyway so it shouldn't look strange."

"You're not going to need to furnish your clinic," Brown insisted.

"We should dig into the duster," Danica said to Erynne. "We've never fired it up, we should make sure it'll work when we need it."

"Without actually turning it on, because that would warn people. We have to assume if they're watching the crew's movements, they're also keeping an eye on the ship." Erynne tapped her chin. "That'll be a challenge. We can run simulations all day but it's hard to check the hardware without lighting it up. But there's the power generation module and the field generation module, maybe if we turn them on independently...."

"Wouldn't that create a strange energy signature?" Meri interrupted.

Brown raised her hands. "You're not going to need the duster!"

"Because we're going to try to present ourselves as pirate recruits?" Leo asked brightly.

"Because you're not going to be involved!"

The *Earthrise* crew stared at their guest for several moments after this outburst. Then Danica said to Ra'aila, "I think we should look into a serious halo shield install. The duster gets us over halfway there as it is… it shouldn't be too much of a drain on resources."

"Let them game it out," Dawson said to his partner.

Brown grasped blindly for her chair. "They're not going to get involved."

"Reese had a long talk with me before we left," Ra'aila said. "She told me she got a civilian citation for the work she did for Fleet on this ship." The Aera pointed down at the deck. "This very ship. This one."

"Did she really?" Erynne asked. "I had no idea the *Earthrise* had such an exciting history!"

Brown covered her face with a hand. "It's like the ship is jinxed."

Her partner smacked her lightly on the arm. "You don't say that on a vessel underway."

"We're not jinxed, we're blessed," Meri said, causing everyone to pause and stare at her. The felid's face was stern. "You think I'm joking? Pirates tore up the Alliance border during the war. Then they showed up and picked at all the pieces the Chatcaava left behind. You want to tell me we're not lucky for having a chance to shut them down? Anywhere? If you two are right, we could make space safer, not just for us, but for everyone in the quadrant. I'll take it."

Saul, who had been conspicuously silent through the discussion, said nothing, but Surela glimpsed his brows rising.

Dawson stretched and slid his elbows onto the table. "I don't anticipate any of you having to do anything in the op, but it doesn't hurt to be prepared. Tell me what you're good at, we'll see if we can use it, and how."

Surela excused herself not long into that session, and Saul followed her. In the corridor, she said, "Is he correct?"

"That they're not going to be part of it?" Saul shook his head. "I'm not Fleet, and I'm certainly not whatever he is, which is something over and above that. I'm sure getting the crew involved is not his Plan A, but someone like that is going to have a Plan B through Z."

"He will use them, if he must, to accomplish the goal."

Saul glanced at her. "They're not being used, Rel. They're volunteering. Remember that, if the guilt gets too heavy to carry."

"I don't—" She halted, cheeks tinting.

Her wolf nodded. "See you at dinner." A grin. "Bet they'll still be talking."

CHAPTER 29

"Y ou go, you say your piece, you get out," Brown said, wedging a bead into Surela's collar so small it was lost against the stitching. "Just remember what we practiced."

"I shall."

"And the two of you, too."

"We'll be *extremely* convincing," Leo promised with a sashay that displayed his outfit to advantage, for he'd dressed the part of a pampered pet in something more hole than fabric. Saul, who was the fixed point of the purser's rotation, remained motionless, but Surela could read patient amusement in the relaxation of his shoulders.

"Bast and An willing, you'll be done before the day's out. The rest you get to leave to us."

"Goddess willing," Surela agreed.

"Move out," Brown said to the two men, who complied as their natures dictated: Leo with a swagger, Saul striding, tail behind him low. Surela watched them descend the ramp, waiting for Brown to finish with the pin that would passively record everything that transpired. With the moment at hand at last, some part of her suspired into a strange calm. Eddings had told her once that to suicide before she'd attempted amends for her acts was the choice of a coward. Dying now, while working to curb an attack on her people, was manifestly not pusillanimity.

Brown stepped back. "Good to go." She raked Surela with a glance, nodded. "You look the part."

Of what? The traitor? Inhaling, Surela stepped toward the ramp, only to be arrested by a hand wrapped around her arm... a hand, and the mind behind it, so complete a blank that she could only envision steel vaults. Dawson was shorter than her but his height didn't signify as he looked up into her face. "You need to make these people believe you're on their side. No matter what. And do what it takes to stay mobile— the moment they pin you down, your chance of survival plummets."

Startled, Surela could only stare into his eyes: such an unprepossessing brown, even less memorable than Saul's. How would she have described them? Not by their color, certainly. Their implacability. He was hard the way the pirate was hard, and that frightened her, because she knew neither she nor Saul nor Leo were. How would they manage?

Dawson's thumb pressed slightly against her arm. "Understood?"

"Yes," Surela answered.

He stepped back. "Godspeed, then."

Relieving her dry mouth would have entailed swallowing, and that would have revealed her unease. She sailed past the twain and down the ramp, where her two furred minions fell in behind her. And so she would have to think of them, for however long it took to be quit of the pirate. She must be Surela Silin Asaniefa, who had vowed revenge on her enemies and still thirsted for a throne. It surprised her how difficult it was to remember how to be that person again... particularly having realized that while she was prepared to die for the Eldritch, she was not prepared to sacrifice the two Pelted quite as easily.

———

That the pirate was awaiting her at the café was surely a test —would she approach of her own volition, or did she have to be corralled? Surela strode to his table and pulled out the chair with a jerk of her hand, for the head of House Asaniefa would have been galled to be forced to attend to her own seating like a peasant. Lighting on the edge of the chair, she folded her hands on her knee and looked down on the human male with an ever-so-slight sneer. She had mastered the look long ago to depress the pretensions of her various relations; in many ways, it was an easier expression than the careful amiability she'd adopted with the *Earthrise* crew. "You are punctual," she said.

"And you brought muscle." The human sipped his wine. "You didn't need to send them in early and to different tables. It's not as if we would have missed them."

"I did not send them in early and to different tables to hide them from you," Surela said disdainfully. "I did so, so that I need not be close to them." Remembering Leo's role, she added, "Though the yellow one is… acceptably servile."

The man laughed. "So the high and mighty Eldritch keeps pets."

"I thought I did say I wanted the minister of war for one."

"You did, but that's a vendetta, yes? Liking the furries is more in the way of a perversion."

"I suppose if one conceived of them as people."

He studied her over the rim of his glass. "You came back angry, did you."

Be the woman she'd been. Surela allowed that woman's outrage to bleed into her eyes. "They have made over my world in a false image, clasped its succession in the arms of deviants, and summoned dragons to oversee its protection—dragons! You speak of perversion? They allow the shapechangers license on the surface of my homeworld. They give land to dragon-whores!"

His brow cocked. "Sounds like you learned some useful things."

"I have a cousin who escaped their culling," Surela said, wondering if Edorinassa had. "We spoke at length." She allowed her gaze to move to the wine and back to his face. "I believe it is your turn to buy."

He laughed. "'Peasant'?" He waved a hand to summon the waiter. "No, don't give me that look. I don't expect you to respect me. Yet."

After she'd been given her own glass, the pirate said, "So. What do you know?"

"My compensation?"

He rolled a wand across the table. "Check it."

Brown had shown her several options for this clandestine payment, and the wand had been the least likely. "It's the most expensive choice, and the most secure," the Karaka'An had said. "A valid wand will be clear. Unlike data transferred other ways, the wand will be the security code; you'd insert it in a reader to unlock the funds or vault. If one shows up, don't question it. Act like you expected him to give you the best."

"Don't be vulgar," Surela said now, sliding the wand into a pouch.

He watched. "Honor among thieves? Really?"

"We are about more ambitious aims than mere brigandage. Are we not?" She paused, arch.

"I suppose we are." He lifted his glass. "To a productive association."

She tapped her glass against his, deploring even this false camaraderie, and allowing her distaste to fuel her deception. "Indeed. So then. Their military is, as you presume, a sham.

Ten vessels, but only three fully crewed, and those mostly aliens. All ten will be accompanying the false heir's ship, and they are leaving in a week and a half."

"Is the 'false heir' an actual decoy or are you expressing a personal opinion?"

Surela sighed. "The latter. They are sending Liolesa's pathetic creature, and her puling husband, and some assortment of aliens and sycophants seeking to curry favor with the monarch. The heir will not be on the flagship, however, which has some sort of…" Surela allowed a languid wave of a wrist. "Issue. With its 'readiness.' She will be on the *Corel*, which will also be the best crewed vessel."

"Interesting. And how exactly did you find all this out?"

"That cousin," Surela said, "thought she would need to flee, and cultivated several disaffected males."

"Several of them?" He sounded amused.

Surela allowed her voice to chill. "They were bred to serve us."

"Of course they were. So did this cousin of yours find out anything else?"

"You must plan for the dragons," Surela said. "They have their own errands in the system, and nothing I learned could tell me what those errands were. But they bore easily, and are restless. Unless they are distracted, chances are good they will accompany the others, and swell their numbers by another ten vessels."

"Interesting. Carriers, I'm guessing?"

"I was not able to ascertain."

"I don't guess you were." The pirate sounded pensive now. "Are they typical dragons?" At her tilted head, he clarified, "Do they like plunder? Slaves? They're hanging around your homeworld… either they're lying about their interests, or they're not interested in the usual Chatcaavan things. Which is it?"

"I hardly believe they have changed their natures," Surela

said. "Did they not lie at the Alliance's treaty tables to lure the creatures into complacency? No doubt they have done it again to end the war on their terms. This is more of the same... what else, with such a prize awaiting them?"

"This might be hard to believe, but a single world isn't much of a prize to people with hundreds."

"My world," Surela said icily, "is not valued solely based on its size."

"Maybe not... but forgive me, princess—" A mocking half-bow from his seat. "Your world couldn't stop a single Chatcaavan squadron from capturing it. They must be playing some other game."

She gritted her teeth. "I have no doubt that they are. And I am no princess."

"Maybe not, but you're not a queen either. Yet." He grinned that corpse-grin again, the one that didn't warm his pale eyes. "But we'll fix that, and then we'll see what the Eldritch can do for us. Yes?"

"I am anticipating a mutually beneficial relationship."

"So am I. Did you learn anything else?"

"There are tiresome rumors that the false heir is capable of some sort of mind-magery," Surela said, embarking delicately on the road the two operatives had suggested might provoke a revelation. "I don't suppose our benefactor said anything more about it."

He smiled faintly. "Don't trust her, do you."

So, a woman. "No more, I suspect, than she trusts me."

"What are you planning to do with her? She insists she's going to be queen."

Surela laughed. "I'm sure she does."

"Is she lying about her credentials? I was curious."

Eddings had told her not to endanger herself in an attempt to uncover the identity of their traitor, but it had been obvious they'd wanted to know. And now... they would. A credentialed traitor who claimed she would be queen could only be the displaced heir to the throne, the one tussling with Liolesa's current choice. That displaced heir had been captured by Chatcaava and rescued from one of their harems, and once upon a time, she would have been Surela's natural ally in the fight against embracing outworlders. But not even Surela's wildest imaginings could conjure a scenario where a woman once trusted by Liolesa with the future of the Eldritch could willingly invite slavers to predate on their people. Surela hid the rising of her gorge with a sip of the wine. "She is not lying, no. But it matters not a whit. Not in the end." How much to reveal? "She met the dragons and was laid low. I met them and lived to plan their end."

"No fear, is that it?"

Surela said, "It will go better between us if you cease to try my patience with these tests."

He laughed. "Will it."

"My goodwill is a useful thing."

"More useful than all my weapons and ships?"

Goddess. What to say? To trade on the Eldritch mystique —would it work? "There is wealth on my world that will unlock solely to those with the proper blood." She considered him. "The mutually beneficial relationship we have been contemplating would avail us more."

"I'm glad you think so." He rose. "Let's go, princess—or, sorry. I can't call you queen, since you aren't one yet. Duchess, then."

"I beg your pardon?"

His smile was once again the monstrous one. "We're starting our mutually beneficial relationship by heading to my fleet. Together. Don't worry, we're bringing your pets." At the distant tables where Leo and Saul had taken position were new men, standing there with equally ghoulish smiles. "I wouldn't want you to have to cut your own food, after all."

If she objected... she couldn't, could she? To say the *Earth-rise* crew would demand an accounting of her absence would paint them as her companions, and make targets of them. If she declined, would he decide she needed killing? Brown and Dawson were purportedly loose on the starbase, but there was no guaranteeing they would be able to protect her. Or be willing, for they'd made their mission clear: their priority was stopping the ambush, with a secondary objective of identifying the traitors who'd summoned the pirates to the attack. If saving her imperiled either objective, they would let her die.

Her silence had drawn on too long. "I admit," she said, "I had not believed you would trust me so readily."

"I don't. But having you at hand and surrounded by my people takes care of that problem." He chuckled. "You understand."

"And yet... you give me this priceless opportunity," she continued, her mind racing as she considered and discarded ways to play the role. "To see your operations. And to win your trust."

"Is that what it is? An opportunity?"

"What else?" She rose slowly. "My enemies have long held against my throat the threat of war vessels."

"And my fleet isn't yours."

"No. But we might pursue that... productive... association."

He laughed. "Don't think you can seduce me, duchess. I don't sleep with business partners."

"That you consider me such greatly intrigues." She pushed in her chair. "We might go far together."

"Maybe." He studied her. "I admit, you've surprised me already. Our benefactor made you sound stupid."

Surela laughed. "What else?"

He grinned back, and this one almost reached his eyes. "Jealousy, is it?"

"She is four hundred years my junior and feels it."

That shut down the glib façade. "Ah. Yes. I forget how

long you people live. But you die just as easily as the rest of us, don't you."

"Yes, thankfully," Surela said. "For I have many enemies I wish to serve a taste of their deserts."

He shook his head. "Let's get going, shall we?" He gestured. "After you, duchess."

That she was walking very probably to her end made a great many things easy. She straightened the folds of her tunic and made much of tidying the fit along her shoulders and collar. The underside of her nail caught on the bead, as she hoped it would, and a careless flick liberated it from her throat. Leaving without it would make her confederates' lives much more difficult, but not as difficult as their lives would be if she was discovered with it. If she was fortunate, Dawson and Brown would recover it, and the information about their betrayer would return to Eddings. That… that would already be enough.

As the others herded Leo and Saul in her wake, Surela forced herself not to glance behind her. To betray any interest in them would spell their doom, and the pirates would never allow them to go free, assuming that they would warn someone of her abduction. Correctly.

"So," she said. "What shall I call you?"

He chuckled. "Oh… I named you. It seems fair to return the favor."

So many traps. "Then I shall call you Basilisk."

"Aren't those chickens with scales?"

She sniffed. "Hardly. They are the most dangerous predators on my planet."

"I choose to be mollified." He offered his arm. "My lady."

Did he know about the Eldritch ability to sense emotions through touch? From the malice in his eyes, he did, and did not fear her. Surela wanted not at all to sample his emotional state, but she had borne worse when beaten by her captors. She twined her arm with his, and accepted the evidence of

her finer senses, which reported nothing new. He was dangerous, and calculating, and cold: there would be no inspiring
him to intemperate urges. Her virtue was safe with him, but
the same lack of interest that protected her also deprived her
of the ability to use her body against him. Would she have?
She thought she might.

A match of minds, then. She would have to hope she was
as smart as she'd believed, deposing Liolesa, and that she'd
learned the lessons Baniel had tortured her to teach.

CHAPTER 30

Basilisk did not guide her to some disreputable vessel in the port, as Surela expected. Rather, she found herself at the ramp leading into: "A passenger liner?"

"A nice one, at that." He smiled. "Don't worry, duchess, I was able to get us the best suite. We'll be very comfortable together."

She kept tight rein on her reaction. "And my servants?"

"Naturally, in the same suite, so you can enjoy their company. And mine. We're a big happy party, you know... heading to a conference on Allegresse. A private conference. Ah, thank you, boys." He smiled at the looming ruffians who'd accompanied them. "They have our luggage in hand, dear, so you don't have to worry about a thing."

"Whyever would I worry?" Surela said.

"Don't be that way. We started out so honest with one another, after all."

She glanced at him, narrowed her eyes. "Very well—dear —we shall say that I am disappointed in the accommodations. I expected something less pedestrian."

"Now, now… you haven't even seen the suite."

The suite was, Surela supposed, palatial for a vessel, composed as it was of a drawing room, two bedrooms, and a bathing chamber. She carefully did not meet the eyes of her companions as they were prodded into one of the cabins, electing to have a turn around the reception area. "I suppose it will do. Though I was hoping to sample your hospitality."

He laughed. "You thought we'd show up at the starbase in one of our ships?"

"I did not assume you would have ships that registered as obviously illegal," Surela said breezily. "Or am I incorrect?" When he paused, she said, "We have started out so honest with one another, have we not?"

"Let's just say," Basilisk replied, watching her like one of those monsters must have its prey, "layers of security are preferable." He nodded toward his lackeys. "Check them, and her. Separate rooms."

When one of them advanced on her, Surela raised her chin. "You will not touch me."

"They'll do a lot more than touch you, duchess." A monster's smile. "We need to check you for devices."

Calmly, Surela reached toward her ear and prised the telegem loose. Then she bent to her boot and pulled her dagger free, inspiring oaths from both the thugs. She ignored them and offered both device and weapon on a palm. "Shall we continue with the honesty?"

He eyed the dagger. "Somehow I didn't think of you as quite so hands-on, duchess."

"Do you travel unarmed?"

The pirate plucked both telegem and dagger from her hand. "I don't, no. Forgive me if I insist on the full search. Just in case you're hiding any other interesting surprises."

Surela eyed the brute hovering near her. "Then I will allow you to have the testing."

"I'm sorry?"

"You are about to strip me, is that it? To seek other devices? Then I am expressing a preference."

He snorted. "Don't think you can seduce me, duchess. I'm not into pasteheads."

Goddess, what a horrendous slur. "Excellent. I have nothing to fear from you, then, do I?"

For a long moment he stared into her eyes, his own narrowed, as if seeking any sign of a trap. Finally, he waved a hand toward his minions. "Take the others. I'll handle her. Though you're going to regret it. I'm not going to be less thorough than my people would have been."

"I would expect not."

Another long pause. Then he shook his head. "Fine. Start stripping."

She did not dare glance at Leo and Saul as they were pulled away. How long would she have to disavow their relationship? What would be better, to demand their company, or to make peace with the separation? Perhaps parted, they would have more of a chance to escape? Surely they could escape from a civilian liner. There would have to be an opportunity when they disembarked at this Allegresse.

Until then… she waited for the doors to slide into their pockets, then began pulling off her tunic. Obvious attempts at enticement would not move him, she judged. But her goal was not to seduce him. Her goal was to create a bond between them that was not shared by others. When he thought of her, she wanted him to picture himself facing her, not his menials. To begin to link himself with her, and so associate her with power.

After the tunic, she sat on the coffee table to begin on her boots, without rushing. If she pretended she was with Thaniet… yes. What would Thaniet have thought of this conveyance? Would she have enjoyed traveling the alien worlds in Surela's company? How good it would have been, to experience the wonders of the Alliance with someone she loved.

"You're calm."

"I have no reason to be concerned." Alien footwear was so much easier to remove than Eldritch riding boots. Surela peeled off her stocking. "You are seeking evidence of duplicity and betrayal. I have already given you the one piece of technology attached to my person, and the sole weapon. I have nothing to hide."

"And if I call your bluff?"

"What would that look like?" She drew off the second boot.

"Do a cavity search. By hand. And by that I mean check every hole in your body."

Worse had been done to her by the villains on her world. She forced herself to pause, though. "What counts as a hole? I prefer not to have anything in my ears."

"You're not fooling me."

Surela removed her second stocking and rolled her pants down her hips. "You may believe what pleases you. I do ask that if you search me in said fashion, you warm your hands first, if they tend toward chilliness. I had a dresser once with cold hands, even gloved. Her touch was unpleasant."

"Wiggling your hips isn't going to tempt me."

"I beg you to attempt the removal of these trews without shifting."

His pause that time was longer. At length, he said, "You really are this cool, aren't you."

Surela removed the vest and the blouse. The scraps of cloth that passed for underthings among aliens went last, and she held her arms out. "Perform your check."

"This is your way of getting me to touch your skin so you can read my mind," the pirate said, but he advanced on her anyway. Warily, but without hesitation.

"I am no mind-mage to read thoughts so easily. Even

touching, I would be fortunate to receive your emotions. Not all of us are endowed with the powers ascribed to us by rumor."

"Which is exactly what I'd tell someone I wanted to lure into doing it."

Surela allowed herself to be seen sighing in frustration. "And what precisely would I learn from reading your emotions? Your thoughts? That you distrust me? That you plan my demise or my betrayal? That you believe you have already extracted all the benefit from me that you feel likely, and you wish only to draw me far enough from civilization that you might dispose of me without being caught? What, exactly, do you expect to reveal that I might not already be assuming?"

The man stopped, staring into her face. His light eyes were inhuman. "Damn, woman."

She lifted a brow. "I cannot seriously have surprised you."

"And if you have?"

"Then perhaps we have both learned something."

He tossed her vest at her. "Then let's keep learning. You're free to dress, duchess. I won't check you for any tech. But if I find out you've betrayed me, you won't like what happens."

"Torture, I suppose."

He grinned. "Don't sound too bored. You might spur me into a demonstration. Just to hear what you sound like afraid."

"Don't be coarse," Surela said, donning her underthings. "It doesn't suit you."

Again, that hesitation. "You don't know me at all, duchess. Don't forget that."

"I shan't. May I have my dagger? The device you may keep."

He laughed. "Good try. No."

She'd hoped he would leave, but he settled on the couch, his eyes never wavering. Ignoring him, Surela dressed, giving each item of clothing her full attention. When she'd finished, he said, "I'll say this... you haven't bored me yet."

What a priceless clue into himself to have thrown away so casually. But what Surela said was, "Do you expect such a comment to be flattering?"

He laughed as the first door opened, revealing his minion and Leo, who was prancing cheerfully in the thug's wake. The sight quelled Basilisk's amusement so completely Surela wondered if it had been feigned. "Did you do the job, or did you sample the wares?"

"He did both," Leo sighed, fluttering his lashes. "I love a man with muscles!"

Basilisk eyed her. "This is what you consider an acceptable pet?"

"Whatever else would he be good for?" Surela asked.

"I love a mean mistress, too," Leo said with a pout.

Basilisk snorted. "Then go unpack for your dom, freak. Since she loves her pets so much, she can share a room with them."

Another test, no doubt. Surela could see the cast of her future, and it was nothing but threading this incredibly lethal needle... and by that, she understood that she wanted to live through her encounter with the pirates. The intelligence she'd abandoned for Eddings's spies to recover had been priceless enough; the intelligence she'd given Basilisk so that he would be tricked into believing the Chatcaava decoyed from Escutcheon, necessary. But what more could she learn to help shield the Eldritch if she won against this criminal?

Unfolding from her seat on the coffee table, Surela waved a hand. "Come, cat. I find myself in need of a bath."

As she turned to go, Basilisk said, "Aren't you going to ask about your other man?"

"No," Surela said. "Because I expect him shortly. You won't disappoint me."

"I won't, will I."

She smiled over her shoulder and left him behind. The chamber door closed on the pirates and left her with Leo, whose expression, so cheerful, was warning enough. They had to assume they would be watched. "Well, pet?" she said. "Basilisk has provided me with luggage. Let us see what he has so kindly packed for my needs."

———

Saul had been identified as the only threat in their party; that much was obvious from how much longer they kept him, and how they released him into her quarters with a shove that promised worse if he strayed. Were she and Leo so easily dismissed, that a gangly Hinichi of no obvious stature or competence should threaten them?

Ridiculous question, that one.

Before Surela could decide how to approach this interaction, Saul spoke. "Lady, I know you didn't want to hire me and you're not going to want to listen, but these people are bad news. This suite? Bugged, no question. And that's if they didn't do something to our clothes while searching us. You should never have gotten involved with them."

So this was what she had to work with. How little she wanted to play this part for people she had come to value… but better this ugly act than to expose them to worse by confessing to gentler feelings for them. "And now you have as much as told them that we suspect them."

The Hinichi rolled his eyes, and the sight took her aback. Sarcasm was not something she'd been trained to expect in Saul Ferry. "They're not stupid. They know we know. That's what I'm telling you, lady. You're in over your head, and if you were smart, you'd talk us out of this."

"You are a mouthy hireling," Surela said. "When I want your opinion on my actions, I will ask it of you. Do I make myself understood?"

"Yeah, yeah. But don't come crying when they sell you upstream to some Chatcaavan."

"Do they do so, sirrah, you will not be in much better case."

Saul snorted. "I go where the money is. Maybe I'll see if they want my contract once they're done with you."

Leo, on the bed, clutched his ears and whimpered. "I don't like fighting! Please stop fighting!"

Saul sneered. "You're not the boss of me either, slut."

Surela brought out the voice she'd used to quell entire halls of quarreling Asaniefa cousins. "Enough. I will have peace in my room." She pointed at the foot of the bed. "Pet. You will sleep there. Guard. You will remain at your post by the door. And I want no more word out of either of you. I will not have you ruining my plans. These people represent an opportunity of a magnitude I can hardly describe to your plebeian ears. I intend profit enough for both sides. And then..." She sat on one of the soft chairs and crossed her legs. "And then, the galaxy."

Had it been enough? Were the pirates listening? Both Leo and Saul thought so. Hopefully they had enjoyed—and believed—the performance. Goddess grant them swift journey to this Allegresse, and escape.

CHAPTER 31

To Surela's relief the pirate had no interest in parading her through the liner's halls as his guest, or wife, or whatever fiction he'd contrived when purchasing their tickets. She remained sequestered in her assigned chamber, exiting only to use the bathing facilities. Neither of the thugs importuned her when she walked across the reception room, and Basilisk was engrossed in his data tablet and not, apparently, interested in small talk. Relieved, she performed her ablutions and returned to her chamber. She doubted her ability to sleep, and wanted desperately to cease being conscious of her dangers for a few hours, and wondered which of these warring impulses would win when she put her head on her pillow. The answer, apparently, was the latter... until the hatch to her bedchamber opened, spilling light over her hip and into her face.

"Wake-up call, duchess," Basilisk said. "Get dressed."

"Are we there already?" But he had already gone. She exchanged glances with Leo and Saul, and it was the wolfine's warning look that confirmed something else was going on. She donned her clothes in haste and strode from her chamber as the deck beneath her feet dropped, so abruptly she fell to her knees and skidded halfway across the receiving room.

Basilisk caught her by the shoulder. "Time to go."

The emergency lights, subdued but strobing an agitating red, had lit where ceiling and bulkhead met. A soft voice said, "Attention, attention. All passengers, please remain in your cabins. We are experiencing a brief delay. Attention, attention—"

One of the thugs opened the door to a sound Surela hadn't heard since the coup at Ontine: people fighting, screaming, falling. "What have you done?" she asked, before she could stop herself. And then, to cover her mistake: "Goddess, you have attacked a passenger liner barely a day out from a Fleet stronghold?"

He chuckled. "Don't worry, they won't find us."

"You will forgive me if I doubt this."

"Not at all." He gestured toward the door. "Out. And bring your attempt at security with you."

Forcing her face to remain stiff with irritation, Surela beckoned to Saul and Leo, then followed Basilisk's minions into the corridor. There were bodies littering the deck, both passengers and the liner's crew, and if the Alliance's weapons made for neater corpses they inspired a surge of nausea in her all the same. Staying in character had never been more challenging, but knowing that she could easily be the next body left on the carpeted deck concentrated her thoughts marvelously. "What a mess. How will you sell them to your clients now?"

"We don't. At least, not alive. We no longer have a slave-selling arm." At the check in her stride, he snorted. "Don't worry, duchess. We can transport a few high-value prisoners for sale. Your enemies will get what they deserve, and we'll all be paid."

"If you do not sell slaves regularly…. how is it that you fund your aims?"

"We're a DGP organization." At her frown, he elaborated. "Drugs, guns, and pelts."

"Pelts?" Surela repeated, imagining the ice deer and frost wolves of Escutcheon's northern provinces.

"More economical than selling the same people as slaves. Kill and skin them and you can fit more product in each hold. You don't need specialized conversions for the cargo bays, either."

Her thoughts stumbled. Not creatures. But people. He was talking about skinning people. "Do you also skin my kind?"

"No one wants Eldritch leather when they could have the whole Eldritch. Same with humans… leather from humans is such a rare request that we don't bother with it. But the furries, everyone likes that. We can even sell them legally if we forge the origin paperwork and trim them properly. Granted, that's a last resort. They're more valuable whole." He paused at the corridor's bend to prod a dead tigraine woman, her striped arm splayed, palm-up, as if supplicating. "It's more of a sideline, you understand. Gives us some return from the bodies. Guns and drugs are better money-makers. Not everyone's a pervert, but in the right situation, everyone's an addict with a grudge." He grinned at her. "Does that answer all your questions?"

"For now," Surela said.

"Want a pelt of your own?"

"I prefer warmer climes."

"And is that an honest answer, duchess?"

She sighed. "I told you I found tests tiresome."

"So pass this one."

She eyed the body. "I will not pretend to an interest to satisfy your worry that I am not sufficiently callous enough to ally with you. Why would I want the pelt of a creature like

299

enough to an animal to be mistaken for one? Of course you skin them. They're beasts."

"Even yours?"

Surela sniffed. "Beasts have sold my kind to dragons. They feel no more fondness for me than I do for them."

"Mmmm." He eyed her. "So far, too good to be true."

"I doubt it. What precisely are we doing abroad in the ship? What have you done with it?"

Another shiver ran through the deck. "I've stolen it." He grinned. "Let's get to the ramp. We're wasting time if we want to make our rendezvous."

Had Saul said something about guilt becoming a burden? As Surela stepped over the bodies, she struggled not to feel responsible for their deaths. Had she opened the path for the liner's doom as she had for her people on her homeworld? Was she allowing herself to be used again?

What would make it right this time?

———

The pirates had, indeed, captured the liner. It was now engulfed in a cavernous cargo bay that made the *Earthrise* look the small trader she was; there were caves in the cliffs beneath Ontine palace that were smaller. Surela could sense Basilisk's gaze on her as she strode off the ramp, so she made much of surveying the space with lifted chin and half-lidded eyes.

"Surprised?"

"Should I be? I assumed you had significant assets, or you would not have been so confident of your ability to destroy the procession."

He snorted. "Very cool, duchess. Very cool."

"I suppose I have disappointed you by not admiring your tactics thus far. Shall I say that I respect your efficiency?"

"Do you?"

"It is commendable," Surela said. "Capturing the entire liner... will you put it to work in your fleet?"

"We'll break it down for parts. Retrofitting it with weapons would be pointless. They're not built to take hits. Better to steal warships."

Surela thought of the Chatcaavan with the magenta eyes. How would he have reacted? "Your ambitions are laudable. I approve."

He laughed. "So glad to meet your high standards. This way. We're going to be late to our appointment if we don't get underway." A hint of menace. "You could have come faster."

"You wanted information, and I provided it. Had you wanted me to delay the progress, you should have said so."

That interested him from the way he glanced at her. "Could you have?"

"Oh, certes. Perhaps something we might consider in the future."

"And you think there'll be a future."

"But of course," Surela said. "You wish to remove a princess. I am intent on removing a queen." She laughed. "You think your buyers will love the heir? Wait until you offer them an empress who has been scheming in their galaxy for hundreds of years. Liolesa has enemies everywhere, I pledge you. Their thirst when they learn she is within reach will be...."

"Immense?"

"Profitable. So very profitable."

"I'll keep that in mind."

The cargo bay truly was enormous, and the scale of the vessel it implied unsettled her. She wished she could have evaluated it further, but the pirate led her over a Pad and onto some new ship. This one was perhaps smaller? Would the corridors necessarily reveal anything? But they were built with the same harmonious lines and colors used by the liner. She had imagined something dirtier and uglier. If anything, the *Earthrise* suited her conception of a slaver's vessel better than this clean and spacious environment. How she wished she could ask Saul or Leo for their perspectives!

They'd gone around several turns when the pirate stopped and addressed his minions. "Show the duchess's employees to their accommodations."

Surela said, "Is there some purpose to separating them from me?"

"Of course there is. I want you alone and vulnerable." Another smirk. "What else?"

She heaved another dramatic sigh. "You have to know they are no danger to you or anyone here."

"No, actually, I don't." He nodded toward his thugs, who took Leo and Saul by the arms. "Don't worry, they'll be waiting for you in your cabin. I thought you'd like to see the bridge."

Would her persona want that? Or would she be bored by the particulars? Better to be informed. "I admit to curiosity."

"Ah, that was good. You almost look like you believe it. What if I tell you that if you want you can watch the demise of your princess while it's happening?"

"Will you be there? Or will you be in a cabin, assming that your underlings are performing their duties while you sip an aperitif and plan your entertainment with the prisoners later?"

Basilisk rubbed his chin. "You know, I think that was an honest question."

Surela brought out the rippling laugh she'd been trained to use at court. "Show me the bridge."

The walk was not productive of any revelation other than that this ship was larger and more luxurious than the *Earthrise*. The decks were carpeted; the lift taking them to the bridge roomier; and the fore of the vessel, when they debouched, was no cramped compartment. Her impression was of windows onto the blackness of space, and darkness interrupted only by dimly glowing displays, and alarmingly focused and silent watchstanders, manning their consoles.

To be impressed? Or to intimate she'd expected better? But no, she would have treated anyone who undermined her authority in public as an urgent threat. "You maintain a disciplined operation."

"The duchess approves?"

"Efficiency is admirable."

"My," he said. "I've earned admiration!" But he gestured toward the forward screen. "We're just in time to watch the evolution."

That he used a naval term did not escape her, thanks to Meri's tutelage; she would not have recognized 'evolution' as a description of the activity of ships otherwise. What did it mean that he used it? Surela did not love what it implied about Basilisk's thinking, and wondered if it was a clue as to his origins.

She forced her racing thoughts to slow as she turned her attention to the display. There were two other vessels magnified on the viewer. One of them looked like a freighter, but so large it dwarfed the ship at its flank—the latter resembled the destroyers Surela had seen illustrated in her copy of Wiley's. Presumably, the liner had been stowed in the larger vessel's hold, so she watched it coast away. If she scanned the tactical station... yes, the vessel they were on was represented. It was smaller than the destroyer, if she read the tonnage correctly. "So we have left the site of the attack. Will our enemies will be unable to track us?"

"They'll try. If they succeed, they won't survive what they stumble into."

"Do they never assume ambush?"

He shook his head. "Most of them? No. They think the Chatcaava are the threat."

"The dragons did destroy a planet recently."

"Which worked out great for us. Fleet was getting too

interested in pirate hunting until the Chatcaava came along and distracted them. But the big wars are never the problem, duchess. It's the creeping internal corruption that takes you down in the end."

Surela glanced at him. "This sounds like a conversation better served by a meal."

"You want to eat with me?" He laughed. "Really eat?"

"I do occasionally require it." Surela glanced toward the view; the cargo vessel was gone, and the destroyer was shifting trajectory. "I presume it won't be long before we set our trap for the would-be princess."

"Our trap," Basilisk repeated, amused.

"As my data made its success more probable, I believe I may claim some portion of it to my credit."

He chuckled. "Fair. But yes, we might only get two days to ourselves before the party starts. Maybe less. If that suits you."

"The sooner the better. Shall we eat?"

He waved her into the lift, and once they'd gained its privacy said, "I'm still not interested in rhacking you."

Surela ignored that as a digression. "What do you plan to do with your empire?"

That successfully baited him off that line of conversation. "Excuse me?"

"You said on the bridge that it is internal corruption that brings down large entities. Is that your end? To destroy the Alliance? Shatter it into dozens of smaller fiefs that are easier to rob? Or do you mean to decapitate the Alliance leadership and set yourself up as king?"

He eyed her, and while the expression was not friendly, neither was it threatening. She had interested him, perhaps. The lift door whispered open and he stepped through it. "This way."

The cabin he brought her to, however, was not his, because Leo and Saul were seated in it. At her pause, he said,

"We're between meals. You'll want to clean up, I'm sure. I'll send for you."

Leo stood. "Oh, mistress! Come see what we have for you to wear! This way, this way!"

The door slid shut behind her as she stepped into the compartment, and the moment it did, Leo hugged her. She remained rigid within the circle of his arms, wondering who was watching and through what device, until Saul said, "It's all right, Rel. We've got a brief window."

"A… what?"

"I'm sure that for this fifteen minutes we won't be recorded, and hopefully we'll have a longer window later, one where we'll be able to get information out."

"How is that possible?"

Saul's ears flicked sideways. "For now, all I can say is that there's an extraction plan, and that we should be careful not to make these people think we're going to betray them, because we're going to need freedom to get to the right access point at the right time."

Until this statement Surela had not felt, in her marrow, how completely she'd accepted the irrevocability of her death. Her shudder caused Leo to squeeze her more tightly, and she leaned into him, grateful for the emotions he projected through his skin: a distracting combination of optimism, pragmatism, and a manic exhilaration that papered over both their fears and horrors. Reluctantly, she pulled herself away. "Do not tell me, Leo, that you are enjoying yourself."

"Even if I am, a little?" He ruined his apologetic look with a nervous grin. "I like adventure."

"This is rather more than adventure—"

"Danger's even more exciting?" He caught her wrist in a gentle circle of furred fingers. "Don't make me look too hard at it until it's over, arii. We're holding it together, right? Let's pretty you up for your date! Is he trying to get into your pants?"

"Trying to—" The idiom caught up with her. "No, he is very much not interested in allowing me to cloud his mind in that fashion. He is too cunning for simplistic approaches."

"Are you having any luck with less simplistic ones?" Saul asked.

"So far he has not killed us?"

"It's a start," Leo said.

Surela looked at Saul, whose face remained friendly and gaze direct. That expression was, she realized, his way of masking his feelings. And in the best way, because of its consonance with his personality. Few would think to look past it. But his spine was too straight, and the fold of his hands in front of his body too loose.

"Saul," she said, low. "If you have done aught that imperils you to secure my safety—"

He held up one of those hands. "Later, Rel. I promise."

Leo nodded and pulled at her wrist again. "Listen to the man, peach blossom."

She allowed herself to be led away. Had Saul truly been one of her retainers, she could have ordered him to explain himself, and more importantly, to promise he hadn't embarked on some bit of recklessness to please her. But she was no longer a great feudal lady, and he was not a knight, and she feared they were walking those roads anyway without any of the protections custom and tradition would ordinarily furnish as armor against grief.

"You'll like this," Leo said. "He's obviously had people watching where you shop." At her flinch, the Harat-Shar finished, "You've got all of two or three minutes to decide that you're all in favor of having been the target of his surveillance because it saved you the trouble of telling him what you want before those cameras go back on. Smile, beautiful."

"I suppose a bath is out of the question," Surela said, resuming her role early. "I will settle for the mortal conveniences."

"Very good, mistress."

————

Surela used the subsequent hour and a half to mull her choices. If Saul's promise proved out, then she should use her dinner with the pirate to uncover more information she could share through this presumably secure communication line. What would be of most material aid to her people's allies? She wouldn't have much time—a day? Two? Two, the pirate had said, at most. Sitting on a chair with the poise of a queen on a throne, with Leo kneeling at her feet and Saul standing at attention beside the door, she allowed her upbringing to inform her expression, her behavior, her carriage, in a way she hadn't needed to since leaving Asaniefa's contentious halls. Let the pirates spy on her and see her at her ease, while she plotted their ruination.

Goddess, someone was planning a rescue. It would be convenient to allow her to die here, but no... they were coming. Dare she hoped it was not solely for Leo and Saul?

When the thug arrived to escort her to supper, she was ready, and glided after him. Had she wondered what the quarters of her guard dog looked like? She had, and yet she had no interest in the cabin of the pirate leader despite the insight into him being of far more use to her. When she entered it, she did so expecting, despite the evidence thus far, a den of squalor, or if not so, then at least a hall full of trophies. But Basilisk's lair was neat, clean, and had very little by way of décor. Some paintings—mythological scenes perhaps? The style had the hallmarks of the classical period that had informed early Eldritch art. He had impeccable taste; even the nudes were tasteful, more scenes from legends. Gods and mortals, all of them… no knights for the Basilisk.

The table was set for two, but not in a way suggestive of formality or intimacy: no tablecloth, no porcelain, no candles or flowers. The food was already waiting on a cart; the sole concession to extravagance was a bottle of wine.

Her host was already sitting, sipping from a glass. He was still in the unassuming attire he'd favored on the starbase; like his quarters, which were spartan save for the sole expense of the art, he spent little on his wardrobe, but she predicted the wine would be superb. "Sit, duchess. We might actually finish a meal, for once. Wouldn't that be novel." His smile was thin. "Do you like the clothes I had picked out for you?"

"They are serviceable," Surela said. "If lacking in elegance."

"Should I have bought Her Majesty something more exciting?"

She seated herself across from him and unfolded the napkin. "The only garb that interests me awaits me on my homeworld. Off of it, expedience is the optimal choice."

"I sense a theme with you."

"That I care little for anything but my concerns? Does this surprise you?"

"That you admit it so easily, maybe." He considered her over the rim of his glass. "I also expected more fear. I have you surrounded, you know."

She gave him her best bored expression, and as she'd honed it over centuries of social warfare in the court, it was an excellent one. "Why should I be afraid of you? You have only enacted the necessary choice concerning me."

"Is that so?"

"Of course. I know you have brought me aboard your vessel to ensure I would not suffer a crisis of conscience and run home to give report of you in return for amnesty." Surela set her empty glass in front of him expectantly. "I applaud your practicality while also anticipating the days we need not bother with such tiresome checks on one another. We have a great deal to do."

A longish pause, but as she expected, he poured for her. The scent of black cherries rose from the dark wine that splashed in the glass, and faintly violets, and walnuts. She accepted the glass when he passed it to her and allowed the aroma to drift to her nose. Yes, the wine was very good. He looked the commoner, but it would not do to underestimate him.

"You asked me earlier if I intended to crown myself king."

"Do you?"

He shook his head. "I don't like cages."

An interesting comment. Should she say so? She gambled. "I find this conception of absolute power... novel."

"Absolute power." He scoffed. "There is no absolute power. You want to be queen? Are you going to tell me you can do whatever you want once you take over? Or will you have to kowtow to some segment of the population? Kill people to convince them you're in charge? Maybe you can swing that for a planetary population, duchess. A small one. For hundreds of worlds? Good luck."

"The Chatcaava managed."

"Did they? Or did they tell us they did? They claim the Chatcaavan War was caused by a splinter faction acting without their emperor's permission. Do you think they're lying? Because I don't. I bet that entire empire only works because every separate faction in it is convinced the other factions don't know they're the ones in control."

"An intriguing hypothesis. This appears to be a topic to which you have devoted a great deal of thought."

"Let's just say... it's relevant."

She made much of considering him over her glass. "So... you do not desire a crown. What do you desire?"

He grinned. "To be my own man." He set his glass down. "Tell me more about this minister of war you want for yourself. What did he do to you?"

Perhaps sharing personal information with him would inspire him to trust her? Or would he think less of her for it? Best to show him a vulnerability she wanted him to see. Surela allowed a touch of ice to chill her voice. "He preferred to marry a human."

"Ah… our old friend Reese Eddings. You know, she's the primary reason you're here." A thin smile, and monster eyes. "She came to us pretending to be on our side. Wanting to work with us. And all the while she had a Fleet mic on her, and was bringing dusted Fleet reinforcements in on us. I wondered if you were pulling the same trick. Our mutual benefactor said you might be soft on Eddings."

"Soft on her! The woman who stole my—" Surela cut off as if angry and looked away. If she thought of Athanesin, and how he'd importuned her with his unwanted proposals, she could sustain the necessary level of pique, both personal and revolted. "Let us speak more directly, shall we? The craven child Bethsaida Emil, our 'benefactor,' probably informed you that I have Eddings to thank for my life, yes?"

"Something like that," Basilisk said lazily.

"And you think for this I would be grateful? That she should arrange for my exile?"

"I'd think that would be better than dying."

"Goddess, if they'd sentenced me to death my family would have smuggled me from the catacombs and into the countryside where I could rally my supporters while my enemies reeled from the coup. Instead I was catapulted into this… this nowhere. Amid beasts and menials." She let her lips curl back from her teeth. "And forced to work as if I was glad of the opportunity! To labor like a peasant! I detested it. But we are a long-lived people, Basilisk. I could be patient, waiting for my opportunity."

"I'm guessing you'll want to kill this Bethsaida then."

"The moment I can, yes. And whoever this... other possible contact was she mentioned to you. Did she tell you more? I should like to prune that branch before it grows."

He snorted. "And if I want to keep that branch, in case I need to prune you?"

"I am your best choice."

"And arrogant about it."

"What else? I know my worth."

He watched her for several moments, unblinking, then smiled again. "You continue to interest me. Shall we eat?"

Before he could reach toward the cart, she set a hand on his wrist. Instantly he stilled, and the look he awarded her from beneath his lowered brows was baleful. But she had leveled similar glares on others before. If she told herself so, she could keep moving. "You will tell me about this other contact."

"Or?"

Surela summoned her sweetest smile and paired it with the clipped precision of her words. "Or you will have to start all over again. You destroy the procession, perhaps net yourself the princess. And then what? A missing heir to the throne of an allied power will require the Alliance to come to Liolesa's aid, and in force. They will scour the area seeking you and yours. You want your vengeance against the Eldritch and Theresa Eddings? You will not have it, for the Eldritch world will become a fortress, and the human will be hidden safely behind its walls. Without me, you must cultivate a new contact. Who is to say the one you have left is worth your time? You were already waiting for them, and in vain. They were not the one who came."

"You talk such a good game," Basilisk said. "It makes me wonder how you lost."

"I did not understand the capabilities of the Chatcaava."

He shook his head. "Their naval power—"

·"Not in space. Their personal power. The ability to shapeshift... it gives them our mental abilities." She smiled faintly. "A dragon who could pass as one of us, and use our talents to read our minds? Well. I know what to expect now."

The pirate sank back against his chair, frowning. "They can do that?"

"They can, and if you have not been so informed by your allies, I leave you to imagine why."

His frown grew more pronounced. "I can't believe the dragon let you live, knowing what you do."

"I would not have, had the dragon in question not desired me for a slave more than he feared me as a threat."

"And you admit that."

Her brows rose. "What point denying it? His error was in believing I might be neutralized so easily. Now... I have divulged something of use to you. You might offer me fair trade."

Basilisk paused, then chuckled. "All right, duchess. I'll play. I don't know the name of my alternate contact, but I was told he was male, and that I'd probably have to make up a story about being an ally he could use to protect the Eldritch from the Chatcaava. Our benefactor said he wouldn't like the truth. She also said she couldn't guarantee he was receiving her messages, because her pings hadn't gotten any returns the way the ones she sent your message tag did."

Pings to her message tag... was that... surely he wasn't talking about the strange, empty messages she'd received when first she'd been exiled?

Basilisk was watching her, and cocked his head. "Recognize him?"

Surela didn't, but she could make up a story. "Oh, the swain she's attached with her tragic tale of suffering. Did she tell you she took a turn in a Chatcaavan harem? She has made a great deal of that little story."

"No, she hadn't. Interesting. Now... are you actually

312

hungry, duchess? We don't have very long before the main event. You'll need your strength."

"Shall I?"

"No doubt you have plans for that slave of yours once we deliver him."

"Ah, yes. And what shall you do with the human? What did she do to earn your enmity? Did her ploy with the hidden Fleet operatives succeed? I admit to curiosity."

He snorted. "And since you hardly know enough for me to keep it back from you... she cleaned out our most lucrative drug arm. We've had to rebuild it from scratch, and doing it took capital we earned by associating ourselves with as nasty a group as they come on this side of hell. The only thing that made that little partnership palatable was that its warlord was all the way on the other side of the Alliance from us... and your princess took care of her. I'd almost be grateful."

"And yet, you are not?"

He shook his head. "Not even slightly. We had to absorb what was left of the warlord's group to shore up our own ranks, and to keep them from selling us out. Now we've got all the problems from associating with people Fleet's actively after—people Fleet's compromised even more completely than they did us—and all the problems of the power vacuum their leadership left behind. Particularly since they were extorting protection money from all the independent groups around here. That was annoying, but at least it kept everyone in line. Now it's a free-for-all."

"Fascinating," Surela said, surprised to discover that she meant it. "And you accused me of living in a cage, surrounded by enemies I must appease? Your political situation does not sound unlike any other afflicting a large body of nation-states."

"Which is why I'm not interested in being king." Another twisted smile. "I just want to be left alone to do what I please. And for that, I need the Alliance too busy to come after us, and my confederates to have other things on their minds."

Centuries of navigating factional politics drew her to the inevitable conclusions. "The attack on the princess is a trap, isn't it. For the elements you absorbed, the ones from this more difficult faction. You intend to give them the princess to please them... and to set the Alliance and the Eldritch on them in a high profile attack." She nodded. "Yes, that is why you are on this smaller vessel. You don't intend to be anyone's target. If all goes well, your force prevails and acquires the defeated Eldritch Navy to take apart for scrap, and the elements in your organization who wanted the princess will be pleased. If it goes badly, you escape with your life and leave these troublesome hangers-on to die, or be earmarked by the Alliance for later destruction. Shall I guess that none of these ships you've commanded to this ambush are from your original organization, save this one?" She paused. "Oh, indeed. That's why you took us on the passenger liner, was it not? And why it distressed you not at all to ambush it so close to the starbase. Fleet would be doing you a service if it followed the freighter to wherever you've sent it, wouldn't it?"

Basilisk had set down his glass and was staring at her.

Reaching past him to the cart, Surela lifted one of the covers and inspected the entrée. Fish, in a light glaze that smelled of citrus. "An inspired plan. You have covered every contingency." When he didn't respond, she looked up, brows lifted. "Do I shock you? But I was already forty years old when the Alliance was established, and had been playing the grand game for almost two centuries when the Chatcaava appeared on the galactic stage."

The pirate said, voice tight, "On a single planet."

"Yours was a single planet for thousands of years prior to the Alliance's formation," Surela said. "Do you mean to tell me that politics on Terra was somehow less complex for being one sole world?"

"I wasn't born on Earth."

"No, but your homeworld matters to you." She let her gaze linger on the nearest painting. "You cherish its treasures." She allowed the lines of her face to soften slightly, so that he could see the approval. "You have good taste."

He grunted, turned to the cart, and started serving. "I hope you're hungry."

"It has been some time."

"Fish?"

"I do love seafood." Such a relief to be confronted with a meal, and an excuse to look down and move her hands.

"You're too good to be true, you know that, duchess?"

"I did say we would have a productive alliance, did we choose to pursue one."

"You make me wish…" He trailed off, smirked. "If it's an act—it's a good one."

"You find me completely at your mercy," Surela said. "What more do you desire? I can hardly hurt you aboard your vessel."

"Ready to be 'done with the testing,' are you."

"I have said. Are you also not bored of it?"

"Not bored enough to forego it. I've been burned enough times. But… if you could be trusted, you would be… an interesting sounding board."

"I am an excellent listener."

He eyed her, and somehow made the next words menacing without changing expression or tone. "I'll remember that in the future."

Somehow, the remainder of their meal involved pleasantries about the food, and Surela's compliments on the wine. Basilisk revealed no more information to her, and though she dearly wished to provoke another revelation, she could tell she had made him uneasy. She allowed him to control the conversation, and dropped her sole challenge when he walked her to the hatch. "I will know when you have decided to trust me when you return my weapon to me."

"Is it that important to you?"

Surela arched her brows. "Do you mean that I should believe you go unarmed?"

He laughed. "Of course not. But a knife?"

"It is a proper weapon for an Eldritch." She lifted her chin. "My vassals kiss it when they pledge their troth."

"Not a ring?"

"The dagger promises their deaths if they betray me. Kissing it reminds them." She smiled. "They must kiss near the edge. If they are not careful, it bleeds them."

His grin didn't reach his eyes. "You make it sound like it's alive."

"Isn't all steel?"

Another longish hesitation. Then: "I'm still not bored, duchess."

"I continue to fail to find your insinuation flattering."

He laughed and keyed the hatch open. "Take her back to her cabin." To Surela: "Good night, duchess. By this time tomorrow, we'll be in the thick of it, so sleep well."

"I shall dream of my enemies laid low."

He shook his head and let the door separate them.

The walk to her cabin took too long in the company of Basilisk's thugs, but it ended, as all interminable things did. As the hatch closed behind her back, Leo looked up from the chair he was lounging in, and Saul, sitting on the opposite side of the room, gave her a sullen look that transformed him from faithful knight to disreputable hireling.

"Truly?" she said, assuming anew they were being watched, "I expected the two of you to do something useful in my absence, even if it was as minor as unpacking... and yet I find you thus, unemployed in any productive activity."

The leonine let his head sag. "Apologies, mistress, there wasn't much to unpack. And… are we staying long?"

"Yours not to ask questions, pet," Surela said. "Kneel. I wish to think."

Leo slid off the chair and pressed himself against its leg, waiting for her to settle. Then he leaned into her calf, communicating… what? Could she sense him through the tumult of her own emotions? She thought he was cheerful, of all things. Caressing his hair until her fingers grazed his scalp confirmed the impression. Leo was not concerned about their fate. Goddess and Lord, if only she could say the same.

"Go back to standing by the door," Surela said to Saul, who trudged there, and there remained.

It had been her intention to brood for however long it took to deliver her to an hour reasonable for retiring, but she must have fallen asleep because her next sensation was of Leo petting her shin. "Rel, Rel, wake up. Wake up, it's time."

Her shoulders and abdomen tensed. "What has gone wrong?"

"Gone right, you mean." Saul was sitting on the ottoman facing her. "How long do we have this time?"

A stranger's mezzosoprano answered in the same fashion a computer would have, but without the computer's wooden diction. "I wouldn't go longer than twenty minutes. They're not firewalled against outgoing transmissions the way they are incoming, but they're nailed down tight and I don't trust them not to stumble onto me."

Surela straightened. "Who is this?"

Addressing her, the voice became markedly cool. "I'm Maia. Empress Liolesa's D-per hire."

Had she read something about D-pers? Were they not… computer personalities? She'd imagined something that sounded much less like a flesh-and-blood person. Certainly no computer she'd imagined developing sapience would have emotions, and this one patently did, and knew who she was. "I see."

"Maia's been tracking us," Saul said. "From Psi all the way here."

"The ship is following us!" Leo added, eyes sparkling.

"I beg your pardon," Surela said, her gut clenching. "The *Earthrise*? Surely not."

"It got an excellent duster," Maia said. "It's holding."

Surela folded her arms around herself. "This is not a safe course for them."

"Of course not," Saul said. "But they're not going to abandon us. Besides, following us was the easiest way to make sure they didn't lose our trail. The biggest problem with these pirates is finding them. They avoid using our infrastructure whenever they can: our navigation buoys, our comm relays, anything that might give them away. But our people knew we were meeting with the pirates, and they were able to track us to the passenger liner, and then off it to the new ships."

"After that, getting into this ship was straightforward," Maia said. "But it's crazy with alarms and tripwires. I don't want to dig too deep or stay too long. I can get a whisker in, and a whisker out, but more than that and we might blow our chance to catch the entire attack force."

Was Surela relieved that someone knew where they were? Or horrified that the *Earthrise*, a freighter with neither armor nor weaponry, had trundled along in the wake of a psychopathic pirate, there to hover alongside and await the arrival of an unknown number of enemy combatants? "If we have only twenty minutes, there is information I must pass to my liegelady."

"Go ahead," said the D-per.

Surela collected her thoughts and recounted everything of note from her last discussion with Basilisk, and then added the trivialities that might offer clues, such as the man's taste

318

in wine and art, for who know but that law enforcement might be able to track those purchases? When she was done, the silence was electric. Saul's face had hardened; Leo looked appalled. And the D-per, when she spoke, sounded suspicious. "And you just happened to find all this out during one dinner date? Did you let him rhack you, or is there some other reason you conveniently know the political make-up of the local underworld?"

"Maia," Saul growled.

"She is required to ask," Surela said. "She is liegebound to Liolesa, and owes me nothing. Less than nothing, as I transgressed against her liegelady."

"You didn't 'transgress.' You committed treason. Why should we trust you now?"

"There is nothing I can say to convince you of my loyalty if my actions do not suffice," Surela replied, thinking wearily that the Eldritch couldn't afford to believe her, and the pirates would not. Where could she belong when neither the bright world nor the dark wanted her? She dared not glance toward Leo to see what he thought of Maia's statement. "But pass this information to Eddings and let her do what she will with it."

"Fine. Saul, Leo, you know where to go so we can do pick-up when the flag drops."

"We do, yes."

"We're going to have our hands too full to come after this ship in particular when the fight starts—"

"Basilisk is their leader," Surela said. "If you take him alive, he will know things that none of the others do. Important matters, that he might be convinced to share."

"You want us to believe that a guy on a ship that small, who has the time to personally pick up contacts on starbases, is going to be the one in charge, rather than some errand boy they sent to take care of their Eldritch turncoat loose end?"

That, though, was all Surela was willing to take, because

the notion that Eldritch would die because of the prejudices of someone who had just met her was intolerable. "You are allowing emotion to dictate your reactions, and we cannot afford that luxury. Give my information verbatim to Theresa Eddings and allow her to evaluate it. Or pass it to the Chatcaavan in charge of the forces in the Eldritch system, who will judge it based on its merits. But we are paying for this information in blood, and I will not see it dismissed because it pleases someone to hate me more than to value the safety of the Eldritch people."

"If you'd cared about the safety of the Eldritch people you wouldn't have staged a coup. And I don't see you bleeding."

"Yet," Leo murmured.

"And she's not the only one here," Saul addd.

That stilled their virtual guest's vitriol.

"I know you intend to save us," Leo continued. "But... that's not very likely, is it? Especially if you've already written Rel off."

"Her name," Maia said, "is Surela Silin Asaniefa, and she's a convicted traitor."

"If you say so," Leo replied.

Saul said, "We're running low on time here. Is there anything else you wanted us to know?"

"No—"

"Then maybe you should go before someone notices you using some of the bandwidth."

A hesitation, which Saul used to rise and return to the door. Then Maia said, "This should be over within forty-eight hours or less, if everything goes well. Be ready. I'm cutting my tether now, you're back under surveillance."

With a long sigh, Leo said, "Mistress, you really should rest. The chair is beneath your dignity. Can I turn back your bed? It's very soft."

Surela searched his eyes for any change, but the Harat-Shar remained very obviously her partisan. Leo had always worn his heart pinned to his vest for all to see. Was that a façade? Or had he not changed his conception of her based on Maia's accusations? She cupped his face, felt through it only the same brightness and zest for life that characterized all his interactions. If she concentrated hard, she thought she caught some vague sense of the foundation beneath that superficial layer, one that struck her as dependable as Saul's, in its own way.

Perhaps she was looking too worried, for Leo rubbed his cheek against her palm. Something in her eased.

"Very well," she said. "I suppose it behooves me to prepare for the excitement to come."

CHAPTER 32

Sleeping… Goddess knew how she managed, only that waking to find Leo at her feet like a real animal rather than a person had been unexpectedly comforting. She rose and forced herself through her toilette, snapping occasionally at her supposed subordinates in a bid to convince the people surveilling that she didn't like them.

Filling the next hours taxed every discipline Surela had learned in centuries of living on a world with few diversions. No prospect engaged her through the windows, which showed only stars; no book had been left for her, and computer access was so curtailed she could not reach so much as a query screen. She retreated to the chair and stared into space, until at last she commanded, "Sing me something."

Had she thought that through, she would have asked for a recitation, since Leo couldn't sing. But before the leonine could protest, Saul said, roughly, "I can't believe you keep asking. I'm not paid to sing."

"And yet, you will," Surela said.

A hefty sigh. Then, Saul consented, and… he could sing.

Not as a trained soloist might have, but with the confidence and lack of ostentation typical of someone accustomed to ensemble work. The lyrics… about longing for home, for the green fields and highlands. The moment she understood the theme, she forced herself to think of something else. To weep while under observation? Never.

Too soon, and not soon enough, she was summoned, and the thugs who came for her did not permit Saul or Leo to follow. "Captain wants you, not them," was all the first said, and Surela was too relieved to argue. If her companions were out of sight, they would remain free to move, as Dawson had required. All she would have to worry about was her own disposition, and that was the only burden she wanted at this point.

The bridge remained dark, but more lights clustered on the displays, and the energy level was markedly higher than it had been. Her host was reclining in a chair in the back of the compartment, watching the proceedings with his cheek propped on a fist. When her escorts left her at his side, he tilted his head just enough to look up at her. "I thought you'd like to witness the fight, duchess."

She glanced down at him and said, "No, Basilisk, you did not so think. You wished to keep me under your eye."

He chuckled. "All right. Yes." Lifting his voice, he said, "Bring a jumpseat for the lady."

In this fashion, Surela was installed at her persecutor's side, and how grateful she was that she'd embarked on her outworld education, because to be trapped here without being able to read the various displays would have been unbearable. But she could read them, and knew through them that theirs was one of sixteen ships, and that the other fifteen were larger than Basilisk's—no surprise—but also larger than the Eldritch Navy's, which was, and an unpleasant one. Not by much; if her reading of Wiley's was correct, the pirates' other warships would be carrying two hundred people each, and the ships acquired by Liolesa were rated up to one hundred and fifty. None of those ships would have one hundred and fifty people, though, not with the Navy so young.

"They will not stop in the middle of their course, I imagine," Surela said, to check her emotions. She thought of the passenger liner. "Is it done the same way as with the capture of the civilian liner?"

His brow rose. "Very good, duchess. Yes. We've got some people here who are very good with tripwires. A bit of technology that can yank ships out of Wellspace if they're placed correctly."

"Interesting. Does this yanking damage them?"

"It can. It also disorients the crew, unless they're expecting to be ambushed. Which they aren't, are they?"

"If they are, you will handily overpower them with this force," Surela said. "Have you held any others back?"

"Maybe." He was watching her now. "I didn't expect an Eldritch to know much about tactics."

"The Chatcaavan War made anyone forced into exile in the Alliance interested in tactics. If they were not idiots."

He snorted. "All right. I'll buy it. For now."

"Is that the countdown until their arrival?" she asked, nodding toward a chronolog in the corner of the main tank.

"It is, yes. A few hours to go. Bored?"

"On the contrary. I am greatly anticipating the events to come."

"So bloodthirsty," he murmured.

"They have earned their fates."

He said nothing to that, and his silence was no hardship. After the complete lack of stimulus in her personal quarters, to be asked to wait out the hours surrounded in data was a relief. So intent was she on reading those displays that she barely noted the man who arrived and murmured something into Basilisk's ear. When the latter snapped upright, she twitched on her chair.

"Looks like we've got an errand, duchess. You're with me."

Here, she thought, was the endgame. She rose and followed.

———

Basilisk brought her to an area she recognized despite its futuristic design because somehow all dungeons looked alike. Held against the wall alongside the second cell was Saul, snarling at his captors; Leo was looking woebegone in the arms of another ruffian.

"And here we are," said Basilisk. "We've caught your man trying to sabotage the engines." He nodded toward his lack-eys. "Make him confess."

Before Surela could inhale, the thug had put his fist into Saul's stomach, hard enough to double him over, and the meaty sound of it drowned out everything else with memories and horror and rage. "STOP!"

"Excuse me?" Basilisk asked.

"He's mine!" She raced through possible reasons to excuse herself before seizing the most likely. "I went through a great deal of trouble to obtain him, for I know him to be an agent of the minister of war."

Basilisk's brows lifted. "You knew he was a plant?"

"Of course," she replied. "Just as I knew you would not allow him serious license to wreak any serious havoc." She wrinkled her nose. "Your security is lax if he was able to escape to attempt sabotage."

"Why… exactly… did you go through the trouble of picking up one of your minister's people?"

She stared at him as if unable to believe his obtuseness. "To lure the minister to me, of course. The man does not normally leave the planet. I could not lay a trap without baiting it. This creature was one of his trusted companions on some colony world where they became intimate in a brangle with the natives. How better to impel the minister to join the others on this procession if not by dangling news of a captive before him?"

Thank the Goddess, Saul entered into her story by renewing his struggles so ferociously he nearly wrenched free of one of his captors. His howl raised the hairs on the nape of her neck. "Bitch! You'll never use me against him!"

Surela sniffed. "That's what you believe, dog."

Hanging limp in the grasp of the third lackey, Leo whimpered. "No, no, this can't be happening, everyone, please stop fighting, stop fighting...."

"You may imprison him until the fight is over," Surela said to Basilisk.

"If you used him to get your slave in position, duchess, then you've got all the use out of him you need." To the thug, "Kill him."

"NO!" Surela forced herself to sound frustrated rather than panicked. "Not until I'm sure the minister of war is in my grasp!"

"If he isn't, you can steal some other furry he cares about."

"Do you know how much trouble it was to acquire this one? A creature I knew, unquestionably, to belong to the minister of war, but who was also pretending to be a criminal? I pledge you, there are not many such people."

His hooded gaze was again on her, and she saw nothing in it but calculation. Had her gambit worked? She met his eyes, refusing fear.

"You keep showing unexpected depths, duchess," he said at last. "You're very smart about things I didn't anticipate you knowing or noticing."

"As I said when we made our deal. We could go far with one another's aid."

"We could, yes." He strolled toward Saul, stared into the Hinichi's furious face, then moved on, his gait loose and unhurried. "I find I want a little insurance, though. A final test."

This was it, she thought. He would ask her to torture one of them. Or kill them... *anything*, she prayed, *except hurting them. Let them live!* And then she staggered, choking. Looking down brought her the sight of her own dagger, nearly hilt-deep in her shoulder, near the collarbone.

"Here's your knife back, duchess." Basilisk shoved it little deeper, grabbing her shoulder to keep her from dropping. "You leave this in until the end of the fight and we can take it out in the clinic. You'll be no worse for the wear. Probably. If you played me straight, and we survive this fight, then... no hard feelings." His grin raised the corners of his lips, a mechanical act that owed nothing to mirth or pleasure. "If you've betrayed us, though, you'd better hope your friends show up in time to save you."

How much easier it would have been had she not been able to see the dagger in the corner of her vision; the violation nauseated her more than the pain, the sense that her eyes kept reporting that something was terribly amiss. She spoke despite it, because she was Surela once Silin Asaniefa, who had endured worse at the hands of slavers and dragons. "After this, Basilisk... we are quit of the testing."

He laughed. "Is that a request or a threat? Rhack, I think it's a threat. If you're really what you say you are, what a partner you'll make! But that remains to be seen, doesn't it." He nodded to the silent watchers. "Brig them. Together." Another grin. "I'm curious to see whether you'll live through your spy's vengeance."

"Not a fair test," Surela said, pressing her hand to her chest beneath the wound. Her fingers skidded on blood, enough to soak her thin vest. "I almost think you plan for me to die."

"I have faith in you. Kill him, or sic your pet Harat-Shar on him." A shiver ran through the deck and the lights flicked from white to red. "Looks like the party's started. See you on the other side."

The thugs were not gentle, tossing her into the cell, and she tumbled against Leo before they shoved Saul in and the forcefield sealed them inside. To her relief, no one stayed to guard them. No doubt their every act was being recorded, but it hardly mattered now. The pirate might say this was the final test, and that if they survived he would heal and free her, but he would never trust her to forgive the insult done her. Some part of him had decided she was too dangerous to leave alive. If, by some terrible circumstance, the Eldritch Navy failed in their charge, she would be sold somewhere, if not killed outright. Or perhaps Basilisk would keep her, having convinced himself at last that he was not as uninterested in her charms as he claimed. He did not sleep with business partners, but a slave? A slave he would use without compunction.

Leo lunged for her. "Rel, oh, angels, Rel!"

"Help her to the floor but keep her propped up," Saul said, ripping something... she couldn't see. It was good to slide down the wall. She was thirsty, and uncomfortably aware that she was oozing around the wound with every pulse of her heart. Careful hands gripped her shoulders, leaning her away from the bulkhead. "Looks like it didn't go all the way through."

"You think it might have hit anything vital?"

"She's not aspirating blood, at least, but... I don't know anything about Eldritch biology." A pause: Saul sounded agitated. "I don't know anything about any biology, almost at all. Unless you count horses. This is Prudence's wheelhouse."

"Should we be talking like this?"

"I think it's a little late to worry about our cover," Saul said. "Right, Rel? Rel, stay with us, arii, please." Aggrieved:

"I was supposed to take the punches for you. Don't die on us."

"No," she breathed. "No, it's well." A hazy sense of rightness suffused her. The last time she'd been thrown in a dungeon, she'd been the hapless victim of her own hubris and ignorance. What had she been accused of at the time? That she was a failure as a queen because she would not do the first duty of a liegelady: to protect her people. This time... this time she hadn't been imprisoned as a powerless victim, used by those around her for their purposes. This time she had been imprisoned for arranging the downfall of her enemies. Her information would save the heir to the Eldritch throne and all the Eldritch manning their newborn navy... because of her, they were prepared for Basilisk and his minions. And if Liolesa's D-per passed along her knowledge, as promised, then all she'd learned since about the pirate organization would end up in the right hands.

Theresa would take care of it. She could trust Theresa.

"Rel? Stay with us," Saul said, urgent.

"Do you think it would help if we hugged her? That would keep her warm, right? That's something you're supposed to do if people are going into shock?"

Yes, she thought. Yes, they should hug her. To drift away enfolded in the feelings of these two people, that seemed right to her. One set of arms: optimism shattered, but a fundamental sunniness and emotional excitability that was focused now entirely on willing her survival... Leo. Another set now, richer and more solid, like bedrock... and tinged with guilt.

"No," she murmured. "You have not failed in your charge."

"Then," Saul's voice murmured, warm against her ear, "don't give up on us now, Surela."

CHAPTER 33

There was a dream then, very distant, of effort, and of voices, a great many voices, lifted and strained and urgent. And then, washing them away, the ocean, in great waves of green that tinted everything a soothing hue, one dappled in sunlit memories of summer courts by the sea and the birds wheeling over the water. She dreamed of those birds more than once, and sometimes they seemed to be dragons. Ridiculous, she thought, until she blinked eyes that dragged as if against water, and found several dragons staring back at her. For a few languorous heartbeats she accepted their regard as natural, and then she wondered where she was, and why she was seeing Chatcaava through a haze, as if she floated underwater. One of them was familiar, though his eyes were some strange brownish hue seen through the tint. He grinned at her, as if pleased, and the sight amused her. The dragon who thought her a worthy opponent. What had his name been? Was it important? Not if she was dreaming.

It felt safe to close her eyes again and drift, so she did.

The dream evolved noises—arguments, she thought, from

their tenor. She parted her lashes just enough to see through the waters, and there she thought she imagined her liegelady, and Saul, and dragons again. Was that silhouette Ra'aila? Perhaps. Someone made a noise, interrupting their colloquy, and their attention riveted on her. How extraordinary, that she would perceive their worry so clearly. For her? What a tremendous piece of self-indulgence, to believe it.

How good the sea was. How she missed it. Why had she never thought to swim? But swimming was not done, of course. They hadn't evolved on their homeworld, and its oceans did not recognize them. Perhaps, now that she was an exile, she might learn? As Prudence had?

Was she dead?

That question occupied her until her thoughts bled into the waters, and once again she lost time until she woke, alert and aching, in a place she did recognize. Sitting up on an elbow, she squinted at the *Earthrise*'s clinic, then winced at the pain in her shoulder. The dagger was gone, of course, and when she palpated the flesh there she felt no break. So... she had been mended. And was not in the hands of pirates anymore. Obviously, because she was not alone.

Theresa Eddings, sitting on a stool in the corner, opened her eyes, straightened. "Thirsty?"

Now that the woman had mentioned it: "I believe so, yes."

Her liegelady fetched a cup for her, then dragged the stool to the bedside and resumed her perch. "How's the shoulder?"

"I do not love the stiffness, but presumably it will pass." Surela wet her mouth. Water had rarely tasted so fundamental to her needs, and yet she still recalled the gentle sea buoying her up. "What has passed? My last memories were of imprisonment among our enemies."

"The Eldritch fleet ambushed the pirates," Eddings said. "And squashed them between themselves and the Chatcaava who surprised them from behind. The Twelveworld Lord insisted on taking the ship you were on personally, and he's responsible for you, Saul, and Leo making it out." Something in the woman's tone made it clear Eddings was unhappy with how that situation had concluded, and that the people she was unhappy with were not present. "The Twelveworld Lord wanted, and got, the captain, and the dragons have been working on him since. Lots of interesting stuff coming out of that, all of it corroborating the intelligence you passed to Maia. The Chatcaava were also responsible for fixing you up... apparently their healing tech works well on Eldritch, it's some kind of gel tank that you float in. Then we transferred you here, because there's no better medical facility available in the sector that isn't technically on Eldritch soil and no one will make an exception for you needing care."

"You are angry about this."

Eddings's blue eyes could look astonishingly hot, and when her mouth firmed Surela could believe the stories of her intransigence. "Yes? When you reported your first meeting with the pirate, you proved your allegiances. You didn't need to go back in, Surela... but you did, and you not only handled it, you did it so well that we now have a tremendous amount of intel to share with Fleet about the pirate network in this quadrant of the Alliance. Your information saved Sediryl and who knows how many Eldritch from dying. And if Saul and Leo are right, you refused to abandon them when you got cornered. I think the least you deserve is transfer to a hospital. In orbit, if not on the planet."

"The dragons appear to have done well by me...."

"The dragons shouldn't have to do well by you," Eddings said. "Because we should be taking care of you. You're one of my people, Surela, and you got stabbed in the line of duty. We owe you for that."

"No." Reflexive, and yet no less true for that. "No, the Eldritch owe me nothing. I owe the Eldritch, and will continue to owe them all of my life, for what I've done."

Eddings's expression was skeptical. "You remember what

I told you about no one being important enough to need to die so a planet could move on? Let's get back to that, with amendment. Your mistakes weren't bad enough to merit restitution for an entire Eldritch lifetime."

"They disagree," Surela said, quiet. "And... I am afraid I can't gainsay them, because so do I."

The woman dragged her hand down her face with a long sigh. "Blood and freedom. Fine. I can do this, too." She drew the dagger from her belt and held it out on her palm. "Are you, or are you not, my liegewoman?"

Surela inhaled sharply at the sight. Had they recovered her weapon? And yet, it could be no other. It had always had a weight, for she'd known it to be one of the daggers issued the guards who warded the empress. Now, though... now the white leather wrapping the hilt was stained a pale pink, and the blade... the blade *knew* her.

"We didn't have this talk," Eddings continued. "Because I didn't know the legalities and wasn't willing to ask. I'm still not going to ask, because I'm acting on my feudal autonomy here. You're already my employee, by Pelted standards. But we've got something to settle by Eldritch ones. I'm claiming you, Surela. I know it's a serious downgrade in rank to go from the head of a big house to a servant in someone else's, but I can't protect you the way I want to unless I formalize this relationship. Will you be Surela Silin Eddings?"

"There... there is no Silin anymore," Surela whispered, trembling.

"Fine, pick a new family name. But take mine and let me give you shelter."

To say that the human did not know what she offered would have been rude... and, Surela suspected, false. Theresa Eddings had the instincts of an Eldritch noble, no matter her species, origins, and plain-spoken ways. "I... I cannot make this decision yet. I do not even know if I have friends left among the crew."

"Why wouldn't..."

"Maia divulged my acts in Leo's presence. And if he has not already told the others what he has learned, then I will have to, because I will not allow them to labor in ignorance if it permits others to surprise them."

"I'd say 'you don't have to do that' but... I can't tell you what to be all right with. If you can't live with them not knowing who you were, that's your choice. But at least sleep on it?"

She had been doing nothing but sleeping since she was stabbed, for surely unconsciousness counted. "How long have I been convalescing?"

"It's been almost a week."

Startled, Surela said, "And the crew is not hanging on your elbows?"

Eddings grinned. "They wanted to, but I sent them away once we were sure you weren't going to need emergency measures. You got hurt fighting my enemies, Surela. I had to be the one who was here when you woke up."

Yes, the woman had the heart of a suzerain. Surela could have done worse. Easily. She was beginning to think, in fact, that she could not do better. "I... understand." She touched her fingertips to Eddings's hand and pushed, just a little. "You must keep that until I make my choice."

Eddings closed her hand on the haft of the dagger. "Then you'll let me know."

"Yes."

The human nodded, rose. "Don't push it for a few days. Gel healing takes a lot out of you, or so I'm told."

"I shall be mindful."

Eddings nodded, paused at the door. "And Surela—well done."

Was it surprising that this encomium should cause her eyes to water? Thankfully Eddings did not stop to see it. Surela blotted her face with the edge of her blanket and tried levering herself off the bunk. She did, in fact, feel weak, like someone fresh from a bout of fever, but she guessed she would only need to make it to the hatch. And she was right, because there she was met by Prudence and Meri and their hugs were enthusiastic enough to keep her on her feet.

"You're awake!" Meri crowed.

"I can't believe they wouldn't take you to a hospital!" Prudence said, with a storm in her eyes.

"But you're awake!" Meri said again, and elbowed the other woman, who shook herself.

"Yes, you are, and we're so glad you're all right. Can you stand? Do you want to lie down? We can take you to your cabin...."

"I think," Surela said, "I would like a shower... and to see everyone."

"And hear about our side of the adventure? Absolutely."

―――

"We followed you!" was Meri's opening over the mess hall table.

Everyone was in attendance, and in one piece, thankfully, because being reminded that they had sent this old and fragile freighter in pursuit of a pirate force chilled Surela's fingertips.... and not solely because she was a little shaky, still. The shower had helped but she definitely felt her week in convalescence. "Was that... advisable?"

"Not even slightly," Ra'aila said wryly. "But it was one of those 'work with the situation you have, not the one you want' moments, or so Dawson told us." She nodded at Surela's raised brows. "They came back aboard, yes—"

"With their tails on fire, practically," Danica put in.

"Thinking they'd have to convince us to help them," Ra'aila continued. "When it was obvious they had no choice. They didn't have access to a Fleet ship, or at least, not one they could pull off duty to go careering off after a random passenger liner. We'd brought them, so we were the logical choice to ferry them around. And even a freighter can follow a yacht."

"Which was news to me," Meri added. "I thought for sure they'd be quick, but it turns out there's a financial balancing act there. They want people on the ship long enough to pay for fancy meals and drinks and entertainment without being on the ship so long that it starts costing more to run her than to get where they're going—"

Surela sensed that Meri had stumbled into another potential educational arena and wondered how long it would be before the woman added hospitality economics to her curriculum. "So, you followed the liner. And when it was captured?"

"Then we followed the pirates. Really, really carefully."

"Such a good duster," Erynne said, satisfied. "They installed the very best this engine class could support."

"She's not telling you she lived in the engine compartment next to that thing the entire time it was on," Danica said, poking the engineer with an elbow.

"That's my job," Erynne replied, unperturbed. "You get used to the vibration after a while."

Ignoring them, Ra'aila continued. "Anyway, it was after your pirate's rendezvous with his fleet that Dawson and Brown contacted the D-per and got her involved."

"The spies brainstormed your escape plan," Meri added. "The one you didn't get to use because you got yourself brigged."

"We didn't plan that part!" Leo said.

"What was our escape plan?" Surela asked. "I never knew."

Saul had taken a chair in the corner and had tipped it until its back was propped against the bulkhead. "We were going to get to an escape pod and either eject it or wait for the ship to be disabled around it. But we would have been safe there until pick-up."

"You almost weren't safe until pick-up," Ra'aila said. "Because once the fighting started it was a mess."

"We didn't get involved in that part," Danica said. "The spies told us to sit way, way out of range of the fighting, so we did. We could barely watch at that distance, but they didn't want a stray shot to head our way."

"And if it hadn't been for the Chatcaava, you would have abandoned there!" Prudence said, ears flat.

"We don't know that for sure," Meri said.

"And we would have gone after them if no one else had," Erynne said. "So there's no use getting worked up about it."

"Anyway, we sat out the fight," Ra'aila said. "But what we saw of it was—"

"Spectacular," Erynne exclaimed, with gusto. "The pirates were using tripwires to pull people out of Wellspace, that's how they got the passenger liner. Since the navy knew where they'd be and what they were planning, they faked their drop out of Well... made it look like the tripwire worked. And pretended to be disoriented, until the pirates came in close. After that, surprise was total. Our side got the first shots in, and by the time the Chatcaava swooped out of Well to pin them from behind, it was nearly over."

The faces arrayed around the mess table, looking at her, showed no signs of fear or dismay. They were proud of their contribution and energized by their success. If someone had asked Surela if the *Earthrise* crew would embark on a military action of such patent danger, she would have guessed not. But they had, and acquitted themselves magnificently, and in defense of a nation none of them were beholden to. She knew, if she asked, that they would say that pirates were everyone's enemy, and they would do it again, and—again—they would downplay the terror and uncertainty they had experienced. What people, these!

337

And she would have to tell them the truth about her past, and lose them forever.

"I am impressed," she said at last. "And grateful for all that you did. Leo and Saul would surely have died without your intervention."

"And you," Prudence said.

"But we know you think you don't count because you were some big bad person before," Erynne said. "Maia said you were a traitor who couldn't be trusted." She snorted. "As if we haven't been living with you for two years now."

Past their shoulders, Saul met her eyes and lifted his brows.

"You... you don't understand," Surela said. "I *am* a traitor, and that bad person."

"You're right that we don't understand," Leo said. "Because, see, you showed up on this ship pregnant with a Chatcaavan baby. One you decided to keep, and not because you had some kind of connection to the father, because if you had, why wasn't he ever around? If you were a Chatcaavan sympathizer—the bad kind of Chatcaava, not the good kind—then why weren't you with them? But you weren't. And you were nice to us."

Nice to them!

"And then the moment a pirate contacts you about killing and enslaving an enormous number of Eldritch," Leo continued, ticking off the points on his golden fingertips, "which would have crippled their navy and left them open to capture, you ran straight to the Eldritch government and told all!" He flashed his palms and waved them dramatically. "Some people suggested that you being willing to go back and talk to them again was your way of luring the Eldritch Navy into a trap, but that's incredibly stupid. If you'd said nothing, they would have walked into a far better trap than any you could fool them into accepting by arranging something differently with those psychopaths. So, I'm sorry, none of it adds up and I told everyone so. Maybe you can explain?"

Beyond them, Saul's steady gaze seemed to demand honesty… without self-flagellation. With a deep breath, Surela composed herself and began. "Prior to my exile, I was the leader of the isolationist political faction on Escutcheon. We wanted no closer ties with aliens than was necessary to ensure we would be left to ourselves. But our empress—queen at the time—led the faction that desired greater enmeshment with foreigners, and so her policies were enacted."

"Did you lose the vote, then?" Danica asked.

The question shattered her focus on the next words she was choosing. "The… what?"

"The vote," Danica said. "Everyone got a chance to have a say about the policy, right? If you were in charge of a political faction, that meant you were on some committee, or part of the government—"

Baffled, Surela said, "There is no voting. The queen rules, absolutely. She makes choices, and the rest of us live with them."

"But then what do the people who disagree with her do?" Meri asked, frowning. "How do they express their dissent? What's their outlet for it? There has to be one, or the queen would never know what her people want. She rules for the people, doesn't she?"

"She does, yes," Surela said. "She does what she deems best for them. Granting that she is a good monarch, and Liolesa is. I did not realize it at the time, however, because I was in ignorance as to the hazards afflicting our world, such as the failing harvests."

"Wait, how could you not know about failing harvests?" Erynne asked, ears flipping back against golden curls.

"Because the Church distributed alms to villages that could not support themselves," Surela said. "We were told those alms came from places of greater plenty, but not that those places were offworld."

The engineer held up a hand. "Wait, they let you believe that there was food being produced on the world when there wasn't?"

"Yes," Surela said. "To keep us from panicking. Had we understood how poorly our world could support us, I believe we would have. The empress solved the problem by buying food from the Alliance and distributing it via the Church— she is also the head of the Church—and so we were led to believe that all was well. Lest you believe her negligent, she was funding multiple research projects to solve our problems. But they had not borne fruit yet."

"Just setting the scene here," Erynne said. "So there's a planet with an absolute, autocratic dictator who was hiding from the population a major food crisis—any other crisis?"

"We also have issues with successful reproduction."

"Okay, great, she was hiding a food crisis *and* a population crisis, in the hopes that she could fix those problems before she ran out of money to patch them over," Erynne continued. "And no one else has a say in what she does or how she does it." The engineer paused, winding a ringlet through a finger. "All right, I can see how that might actually work out for the best, if you can keep the people who don't understand why she's running roughshod over them from rebelling. That was you, I'm guessing."

"Yes," Surela said, astonished at how quickly and accurately the woman had summarized the issues.

Erynne nodded, as if satisfied with a completed puzzle. "You had no idea the planet was in trouble, and you didn't want people showing up and contaminating your culture and changing your way of life and this is the part where you do the traitor thing."

"I'm surprised you waited that long," Ra'aila muttered.

Surela wondered when she'd lost control of this story but

340

she no longer felt herself the master of it. "There was a priest who promised that with his aid, I could depose Liolesa and make myself queen. He had foreign weapons, he said, and it would not be necessary to use them; merely brandishing them would cause our opposition to surrender, because they would know they couldn't win against them."

"Ah ha!" Meri said. "The villain of the piece arrives!"

"I feel constrained to point out that I believed him, and did not want to question how he'd acquired offworld weapons," Surela said. "Had I done so, I would have guessed he was planning to use me. I wanted control more than I wanted to be sure of my methods and my conspirators."

"I'm betting you paid for that," Ra'aila said.

"I did, yes."

"Still, animals backed into corners aren't in a position to think clearly," Prudence said.

"Please, make no excuses for me. I should have known better." Surela exhaled, forced herself onward. "We effected the coup, and in this way I discovered the reasons for Liolesa's actions." Should she tell them about Thaniet? About Fassiana and Araelis? About Hirianthial? Goddess, but this telling could get long, and founder in the weeds alongside the road. "There were many… unpleasant… experiences, conversations, and realizations. I began to question my allies' motivations, and confronted them, and was thrown in a dungeon for my pains."

"Oh," Leo said, ears falling. "This is where the baby comes in."

"Yes," Surela replied. "The priest was involved with pirates and Chatcaava, and he opened the world to them. Nor was that the least of my crimes, for one of my liegemen, in an effort to please me into marrying him, went to one of my opponents' strongholds and… razed it, killing everyone. Not just the nobles, but all the tenants on their lands, in every village. So in addition to revealing the location of our world

341

to criminals and slavers and dragons, I am responsible for the destruction of a good four thousand innocent people."

"Wait, how are you responsible for that, when it was this guy?" Meri asked, frowning.

"And how are you responsible for revealing the location of your world to criminals?" Danica added. "It sounds like your priest friend was the one who did that."

"But I allowed it—"

"You did a bunch of things wrong," Meri said. "But did you want to kill off the people who disagreed with you?"

"No! I wanted to rule them. You cannot rule the dead. I wanted to convince them that my way was the best way to preserve our autonomy."

"And you didn't want to make deals with slavers and pirates…."

"Of course not. I wanted our world protected from them. From everyone. I wanted…" Surela sighed. "I wanted to be left alone. I liked our world the way it was."

"The way it was… which you didn't know was a fiction, because your queen was hiding it from you and everyone else," Erynne said.

"I shall point out at this juncture that the way things were served me. There were people who were not served by the status quo."

"That's always the case, though," Ra'aila said. "Societies are never perfectly fair. I think it's reasonable to want to preserve a way of life that works for you."

"Especially if you're unaware that it's not working in some other way," Erynne said. "Ways that you were prevented from learning were ineffective."

"You are making me sound far too—"

"Forgivable?" Danica asked.

Behind them, Saul hid an expression behind a curled finger that Surela guessed was a sympathetic smile.

"I did wrong," Surela said. "I was arrogant. I was ignorant. I decided to take what I wanted, so that I could run the world the way I liked."

"And the way a bunch of people also liked," Meri said. "You were a leader of a political faction, right? So they wanted it too. You were speaking for them."

"I did it for myself!"

"I doubt that," Danica said. "Or at least, I don't think it's the only reason. Otherwise, you wouldn't be telling us the empress had good reasons for her actions, and you wouldn't have had all these 'uncomfortable realizations', and you wouldn't have tried to confront your allies about it, which… honestly, it sounds like the act of an idealist, Rel. 'If I just tell them they're wrong, they'll fix it.'"

"I am not an idealist," Surela insisted.

"A romantic?" Leo wondered.

"I am not a romantic!"

"I just don't think it's reasonable to run a world autocratically," Danica said, more to the others than to her.

"It seems to have worked for them for a long time," Erynne replied. "Besides, don't the Akubi do something similar?"

"No, I think they fight for leadership. Or breed for it? I can't remember."

"Maybe you're thinking of the Phoenix," Meri said.

"No, the Phoenix say they reject the idea of leadership."

"But isn't there someone who sits in the 'center of the world'?"

"I want to know what happened next," Leo interrupted. "So you got stuffed in a dungeon, Rel, and your allies hurt you. I'm guessing the queen came back and kicked them all out? Then she… did what to you and your priest guy?"

"The priest was killed in the fight to retake the palace," Surela said. "And my liegeman, the one who razed the settlements, was slain in a duel with the Lord of War. I was sentenced to death, but Theresa Eddings intervened, and through her efforts my sentence was commuted to exile. She employed me, and here you find me."

"Oh, fabulous!" Leo exclaimed. "And now, in a perfect storybook ending, you go from accidentally hurting your people to intentionally saving them!"

Her expression must have been leading, because Erynne said, "You have to understand how it looks from our perspective, arii. You have a bunch of people who have no say in how their lives are going to go, having to accept someone else's decisions without even a chance to object? What choice did you have, if your government gives you none? So you seized the only chance it sounded like you had to fix things. Then you were tricked into being the catspaw for a lot of terrible people, and when you found out, you tried to stop them."

"I was cruel," Surela said, thinking of Hirianthial and the things she'd said to him. Thinking of the things she'd believed of aliens. Surela the would-be-queen would have called the *Earthrise* crew mortals, and thought them lower than beasts. "And ignorant. And unkind." She thought of the Twelveworld Lord. "I was ambitious."

"Sounds like you regret a lot of it." Prudence patted Surela's wrist gently, imparting a faint but clear impression of the healer's compassion. "That doesn't sound very villainous to me." Her eyes narrowed. "What does strike me as villainous is not allowing someone the best medical care because of some hairsplitting about whether outer space counts as Eldritch land or not."

"Oh, no, she's going to rant." Meri rose. "I think that means it's time to bring out the cake."

"Cake!" Leo exclaimed, doing an impromptu dance in his seat with lifted arms.

"Cake?" Surela asked, confounded.

"We made cake," Meri said. "Celebratory 'we beat pirates who thought they could beat us' cake. It's white cake. Very fancy."

"We even saved you a big bowl of raspberries to go with it," Danica said to Surela.

"Hey!" Ra'aila said.

"Don't worry, captain, there's enough for you too."

"And over cake we get to tell you our part of the story!" Leo said enthusiastically. "About the amazing acting job Saul did, and how Rel figured out the pirates' political maneuvering with almost no information because she's *that* smart, and how *I* convinced everyone that I was a useless fribble, and then the amazing acting job that Saul did *again* when he had to convince people he wasn't a hired thug, but an Eldritch government plant!"

"Oooh, yes, I want to hear all of this!" Meri exclaimed.

Useless to protest that she had done only what was necessary… and Leo and Saul had gone into significant danger on behalf of a foreign nation, and deserved the admiration. So Surela attended to the delicate cake, and the raspberries her companions had saved for her, and listened to Leo tell the story because neither she nor Saul would. It made her smile to watch the latter's ears flush dark pink at the praise, though, and whenever the crew applied to her for corroboration she was glad to give it. Of her own efforts she was reluctant to speak, but Leo drew her out, so she told… enough of it, she thought. It was easier to digress onto her opinions of Basilisk's personality, motivations, and what the latter implied about the pirate organization. That led, thankfully, onto a different and interesting topic: that of the *Earthrise*'s former accomplishments, because apparently while Theresa Eddings had been captain they had embroiled themselves in the exposure of pirate doings in the sector. How strange, to look back on the woman she'd disdained as the plaything Hirianthial had chosen instead of a proper Eldritch wife, and realize that before Theresa Eddings had set foot on Escutcheon she'd been protecting Eldritch interests more successfully than nearly any Eldritch on the planet.

Truly, Surela thought, tilting her fork in her hand, she could not do better for a liegelady.

The party—for there was no other word for it—did eventually wind down, for which Surela was grateful... though she was no invalid, her energy was not what she could have wished.

It was Prudence who walked her to her cabin, alone, so it was to Prudence that she confessed, "The crew has been too kind to me. I'm not sure... I'm not sure they understand the depth of my sins."

"I'm entirely sure they don't," Prudence said. "But I'm not sure you do, either. That's what makes me sure of you."

Surela drew up alongside her door. "I'm sorry?"

"Bad people invariably think that the things they do aren't as bad as the people around them believe they are," the healer said. "Good people are entirely sure that the things they do are worse. You're convinced you did awful things— you regret them—so I tend to think you're probably exaggerating how bad they were."

"I beg you to understand that I'm doing no such thing. I... I deposed my own queen and oversaw the death of thousands of people! All on account of my own hubris!"

"And when you say it that way, it does sound awful," Prudence said. "But like Leo said, the story doesn't add up, at least to me. Usually things are more complicated than they sound to outsiders. I'm betting this is one of those things. But just because an outsider doesn't understand the nuance, doesn't mean an outsider can't see things clearly. Sometimes, they can see things more clearly, because the details aren't in the way." She looked up at Surela. "I'm sorry, Rel, but I can't hate you for what you did, because I can't believe it. It's like... you're talking about some other person. The Rel who's lived with us for two years isn't a good enough actress to have been some irredeemable villain all this time."

"I was a good enough actress to fool the pirate—"

"The pirate didn't live with you. He didn't feel your arms around him while he cried over his planet. He didn't see you buying baby clothes for your daughter while the rest of us pretended we weren't looking." Prudence folded her arms. "He didn't notice you making sure that we only bought the kind of cocoa that Danica prefers for her evening hot chocolate, after she made faces about the other styles. He didn't see you wear Leo's barrette to make him feel better, or find that weird and specialized course on the intersection of flower arrangement and interior design of shops to make Meri laugh. He certainly didn't know that you subtly shored up Ra'aila's authority when she was still new to her job. If you hadn't, we wouldn't have followed your pirate at all, because it was Ra'aila who made the call and she believed we could do it... so we believed, too."

Stunned, Surela could only stammer, "You cannot know that for certain."

"No, but I can bet." Prudence shook her head. "Saul's not the only person who believes in second chances. If you really were this awful person who betrayed her people, Rel... then you haven't wasted yours. I think that's a lot more important than who you were before." She went on her toes and kissed Surela's cheek. "Don't waste the future you've worked so hard to build for yourself, please?"

"No... no, I shan't."

The healer beamed at her. "Good. Then go rest, and maybe we'll be able to ship out in a few days."

For several long moments after Prudence's departure, Surela couldn't move. Could only stand alongside the hatch, her knees quivering, and feel the throb of skin on her cheek. And yet, for all the intensity of the sensation, the true benison had been the words, words that dared her to imagine moving on from what she'd been. Eddings would have agreed, had she heard them. Had always agreed, from the moment she'd interceded in Surela's fate.

Was it really that easy? Decide, and accept, and wake to each day with the intention to do better?

The bed inside her cabin no longer looked mean, and the walls no longer ugly and barren. Here was a refuge where she need not worry—not about the surveillance of pirates, nor about the intrusion of servants. Here she was alone, and free, and she tipped into her bunk without stripping her shoes, and surprised herself by falling nearly instantly asleep.

CHAPTER 34

I n the morning, there was a dragon at her cabin door, and
that this didn't alarm her was more surprising than his
presence... which, granted, was incredible in its own
right. The sight of this neatly dressed alien reminded her in
no fashion of her attacker. Part of it was that she'd never been
allowed to meet her attacker while on her feet, and this had
prevented her from realizing how short the dragons were.
This one, a tarnished pewter in color with enormous eyes the
blue of cornflowers, wearing a tailored uniform, made her
think of a doll; his head barely reached her ribcage. Even with
her ears flattened, Ra'aila towered over him.

It was the latter who spoke. "This is Detsauk, who's come
to escort you to the flagship of the Chatcaavan force. If you'd
like to go. You're not required to go. He... doesn't speak
Universal."

No? Surela tried her Chatcaavan on him. "You have come
to escort me to your ship?"

The dragon's gemlike eyes widened. "Yes!" he exclaimed.
"The Twelveworld Lord invites you personally for a meal and
a tour."

349

Ra'aila, scowling, said, "What did he say?"

"Their master wishes to eat with me, and show me his ship," Surela said. "And I believe… I shall say 'yes'."

———

A Chatcaavan military vessel was not much like a freighter. It was full of dragons, for one, and all of them short, serpentine creatures in sleek uniforms with their manes trimmed into neat clubs. The corridors were broader than the *Earthrise*'s, and higher, and the deck plating echoed less. And there was a smell… her nostrils flared. Like a combination of the air after a lightning strike and some spice. Cardamom? It distracted her more than the lighting, which was slightly more yellow than she was accustomed to.

Detsauk guided her to the fore of the vessel, which was reminiscent of the pirate vessel's, but with fewer blue lights, longer and narrower displays, and odder seats—unavoidably, since they had to be built for winged creatures. Fewer of these Chatcaava sat at their stations, and the dragons in the center of the compartment did not appear to have seats at all. One of them, turning toward her, was the Chatcaavan she remembered from the painful meeting with Hirianthial and Haladir Delen. At the sight of her, he flashed all his white teeth in a grin, because his magenta eyes had what she would have assumed to be a merry tilt had he been humanoid. "The Eldritch!" he said in Universal. "Welcome! I am glad you did not turn down my invitation."

The opportunity to use her third language was too tempting. She responded in Chatcaavan, "I could hardly reject such a flattering offer."

"Oh ho!" The dragon laughed heartily, dispelling forever any picture she might have carried in her head of him as a humorless villain. "These long-lived creatures, they are dangerous," he said to the male standing alongside him. Indicating that individual, the Twelveworld Lord said, "This is Flagship Prime, who commands this vessel."

"I had thought… you commanded this vessel?"

The new male's smile was slight but genuine, from the wrinkle of his lower eyelids. Yes, their smiles seemed to mound cheeks the way she expected, and the effect was far more noticeable given the size of their eyes. "We are his deputies. He commands all these vessels. To glory, as he proved recently."

"Ha! That was barely a fight. What comes next, though…." That grin was narrower, and she could see the predator in it, and didn't fear it. Basilisk had been uglier, somehow. "But I am a poor host. May I show you the ship, and offer you a meal?"

"I would like that," Surela said.

And… she did. Flagship Prime—did he have a name? Come to that, did the Twelveworld Lord? Accompanied them on this tour, following the other male the way an indulgent castellan did a favored noble when the latter insisted on clattering around the storerooms. The interaction amused her, particularly when she realized the Twelveworld Lord was aware he was being indulged. That interaction, barely a flash of expressions exchanged when the latter said something particularly outrageous, suggested years of trust and camaraderie, and completed the transformation of the Chatcaava into people in her eyes… people she could imagine having concerns and needs and political struggles. She wondered if their Emperor's challenges were anything like Liolesa's. Had they discussed it, long ago, when they'd sat at that parley table in Selnor System?

Flagship Prime was engaging company, so she regretted that he begged off from sharing their meal. But she followed the Twelveworld Lord into his quarters without qualms, and found there another tableau, so like, and so unlike, the one with Basilisk that she paused.

The dragon chuckled. "Thinking of the scum, yes? He wasted that dinner. You played him magnificently."

Surela's mind raced to the inevitable conclusion. "There was a recording."

"There was!" The Twelveworld Lord drew out a chair for her and gestured so flamboyantly that she had to laugh and accept the gallantry. "Your empress has on her payroll a Chatcaavan data specialist out of our navy, and I asked him to crawl through the ship's systems. My goal was to find locations, rosters, passcodes… anything we might use to track the remainder of this pirate organization to its source. But he also unearthed recordings, because every compartment in that ship was under surveillance. Your 'Basilisk' was a paranoid male. And you are a most impressive female. Have you been given a title yet? You deserve one. Something dangerous, like Dagger, or Asp."

The latter words had been offered in the Eldritch tongue, which made her realize they'd been mixing Universal and Chatcaavan. Goddess, what a mess of languages. And yet, how enjoyable, for they had their separate strengths. "I have no title. Other than 'supercargo,' I suppose."

"I forget you people aren't reasonable about such things. Names are meaningless, my dangerous Eldritch guest. They die with you. Titles are eternal, and to inhabit one is to partake, no matter how briefly, of their glory. You should have a title. It would be a crime to waste you as you are about to be wasted." He sat across from her. "You should join me."

Surela allowed herself one heartbeat to indulge in the total scattering of her thoughts before collecting them. "I should do what?"

"Join me." The dragon poured her glass full of a clear liquid the color of flax. It smelled floral and pungently alcoholic. "The information Uuvek pulled from that ship's computer is enough for us to hunt the remainder of the pirates to their holes... not just the slaver faction this Basilisk lured into destruction in this ambush, but his faction, the drug-makers and gun-runners. I elicited confirmation from him. There will be killing, and plunder, and for you, vengeance. You should come with us, see it done."

"I doubt I would be of any use," Surela said, shocked. "I know nothing about operating a warship."

"You would learn quickly. Those meetings with him...." The Twelveworld Lord laughed. "Living Air, female! You think *fast* and you think *complete*. It was such a pleasure to watch. A high. Competence is always exciting, don't you think? If I put you in a remedial training program, you won't stay in it long. Especially since you troubled yourself to learn Chatcaavan. Even that is an indication of your intelligence. Yes? You learned the tongue of your enemies, and without being told to do so."

"You are not my enemies," Surela said reflexively.

His eyes widened, and his grin then was triumphant, and amused. "You keep proving my point for me. Your freighter crew is a brave one, and I salute their loyalty and courage. But you were a female who dared reach for a throne. You belong somewhere you can achieve the power you crave."

Goddess, could she even identify a single emotion in the welter those words inspired? "I am not sure I should be chasing power."

"You would let your puling masters tell you so?" Said with relish in Eldritch, shaded with the black mood prefixes for cynicism. "They would squander your talents out of fear of your ambitions. Useless! They should be guiding you so that your ambitions serve them." He huffed. "Well, I am not afraid of you. You could be an incredible resource, and one day a power to be courted. So you reached too high and failed. Does that mean you should stop reaching?"

"My first attempt was…" What? Ill-advised? Informed by ignorance and hubris? "Productive solely of terrible results."

"So? Learn so your next attempt will have better ones." He extended his long neck toward her, and scrutinized her with those enormous eyes. "Tell me the true thing. What holds you back?"

"I don't know that… that I can be trusted," Surela said.

"That's not it."

This statement was so confident that she had to laugh. "Isn't it? Then by all means, enlighten me as to what troubles me."

"Tell me why you strove for power before."

"To protect my people from the outworld and the alien." She reconsidered. "No. To protect my people from having to think about the outworld and the alien, because I was too ignorant to understand that I couldn't keep them at bay simply by deciding not to engage with them."

"Why are you not continuing to strive for power to do this thing?"

"Because Liolesa is already doing it better than I could have," Surela said dryly.

"You think this empress of yours needs no deputies?"

Surela shook her head, took up the glass. "She could never trust me."

"More fool she," the Twelveworld Lord declared in Eldritch. His use of the language was outrageous; most Eldritch only color-shaded one or two words per sentence, but he insisted on slathering them on every word. They exploded in her mind's eye with a confetti-like palette, and made her think of enthusiastic girls eager to use every ink in their sets as they embarked on their first letters. "I will tell you a truth from our religious tenets, dangerous female, that apparently no one on your planet understands: the purpose of power is to be worthy of power. So how, I ask, will you become worthy, without enough power to prove it?"

"I'm not sure it works that way—"

"It very obviously works that way, because no one will ever know a person's moral mettle if they are not tested. If you cannot show yourself able to turn from wrong choices, and make right ones, how can you be trusted? And the more chances you are given to make the right choices, the more worthy you will become of power, and even greater titles, and eternity." His nostrils flared like a restless horse's. "They would bind your wings to prevent you from rising, expecting you will always fly against them... and so make it impossible for you to prove you can fly for them. To do this to someone with the will to fly the highest winds, the hardest storms... it is criminal. I will not do the same. You should join me. I will train you to command warships. We will hunt pirates and traitors. It will be tremendous."

The absurdity of it struck her moments after the longing: that she should be able to help her people... but only from the bridge of their former enemy's warships? If she had been offered this opportunity by Haladir Delen, the head of the Eldritch Navy... Goddess, she would have said yes. But how could she willingly leave behind not only the Eldritch, but the *Earthrise* crew and the fascination of the Alliance, to be plunged into mayhem while surrounded by dragons?

Then again, she would live so long... what would it matter, ten years, twenty, even fifty learning to command a dragon fleet?

"You intrigue me," Surela said at last. "But I will need time to consider it."

He settled back against his chair with a woeful expression. "You have chosen against me. Alas! We would have been dangerous together." He brightened. "But you might change your mind. We shall see. Let me offer additional incentive in the form of a delicious meal and stimulating conversation."

That made her laugh, and she did, in fact, enjoy the meal and the conversation, which included a recounting of how the

Twelveworld Lord had pried the information from Basilisk. Using the data coaxed from the pirate computers by this specialist, whose skill was apparently legendary, the Twelveworld Lord had changed shape into an Eldritch and threatened to read all of Basilisk's secrets from his mind. "I petted his arm," the Twelveworld Lord said, "and told him 'I am sensing the name of a system... is it... Noctis...' Which was one of the locations Uuvek had found, you understand. And this distressed him so much that when I began caressing his hip he started talking."

Like something out of a farce, Surela thought, imagining it. "Could you really read his mind?"

"Oh, his emotions," the dragon said, refilling her glass. He'd called the drink distillates of tea-wine, and she was grateful the meal had been heavy enough to offset its effects. "Much as any of you. But could I dig into his thoughts and liberate his secrets from them?" He shook his head. "No. One of your mind-mages could, but I have not heard of a Chatcaavan becoming a mind-mage after taking your patterns."

"You learned our shape," Surela murmured.

"It is an excellent shape! I had it from a friend."

From a friend! How extraordinary. She wanted to ask, and didn't, because the mystery was somehow more satisfying.

"What did you do with him?" she asked near the end of the meal.

"The pirate lord? Killed him. Do you approve?"

"Goddess," Surela said. "Yes. I'm sorry to say that I do."

"Are you truly?"

"I am a villainess myself, and you, by your admission, were as well. If we'd been killed...."

"Ah," the Twelveworld Lord said, scattering gold and shadows and white and silver mood shadings all over the Eldritch words. "but we were useful villains, with good intentions!"

The idea was risible, and he said it with such gusto that she couldn't help her amusement. "You are ridiculous."

He laughed. "I can't help it. Your language brings out the jester in me. And I like being here, and my lover likes being here, and I have enjoyed beating your navy into shape, and I enjoyed this ambush and am about to greatly enjoy this pirate hunt. Which you should join me for. Because you will also enjoy it."

"I am not a huntress," Surela murmured.

"A bringer of justice, then."

Was she that? What was she, anymore?

"But you should reconsider the huntress title," the Twelveworld Lord mused. "You would make a very attractive picture with a boar spear and a horse to throw it from. I have ridden a horse, you know!"

———

Surela returned to the *Earthrise* from that extraordinary interview with all her emotions in tumult, and the sight of Ra'aila on the other side of the Pad brought her up short... because of how patently obvious it was that her captain had been worried enough about her to lurk in waiting.

"They were all that was kindness," she assured the Aera before the woman could speak.

The giant ears sagged. "Oh, good. I couldn't exactly say no if you wanted to go, but...."

Surela chuckled. "The worst I suffered was an excess of drink."

"Is that all? There's a pill for that." Ra'aila eyed her. "You're sure you're all right? You look a little unsteady."

"It was rather a lot of drink," Surela said, because admitting to the rest of it was beyond her.

"Then I'll get you the antidote right now."

Surela escaped with the pill to her cabin and the solitude

she craved to evaluate the Twelveworld Lord's offer. He'd claimed she'd already made up her mind, but... she couldn't deny the allure of that destiny. To chase down the pirates who'd used her to open the Eldritch world to slavers? Would that not be payment for her sins? And was that why she wanted to do it, or was some part of it a desire to be relevant? To be a power again, the way she'd felt herself to be prior to her exile?

How long she sat her on her bunk, her spine and the back of her head pressed to the cold bulkhead, she didn't know. But she bored of it, as she always did of her own maundering, and forced herself off the bed and to her computer. She could do research on dragon culture—

The computer interrupted her thoughts. "You have new messages. Read now?"

"Yes," she answered, reflexively.

The first did not ease her internal turmoil even slightly.

The service you have done for the Eldritch people, in informing us of the threat to the procession, and in volunteering to misdirect our attackers, deserves more credit than you will be given because of your past actions. I cannot commend you publicly as I feel you should be commended, but your service will not be forgotten, neither to the Eldritch, nor to me, personally, for guarding my daughter.

—Haladir Delen Galare, First Courser Lord

It was so handsomely done, and so unnecessary. She hadn't expected anyone to thank her. The first tears stung her eyes and she pressed her hands to them to forestall any further flow. Wiping her cheeks jerkily, she advanced to the next message to erase Haladir's from view.

Good job. Also, you're welcome.

—Dawson

It was so brief that for several moments she couldn't remember who 'Dawson' was. Then she remembered the operatives placed on the *Earthrise*, Mina Brown, the Karaka'An, and her partner, the human. Montie Dawson.

The 'good job' made sense. 'You're welcome,' though? For what? The training they'd given her, that had enabled her to survive? She hadn't stayed mobile... that thought made her smile ruefully. Had she been able to follow that instruction she might have saved the Twelveworld Lord the trouble of extricating them from the ship. But then, from what he'd told her over their meal, he'd greatly enjoyed leading the boarding team and personally killing the pirates he'd met in the corridors on his way to his daring rescue.

There was a final message in the queue, and the header claimed it had come from the Selnor system itself, from Fleet Central. It was so formally worded that she had to reread several parts of it twice; she wasn't accustomed to Universal being quite so recondite. But it was notification of an impending citation from Fleet for her aid in uncovering and abetting the neutralization of a threat to an allied power, and it promised a medal (awaiting her at Starbase Psi for pick-up) and... a reward. A monetary one. It was, in fact, the payment she'd been promised by Basilisk, the amount that would have presumably been unlocked by the data wand he'd given her. Had she kept it all that time? Leo must have put it in her luggage, for he'd had the dressing and undressing of her while in captivity.

Surela stared at the total and strove not to hyperventilate. She'd asked for an enormous sum from the pirate, because what else would be believable in someone offering to betray their nation? And Fleet had passed it on to her in full.

She could buy a private ship with this much money, with more than enough to spare. She could overhaul the *Earthrise* with it. Goddess, she could buy two more Martian clippers and hand them to her liegelady to work as a freighter fleet.

It was too much. She shut down her display and left her cabin.

CHAPTER 35

No one had moved Saul's altar, so Bay 4 had evolved into the ship's chapel. It had been Saul's chapel until the war; after that, other people had begun sitting in it, now and then. Surela had never felt the need until this moment, when she had at last surrendered to her inability to her discipline her emotions. She sank onto the bench someone had put in front of the altar and stared at the candle-glow, so modest to also be so comforting. What did her fellow crew pray to when they came? Or did they pray at all? Perhaps, like her, they simply sat and hoped for their personal puzzles to resolve.

"It's my turn to ask if I'm bothering you."

She glanced toward the open hatch, where Saul had paused, a silhouette against the light welling from the lift. "No, you are welcome." She thought through her feelings, said honestly, "You are always welcome."

He began walking toward her, and the door slid shut and returned the bay to its warm, dim shadows. "I don't see how, when I was supposed to keep you safe and I failed."

"But you did," Surela said. "You kept my soul safe, which

was of more consequence than my body. What good the safety of the latter, with the former compromised?"

That stopped him. "That's... incredibly kind of you."

"You have been a friend to me, when I did not ask for one," Surela said. "You deserve to hear it."

He still hadn't moved. "That sounds a lot like a goodbye. Are you leaving?"

"I don't know."

Perhaps that comforted him, for he resumed moving, until he could sit on the other end of the bench. Together they faced the light.

"I am at a crossroads," Surela said at last. "Where I could take one of... three... paths. Yes, I think three."

"Those being...?"

"The Twelveworld Lord would like me to accompany him on his hunt for the remaining pirates. He offered to train me to command a Chatcaava warship."

Saul's tail sagged. "Seriously?"

She nodded.

"That's... quite an offer."

"I know," she said. "Theresa Eddings has also made me an offer, to take me into her House. This would formalize our relationship as liegelady and tenant. She would protect me, and I would serve her and her interests. It is a sacred bond, and one she implied but did not claim outright initially, for fear it would be blocked by those who mistrusted me."

"And now that you've done something that demonstrates your allegiances, they'd have a harder time protesting, is that it?"

"Yes."

He nodded. "Then you'd stay on the *Earthrise*, probably, and keep doing this sort of work."

"I imagine so, as my exile would not be revoked by her act. I will have to remain in the Alliance, even if I become a Laisrathera tenant."

His 'mmm' sounded noncommittal. "What's the last choice?"

"Fleet has given me a citation and… all the money the pirate set aside for me."

"A lot?" She told him the sum, and he whistled. "So your last choice is… whatever the heck you want. You could go anywhere, do anything. Be a free—and very rich—agent."

"Yes."

"Hard choice," he said. "What will you do?"

She started with the one she was fairly sure of. "To hunt the pirates… is it wrong to admit that I thirst to do this?"

"Why would it be wrong to want to fight evil?"

"Because fighting is uncouth." He snorted, and she smiled. "Yes, I know. An unreasonable attitude, and very like the one that landed me in my troubles to begin with. To not dirty oneself with the hard tasks, in the hopes that they will magically resolve themselves… that philosophy failed me as One Week Usurper, and would fail the universe at large were it broadly employed."

"Everything needs maintenance," Saul said. "Entropy wins, without maintenance. So you like the idea of hunting pirates with dragons."

"I like the idea of hunting pirates. But I do not want to be forced to join a foreign navy to do so." She sighed. "It is not enough to want a thing. The way you want it matters, I find."

"As it should. So the dragon path is a 'no'."

"Yes."

"So your choice is between striking out on your own and pledging to your people, through Reese. Is it that you don't want to do the latter, when you know they won't ever let you rejoin Eldritch society?"

"But I would be part of Eldritch society," Surela said. "To be a member of a House is to be Eldritch, no matter how far from home you go." She thought of the various Eldritch who'd participated in the war. They had remained them-

selves, extravagantly so, while embroiled in the most important and far-flung conflict in the galaxy. "I… could not step
foot on any of the Eldritch facilities, or worlds, it is true. But I
could serve my people's interests. If Theresa allowed it, and I
think… she would listen, if I expressed a desire."

"Definitely."

"But… to be free…" She stared at the light.

"Can you be?"

That made her look at him… look at him and feel a surge
of gratitude that he was sitting beside her, when neither of
them might have survived to do so. Had she thought him
homely once? But there was strength in him that transcended
his features, which were, now that she considered them, far
more fortunately arranged than she once deemed.

If he was aware of her regard, he showed no sign of it. "I
often wonder. Don't we all serve someone, or something?"

"I once served myself," Surela murmured.

"You tell yourself that, but you were striving toward
something and it wasn't all about you. Your identity and
desires were wound up in it, but how could you avoid that?"
The light bobbing serenely on the altar reflected off his eyes
as he watched it. "I think hating ourselves is too easy. And
regret is like a drug. It feels good to regret. Much better than
working on the things we've been tasked with. So, what will
you do?"

"I don't know," Surela said, but she did, and maybe Saul
knew it because he smiled at her and pushed off the bench.
As always, when the danger passed, he considered himself
free to go.

For some time, she tarried, because the quiet gratified her. It
was not the true silence she could have enjoyed in the stone
walls of an Eldritch chapel, because even at rest the *Earthrise*'s
engines created a slight hum… in places where it did not inspire
rattling in the deckplates. A chapel would have allowed her to

imagine herself alone far better than this place, so tangled with the needs and desires and trajectories of other lives. But imagining the Eldritch as singular, and without need of the outworld, had been wrong. Imagining herself that way was, also. And how could she turn her back on her people, when her daughter lived among them? And Thaniet… had they buried her with dignity? What of Surela's remaining family, if anyone had survived the coup? Some of them had mattered to her.

And she liked Theresa Eddings, and could admit it. And liked the crew of the *Earthrise*. Two years was not enough to learn what the Alliance had to teach her, and while she could learn it alone, was it not easier to go in company?

Was it not also more enriching?

How far she'd traveled, to arrive at this place. Where might she end up, if she continued? She wanted to find out.

———

In her cabin she sent a message to Theresa, accepting her offer. And then she shut off her display and considered. No one would be in the mess while the ship was docked, but someone was always watchstanding. The corridors as she strode them no longer struck her as barbarous or ugly, though comparing them to her memories of the more spacious dragon flagship made her wonder how far her money would go if she used it to overhaul the freighter's living spaces. They were due some comfort for their troubles, surely, and it would be pleasing to provide it.

In the fore of the ship she found both Danica and Ra'aila, and her arrival caused both to glance at her. The former's bicolor ears were splayed, and the reason for her bemusement was made clear in her greeting. "Hey, Rel… did you get a citation from Fleet?"

"I did," Surela replied. "Did everyone else also?"

"So far, it sounds like it," Ra'aila said, dumbfounded. "Seriously, can you imagine us as Fleet heroes?"

"The most unlikely heroes in the Alliance," Danica added, shaking her head. "There's a pot brewing if you want something to drink, arii. Ra'aila and I were talking through our next set of requests before we got hit with the news."

"Do we have them already?"

"Pirates and wars and fleet actions come and go," Ra'aila said, "but people still have to eat."

Danica nodded. "Life goes on."

Surela filled her mug and perched on one of the spare seats. "Do you suppose we could go somewhere different to fulfill these requests?"

Ra'aila looked up sharply.

"We might, might we not? It would be interesting, to see more than one place."

"It would be," the Aera said. "And Starbase Ne is apparently one of the nexus points the princess wants to establish. For agricultural equipment, or so I've heard. We could go there... the city-sphere's run by the Phoenix. They supposedly have cute flying fish things."

"I'd like to see cute flying fish things," Danica said, ears perking. She winced. "Though we're supposed to pick up our medals at Starbase Psi."

"They did not say when," Surela murmured.

"I thought 'as soon as possible' was implied but... you're right, technically." Danica brightened. "It would be great to see a new place."

Ra'aila said, diffident, "So... you're staying?"

"Goddess," Surela said. "You people went into the maw of a pirate attack to rescue me. And you would have me abandon you in trade?"

"That does sound pretty rude." Ra'aila was grinning now.

"It's almost like we're fond of you," Danica said, eyes twinkling.

"Truly, I am fortunate," Surela said, and felt it. Sitting here, on the cramped bridge of this cargo ship, among aliens and foreigners, she truly understood the magnitude of her blessings. What had Prudence said about not wasting second chances? Well, she would endeavor at least to not make the same mistakes twice... and that left a broad universe of choices before her, and excellent companions to make them with. "Let us have the starmap, and scandalize everyone by postponing our date with Fleet and going farther afield than suggested. And when we arrive... I will be the one buying dinner."

"I'll get the restaurant listing!" Danica exclaimed. "Maybe we can find a place with souvenir sunglasses!"

"It would go with the souvenir hats," Ra'aila said, but they'd already lost the first mate to her data tablet. Quieter, the Aera said, "We're glad you're with us."

Surela smiled back. "I'm glad to be here. Right here."

AN EXILE AMONG STARS
SHIELDMATRON BOOK 2

For seven years, Surela "Rel" Silin Eddings has been plying the galactic waters on the merchant vessel *Earthrise*, picking up sundries for the home system from which she remains exiled… and enjoying herself despite it. How else, with a congenial crew, dozens of worlds to explore, and so many things to learn? Most days, she can even forget she's a criminal to her own people, and that's the way she likes it. The last thing Surela wants is a new mission… particularly one that involves haring off into the unknown reaches of space in search of an Eldritch from a House predisposed to hate her for her misdeeds. But the Empress has decided one of the Eldritch's waywards needs to come home, and Surela's the woman to fetch her.

As usual, nothing goes as planned…

Watch for Book 2 in 2024

APPENDICES

THE SPECIES OF THE ALLIANCE

Three major groups of sapients are known to exist in the Peltedverse (so far): **the Pelted**, who founded the Alliance, and who are the descendants of animal-human bioengineering experiments on earth; **humans and their offshoots**, the Eldritch; and the **true aliens**, who evolved naturally on alien planets. The following, alphabetically, is a list of known peoples.

- **Aera (Pelted)** – This brightly colored race is tall, hare-eared and long-muzzled like foxes, and tends toward nomadic cultures. Some variants also have winged ankles.
- **Akubi (Alien)** – The Akubi are giant bird-like/dinosaur-like creatures, nine to twelve feet tall, with thick razor beaks and large wings. They have three sexes, and the neuters are the ones that tend to travel to see the interesting little mammals. They are excellent mimics and enthusiastic observers of alien culture.

- **Asanii (Pelted)** – One of the more numerous of the core Pelted races, the Asanii are plantigrade people with humanoid faces, but a veneer of domestic feline. They have five fingers and toes, catlike tails, and nails rather than claws. They are excellent jacks-of-all trades, socially and skills-wise, thanks to a culture that emphasizes mutability.
- **Chatcaava (Alien)** – A species of shapeshifters, in their natural form, the Chatcaava look like bipedal winged dragons. Some females are also winged, but most have two sets of arms rather than arms and wings. They sat on the other side of a cold war with the Alliance for a long time, and their Empire is substantially larger than the Alliance thanks to an expansionist warrior culture permeating the upper echelons of their society.
- **Ciracaana (Pelted)** – A race of gengineered centauroids, the Ciracaana are very tall, very lanky, and have furred and pawed lower bodies with long tails and faces with pointed muzzles and large pointed ears. They come in any number of riotous colors and patterns. They were another of the three races created by the Pelted in an attempt to understand their origins.
- **Crystalfolk (Aliens)** – Not much is known about the crystal people, who were found on a single moon and have made no move to join the Alliance or leave their habitat. Their first (and only significant) mention is in *Earthrise*, the first book of the Her Instruments trilogy.
- **Eldritch (Human Family)** – The Eldritch are an offshoot of humanity, altered with greater longevity, light gravity bodies that are long and delicate, and uniform skin and hair color and texture (pearl and fine/straight, respectively). They

are one of the only known esper races in the universe.

- **Faulfenza (Alien)** – This heavy-gravity world race is tall, furred, powerfully muscled, standing on digitigrade legs. They have muzzled faces and long ears that fan open, long tails with two tufts, and six fingers/toes. A race of dancers, they are also gifted with the Mindfire, which allows them to burn/heat things with their hands.
- **Flitzbe (Alien)** – The alien Flitzbe are plant-like creatures that reproduce via budding and photosynthesize for energy; they communicate empathically and travel in clods that stick together using their flexible neural fur. In appearance, they look like small furry basketballs that change colors.
- **Glaseah (Pelted)** – The second of the two engineered centauroid races, the Glaseah are compact, dense people with the lower bodies of great cats and a humanoid upper body with a short-muzzled face and feathered ears. All are skunk-patterned; some have membranous wings on their lower body, and some don't. A phlegmatic and practical people, they were the last species created by the Pelted in an attempt to understand their origins.
- **Harat-Shar – (Pelted)** The party people of the Alliance, the Harat-Shar are big-cat-based, and can be either plantigrade with finger fingers and toes and nails, or digitigrade with four fingers and toes and claws. They can have any big cat pattern, though some are more common than others.
- **Hinichi (Pelted)** – Built primarily from lupine additions, the Hinichi are the wolf-like people of the Alliance, clannish and stubborn and noble. They can be plantigrade, with five fingers and toes

and nails, or they can be digitigrade with four fingers and toes, and claws.

- **Human (Human Family)** – Our descendants. Humans from Earth come in the expected shapes, sizes and colors… there are also Martian humans (short but tending toward less mass) and Lunar humans (very ethereal thanks to their light gravity builds).
- **Karaka'A (Pelted)** – The Karaka'A are another felid race, domestic cat-biased, but they're all short, with digitigrade legs and four fingers and toes and claws. Because they were offshoots of the very first Pelted experiments (which were foxlike), they can have fox-like patterns as well as catlike ones.
- **Malarai (Pelted)** – A small populace, the Malarai were built off the Asanii base (humanoid with thin veneer of cat) with feathered wings grafted on. Their feathered wings are too small to fly with in normal gravity, and their original design left them with a predilection toward lower body disorders, mostly nerve but sometimes joint-based.
- **Naysha (Pelted)** – The most alien of the gengineered races, the Naysha are mermaid-like creatures, with the lower bodies of porpoises and the upper bodies of humanoids, with heads that are somewhat otter or seal-like, with enormous eyes. Lacking the apparatus for speech, they speak via sign.
- **Octopi (Aliens)** – A relative newcomer to the Alliance, the octopi aliens look like enormous octopuses with translucent veils connecting their limbs. They are one of the two inhabitants of the planet Amity; the second, the sapients who lived on land, have died out. Their first contact story is told in the Stardancer novel *Either Side of the Strand*.

- **Phoenix (Pelted)** – The Phoenix are mammalian bipeds with birdlike features, like long beaks and crests and feathered wings and tails. They were engineered by the Pelted, who subsequently found them more alien than many of the true aliens. They come in any assortment of metallic colors.
- **Platies (Aliens)** – Another sea-based alien, the Platies look like colorful flatworms, except without mouths or eyes or any visible organs. They begin palm-sized and can grow to the size of a shuttle. They communicate only with the Naysha, who can't explain how that communication works, and are capable of traveling by folding space (also poorly understood). Some Platies can be found on Fleet warships as adjuncts to the navigation/propulsion systems.
- **Seersa (Pelted)** – The other elder Pelted race, the Seersa are short fox-like people, digitigrade with four fingers and toes and claws. They can have fox or domestic cat patterns, being very similar, biologically, to their sister-race the Karaka'A.
- **Tam-illee (Pelted)** – The last foxish race of the Pelted are the Tam-illee, who are also the most humanoid of the group. They have five fingers and toes and nails, and stand plantigrade, and have human-like faces with fox ears and fox tails. The Tam-illee are also one of the few Pelted races that can often be born completely furless.

THE SPECIES AND RACES OF THE PARADOX PELTED UNIVERSE

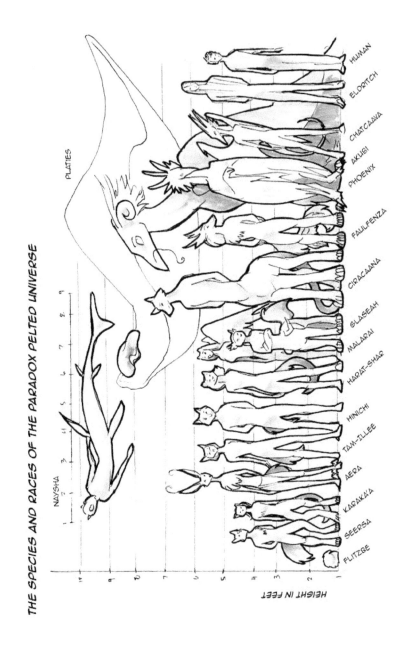

HEIGHT IN FEET

DRAMATIS PERSONAE

Being a brief catalog of major and minor characters in the novel. More information can be found on the peltedverse wiki at peltedverse.org.

Araelis Mina Jisiensire. Eldritch. The current head of House Jisiensire, which was nearly destroyed by Surela's liegeman Athanesin, Araelis defied Surela when she was briefly queen, and was one of the first to make her question her beliefs. Araelis appears first in the novel *Rose Point*.

Athanesin Fesa Sovanil. Eldritch. The liegeman who razed the province of Jisiensire, purportedly in Surela's name. His misdeeds and their effects on Surela's short reign are chronicled in the novel *Laisrathera*. He was executed for his actions by the Lord of War, Hirianthial.

Baniel Sarel Jisiensire. Eldritch. The former High Priest of the Eldritch Church, Baniel consorted with pirates and slavers in order to bring down the Eldritch monarchy. He used Surela as a catspaw in his plans. His story is told in the Her Instruments series, and he appears first in the novel *Rose Point*.

Basilisk. Human. Pirate. Dangerous, but not more so than a dragon.

Breath of the Living Air/Chatcaavan Queen. Chatcaavan. The consort of the Chatcaavan Emperor is only briefly mentioned in this novel as the woman who pardoned the Twelveworld Lord for his treasonous acts. Her evolution from powerless slave to the most powerful woman in the Empire begins in the novel *Even the Wingless*.

Danica Blakesley. Karaka'An. First mate of the TMS Earthrise at the time of *Exile*. She herds cats, that's why Ra'aila hired her.

Emperor (Chatcaavan). Chatcaavan. The head of the Chatcaavan Empire had a redemption arc from villain to great moral power even more extreme than Surela's. His story begins in the novel *Even the Wingless*.

Erynne Seyvald. Asanii. Golden-haired engineer of the TMS Earthrise at the time of *Exile*. Competent and always ready to fix the things.

Haladir Delen Galare. Eldritch. The father of the current heir to the Eldritch Empire (Sediryl Galare), and currently the head of the nascent Eldritch Navy. Divorced from Sediryl's mother, Thesali Nuera Galare. He appears briefly in Sediryl's origin story novel, *Girl on Fire*, and again in his own novel, *Fathers' Honor*.

Hirianthial Sarel Eddings Laisrathera (once Jisien-sire). Eldritch. The Lord of War, and Theresa Eddings's husband. He was instrumental in the defeat of Baniel, Surela, and the pirates, and in the restoration of Liolesa to her throne, and has significant history with her which is described in the novel *Rose Point*. *Rose Point* is also the novel where Hirianthial meets Saul Ferry.

Leo (Leonid). Harat-Shar, lion-based interface. Purser on the TMS *Earthrise* at the time of *Exile*. Heart of gold, complete with flaky-looking exterior.

Liolesa Galare. Eldritch. Queen and later Empress of the Eldritch Empire. The story of the coup she defeats with her various allies is told in the Her Instruments series, starting with the novel *Earthrise*.

Lunet. Chatcaavan. Daughter of Surela Silin Asaniefa. A winged shapeshifting dragon girl, remanded to House Laisrathera's, and Theresa Eddings's, care.

Maia. D-Per ("digital personality"). The sentient AI hired by Empress Liolesa to help her manage the Eldritch expansion. Maia made her in-canon debut in the Princes' Game series, in *Amulet Rampant*.

"Meri" Merina York. Pilot of the TMS *Earthrise* at the time of *Exile*. Inexhaustibly curious and always learning.

Mina Brown. Karaka'An. A Fleet intelligence agent, partnered with Montie Dawson. She and her partner are currently stationed in the Eldritch system to lend their aid to the Empress.

Montie Dawson. Human. A human intelligence asset on loan to Fleet, Montie and his partner Mina have made sporadic and mysterious appearances (as is proper for their profession) throughout the events of the war. We first meet them in the collection *Major Pieces*, however, in the short story "Jackal Chest."

Prudence MakesShift. Tam-illee. Healer on the TMS *Earthrise* at the time of *Exile*. Gentle on her own time, ferocious in defense of her patients.

Ra'aila, Clan Flait. Aera. Captain of the TMS *Earthrise* at the time of *Exile*. She met Reese during the same incident that introduced Saul, on the planet of Keryale during the novel *Rose Point*.

Saul Ferry. Hinichi. Mechanic and guard wolf. Saul meets Reese and Hirianthial on the colony world of Kerayle during the novel *Rose Point*; his actions there led Reese to offer him employment during the short story "The Call," which appeared in the collection *To the Court of Dragons*.

Sediryl Galare. Eldritch. The current heir to the Eldritch empire, a mind-mage in her own right. Her origin story is told in the novel Girl on Fire, and her involvement in the Chatcaavan War begins in the novel Amulet Rampant.

Surapinet. Human. Former head of an interplanetary drug cartel; Reese Eddings got him imprisoned through her actions in the novel *Earthrise*.

Surela Silin Asaniefa. Eldritch. Antagonist to the aims of the Queen, Surela's attempt to take power saw her condemned as a traitor. She first appears in the novel *Rose Point*.

Thaniet Irys Asaniefa. Eldritch. Surela's dearly beloved lady-in-waiting, who was killed by Baniel's pirate allies. She appears (and meets her end) in the novel *Laisrathera*.

Theresa "Reese" Eddings. Human. The merchant and original captain of the TMS *Earthrise* who became a landed Eldritch noble during the events of the coup, as told in the Her Instruments series. Her story begins in the novel *Earthrise*.

"Third." Eldritch. Briefly mentioned during the conference at the beginning of Part 2, "Third" is the Chatcaavan title of Lisinthir Lauvet Imthereli, once Lisinthir Nase Galare, whose part in the war is explicated in detail in the Princes' Game series, beginning with *Even the Wingless*.

Thuliven Mel Deriline. Eldritch. Liolesa's Royal Procurer, who was charged with helping her feed the populace. Became sympathetic to Surela during her short reign after assessing her motivations and personality; he appears briefly in the novel *Laisrathera*.

Twelveworld Lord. Chatcaavan. Lord over the historically significant and powerful Twelveworld area of the Chatcaavan Empire, he is currently detached to Eldritch space to aid their navy and search for traitorous Chatcaava who might have fled past the Eldritch world. He enters the story during the Princes' Game series, at the end of the novel *Amulet Rampant*.

"Val" Valthial Trena Firilith. Eldritch. The current male head of the Eldritch church, Val is a mind-mage who was involved in defeating the coup against Liolesa, with the aid of Reese Eddings and Hirianthial. He appears first in the novel *Laisrathera*.

BRIEF GLOSSARY

Alet (ah LEHT): "friend," but formal, as one would address a stranger. Plural is *aletsen*.

Arii (ah REE): "friend," personal. An endearment. Used only for actual friends. Plural is *ariisen*. Additional forms include *ariihir* ("dear brother") and *ariishir* ("dear sister").

Dami (DAH mee): "mom," in Tam-leyan. Often used among other Pelted species.

Fin (FEEN): a unit of Alliance currency. Singular is deprecated *finca*, rarely used.

Hea (HEY ah): abbreviation for Healer-assist.

Kara (kah RAH): "child". Plural is *karasen*.

Tapa (TAH pah): "dad," in Tam-leyan. Often used among other Pelted species.

THE ELDRITCH LANGUAGE

One of the unique features of the Eldritch language is the ability to modify the meaning of a word with emotional "colors." In the spoken language, these are indicated by the use of prefixes, which can be used as aggressively or as infrequently as the speaker desires; a single prefix can color an entire paragraph, or the speaker can use them to inflect every word. Uninflected language is considered emotionally neutral. This modifiers are not often used in the written language, but when they are, they take the form of colored inks.

There are three pairs of moods, with the gray mode not necessitating an opposite. Each mood in a pair is said to be the 'foil' of the other.

> **Gray (normal)** – No modifiers are required to denote the neutral mood, however there is a prefix associated with it, and using it can be interpreted as a way of calling attention to one's lack of mood.
> **Silver (hopeful)** – Silver Mode is the foil of the Shadow mood, giving a positive flavor to words. This is the color of hope.

Shadowed (cynical) – When Shadowed, most words bear a negative connotation, usually cynical, sarcastic, or ironic. It can also be used for dread/foreboding or fear.

Gold (joyful) – The best is always assumed of everything in the Gold mood, and all words take on that flavor.

Black (dark) – Black, the foil of Gold, tends to violent, angry, or morose connotations of words. Whole groups of words radically change definition when referred to in the Black.

White (ephemeral/holy) – Whitened words refer to the spirit, to the holy and pure. You often find this mood used for weddings and in the priesthood, and in the schools that teach the handling of esper abilities.

Crimson (sensual) – The carnal mood gives words a sensual implication, and inflect speech to refer to things of passions and things of the body.

AUTHOR SKETCHES

It's typical for me to do sketches while writing, a sort of mental doodling as I work out events and character arcs. These sketches are not intended to be the final word on what the characters look like! In fact, I usually have trouble pinning down people's looks. But I find I work better when I'm thinking with a pencil as well as a keyboard. Here are a few from my writing of *Exile*:

- *Earthrise* **Crew Members** - As we learn in this novel, this is the second crew the Earthrise has had, and I wanted to have a good spread of personalities. Here was my initial ensemble sketch.
- *Earthrise* **Schematics** - I somehow went through an entire series previous to this novel set on this ship without ever drawing layouts for it. I fixed that this time around.
- **Surela and Saul** - Prior to my writing the scene where Surela tells Saul about Basilisk, I had envisioned it taking place in the cargo bay, which is how I doodled it originally here.

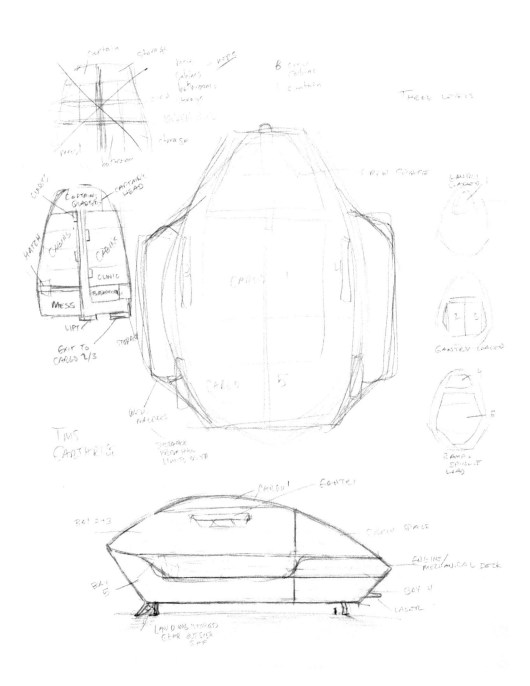

captain   storage

mess + WSFC
cabins
bathrooms
lounge

B crew
cabins

captain

THREE LEVELS

storage

CREW SPACE

GANTRY
LOADED

captain
quarters

CAPTAIN'S
LEAD

closet

HATCH

CABINS   CABINS

CLINIC

BATHROOM

MESS

LIFT

EXIT TO
CARGO 2/3

STORAGE

WIND
NACELLES

2   3

GANTRY LOADED

4

5

RAMP +
SPINLIT
LEAD

DISTANCE
FROM HULL
LIMITS SPEED

THIS
CAPTURES

CARGO 1   GANTRY

BAY 2+3

CREW SPACE

ENGINE/
MECHANICAL DECK

BAY
5

BAY 4

LASER

LANDING STORED
GEAR OUTSIDE
5 HP

ABOUT THE AUTHOR

Daughter of two Cuban political exiles, M.C.A. Hogarth was born a foreigner in the American melting pot and has had a fascination for the gaps in cultures and the bridges that span them ever since. She has been many things—web database architect, product manager, technical writer and massage therapist—but is currently a full-time parent, artist, writer and anthropologist to aliens, both human and otherwise. She is the author of over 50 titles in the genres of science fiction, fantasy, humor and romance.

An Exile Aboard Ship is only one of the many stories set in the Pelted universe; more information is available on the author's website. You can also sign up for the author's quarterly newsletter to be notified of new releases.

If you enjoyed this book, please consider leaving a review… or telling a friend!

mcahogarth.org
mcahogarth@patreon
studiomcah@locals

Ingram Content Group UK Ltd.
Milton Keynes UK
UKHW020711270723
425883UK00016B/675